immortally yours

angie fox

This is a work of fiction. All of the characters, organizations, and events portrayed in this novel are either products of the author's imagination or are used fictitiously.

IMMORTALLY YOURS

For information address St. Martin's Press, 175 Fifth Avenue, New York, NY 10010.

ISBN: 978-0-312-54666-3 *4968 0266 09/12*

Printed in the United States of America

St. Martin's Paperbacks edition / September 2012

St. Martin's Paperbacks are published by St. Martin's Press, 175 Fifth Avenue, New York, NY 10010.

10 9 8 7 6 5 4 3 2 1

*To my friend and first reader, Kristin Welker,
who always has my back.*

acknowledgments

Special thanks to my amazing readers. Your e-mails and enthusiasm mean more than I can say.

Let him that would move the world, first move himself.
—SOCRATES

chapter one

Attention all surgical personnel. Attention. Incoming wounded arriving on chopper pad two. Come and get yours while they're fresh.

Also, tonight's movie is the documentary Clash of the Titans.

And will whoever released a kraken in the officers' showers please report to Colonel Kosta's office on the double.

I couldn't help but grin. Little did they know a few of the girls and I had relocated the kraken to the men's john. It hadn't been easy. But it'd be worth it.

Back to work. I adjusted my plastic surgical goggles and took a look at the immense demi-god on my operating table. "Stick with me and you'll be out of here in time to see that movie."

The soldier tried to smile. "Gotcha, Doc." He still wore his rusty red combat boots and the remains of his army fatigues around his ankles. Ripped abs, built chest, powerhouse arms—he definitely had the body of a minor god.

And X-ray vision, given the way he was ogling my chest. "Eyes up here, soldier. I have a tray of scalpels and I'm not afraid to use them."

A tech rushed behind me with half a dozen fresh units of blood. "Coming through!"

We'd squeezed two extra tables into the operating tent

last week and I wasn't sure if it was hurting or helping. One thing was certain—the noise level had gone from a large racket to a small riot.

My nurse tucked a surgical blanket over my patient's lower body while I took a look at a nasty slice on his side.

"Yeti claw to the torso," I said, as if it weren't obvious from the swarthy black spike jutting from between his thirteenth and fourteenth ribs (and yes, the minor gods had extra—their ancestors didn't give anything up in the Garden of Eden).

"And I lost something," my patient said, dropping his chin. His tousled golden hair parted to reveal a pair of thick devil horns. Make that one devil horn. The other had popped off, the wound completely healed. It was one of the things about divine warriors that drove me slightly crazy. They healed so fast, their bodies sometimes forgot parts. I swear some of these guys would lose their heads if they weren't attached.

"Do you know where you left your horn?" I asked, testing the wound beneath my gloved fingers and fighting the urge to lecture him about absent body parts.

The side of his mouth tipped up, and there was no mistaking the gleam in his eyes. "I think I had it when I got here."

I remembered him. This was the one who had us searching half the camp for his missing eyeball. He thought it'd be funny to put it in someone's soup. Har-de-har-har. Served him right when a selkie ate it.

Of course, three days later he got it back.

Everybody was a comedian. And people like me had to deal with it.

"Horace," I called across the crowded operating room to the nearest orderly.

Horace zipped to my side and hovered just above eye level. Golden wings fluttered on his heels and at his shoulders. "Yes, Petra."

I ticked my chin up a notch. "That's Dr. Robichaud," I reminded him. Again.

"No." The attendant's eyebrows spiked toward his overly large surgical mask. "I do not speak Cajun."

"Well, learn." It wasn't my fault if some of the old-world creatures had a chip on their shoulder against mortals.

Just because we hadn't hung around for thousands of years, guzzling wine and smiting our enemies, didn't make us second-class citizens. And if they wanted us to go back to worshipping them, they could forget it.

Times had changed, and if I had to learn to live in this place, Horace could figure out how to play nice with a half-human. "See if you can't find a horn floating around here. About two inches wide, three inches long. Red."

"Actually"—the demi-god on the table leaned his head forward—"it's more of a garnet."

Like anyone around here would know the difference. "Red," I repeated. "With a little curve on it."

Horace raced off, and I leveled a stern look at my patient. "I'd better not find it in my Spam carbonara or I'm going to reattach it to a place that doesn't see the suns."

Although frankly I didn't think anything could make that night's dinner worse.

A cold hand touched my arm, and dread slithered down my spine.

Not him. Now now.

"You need help here, Doctor?"

I braced myself as the watery voice seeped over me. The air temperature dropped, and I saw my patient shiver.

Ghostly fingers tightened on my arm. "Doctor?"

I took a deep breath and glanced to my right. It was Charlie, the nurse I worked with for the first six years I'd lived in this hellhole. He was killed last year before HQ had wised up and moved us another half mile from the front.

Charlie looked like a teenager, too skinny for his rusty red army scrubs. His mousy brown hair was scraggly at the ends, and he wore an earnest expression.

He didn't know he was dead. And I sure as heck didn't need anyone seeing me talk to thin air. "Go, Charlie," I murmured. "I've got this."

My patient's eyes clouded with confusion. "My name's not Charlie."

"Of course it's not," I said, as if this were a normal conversation.

The soldier flinched as Charlie took his vitals. He couldn't see my former assistant's ghostly stethoscope or sure hands, but I'd bet anything he felt the chill.

My heart squeezed with regret. Charlie had a mom and a dad. He'd been so very young. He never should have been down here. I'd tried to explain to him that he was dead, but he hadn't been willing to accept it. We'd try again later. Alone.

Charlie's milky eyes caught mine. "Dr. Robichaud?" I knew that sad, hopeful look. The kid needed a little reassurance, a comfortable word—hell, even a joke. Charlie had been assigned to me straight out of nursing school. I'd laughed and called him my young squire. He was my responsibility.

I looked straight through him. It cut me deep to do it, but I couldn't risk being exposed. Not here. My power to see the dead, to talk to them, was outlawed by the gods. And the gods had a thing for strange and horrific punishments. It was like a divine version of *The Godfather*.

Only these sicko bosses turned women into spiders, fastened "friends" to burning wheels for eternity. Oh, and tied one of their own to some far-flung rock so he could have his liver pecked out by an eagle until the end of time.

No thanks.

My patient studied me. "You with me, Doc?"

Of course. "Yes."

The tightness in my chest eased as Charlie faded away.

The demi-god cocked his head, blond hair spilling over the spot where his horn should have been. "Your face looks funny. And I've been staring at your breasts for the last two minutes and my balls are still intact. What gives?"

I reached for the Betadine, breathing in the familiar sweet scent. "That's it," I said, swabbing his chest with the amber liquid, careful of the yeti claw. "I'm going to quit surgery and dedicate my life to discovering an anesthetic that works on you people."

"You know you can't quit," he said, teasing, but hitting way too close to the truth.

I was stuck here for the rest of my life. I knew it the day I'd sat in my little paranormal clinic in New Orleans and opened the New Order Army draft notice.

Involuntary conscription until the end of the war.

Which for me was a life sentence.

The younger gods had declared war against the older gods. Again. Neither side had so much as called for a cease-fire in the last seven hundred years.

Both armies were allowed to recruit anywhere on Earth. And I use the term *recruit* lightly. It was more like a shanghaiing. A rep from the young gods spotted me first. Army officials had given me one hour to close my practice and say my good-byes. There would be no home leave, no return.

My dad couldn't even see me off as they led me out into the depths of the bayou to a portal that hung like a misty cloud amid a tangle of cypress trees. Before I could say *Bad idea,* I was in the red, flat wastelands of limbo.

I snuck a glance across the crowded operating room, with a dozen tables like mine.

We worked to save as many lives as we could. And to get the soldiers back onto the battlefield. If the armies of the gods were evenly matched, they'd kill each other, which was bad enough. If one side got the upper hand, it meant earthquakes, tsunamis, disasters of biblical proportions on Earth.

I'd seen it firsthand.

So I'd stay here. I'd patch up our people and get them back to the Limbo Front. We'd keep the terror on Earth at bay and maybe, just maybe someday there'd be an end to the fighting.

Until then, we had to hang on.

I reached down to make sure the claw hadn't worked its way too far out of my patient's chest. Immortals could die. That was the big secret they liked to keep from the mortal world. The yeti claw had missed his vital organs. It wouldn't kill him, but I didn't want it healing wrong. I tested the edge, careful not to cut myself.

Yeti infection was bad for immortals. It could be deadly for me.

"You know I got into medicine to make a difference," I caught myself mumbling.

I wanted to help people who didn't voluntarily mix up their vital parts. Creatures with real problems who couldn't go to human hospitals. I'd been one of the last paranormal surgeons in Orleans Parish. And the only one who specialized in thoracic medicine.

I glanced at Nurse Hume, who was swathed in scrubs and a surgical mask. He looked like a child next to these immortals. We all did.

"Brace yourself," I told my patient.

I clamped the skin back. Blood smeared my surgical gloves as I manually retracted the spikes from the surrounding muscle tissue. "I'm going to remove it on the count of three." I flicked my eyes up and found him watching me. "One." My fingers tightened. "Two . . ."

In one quick motion I made the extraction.

"Alala!" My patient bellowed the Athenian war cry.

And why not? We fought the war in the operating room as sure as they fought it on the battlefield.

I tossed the claw into the metal pan. "It's easier on you if you don't stiffen up."

He flopped his head back on the table. "You MASH docs always go on *two*."

I shook my head as I inspected the wound for splinters. "*Merde*. I hate being predictable."

The wound was clean, and healing, even as I stitched it up.

I tugged off my gloves and tossed them into the bio waste can.

My dad had worked a factory job all his life. He spent forty-three years shaving the sharp edges off Folgers coffee cans. He called it good, steady work. And he kept on doing it until plastic containers came along and they forced him to retire. I never understood how he could do the same thing day after day.

He worked long hours to put me through school because I wanted to be different. I'd be a doctor. I'd change the world.

Ha.

If he could see me now . . .

I stepped back and accepted a cool towel on the back of my neck. We had the air conditioners going full-blast, but the operating tent wasn't terribly efficient at keeping cold air in.

"What about my horn?" my patient demanded as Horace fluttered to my side.

"As soon as we find it, it's yours," I said, letting the orderly take him.

I held my hands out as Nurse Hume scurried to fit me with a new pair of surgical gloves. We took a step sideways as an orderly rushed past my table with four units of blood. "How about a real case next time, Horace?"

Horace stiffened, his pointy ears twitching. "Protocol dictates—"

"Screw protocol."

His cheeks colored. "Oh please, Dr. Petra. You don't have the rank or the seniority."

I'd been here for seven years and I was low man on the totem pole. I'd probably be a newbie until I died. That's what happened when half of the docs were immortal.

I took stock of the packed OR. "What about the burn victims?" At least two patients had just come straight from a greased lightning attack. From what I'd seen, Colonel Kosta hadn't called in any of the off-duty surgeons.

"Taken care of," Horace singsonged.

"Just give me something interesting." Or at least the chance to save somebody. We'd lost three patients today. Maybe they'd have died on my table, too, but I owed it to these soldiers—and myself—to try to make a difference.

"Perhaps if you showed me the respect I'm due," the winged god began, "I could find it in my heart to . . ."

Oh please. Horace had been worshipped once for about

five minutes. His cult had died out around the time of Cae-
sar. He'd been trying to get something going ever since.

But I knew I'd get better results with honey. "See what
you can do," I told him. "In the meantime I'll leave an offering at your altar."

The orderly huffed, but I saw him perk up a bit.

"You do still have an altar," I said.

"Yes." He flew a few inches higher. "What will you leave
me?"

"Er . . ." I had to think. "Flowers?"

He looked rather put out at that. "I am the god of three-
wheeled chariot racing."

"I don't have any chariots."

"You're as funny as a bad rash. Enough of the games. I
like copper." He squared his shoulders. "You have three
pennies in the bottom of your footlocker."

"Fine." And interesting to know. Perhaps the little god
had some power in him after all.

He sniffed, as if he knew what I was thinking. "Make sure
they're neatly stacked."

"Done," I said.

"All right. Perhaps I will help you," he said, wheeling away
my patient. "Although I must say your entire style of worship leaves something to be desired."

I didn't doubt that. This place was killing me.

"So what's next, Nurse Hume?"

Nurse Hume simply stood there and waited, all the fire
gone from his pale blond hair, pasty skin, vacant eyes. He'd
had been here for decades. This place had turned the man into
a total drone. Some days I wondered if Charlie were more
alive.

Well I wasn't going to let it happen to me. I wasn't just
going to stand here and yank out claws. I wasn't going to
spend my life tracking down lost horns and eyeballs.

Or was I?

Nurse Hume took the next set of charts and shuffled his
way around the table. "X-rays indicate our next patient has
ingested a horse."

"Excuse me?"

He posted the images to the light board next to my table. "His colleagues bet him that he was not, indeed, hungry enough to eat the unfortunate animal. And so he did."

I stared at Nurse Hume. Then at the X-rays.

"Son of a bitch."

He cleared his throat. "As you can imagine, hooves and harnesses are not digestible."

"So this is my life," I said to no one in particular.

"I can't imagine . . . ," Nurse Hume began before his voice trailed away.

"What? Do you want to say something to me?" Frankly, I wished he would. If Hume started getting opinions, there might be hope for the rest of us.

"No," he murmured. "Never mind."

Just when I was about to bang my head against my steel operating table, I heard a commotion on the far side of the tent.

"We need a doctor, *stat*!"

Ambulance workers loaded an immense New Order Army soldier from a stretcher onto a table. He must have just come in. They were still cutting his uniform from his body.

His face was hard. His jaw could have been cut from marble. He was well over six feet, with scars slicing across one impossibly wide shoulder.

He had powerful arms, cut abs. He was like a Greek statue come to life. Only he was more. Much more. Even prone, he was intensely powerful—striking in a way that went beyond mere physical strength.

He was commanding.

I stared at him, raw excitement thudding through me. I'd seen a lot of demi-gods, but none of them as astonishingly regal as this one.

He was rough, dangerous.

He was a work of art.

My breath caught. He was watching me.

I crossed the crowded ER, intimately aware that he never took his attention off me. It was as if he'd come to find me.

Ridiculous.

He needed me because I was there. Everyone else was busy with the greased lighting victims. I was the only one who could handle this.

"What have you got?" I glanced at a sandy-haired EMT.

"Stab wound to the upper chest. Possible punctured lung."

Finally, a real case: a soldier who needed my skills, my expertise—me.

No wonder it felt good.

I ran through my mental checklist as I inspected the bronze knife lodged in his upper torso and took stock of his vitals.

He must have gone down during the storm. His clipped brown hair still held water droplets.

"What's his pressure?" I could feel my fingers shaking.

"Ninety-seven over fifty-six."

My patient fought for every breath, his impossibly blue eyes locked onto me.

"I'm going to save you," I told him.

The soldier closed his fingers over mine and squeezed, leaving a smear of blood across my hand.

"Get him over to my table."

I grabbed his file. His heart rate was dropping. Blood pressure down. He was hemorrhaging. I was glad to see Nurse Hume already at the table, prepping my instruments. "Patient is a male, mid-five-hundreds. Blood pressure's down to eighty over forty. Pulse is up to one twenty-six. Hook him up to both blood and saline." I took a final glance at his chart.

Galen of Delphi. Rank: Lokhagos. Decorated unit commander and head of the Green Hawk Special Forces team.

"You're in good hands, Galen of Delphi."

He nodded, wincing against the pain.

"Don't worry," I said for his benefit, and mine.

I could feel my blood pumping as I handed off his file.

Metal weapons wounds could be dicey. The commander's head slammed against the table as he began to convulse.

My gut clenched. "Let's get a move on, people."

Horace posted the X-rays. The knife was dangerously close to his heart. And convulsions meant poison.

"Get me one hundred twenty cc's of toxopren."

The drug was highly toxic, and flammable.

Nurse Hume offered me a prepared injection the size of a horse tranquilizer.

Both armies liked to poison their weapons. They usually used the blood of Medusa, or spittle from Cerberus, the three-headed dog of the underworld. I'd even seen them use Britney Spears perfume. We actually preferred that last one. It smelled nice and it wouldn't kill any mortals on staff.

The commander thrashed harder as I injected him with toxopren. Soon his entire face went red.

Toxopren burned as it neutralized the poison. The commander was lucky he was delirious. It was the kind of pain that made even the gods scream.

But that was the least of my worries. The poisoned blade was designed to split as it came out—over and over again. The shards would slice him apart, from the inside out, until he was well and truly dead.

"I hope you know what you're doing," Horace said.

"Don't you have some chariots to bless?"

I rubbed at the trickle of sweat working its way under my surgical cap. *Focus.* Of course I knew what I was doing. I'd looked this man in the eye and told him I'd pull him through. I just needed to concentrate.

The commander thrashed on the table.

"Hold him steady," I said. "I need him motionless."

It took both ambulance drivers to pin his arms and legs down.

I double-checked my grip on the leather handle of the knife and used the nervous tension to help me focus. The blade was millimeters from his heart. One wrong twitch and he'd be dead. One really bad move, the knife would shatter and we'd both be dead.

"Okay." I cleared my mind and tugged at the blade.

My stomach churned as I felt a droplet of sweat snake

down the side of my face. I held steady, my fingers working the poisoned knife.

"Halfway there. We're doing good." Bracing my left hand against the closing wound, I extracted the knife with my right. I kept my grip steady, and followed the entry trajectory, until a piece broke. I watched it snap and disappear.

"Shit!"

His vitals plummeted. I tossed the remains of the dagger into a silver-lined tray. "Give me suction." I needed to see where the piece went. "Now."

The heart rate alarm sounded.

Nurse Hume dabbed blood away from the wound. Too slow. I yanked the suction tube out of his hand and did it myself.

"Stay with me," I ordered.

I needed to see where it went. He wasn't even thrashing anymore. One piece of the blade would kill him.

I saw it under his skin, inching down his chest, toward his stomach and bowels. It could just as easily nick the liver.

"Scalpel!"

"You can't just cut him open," Nurse Hume protested.

"You got a better idea?" I snapped.

Of all the times for him to grow a pair, this wasn't it.

The scary thing was I had no idea if it would work. But I didn't have any other options. Not to mention his original knife wound was still bleeding out.

"Stay with me," I repeated like a mantra.

With my scalpel tip, I followed the bulge of metal under his skin until I got about half an inch ahead of it. Then I sliced. Blood pooled in the wound. I spread my fingers and put pressure on either side as the tip of the shard emerged. I seized it. The deadly metal ground against my thin latex gloves.

Not a good idea.

I tossed the splinter into my tray. "See if I got it all," I ordered Hume as I suctioned more blood and felt for any remaining knife fragments.

A shrill alarm sounded as my patient flatlined.

"No, no, no, no." My mind raced.

Shocks didn't work on immortals. Adrenaline didn't work. His body had to heal itself, and now there was no more time.

His spirit began to rise from his body. "Stop!" I needed a minute more, maybe less. "I need more time."

The commander's spirit blinked at me, as if wondering where he was. I stared at him, throat dry, heart pounding. When he'd arrived on my table, I'd held his hand and told him I'd save him.

His spirit didn't show the blood or the gaping knife wound. He was healthy and strong. I took in the scar that cut across his right eyebrow, the sharp lines of his face, the vivid blue of his eyes, and was wrenched by a gut-deep pull, so shocking and so utterly *right* it left me breathless. I stood frozen as we watched each other for a long moment.

Then he began to rise up.

"No!" I grabbed for him. I don't know what made me do it. Pure instinct, or more likely fear. All I knew was that I could not lose this man. Not when we'd come so close.

"Get back in there!" I needed one more minute. One more and I'd save his life.

My fingers closed around his and I gasped as pure energy streaked through me.

Holy mother of god. My pulse pounded in my ears, my entire body quaked, but I didn't dare let go. I held the man's soul in my hands.

He radiated with strength and honor. Yet he was damaged, torn with pain and regret. His innate power washed over me, along with a terrible aching loneliness.

His jaw tightened as he stared down at me with tender ferocity. This immortal warrior. This man who was half god.

The heat of him slid over me, every cell in my body aware of the pull. I felt my own self reaching out to him, tangling with him. In that moment, I was helpless, innocent and wide-eyed as I hadn't been in so long. I couldn't move. I didn't want to lose him as his strength, his sorrow, his need pulsed through me.

This was a man who deserved a second chance, who

deserved to be loved. Raw energy tickled my fingertips as I lifted my hand to caress his ghostly jaw.

Gods in heaven! What was I doing?

Horror crashed down on me. This had to end. Now. I held on tight and flung him back into his body.

"We have a pulse," Nurse Hume announced.

I couldn't believe it.

"Doctor?" Nurse Hume called.

My head pounded. Crisp power sizzled over my skin. I'd felt him. I'd touched him. I'd never touched a spirit before.

What did I just do?

"Doctor, he's bleeding out."

Of course he was. He almost died.

What was I saying? He did die.

"Clamp," I said automatically, numb from shock. I worked on his chest wound first, checking to make sure the vital organs were intact, cutting away the tissue burned black with poison, stitching the muscle and flesh and skin back together.

Focus on the task at hand.

Don't think about what just happened.

Because it scared the hell out of me.

chapter two

I burst out of the OR without even bothering to rip the plastic covers from my military boots and nearly tripped as the stifling heat of limbo hit me square in the face.

Yanking off my surgical mask, I used it to wipe at the sweat that was already beading on my forehead. Steam rose off the ground as the heat from Hades burned off the last traces of an early-morning rain.

I'd saved Galen of Delphi.

He'd live, with no lasting complications from the poison or the knife that had almost killed him.

But at what price?

Would he remember what I did?

I knew I'd never forget.

A bone-deep shiver nearly sliced me in half. What if Galen of Delphi decided to come after me? The desert vistas of limbo left absolutely nowhere to hide.

I jumped as an EMT bounded up next to me. "Nice work in there, Doc." It was the sandy-haired ambulance driver who had held the legs.

"Thanks," I said. I kept my face neutral and my mouth shut. If anyone asked anything, I'd deny it. Sure, I may have acted funny, but no one else would have been able to see the spirit. I'd saved Commander Galen's life. End of story.

Now I just had to hope and pray that he wouldn't remember.

A wide desert stretched beyond the tents of our MASH unit, the bare, red landscape littered with rock. My stomach tightened as I focused on a spot where palm trees clustered. Colorful birds dived among that narrow strip of paradise.

The tropical gardens bloomed over hell vents, tempting the foolish.

Gods. They tempted me. A long drop into hell seemed a lot more pleasant than answering for what just happened.

I'd never forget the way Commander Galen had looked at me—so ardent, so powerful. So achingly alone. I knew how he felt. At least when it came to being by myself in a crowd.

Loneliness was simply a part of war.

It was something I'd learned to accept. It shouldn't even bother me anymore.

Shake it off.

The ambulance driver had fallen into step at my side. "Are you okay, Doc?"

"No," I said, taking a hard right, making my way for my tent.

My mentor in medical school had had the gift. He'd sensed it in me and sought me out. Dr. Levi believed it was a blessing to connect with recently deceased patients. He'd even helped some cross. But he'd been careless. The gods discovered him.

Goose bumps skittered up my arms when I thought about what they did to him.

I wondered if the gods would have been so vengeful if it weren't for the prophecy attached to this particular gift.

Then again, if doubts were donuts, we'd all have a Krispy Kreme hangover.

I suddenly felt very tired.

No wonder. We'd been in surgery for almost ten hours. I squinted against the twin suns of the in-between worlds. Our MASH unit had been on this blighted spot for nearly a year, long enough for us to set up regular supply routes, postal service, and badminton courts on the edge of the tar swamp. In retrospect, that might not have been the best idea.

Ambulance workers in maroon jumpsuits unloaded boxes of medical supplies into the triage locker while a maintenance worker hummed "Puttin' on the Ritz" as he raked fresh dirt over spilled blood. I wondered just how long he'd been with us.

I nodded as I passed them and resisted the urge to check on a few patients in the recovery tent. If I could, I would have kept going until I made it back to New Orleans.

Ah, what I'd give for a plate of Dad's boudoin balls, served up crispy and hot with a side of crawfish étouffée.

Instead, I reached in my pocket for a half-eaten Power-Bar and chased it with a stick of Fruit Stripe gum.

It was better than what I'd find in the mess tent.

I made my way south through the red canvas compound until I came to a series of low hutches that made up the officers' quarters. They were basically wood frames draped in canvas.

Oh yes, I was done with delusions of grandeur.

Which I supposed was fortunate, since I'd made it to my military hovel away from home. I banged open the door of the asylum I shared with a moody vampire and a vegetarian werewolf.

Clotheslines crisscrossed the ceiling, and if I didn't know better I would have sworn somebody had been cooking Beefaroni. My roommates had the back two cots, which normally boasted a lovely view of the tar pits. This morning, the light-blocking shades were down, lanterns blazed, and my vampire roommate was still awake. Arguing.

"All I'm saying"—the undead Marius bit off every word, his layered blond hair falling in his eyes—"is get it out of my face! It stinks!" Dramatic as ever, he yanked a black silk handkerchief off the clothesline and stuffed it under his Roman nose.

I eased onto my cot by the door and shucked off my boots.

Marius had a pathological need for privacy, which was impossible to pull off in a MASH unit. There were times I felt sorry for him, and then he'd open his mouth.

Rodger, who'd been lounging in his cot, sat up on his elbows. "You're saying my wife stinks?"

Marius towered over him. "Whatever she put in that bottle sure does."

"Rodger—" I began, wondering if I really wanted to get between a high-strung vampire and an emotional werewolf. I was used to crazies, growing up around a large Cajun family, but I'd never had to live with them.

Rodger leapt up and shoved a cloudy pink bottle at the vampire, who backed away like it was holy water. "This is her scent. My mate's scent. And I'm going to put it wherever I want." He swiped a handful over his barrel-shaped chest and through his wavy brown hair before he began sprinkling it over his cot and the bookcase next to it.

At least now I knew what smelled like Beefaroni.

Marius bared his fangs. Rodger snarled. At least they wouldn't eat each other. Marius was allergic to werewolf blood and last I heard, angry vampire didn't taste nearly as good as tofu.

"Hey, that's my table!" Marius shrieked as Rodger dumped large wet splotches onto an old wooden door that they'd laid between two sawhorses.

"Oh yeah?" Rodger slammed the perfume down. "Half this table is mine."

"I know," Marius looked angry enough for heart palpitations—if his heart still beat—as he gestured toward the photo frames, *Star Wars* figurines, and handwritten letters strewn across Rodger's half of the knotted wood board.

"I am a vampire. I can smell. Everything!"

"Then stop dousing yourself in Drakkar."

Marius whirled and stalked for his own cot on the opposite side of the table. "Oh for the days when I could brood in peace! I had minions, a loft full of black leather furniture, I had a grand piano, mirrored walls and ceilings, crystal wineglasses. Orgies with sweet desirable mortals!" His voice shook. "Now I get a tent full of puppy pictures and a nail salon in the corner."

"Hey," I said, reaching for my towel and my shower kit, "don't bring me into this." Besides, two bottles of half-dried OPI was not a nail salon. Unlike Rodger, I didn't get care packages.

The polish bottles clattered with Rodger's stomping.

I grabbed a fresh set of scrubs from my footlocker. "You two can tear the tent down, just stay away from my book-shelf."

"What?" Rodger clomped up.

Oh for the love of Pete. I reached to steady the colorful mosaic picture frame on top of a stack of Sookie books. "What did I just say?"

"Sorry," he muttered, in what I could only assume was a supreme act of sacrifice.

"Yeah, well keep the pity party over there." Hand on his back, I steered him over onto his side. The army had allowed one bag from home. I'd taken some clothes, my "keeper" books, and the only picture I had of my parents together. I wasn't about to let an undersexed werewolf grind it into the red dirt floor.

"You're not with me on this?" Rodger pleaded. "The only thing I have from home is in this bottle."

"Oh I'm with you," I said. Marius was as arrogant as they came, with his talk of mirrored love nests and mortal women. "I'd like to send him back to his loft with a bottle of Windex and a twelve-pack of Viagra."

"Rude and crude, as usual," Marius sniffed.

"But I don't think he's going," I added.

And really, Marius had it worse than anybody. Were-wolves only lived to about one hundred. Being half fae, I'd make it maybe fifty years longer than that. But our vampire buddy was here for eternity.

Long after lights-out, I lay staring at the shadows on the ceiling of our tent. Liquid tar gurgled in the pit out back. The acrid smell didn't bother me much anymore. Most nights the purr of the bubbles put me to sleep. I rolled over and wadded my pillow under my cheek. I should be bone tired from the OR. And I was. Still, I didn't think I'd be able to relax until Commander Galen shipped out.

Not to mention I probably shouldn't have walked out of surgery. I was thirty-four, not six.

I didn't ask for the power to speak to the dead. It was just one of those things that had always been there. Dr. Levi believed it was a rare, recessive trait that had originated in Faery.

My mom had been fae, but I didn't know much else about her. Well, except that I had her rich black hair and high cheekbones. I also had her height. I was six inches taller than my dad.

My mom skipped out on Dad as soon as she had me. He was proud of her for staying that long. I thought she was a jerk.

It didn't get me out of going to Supernatural PSR until I was fourteen. I was the only kid in my class who knew Marie Laveau personally. You don't know how hard it was as a teenager to have a famous friend and not be able to talk about it.

A small fist rapped at the door. "Petra!" Horace whispered.

"That's Dr. Robichaud to you," I grumbled.

"He's awake."

I squeezed my eyes closed with dread. Still I asked, "Who?"

"You know very well who. The immortal you saved. He wants to talk to you."

Naturally. I hoped it wasn't about what I thought it was about.

Groaning, I dug my feet into my sneakers.

This was my secret—my butt on the line.

Horace zipped backward as I banged out of the hut, wearing surgical pants and a tank top with no bra. No sense worrying about it. It wasn't like I had much to cover.

"Where are my pennies?" he demanded.

"I'll do it first thing tomorrow," I said scraping my hair back into a ponytail, wondering just what I was going to say to Commander Galen.

Deny it all.

"This isn't worship," Horace growled. "This is charity. I need to bust out of this camp and find some real followers."

I eyed the pint-sized thundercloud, from his starched red uniform cap to his sparkly military boots with wings poking out the back. "You really think that's the problem?"

"Of course it is. I'm cooped up here. If I could just get out in the world, I could get my entire three-wheeled chariot cult going again."

It *would* be a solution to the energy crisis.

Horace brainstormed modern worship solutions the entire way to the recovery tent. "I just can't figure out how to reach people, you understand? I need to break through the clutter. Everyone is so busy these days."

He held open the door for me and I walked into the tent with my head held high and my fingers trembling only slightly.

chapter three

I pulled my white physicians' coat off a wooden peg by the door and slipped it on. I needed to take it easy.

Yes, he was striking and yes, I'd saved him. But that didn't mean I should get carried away. "He's just a patient," I murmured to myself. I'd done this hundreds of times.

Yeah, right.

At least the place smelled familiar—a mix of antiseptic and desert dust. I nodded to the night nurse, who acknowledged my presence from behind a brick-red metal desk, lit by a simple one-bulb lamp.

The door banged behind me and I glanced back to see Horace bugging out. How bad was it that I wanted him to stick around? Talk about desperation.

I walked down the long, narrow tent like a convict facing the firing squad. Military beds lined either side. The blue lights came on at night and cast more shadows than they illuminated.

It was important for patients to rest in order to gather their strength. I was glad to see most of them asleep. At least some people would have a relaxing night.

Commander Galen had been assigned to bed 22A, almost at the end.

Would he know?

Would he remember what I'd done?

Sharp anger speared through me. I didn't ask for this.

I could feel his eyes on me as I stopped to check my one-horned patient, who was snoring like a banshee. His chart indicated they'd found his missing appendage. I reached in my pocket and clicked open a pen, noting I'd do the reattachment in the morning.

Things had to look better once the suns came up.

Jeffe, the security sphinx, padded toward me. He was as large and muscular as a full-grown lion. His thick, tawny hair cascaded into a long, straight mane that framed his sharp, human-like facial features. Well, what I could see of his face. Jeffe was in the process of growing a goatee and had hair sprouting everywhere from the nose down.

Sphinxes weren't allowed in the OR. They'd been bred as soul eaters for thousands of years, and, well, why risk it? But they made great night guards for our non-critical cases.

Jeffe snarled, shaking his abundant mane over his shoulders. "The one at the end is awake." He spoke like every sphinx I'd ever known, deep and guttural with a hint of Egyptian. "I'm going to go ask him a riddle."

"No. I've got it." There was a reason we employed the sphinxes after the patients went to bed.

Besides, I didn't want Jeffe around to hear what kind of questions the good commander had for me.

I caught sight of my patient through the scattered pools of light. He was even more chiseled, more raw, more breathtakingly powerful than I'd remembered.

I felt it the way a deer scents a wolf.

Jeffe growled low in his throat as he retreated. "You will call to me if you need me."

No, I wouldn't. I had to do this alone.

Commander Galen sat propped up in his bed, studying me with naked interest.

My stomach tightened.

He was seductive in a way that was almost a physical caress. I refused to react, even as warmth shot down my spine, gathering in my core. It was as if he'd already touched me in the most intimate way possible and had memorized every inch of me.

Damn, it was no wonder there wasn't another one like him. The females of the species wouldn't stand a chance. Even with my years of training, I was going to be a puddle on the floor if I didn't watch it.

Focus.

I had to think of him as a patient, and not the man who had been on my table yesterday afternoon.

Not the man whose soul I'd touched.

A small shiver ran through me.

Get it together, Robichaud.

This was no time to get personal. I needed to keep my distance and my wits.

Steeling myself, I gave him a tight-lipped smile and drew my clinical persona around me like armor. "I'm glad to see you awake," I said, taking his chart.

According to the blue ink scrawls, the nurse had changed his dressings an hour ago. Both wounds were healing well. I'd saved his life. Now we'd just have to deal with the consequences.

"What happened?" he asked, with the tone of one used to commanding attention.

My chest tightened as I flipped to the second page in his chart. "I'm not going to lie to you. It got ugly." Blood pressure normal. "But no worries. We patched you up." The rest of his stats looked good.

"I remember dying." His gaze traveled over me, as if he was waiting for me to give something away.

I kept my face blank and my mouth shut. I could feel the weight of his inspection.

"You touched me."

"I don't know what you mean," I said, my expression carefully neutral.

It had been one of the most incredible things I'd ever done, a pure, raw moment of clarity.

He trailed blunt fingers across a battle-hardened arm.

"I saw you," he said, almost to himself. Confusion flickered across his features. "I could have sworn it."

I'd been as close as one human being could be to another. I'd never touched anyone that deeply, or let him touch me back.

It was both illuminating and frightening. I'd held his life in my hands and felt his strength, his dedication. His isolation.

That last one had really gotten to me. This was a man who put his life on the line every day. Commander Galen endured death and blood and pain. He was willing to go through hell so that people like me didn't have to.

It saddened me to think he was alone in the world. He at least deserved to have someone care.

I took a deep breath. "You were very heavily poisoned."

He stared at me, *into* me, calculating every breath, every stuttering blink. I felt exposed, laid bare, as if he could see and comprehend even the smallest emotion that flickered across my features.

"Tell me what happened," he said, as if he already knew.

I found myself wanting to open up, craving the connection. "You didn't die," I said quickly. "Or you wouldn't be here."

Galen drew himself up on his elbows. "I remember standing outside my body. Watching you."

Part of me wondered what he'd seen in that moment.

Seven hells.

"You need to lie down," I said. He was going to pull his stitches open. I forced myself to once again touch his smooth, tanned skin as I eased him back onto the bed. His heat soaked into my hands as I checked his vitals.

"What aren't you telling me?"

I felt myself flush. One slipup and he'd have me. So I did what I'd always done to keep my emotions in check. I focused on my job.

"Doctor," he began.

"You got lucky," I said. It was the truth and then some.

"You had a serious knife wound, a poisoned bloodstream, and an acute reaction to the one hundred twenty cc's of toxopren we pumped into your system." I hooked my stethoscope around my neck. "You're going to be fine. But it's normal to feel out of sorts after what you've been through." Normal for him and for me. We both needed to relax, let it go.

His eyes narrowed, trying to remember.

I glanced back at the shadow-drenched unit and fought the urge to pull a repeat of my dash from yesterday. This entire conversation was making me feel claustrophobic.

"Why don't I have Father McArio stop by to see you?" I asked, standing. "He's a good guy." The kind without deadly secrets.

A muscle in Galen's jaw twitched. "Dr. Robichaud."

He would have to pronounce it like a true Cajun.

Still, I'd stood my ground. I'd secured my distance and it would take a lot more than that for me to give it up. I replaced his chart at the foot of the bed. "Get some sleep." I buried my hands in my pockets and walked away.

"Tell me you didn't see it."

And in that instant he tore it all down.

I turned. Sure enough, the clean-cut, square-jawed commander was trying to get out of bed, naked.

"Oh, for heaven's sake." He couldn't follow me. If he tried to stand, he'd end up on the floor.

Jeffe rushed to my side. "Patient out of order!" He thrust his chin at Galen. "What's the capital of Saskatchewan?"

"Pipe down, Jeffe."

The rest of the patients needed their sleep.

"Commander Galen," I protested, ready to catch him as he stood. He couldn't have been steady on his feet. It was too soon. It was also impressive as hell to see at least six and a half feet of pure muscle and man unfold right in front of me.

Galen held his sheet around his waist, not tight enough in my opinion. It slung low over his narrow hips. I felt my throat go dry before I caught myself staring.

"You want me to eat him?" Jeffe snarled.

If he didn't, I would. I gave myself a mental shake. I was not going there.

Jeffe danced at the foot of the bed on massive paws. "Or I can suck out his liver, maybe boil his ears in oil. You know, give him the full Egyptian treatment."

I cleared my throat. "Thanks, Jeffe. I'm fine."

If only that were true.

Galen loomed over me. I could tell he was having a devil of a time standing, but it didn't stop him. He squared his shoulders and I felt it down to my core. He was too solid, too wide, his jaw too set to be considered classically handsome. No, he was something more. He was unapologetically male. It was as if he commanded the recovery tent and everyone in it. Never back down. Never surrender. If he was this impressive injured, what would he be like when he was healthy enough to fight?

"I'll let you go," he said, "on one condition."

"Name it."

His mouth curled up at the corner. "Give me five minutes."

Oh my. "You got it," I said, ignoring that little voice in my head that told me I was sinking in deep. Too deep.

"That wasn't so hard," he said in an all-too-familiar tone as he eased himself back into bed.

This man was going to be trouble on wheels.

Get a grip.

Jeffe plopped down at my side. "I think he needs another riddle."

"No." Because if Galen got it wrong, Jeffe would be honor-bound to eat him, and that had about a zero percent chance of working out.

The sphinx wrinkled his long, Egyptian nose. "Puzzle?"

"No."

"How about a game of Parcheesi?"

"I think I have it handled."

"Right. Sure. Who cares what I think? I've only been doing this since Ramses was in diapers."

"Give us a break, Jeffe." I'd promised the commander a

conversation. If I kept my wits about me, I might be able to convince him to back off.

The sphinx rolled his eyes and sat down next to me, his lion's tail swooshing against the leg of my scrubs.

"Away, Jeffe."

"Fine. I get it. You don't have to tell me twice," said the sphinx, lumbering off.

Lovely. I wiped my brow with my sleeve. I'd owe him my last Tootsie Roll for that one. It was amazing how easily the sphinx's feelings got hurt, and how much chocolate seemed to help.

At least my encounter with Jeffe had allowed time for me to gather myself—and for Commander Galen to adjust his sheet over those abs of his. I was a professional, but even I had my limits.

I leaned over him, bracing a hand on the back of his metal hospital bed, the sleeve of my white coat nearly brushing his ear. "You need to relax and take care of yourself."

Besides the fact that he was naked and injured, I didn't see what he had to gain by following me out of the tent. I'd already told him as much of the truth as he was going to get.

He met me halfway, the sheet pooling at his waist. The air between us thickened.

"It's the damndest thing, Doc. I can almost see what happened, only my mind won't let me. It's like I had something right here." He held his wide hands open, palms up, empty. "I had it."

Hellfire and brimstone. I fought the urge to glance at Jeffe, who would zip to my side the moment I did.

I tucked my hair behind my ears. There had to be an answer that would satisfy him. I tried to look at it intellectually. Forget what happened and focus on normal, everyday fears. No doubt the concept of death was tough for these so-called immortals. "Look, I'll go get Father McArio myself."

Galen sat up straighter. "I don't want him. I need *you*."

Lord help us. I knew what this soldier wanted even if he didn't. Galen craved that soul-deep connection we'd shared in that operating room. He ached for it like I did.

I gave him a cockeyed look. "Of all the immortals in limbo, you had to show up on my table."

He grinned at that.

"I'll stay," I said, ignoring the glint of victory in his eye. "But lie back down," I added, mindful of his injury.

I pulled up a cramped military chair next to his bedside.

Galen leaned in close. The scent of the harsh astringent we'd used on him wasn't enough to mask the spicy male scent underneath. Perhaps this wasn't the best idea.

His breath felt warm against my cheek. "I feel strange," he said. "Like the fates have tied us together somehow." He shook his head slightly. "I can't tell you why it's there, but it is."

I knew all about it.

I worked with soldiers every day, men in pain, men who needed me. There was no reason why Galen should be different. But he was. Saving him, touching his soul had affected me in ways I was only beginning to understand.

"It's not fate," I said. It was an absurd fluke, one I wanted to forget. A short laugh bubbled out of me. It was all too much. "I don't even read my horoscope."

There was no point anyway. By the time any magazines or newspapers got down here from Earth, they were a month old.

The look he gave me cut straight through the web I'd tried to spin. "It's supposed to be a healer who ends this war."

"True." One with a forbidden power. The gods had probably killed the person already, or chained them inside a volcano where they could be dipped in lava twelve times a day.

A moment of silence passed between us.

"Do you believe in oracles?" he asked.

"No." Not anymore.

He seemed surprised at that.

I shrugged and leaned back in my chair. "I'm from New Orleans. I've heard a lot of ghost stories."

And since I'd gotten here, I'd seen a lot of soldiers.

Damn, I was in trouble. I tilted my head, studying Galen of Delphi. A triple scar sliced across his lower belly, as if something had taken a swipe at him. A bandage from his recent wound covered his heart and trailed over a broad shoulder. He had legions of nicks and scratches from count-less hurts. I found myself wanting to fix all of it, even though I knew I couldn't.

Instead I asked, "How many times have you been in-jured?"

A muscle in his shoulder twitched. "Too many to count."

I knew. I'd felt it firsthand. This man was different from the one-note, hotshot soldiers who crossed my table. Galen had the passion of an immortal, and the intensity. Yet he hadn't lost his humanity. There was no mistaking his suffer-ing and his pain. It was comforting and disturbing at the same time.

I couldn't imagine what he'd been through. I'd never wit-nessed a battle up close. But I did see the men as they came off the field, injured and dying.

No doubt he wanted to bring an end to it all. It was more than our startling connection. He *wanted* the prophecy to come true. But in my experience, life didn't work that way.

I touched him lightly on the arm. His skin was sleek, the muscle underneath hard. "You've suffered." Surely he'd lost friends as well. My chest tightened. "I understand."

"No, you don't." The ice in his voice sent a shiver through me. "I wouldn't wish it on you if my life depended on it. You have no idea what's about to happen."

It was true. I didn't know what he faced. And he didn't know me. We would leave it at that.

I stood. "My time is up."

He ground his jaw, watching me as I slid a rust-colored military blanket over his shoulders and made a notation in his chart. Commander Galen would ship out tomorrow to the MASH 8071st—the farthest unit from us. I'd figure out a reason later.

"Thanks for talking, Doc," he said, grudgingly taking my hand. His touch rocked me to the core.

He inhaled sharply.

Our eyes locked and I could see that he felt it, too. I let out a shaky breath.

It was the first time we'd touched like this since the incident in the OR, and it hit me with stark clarity just how dangerous this man was.

Like an idiot, I didn't let go right away. I let him hold my hand for a long moment. His eyes searched my face, as if he was struggling to remember.

I drew back. "I've got to go."

"Right," he said under his breath, recovering. "I promise not to scare you if you come see me tomorrow."

"Sure. I make rounds at noon."

I watched him ease back onto his military recovery bed, aware that I'd gained a much-needed reprieve.

Technically, we could talk at noon tomorrow. If I hadn't just scheduled him to ship out at dawn.

chapter four

The wooden door of the recovery unit banged closed behind me as I breathed in the stuffy night air. The shadows of the camp slung low against the desert. Torches lined the walk, casting pools of light in the darkness.

We'd talked the new gods into a generator for the hospital, but otherwise they insisted we go old-school with lanterns and anything else we could set on fire. For progressive gods, they sure needed to get with the twenty-first century.

I rubbed a hand over my gritty eyes, trying to ignore the pounding in my head. I wished I could do more for soldiers like Galen. I tried to make a difference. Sometimes, though, it seemed like all we did here was patch them up so somebody else could blow holes in them again.

Cripes. I had to let it go. I couldn't change anything about this war or the soldiers who fought it.

I blew out a breath. As much as I didn't want to think about it, Galen was different. I'd seen wounded heroes before, but he was the first one who'd tried to charge out of bed after me. I wondered how many times in his life that man had ever given up command. Let himself be vulnerable. Rest, for gods' sake.

Talking to Galen tonight had felt like running a mental marathon. Shipping him out of here would be like crossing the finish line.

So why did I feel so guilty?

I started walking. Forget about it. I'd done the right thing—the only sane thing—to do.

It was more than I could say for some of the generals in this war.

Or the gods. The original war had stemmed from an argument over where to house the capital city. The old gods wanted Atlantis. The new gods wanted El Dorado. Seeing as both cities had been destroyed in the war, you'd think they'd stop fighting.

But no. In a grand show of immortal egomania, both sides refused to back down. Now they were locked in a senseless, deadly game of one-upsmanship that no one could possibly win.

The PA speaker above my head crackled with static.

Attention. Doctors on call. Incoming wounded.

I snapped to attention, almost ashamed to notice that it felt good to be back on familiar ground.

My life made sense again. I was Primary Team on call tonight. Adrenaline surged through me as I jogged to the operating tent, my sneakers crunching against the sandy soil.

In the narrow prep room just outside the OR, I donned my mask and scrubbed up to the squealing of ambulance brakes and the shouts of the drivers. I could hear more doctors arriving in the yard, prioritizing cases as I finished up.

"What do we have?" I asked, sterile hands up as I banged into the front of the OR. Nurse Hume had beaten me out to the floor. Silent and efficient, he helped me fasten my gown and gloves.

The immense steel lights above our tables hummed as EMTs and nurses hustled the new arrivals in.

"Cannon shot to the lower abdomen," an ambulance worker grunted as he and another EMT carried the patient to my table.

I took a look at the chart. "Good." At least it wasn't fatal.

The gods hadn't made a poison that could withstand the heat of an artillery shot. Yet.

"Get me some more light over here," I ordered.

I kept my head down and handled a total of two gut shots and a severed spinal cord. It seemed I was back to my normal caseload, although a broken neck can be a challenge on an immortal.

The trick is to get the bones lined up before it heals wrong. Otherwise you have plant your hands on either side of the neck and break it again before you can set it. The weak spot breaks first. Easy peasy, right?

Don't think about it.

The night passed quickly as I worked on case after case. I was back to handling the routine traumas, and this time I did it without complaint. Galen had given me enough excitement to last the rest of the war.

Afterward, I tossed my gloves into the bio hazard can and headed for the surgeons' locker room.

At least it kept my mind off Galen for the night.

We changed in a square room just behind the surgical prep area. Lockers lined up on opposite walls, with a few benches in the middle.

I yanked the surgical cap off and unwound my hair from a tight bun. There's nothing like setting it loose after tying it too hard. I bent over at the waist, letting my hair flow as I drew my fingers against my scalp. Sweet freedom.

A leg scraped up against my hip. "Do you mind?"

I kept my eyes closed, ignoring the scratchy voice of Captain Thaïs. The man was like sandpaper.

"I have a bone to pick with you," he said, banging around in his locker.

Thaïs was from the immortals-are-superior school of thinking. Frankly, I didn't feel like dealing with it.

Brushing my hair out of my eyes with my fingers, I stuffed my operating gown in the bio hazard can.

I could practically feel him invading my personal space.

"Hey, are you ignoring me?"

"No." Yes. I couldn't help it. It was standard protocol at this point. In fact, I was surprised that tips for deflecting, ducking, or otherwise avoiding Captain Thaïs weren't included in the MASH 3063rd handbook. Maybe they were. Come to think of it, I never read the handbooks they issued every year. I just used them to prop up my wobbly bunk.

"It figures." He stood inches away from me. The man looked like Mister Clean, minus the earring. And the smile. Thaïs wore a permanent scowl. "You're going to have to write up your nurse for failing to retrieve the proper neck brace for your patient back there."

My nurse was timid enough. Writing him up wouldn't help.

I nudged my way around him and dialed the combination to my surgical locker. I needed a hairbrush and some duct tape for Thaïs's mouth. "The neck brace was close by. I grabbed it."

No big deal.

He stiffened. "The nurses need to learn respect."

"They're not the only ones," I said. I opened my locker and about fell over. I slammed it closed again.

"What?" he demanded, trying to see around me. "What did you just say to me?"

"Nothing," I said automatically. My splayed hand blocked the door. My heart was pumping like mad. There was a bronze knife in my cubby. Either it was a sick practical joke or the knife from surgery had made it onto the shelf next to my PowerBars.

Somehow I knew this was no joke.

Thaïs scowled. "Well, if you ask me, you're acting stranger than usual."

No kidding. I'd get the knife later, when there were no witnesses around to see it.

I fought to keep my voice even and even managed a half-hearted smirk. "Yeah, well, they shouldn't let half-breeds into the operating room."

Thaïs propped a foot up on a bench, tying his rusty red combat boots. "You said it, not me."

It would have suited me just fine to leave the fighting and the dying and the entire bloody mess up to demi-gods like Thaïs. Only a birth defect had kept him out of the line of fire. "If I could fix your leg and hand you a long sword, I would."

"Ha, ha," he grumbled, before limping out of the tent.

When I was sure he was gone, I opened my locker again. The bronze knife sat on the top shelf, dull with dried blood. It was as long as my hand, with a compact handle and a triangular blade. I picked it up. It wasn't army issue. It was old and ornate, with a newer leather-wrapped grip. Just above, the top of the knife curved to form the head of a snake, or some sort of serpent-like beast.

Intricate, time-worn carvings wound down the blade. A chill ran through me as I saw the sliver missing from the tip. I was pretty sure this was the knife I took out of Galen. Hades knew what it was doing in my locker. It was supposed to be in weapons waste.

I ground my jaw. *Nobody saw me.*

Except for Galen.

That wasn't as comforting as I'd hoped.

Still, Galen couldn't have planted the knife. He'd been under guard. And no other gods knew about my ability or I'd be dead.

I was tempted to take the dagger straight to the biohazard pit. I would have if I could be sure that would be the end of it.

No, I'd take care of it myself.

With one last glance at the door, I carried the knife over to the prep sink. Holding it like the deadly weapon it was, I carefully washed any remaining poison from the blade. Then I wrapped the whole thing in a used surgical cap and eased it into the pocket of my scrubs, pointy-side down. It didn't fit all the way, but at least it wouldn't stab me.

I dried my hands on my scrub pants. There were windows high up in the locker room, and I could see morning sunlight peeking in from the sides of the drab army-issue shades. Father McArio would be up by now. He'd know what to do.

A dusty breeze hit me as I nudged my way out of the operating tent. It was still fairly cool. In another hour or so we'd be hit with the full heat of the day.

On my way toward the south end of camp, I saw Rodger coming out of recovery.

He waved. "You eat?" he called. The wind tossed his hair up in a frenzy, as if it weren't wild enough. His wife had sent him another new shirt from home. He wore it under his white doctors' coat. This one said TROPHY HUSBAND.

I caught up to him. "I have to go see Father McArio."

"He's in the mess tent," he said, cocking his head in the direction I'd been heading.

"Then let's eat." I fell into step next to him. No need to draw attention to myself. I'd get a hold of the father on the way out. Besides, if you were going to eat, breakfast was the safest. It's hard to screw up powdered eggs and dehydrated bacon. "Nice shirt, by the way."

"My wife made it," Rodger said, with a hint of pride.

I could tell by the crooked T.

"You're a lucky man," I said as we ambled down the sandy main drag through camp. I nodded to a pair of doctors passing the opposite way.

"I took care of your one-horned patient this morning," Rodger said.

"I was going to do that." I should have had them bring him in at the end.

"It's okay." Rodger shrugged. "Although considering the way he was grumbling, I don't think he had as much fun staring at my chest while I reattached it."

"Served him right," I said. "Thanks," I added, meaning it. "It's been a hell of a few days."

Rodger squinted against the rising suns. "Recovery is jammed. Jeffe is fit to be tied. Keeps trying to play twenty questions with your knife-wound patient."

Dread punched me in the gut. "I shipped him out."

"No, you didn't," Rodger said, far too happily for my taste.

I ground to a halt. "What?"

Rodger took three more steps before he realized I'd stopped walking. He turned. "Commander Galen, your knife patient. He's in recovery."

"You've got to be kidding me." I'd transferred him. I'd handed over the paperwork myself. "Son of a—" I took off for the recovery tent. A surprised group of nurses and a departing ambulance team made way.

"Hey," Rodger called from behind, "what about breakfast?"

I didn't need eggs. I needed an explanation as to why the hell my patient was still here.

Sure enough, Galen was down near the end of the row, in bed 22A, smiling at me.

I placed both hands on the desk of the attending nurse. The knife felt heavy in my pocket. "I ordered that man transferred."

Marjorie was a calm, thin woman with generous lips and large eyes. She looked up from her laptop. "Transport made a paperwork mistake," she said, patiently. "They were gone before we realized he had to go."

I stared her down. I couldn't help it. "A paperwork mistake?" I repeated, emphasizing every word. I was trying to believe it was a coincidence. I really was.

She leveled a steadying gaze at me. "It happens."

Not often. I strode outside to where I saw the ambulance team preparing to leave. "Where are you going?"

The tattooed paramedic glanced up. "To the 4027th," he said, tightening down a loaded stretcher. The ambulances could take up to six patients.

"Got room for one more?" I asked, seeing two empty bunks.

"Yes, ma'am."

"Bed 22A." Hand shaking, I braced a clipboard on my hip as I drew up orders. Dr. Freiermuth would know what to do with him. I hoped. At least I was pretty sure she didn't see spirits.

Two EMTs headed inside to retrieve Galen. "Better take a third man," I said, scrawling my signature at the bottom. "And strap him in," I added, despising myself just a little.

I hated to order restraints. Galen would be ticked. But I

couldn't have him getting up and walking away. He'd do it, too.

I stood at entrance to recovery and cringed as three immortal orderlies struggled to tie Galen down. When they'd finally subdued him, two of them hustled him out. The third orderly followed, rubbing at his left hand.

Galen's muscular shoulders shook as he fought the leather straps on his wrists and across his upper arms and torso. They strained against the metal supports that held them in place. "Stop," he demanded. "Tell me where you're taking me."

I followed them out, toward the waiting ambulance. "Can I have a minute?" I asked the orderly before he eased Galen's stretcher inside.

He nodded and left my patient on the slide-out rail of the transport.

Cripes. Galen was busy working a hand loose. I knew better than to think he couldn't pull it off.

At least I was used to delivering bad news. I placed a hand on Galen's chest where the blanket had fallen away. I hadn't wanted to do this out here, in the yard. Or heck, at all. "We're sending you to the 4027th for additional treatment."

He went from confused to calculated in about one second flat. "What the hell," he swore under his breath. "I have an honest to god conversation with you and you ship me out?"

My breath caught as his eyes narrowed.

"I don't know what you mean," I said.

"I really did see something, didn't I?"

He knew. We both did. A moment passed between us that I couldn't take back. I looked into his piercing blue eyes and felt the weight of my betrayal.

Heart pounding, I opened my mouth, then closed it again. It had to be done.

Right now, he had no proof, but if he stuck around here there was no telling what he'd find out. Something had happened between us and I didn't know if there were traces or what—or hell, if I'd end up giving something away. Or if some treacherous part of me even wanted him here with me. No matter what, this had to end right now.

I leaned close, my voice barely a whisper. "I can't do it." This was as far as I went.

His hand cupped the back of my head. I jumped, but he held me close.

I trembled as his fingers wound through my hair. "How did you—"

"I escaped," he said simply, his touch scorching me. His breath was ragged. "Whatever happened on that table, your secret is safe with me. I won't hurt you." He guided me closer. "What are you afraid of?"

I could barely find my voice. "You."

"I know," he said, fingers caressing my scalp as if to calm me. It didn't work. A riot of sensation flooded me. I could swear he saw through me, into me, like I had him. But that was impossible. "Let me in," he urged, "I can protect you. It's what I do." His breath touched my ear. "You don't have to fight this battle alone."

Warm desire sluiced through me. I shouldn't feel this. Or anything. And I didn't have to fight any battles at all. He could get me killed just talking about this.

I broke away from him. "You need to go."

"You can't pretend this isn't happening. It won't work," he said, with way too much conviction for my taste.

I stood. "You're in the hands of the New Order Army now," I said to him and anyone else who wanted to listen. "Beware of the paperwork."

This was the way it had to be.

"This isn't over," he ground out.

It was. "I'm sorry, soldier. It was an honor to meet you."

Galen watched me as the orderly slid his stretcher into the ambulance.

It hurt to watch him go. I wanted to say something more, to tell him to be safe or to take care of himself. But I knew that was impossible. I'd given what I could. There was no safe place anymore—not in this war.

The only thing we could do was survive. I handed the driver the completed orders.

Good-bye, Galen of Delphi.

I tried to forget about him the best way I knew how. I stopped back by our place and talked Rodger into hitting our favorite fishing spot near the edge of the tar swamps. Then again, with Rodger it didn't take much convincing.

The day was heating up, but I didn't care. I was used to this place. I could handle it.

I unfolded my beach chair, wedged my pink flamingo iced tea cup into the sand. One good thing about the gods— justice was swift. If anyone in the yard had suspected my forbidden gift, I'd be serving my sentence by now.

Rodger clapped me on the shoulder. "Why so glum?"

"No reason." I eased back into my chair.

Despite what Galen had said, it was over. He was at least halfway to the third quadrant by now.

It shouldn't have affected me as deeply as it did.

Galen had his duty. I had mine.

End of story.

One Greek commander couldn't protect me from the wrath of the gods, no matter how fearsome or drop-dead sexy he was. Which was why he had to go. And why I shouldn't get personally involved with my patients.

Damn. I gazed out over the bubbling lake of tar. I was turning into a complete sap. As a doctor, I'd learned to block out personal feelings. Sure, I cared about my patients and wanted to help them as much as I could. But I couldn't get caught up in every struggle or it would kill me.

"I saved you some powdered-egg-and-bacon-bits casserole," Rodger said, nudging a brown sack with his foot.

Yum. "I just wish I hadn't missed Father McArio at breakfast."

The priest hadn't been in his office, either. I'd checked three times.

Rodger gave me an encouraging smile from under a

floppy hat decorated with beer company logos. "Relax. He's around somewhere."

I eased the knife out of my scrubs. It was still wrapped in my surgical cap. I knew I'd rinsed it long enough to wash away the poison. Still, I didn't want it in my pocket for the next couple of hours.

I stored the knife under my beach chair and took a bite of the eggs. They managed to be both dry and sticky at the same time. "Someone should tell them to add water to the powder."

"And bacon to the bacon," Rodger said, baiting a hook with popcorn. "That meat is so far away from the pig, *I* could probably eat it."

He cast his line into the swamp. The weight on the end made a small *plop* before it sank under.

"Got any more popcorn?" I asked.

He smiled at me like he would one of his kids. "Just five pieces and they're for the fish."

I washed the rest of the eggs down with a large gulp of warm tea. We were each issued two ice cubes with any beverage, and it seemed I'd used mine up.

Ah, the joys of camp life. I should be back in our hutch sleeping, but I couldn't get Galen of Delphi out of my mind.

If he'd only gone the first time. If only I could have let him go this time without having to restrain him.

If only he hadn't touched me.

He was the most unhelpless tied-up guy I'd ever seen. Now he was out there somewhere putting together the pieces of what had happened on that operating table. It shook me in a way that I hadn't been, not in a long time.

But what I'd done was right. I'd saved both of us from a world of hurt. I ended this pursuit of a doomed prophecy that could only serve to expose me. I'd kept Galen of Delphi from learning anything else, and I'd be rid of this knife as soon as I could find our resident exorcist.

Then I could rest easy tonight. I hoped.

In the meantime, I lowered my sunglasses, stretched out my legs, and leaned back in my chair. "Wake me when you catch the big one."

"You're the Sleeping Beauty of the swamp."

I sank back, becoming one with the chair. "Just as long as I'm sleeping."

Our roommate, Marius, had left his German club music on inside the footlocker that doubled as his daytime coffin. Again. And even if I lowered the light-blocking shades, it's not like I was really up for cracking the lid and waking the vampire to make him to turn it off. I could still hear the *thump-thump* techno beat from our tent at the far end of the swamp.

I squeezed my eyes shut, trying to turn a deaf ear. "How does Marius listen to that junk?"

"Got a few pennies? We can have Horace blow his speakers."

The warm sunlight seeped into my skin. "I'm done offering Horace pennies," I said, refusing to move a muscle.

"Well, I'm not going anywhere near those speakers," Rodger mused. "It seems like every creature with a nose has been able to scent me lately."

Yes, well, love is not telling your friend that he smells. "I don't know why you even bother fishing for sea serpents," I said, changing the subject. "They taste worse than mess hall food."

"They make cute pets."

If you liked scraggly, nibbly little dinosaurs. Rodger had at least six. I shuddered to think what would happen if Marius ever caught on. If I were a psychologist, I'd say the wee beasties were an unconscious replacement for the four pups and a wife Rodger had left behind in California.

We weren't allowed to keep pets—or ship them home. Not since a sea serpent got loose in Loch Ness.

Colonel Kosta, our camp commander, was a real hard-ass. The old Spartan liked to sleep on a plank of wood and ran the camp with ironclad efficiency. He was squarely on the side of duty and order. I was on the side of whatever kept us sane.

Rodger's chair squeaked as he leaned back. "Nice job on the kraken in the shower, by the way."

"Oh, it wasn't my kraken. I just moved it." Kosta had

already showered. Ugly sucker—the kraken, I meant. Well, Kosta, too, come to think of it. "Whoever did it needs to pay attention to the colonel's schedule." He was long gone by the time they'd dumped the adolescent sea monster into shower stall three.

We had a bet going to see who could prank Kosta first. It started off with just me and Rodger, then the nurses, then the motor pool. That's when the stakes went way up.

"What's the pot up to now?" Rodger asked.

"Three weeks, one day, six hours, and twenty minutes." Army money was useless unless you were headed to the officers' club. So we bet what really mattered—time away from this joint.

Rodger whistled under his breath. "You don't want to know what I could do with that."

"Make more pups?" I asked. I couldn't resist.

He grinned. "Mary Ann and I wouldn't mind trying."

His face fell and I knew he was thinking about his wife. There was nothing I could say to make it better, so I kept my mouth shut. Sure, I missed my old life in New Orleans, but Rodger had a wife and family. He'd been here for three years with no hope of ever seeing his kids again.

The army granted each soldier twenty minutes topside for every year served. That meant in the last three years, Rodger had earned an hour of vacation. Regulations prevented anyone from cashing in leave until they had a week. It would take more than five hundred years to get that kind of break.

So if we couldn't spend it, we bet it. Pretty much everybody in camp had put their leave minutes into the pool. Whoever succeeded in pulling one over on Kosta would get the whole pot.

Kosta knew it, too. That's why he was so hard to get.

I listened to the bubbling tar and focused on the warm sun against my face. I was nearly, maybe, possibly asleep when a cool breeze whisked against my shoulder. It almost felt like the winds off the river back home until a bony finger dug into my arm.

"Oh, Petra . . ."

I was instantly awake—a trick I'd learned in residency.

"He's back," Horace said.

I got a sinking feeling in my gut. "Who's back?"

The orderly hovered at my left, the wings on his ankles fluttering like hummingbirds. "Your balls-to-the-wall special ops patient," he said. "The ambulance broke down."

"For the love of the gods." I sat up.

"I never heard of that," Rodger said, his fishing pole braced between his knees, a mess tent coffee cup in his hand. "The EMS fleet is in top shape."

Rodger was right. The army took impeccable care of equipment. We couldn't afford for something not to work.

I shuddered to think it, but, "Did Galen break it?"

"Who?" Rodger gave me a look like I was the crazy one.

Horace crossed his arms over his chest. "Imps nesting in the engine."

I felt my back stiffen. "Put him on the next one."

"They did," he said, managing to sound both superior and offended. "That one ran over a horny-backed boar. The pig is fine, but the ambulance blew out two tires. Then they used the smaller ambulance."

My belly sank. "The one that holds four patients?" I knew where this was going.

"He didn't fit."

I dug my fingers under my sunglasses to rub at my eyes. "Let me guess. The smaller ambulance left without a hitch."

The sprite nodded.

Cripes.

Rodger's bushy eyebrows wrinkled like he didn't get it. "I saw Commander Galen this morning. He's fine. He can recover here."

No, he couldn't. "He's a troublemaker," I said in the understatement of the year.

Rodger settled back into his chair, tugging on his fishing pole. "He seemed okay to me."

"What do you know?"

"I know enough to keep my foot out of the popcorn bowl."

"Sorry." I moved my foot and sat with my elbows planted on my knees. "Maybe I can put him on a chopper."

"The winds are coming up," Horace said, scanning the horizon. "Nobody's flying."

"Of course they're not."

Besides, I didn't want to break any choppers. The ambulances were bad enough.

I eased the knife out from under my chair and stood.

"Hey, where you going?" Rodger asked.

"I'm going to see Galen of Delphi."

chapter five

Galen lounged in bunk 22A, chest bare, waiting for me.

Part of me was almost glad to see him, which was ridiculous. I was in charge of this operation, not him. At least I hoped that was still the case.

I made my way down the long row of beds, nerves hammering even as I tried to retain the aloof casualness that had served me so well throughout my career.

If I had any less pride, I'd be cringing.

I took his chart off the end of his bed. "Heck of a day. You must be tired."

His expression was stone cold. "You wish."

Okay. I probably deserved that. "What can I say? I'm used to running the show."

"So am I." I saw a glint in his eye. A challenge? Oh hell.

I replaced his chart. He was healing well. No signs of infection. With any luck, I could ship him back to his unit in the next day or two.

And he would be sent into battle again.

I clicked my pen closed a little tighter than necessary. I'd told him I'd save his life, and I had. I couldn't save him from anything else.

No matter how much he fascinated me.

He rested his hands behind his head, a move that only

served to draw attention to his well-developed arms and pectoral muscles. The man was built like every woman's dream.

Too bad I couldn't afford luxiuries like that anymore.

Especially not with him.

"Do you want to know what's happening here?" he asked.

Not particularly, but that wasn't going to stop him.

"It's fate," he said.

"I'm a woman of science." Maybe I could dazzle him with my logic. I had to at least try before I lost my nerve. "You have pajama bottoms on?"

"Why do you ask?" he prodded, amused and absolutely unwilling to make this any easier.

Because I was done with this hot soldier wearing nothing but a sheet.

Lucky for me, I saw the start of cotton sleep pants where a fine line of hair on his stomach snaked past his lower hips. "Come with me," I said, motioning for a wheelchair.

Horace hovered off my left side, frowning.

Tell me about it.

Galen stood easily. He was recovering faster than I'd expected. Good. If I could just hold him off for a day, I could ship him out.

"I don't need a wheelchair," he snorted, towering above me. I stared straight into lean, hard muscle. And at that moment I saw, too, the absurdity of cramming this powerful soldier into a chair.

He looked like he could wrestle a minotaur. Still, if I wanted to get him out of here, I had to follow protocol. "It's the only way you're leaving with me."

He gave me a faint, salty smile. "Are you sure about that?"

No. "Listen." I lowered my voice. "You want to talk, right? Well, then I've got to get you somewhere private. In this." I pointed to the wheelchair, the other hand balled into a fist in the pocket of my scrubs. "If anyone sees you walking around, you run the risk of getting sent back to your unit, with or without any interference from me. And you know what? I'd be just fine with that." I'd fall down drunk with relief. "So if you want to talk, get in the chair."

The corner of his mouth tipped up. "Do you know your cheeks flush when you're angry?"

"Can it. Five more seconds and I walk."

If I didn't know better, I would have sworn I saw a flicker of surprise. He stared at me for a long moment, almost daring me to bolt before taking two powerful strides in the direction of the feeble chair. "Shall we?" he asked drily, sprawling over it like a king at court.

Good enough for me. I grabbed the handles and steered His Highness down the long hallway toward the door, ignoring the catcalls from the soldiers.

The doctor needs to see you alone?
Have fun with that exam.
Ask her if she makes house calls!
I'm next!

Galen grinned like he was in the Macy's Thanksgiving Day Parade. I, on the other hand, blushed down to my toes. Didn't these guys ever grow up?

Didn't they see that I'd won? I'd gotten my way. Galen was going outside with me, per regulations.

So why did I feel like I'd just handed him the battle?

Jaw clenched, I focused straight ahead as I steered him toward the door. What I had to say to the commander was better said in private. There were very few options if you wanted to be alone in a MASH camp. Walking was one of them.

Maybe it would even clear my head. Over the years I'd made a habit of wandering the red dirt paths. It was the only place to go. Outside camp was too dangerous, what with packs of imps on the loose. Not to mention enemy patrols. And if you could manage to avoid those, you risked sand traps that could swallow a person faster than quicksand.

Besides, the camp walkways weren't half bad, especially in the evening as the twin suns set. It was cooler then, with fewer people rushing around.

At last, we made it out of the recovery tent.

"That was brutal," I said as the door slammed closed behind us.

"Best time I've had all month," Galen said, throwing an arm over the back of the chair. He gave me a conspiratorial grin. "Maybe I should start letting you order me around."

I kept my mouth shut and my eyes on the road. Once I got him somewhere private, it would be worth it.

We passed the supply hutch. Naturally the female clerk had to whistle. Then there were the two nurses at the bulletin board, who openly nudged each other and smiled.

What was with these people?

"Hey, Petra," one of the nurses called, "where are you taking that half-naked demi-god?"

"Mind dropping him off at my place?" the other one said, giggling.

What? My stomach twisted. "He's not—" *Merde.* Yes, he was half naked, and had somehow managed to look both gorgeous and in charge. I didn't know if I wanted to slap him or kiss him.

"Sorry ladies," Galen called, "I'm all hers tonight."

"Stop encouraging them," I hissed.

"It's true," he said, to them and to me.

"Yes, but not the way they . . . forget it." I said, wheeling him faster.

I headed for the shadows, past the rectangular shack that served as the officers' club. The tin roof was loud as heck during the monthly rainstorm, but it gave the bar its bite. Large gutters funneled down into tanks that captured Hell's Rain. Rodger had measured it at 180 proof. I didn't like to touch the stuff. Only now it didn't sound half bad. If anybody could drive me to drink, it was Galen.

Maybe I should have stopped for a glass because horror of horrors, Colonel Kosta emerged from the shadows, coming our way. Oh, this was just great.

Colonel Kosta held himself impossibly erect, shoulders squared, his shaved head gleaming under the outside floodlights. An angry scar cut down his right cheek and over his mouth and chin, a souvenier from the Battle of Thermopylae.

Maybe he'd let us pass. I gripped the wheelchair handles

tighter. It's not that I'd necessarily be in trouble. But I didn't want any questions, either.

Leaning down, I whispered against Galen's ear, "Be casual."

I could feel him grinning. "What? Do you want me to take something else off?"

Maybe I'd died and gone to hell. I tried not to let my mortification show, which was probably impossible.

Kosta's sharp gaze lingered on my patient as he passed. "Evening, Robichaud."

"Colonel," I said, straightening. Maybe I could just be struck by lightning and be done with it.

Somehow—I think I blocked it out—I managed to get Galen past the medical supply tents, past the enlisted club, the general supply depot, and the ambulance lot. The suns had almost set and the motor pool was lit with lanterns and torches. A few mechanics had a jeep up on blocks and were working underneath.

One of the smart alecks called out to us as we passed, "You two going to see the good father?"

"At least I've been invited, Lazio," I shot back.

Galen drew a hand through his short spiky hair. "Something I should know about?" he asked, watching Lazio chuckle with a few of the mechanics.

"Oh, it's dumb." Which is what made it kind of fun. "There's really nowhere to be alone in a MASH camp, so when people want to get a bit amorous, they head back to this huge outcropping of rocks past the cemetery and beyond the minefield."

"Minefield?" He sounded surprised.

"That's what we call the junkyard. I mean, you can't let frisky couples sneak in and out of there without wiring the place with a few pranks."

He seemed amused at that. "And couples? They still risk it?"

"For half an hour alone? You bet."

"How romantic."

"I wouldn't know." Now, why had I told him that?

"Anyway, our chaplain has a hut out that way. He likes to minister to the semi-demonic creatures, try to help turn them around. As you can imagine, they're a bit reluctant to show up in camp during office hours."

I parked the chair. Galen was up and out of it before I could even get the emergency brake on. I let it slide. We were finally alone. Now I just had to think of exactly what to say to the man.

The torches cast an uneven light as full night came upon us.

His back muscles bunched as he squinted out past the cemetery, toward the mounding scrap yard beyond.

"Believe it or not, there's a path through it," I said. "Toward the end, you come to a fork in the road. Go left and you come up on Father McArio's hut. Go right and it's make-out city."

"Ahh." He turned back to me, eyes glittering, "so when you want to be alone with your sweetheart . . ."

"You just invite them out to see the good father."

He gave me a long look. "And what does your camp commander have to say about that?"

"As much of a hard-ass as he can be"—and Kosta definitely took pride in driving us to our limit—"he ignores the junkyard and the rocks." It happened outside the main camp. Besides, the old Spartan knew when to throw us a bone.

Galen had fallen silent. Thinking, no doubt. No good could come of that.

"You have a target range?" He indicated a series of lumps in the field beyond the motor pool.

My voice caught. "That's our cemetery."

He didn't get it right away. "Soldiers are cremated."

"Yes." Demi-gods were lit upon a funeral pyre, as tradition demanded. "These are the doctors and the nurses. Mechanics and clerks." These were the people who never made it out of limbo. Someday I'd be one of them.

He studied the crude wooden tombstones. We couldn't

exactly quarry stone, not with a war going on. But we did get a monthly shipment of wood.

"We're here for life, too." Or until the end of the war. "Families can claim a body, and the army will ship one of us home. Those without families stay here."

My throat closed.

His eyes cut to me, as if he knew what I'd been thinking.

"You are one of the ones staying."

I tried to smile and failed. "Yes."

I didn't have anyone left. Well, anyone who knew I had a supernatural side.

My boyfriend during med school had been a shapeshifting dragon. Marc had been drafted by the old gods while he was still in his surgical fellowship. He'd been killed almost immediately.

My dad had been human. He'd kept my secret almost too well. He'd told the family I'd gone off to serve the poor in Haiti. A necessary lie. No one in my extended family knew about my mother's fae nature, or my military service for the new god army. Now, with Dad dead, there was no one left even to know I was here.

I'd been alone ever since.

Galen touched my shoulder. In an absurd moment of weakness I let him.

"I'm sorry," he said simply.

I shrugged. "For what? It's not your fault."

He remained 100 percent focused on me. "It will be if I can't stop this," he said, refusing to let me discount my pain.

I glanced away. I didn't want to go there.

"You can't save everyone," I told him.

Deep in the cemetery, a ghostly soul shimmered between the graves. It took me a moment to realize who it was.

Charlie.

The wind ruffled his sandy brown hair as he stared out past the camp, into nothingness.

I squeezed my eyes shut. That's it. I was done. I grabbed the wheelchair, steering it away from the civilian part of the cemetery. I should have tried to get Galen back in it, or at least examined him, but who was I kidding? There was no trace of his injury. And I didn't want to argue with a half-naked demi-god.

Suddenly this place didn't seem like such a good idea.

"Let's get you back. It's cold."

"I'm not cold." He stood in front of me, blocking me. Cripes, he was bullheaded. I'd never known anyone so determined to insert himself into my own personal hell.

He stared down at me, positively dripping with challenge. "I stayed for you," he said, as if he could make me face it by sheer force of will.

"The ambulances broke down," I bit off every word. Maybe if I said it enough, I'd believe it.

"Bullshit." He caught me by the shoulders. "I didn't choose this any more than you did. When I took that poisoned dagger to the chest, I thought I was going to die."

I'd seen. I knew.

"What was it like?" I asked, startling him.

His fingers loosened and he fell silent for a moment, as if he was hesitant to say more.

"It was almost a relief for it to be over." Guilt flickered across his features. "The worst part about war isn't the fighting," he went on, almost to himself. "It's when you're helpless to stop the horror from reaching innocent people. Kids. Families. Not everybody signed up to have their guts torn out. I didn't know how to stop it. But now maybe we can change things."

I didn't understand what he wanted from me. "I hope you do. You're a good soldier."

He made a low sound in his throat. "That's not what I meant and you know it."

Okay, fine. This place was a nightmare, and the stark truth was—there was nothing we could do about it. Well, except pursue a doomed prophecy, which was a surefire way to fail again and get me killed in the process.

He caressed my skin, watching goose bumps erupt on my shoulders. "You're good at deflection, Doctor. Why is that?"

Years and years of practice.

"Let's go," I said, pulling away.

This time he let me.

We began walking again. At the edge of the cemetery, we passed three smoldering funeral pyres. It had been a rough day yesterday.

"Where were you when you were stabbed with the dagger?" I asked.

He owed me that at least, to help me figure out why this thing was following me.

His eyes lingered on the funeral pyres. "It's classified."

"Who stabbed you?" I asked, more tartly than I'd intended. "Is that classified, too?"

"I don't know," he said, frustrated. "It doesn't matter." He stopped. "I understand you're afraid. It's part of the job. But it doesn't mean you can step away and pretend this isn't real."

"Pretend?" That was rich. "Just because I don't happen to agree with you, you think I live in some god damn fantasy world?" I felt every slice of humanity this place cut out of me. I was raw with it. "Do you think I was pretending when I pulled that knife out of your chest?" I'd given everything I had to this job and to him.

He brought a hand up to his chest and ripped the bandage away. An angry red scar sliced across tan skin, the only indication he'd nearly died yesterday. "We were brought together for a reason. I can feel it. You can, too."

Feeling? What did he know about feeling? If I felt any more, it would eat me alive. "Listen, hotshot, this war isn't my fault. What may or may not happen to those kids you're talking about is not my fault. What happened in that OR is not my fault."

"No," he thundered. "It's your fucking obligation."

I turned and walked away.

He followed me.

Fuck. I couldn't stand it. I couldn't take it for one second longer. I spun back to face him. "What the hell is your angle, Galen? What do you want?"

In two rough steps he was right there with me, on me. "I want the right team on my side when the real battle begins. Otherwise there is no hope—for you or my men or anybody else."

He was positively lethal. And frightening. And exactly the man I'd want on my side if all hell broke loose.

"We have to end this," he stated, as if it were inevitable. "Soon."

"Impossible," I said. I could feel the heat rolling off him, and me.

He didn't give an inch. "I know things," he said, his voice low and intense. "I'm out of the loop now," he added, almost to himself.

"Good."

"I think that's fate, too," he continued, as if I hadn't even spoken. He locked eyes with me. "I need to stay here, but my men could be on the move as we speak."

My stomach fluttered. "Doing what?" I didn't like the way his voice sounded, or the fear behind his words.

"It's classified."

I hated the military.

He inhaled sharply. "I can't tell you. I don't need to tell you. You only have to understand that it will be bad for all of us. And disastrous for those on Earth."

I rubbed at my eyes. He would have to say that.

"Listen to me. I'm here for a reason. We came together for something bigger than just saving my life." He was absolutely convinced, driven. On a collision course with death and ruin. "Help me figure this out."

"I'm afraid," I said. Terrified.

The corner of his mouth turned up. "Good. It'll help keep you alive."

chapter six

I returned Galen to the recovery ward. I hoped to the gods he'd be out of our camp in the next twenty-four hours. Otherwise I wouldn't know what to do with him.

Holly, the charge nurse, leaned her elbows on her desk. Her mop of blond hair was streaked with red highlights. She'd tied part of it into a ponytail holder and left the rest free.

"Do you have the medical history file on Galen of Delphi?" I asked.

She shook her head. "It hasn't come in yet. You want me to let you know when it does?"

"Please." Knowledge was power, and I needed every bit of it when it came to this man.

She wrote a Post-it note for herself and added it to the flurry on her desk. "You heading to karaoke?"

"No." I stole a Starburst out of her candy bowl and unwrapped it. "I'm going to drop in on Father McArio."

She grinned. "Rumor here is that you already went to the rocks."

Of all the . . . "I suppose denying it will only make it worse," I said, cringing.

"Guaranteed."

Hades. I felt the sting of it. And a tug of disappointment as well. If I was going to be accused of stripping down a hot, broody special ops officer, I wanted to actually get a taste of something besides his temper.

Or maybe I really was going crazy.

"Hello," Jeffe rumbled. I hadn't even known the sphinx was behind me.

He twitched his nose like a cat, his copper mane swishing at his shoulders. "I can hold my silence no longer."

Oh good. A sphinx was going to lecture me about my love life.

"You listen to me," he said, as if he were divulging the secrets of the Great Pyramids. "It is not a good idea to go through the minefield right now."

When was it ever a good idea? The vacation pot was up to three weeks. The minefield was the perfect place to give a prank a test run. Now it seemed even Jeffe was getting in on the act. "What'd you do, slick?"

He straightened his front legs and stiffened his shoulders. "I cannot tell you."

I stuffed the candy wrapper into my pocket. "Fair enough." After all, Rodger had gotten the sphinx drunk and encased him in stone last week. Of course it was just plaster of paris and we let him out. Still, Jeffe had his pride.

Jeffe leaned forward. "You will not get me to tell you."

Holly and I exchanged glances.

He was squirming like a kid on Christmas morning. "Okay, I will tell you."

"Remind me never to tell you a secret." Holly grinned.

"I order these baby scarabs from my homeland and then I mummify them. First I had to wait for them to die because they are sacred. But then I mummify them and I hide them in the machines!"

Good on him. "That would definitely scare me"—provided I saw them and knew what they were. But I had to give Jeffe an A+ for effort. "Thanks for the warning," I said, saluting them both as I headed out the door.

Dang, it was getting cold. I stopped by my hutch for my jacket. The place was dark. Both Rodger and Marius were out. At least neither of them had seen me giving my patient the grand tour of camp. I'd never hear the end of it.

Kosta was bad enough.

I grabbed a piece of Fruit Stripe from my candy stash and pulled the dark blue New Orleans Zephyrs jacket from its peg. I was a minor-league baseball freak. Or at least I had been until my dad stopped sending box scores.

We used to go to games all the time when I was growing up. He'd quiz me on state capitals between innings. One summer it was the periodic table.

He told me I was smart, said I could do anything. Of course that didn't stop him from hitting the roof when I'd gotten a "Fleur-de-Z" tattooed on my right hip.

I squared my shoulders against the wind as I crossed the street, away from the familiar bubble of the tar swamps.

Father McArio would have sage advice. And hopefully some chocolate chip cookies. He gave them out every Sunday after mass, which was why he had so many minor gods in attendance. Their supreme deities may have gotten us into this mess, but Father McArio and his God had a direct line to Mrs. Fields.

Torches cast flickering light on the path in front of me. Farther down, shouts of laughter poured from the officers' club. I glanced at the closed door as I passed. From the sound of it, they had the Lounge Lizards in Limbo karaoke contest going in full swing. Rodger was belting out "Like a Virgin" and howling half the notes. He was either throwing the contest or hopelessly drunk.

With Rodger, it was hard to tell.

On the other side of the cemetery, I grabbed one of the last torches lining the path near the funeral pyres. This was the end of the road, at least for the civilized section of camp.

The flame cast flickers of light on the uneven ground in front of me as I entered the minefield. The sign said JUNK DEPOT, but I knew better.

Hulking skeletons of half-rotted ambulances and jeeps

lay rusting on either side of the rock-strewn path. I didn't
come back here that often—for obvious reasons. I had no
love life, so I wasn't about to take the right fork in the road.
And as much as I liked Father McArio, it was easier to see
him in camp, when I wasn't in as much danger of having a
pot of clams dumped over my head.

But this knife, and whatever I had with Galen, couldn't
wait. I hadn't felt this on edge in a long time.

The real kicker was, Galen had gotten to me. Despite the
mess. Damn it all. I hadn't let myself get personally involved
with a patient since I'd left my practice in New Orleans.
Those people I could help. All I could do for these soldiers
was send them back to the front.

Of course, the problem was that Galen was no longer just
a patient to me. He was a man. A take-charge, daring, utterly fascinating man.

I ran a hand along the charred remains of the last VIP
shower tent. Finally, something I understood. It seemed like
only yesterday that it had gone up in glorious flames.

The prank had gone wrong, as usual. If only the visiting
General Fiehler had stayed in his hutch like he was sup-
posed to. Dale Fiehler was a legendary tactical genius. Still,
I had no idea how he even got out. We'd nailed his door shut.
He escaped anyway, and then headed to the showers and
tripped a Fourth of July fireworks extravaganza.

A minute later and Rodger and I would have gotten Colonel Kosta. But one minute could mean an eternity around
here.

I drew the collar of my jacket up and skirted a suspicious-
looking van parked in the middle of the path. Gloppy footsteps echoed inside. Uh-hum. Hickey Horns. They were
technically a plant. The green, spindly things fed on human
hormones, so they'd basically scramble up to your neck and
make you look like a teenager in love.

I stopped mid-step and held the torch low. I scanned out-
ward, the firelight traveling over rocky soil and dirt until it
hit upon a series of trip wires that ran straight to the door of
the van.

Impressive. I'd have to find out who did it.

Rodger and I could use a co-conspirator with an expertise in triggering mechanisms.

In the meantime I stepped lightly and left the hickeys to the next poor fool who wandered this way.

McArio had better be home. He'd talked about moving his hut closer to camp, so that people like me wouldn't have to skirt half a dozen pranks in order to visit. But then there was his "other" ministry. And frankly, I figured he liked living on the edge.

I glanced at the dense maze of shadows behind me.

At least I was still technically in camp. I didn't even want to think of the nasties lurking outside the wards.

When I reached the fork in the road, I let out the breath I hardly realized I was holding. "Hallelujah," I said, taking the wider, safer path to the left.

Jeffe would be disappointed. Well, maybe I'd tell him I was spooked by a few mini mummies.

In the distance, lit by the full moon, I spotted McArio's small hutch. The light was on inside. He'd also left a dinged-up camping lantern out by his sculpture garden. Father liked to work with junk metal, and he had quite a collection of pieces.

Most of it consisted of birds and other winged creatures that appeared as if they'd take flight any second. There was even a beautiful Pegasus, with its mighty head directed toward the sky.

I gave the father's door two swift knocks, sending a multicolored Talavera cross slapping against the wood.

"Come on in," he said, as if I'd braved the minefield a hundred times to come visit him.

I batted at the pine tree air freshener above the door and entered to find Father McArio sitting at his desk. A single lantern hung overhead. He wore army boots and fatigues, topped with a black shirt and a clerical collar. He had to be at least sixty-five, although you wouldn't know it from his thick black hair.

"Petra," he said, his voice warm. He turned toward the

darkened corner behind him. "It's okay, Fitz." He pinched two fingers together and waggled them at the shadows. "You can come out."

A coal-black puppy tottered forward, bashful with its head bent. "There you go." Father lifted it onto his lap and grinned as the dog started gnawing on his hand. "He's a little shy until he gets to know you."

"Aww." I reached down to pet the doggy behind the ears. I loved soft puppy fur. The dog licked at my wrist. His red eyes blazed up at me.

I snatched my hand back. "You're keeping a hellhound?" Of all the . . . Those things came straight from the underworld.

"A friend of a friend's hellhound got frisky and fathered some puppies," he said, as if he were the proud dad.

"What? In Hades?"

The puppy began gnawing on the father's shirtsleeve. "Of course not." He rubbed him on his round puppy belly. "Fitz came from Las Vegas."

It figured. Father used to be an exorcist there. But still, it didn't make it right. "Colonel Kosta will skewer you if he finds out."

Father fed more of his sleeve to the beast. "We're in limbo. How much worse can it get?"

"I'm not sure I want to know."

He shoved a camp chair at me with one foot. "Take a load off. Tell me what brings you here."

Okay, well, if a hellhound couldn't get him going, maybe this could. I dug into the pocket of my scrubs and withdrew the dagger.

Father leaned forward as I slowly unwrapped it and laid it out on my lap. The smooth metal glowed in the low light of the lantern. The head of the snake looked even more ominous.

"It's bronze," I said.

His eyes flicked to mine. "How'd you get it?"

Guilt tugged at me. I didn't like to be reminded that we'd been in this situation once before. Father was the only one who knew my secret, and what I'd done after I first arrived.

"Don't worry," I said quickly. "I didn't make another mistake, if that's what you mean."

"I didn't doubt you," he said, without a trace of irony.

Father's expression remained neutral as I explained about Galen and the surgery gone wrong.

The Jesuit held still, absorbing each word. It was a gift few of us had—to truly listen without judging.

When I'd finished, he leaned back in his chair. "What do you think?"

"Me?" The blade glistened in the pale light. "I don't know." Science couldn't explain this away.

He lowered the hellhound to the floor, where it immediately began gnawing on Father's pant leg.

"May I?" he asked.

I let him take the dagger. He held it by the handle, touching his fingers to the smooth part of the blade. "This is old. Beautiful as well."

"I think you need to exorcise it," I said.

He gave a small smile. "It's not possessed."

"How do you know?" I answered quickly. Then I remembered whom I was talking with. "Fine." It was a mere technicality. "Is there a way to destroy it?"

The creases in his forehead deepened as he continued his observations. "If you don't mind, I think I'll pray on it."

"Why?" I asked, apprehension creeping up my spine.

He placed a steady hand on my knee. "I'm a Jesuit. It's what we do."

I was all for faith, but, "What about mashing it to bits?"

"Patience," he said, wrapping it carefully. When he finished, he held it out to me.

Heck, no. I didn't want that thing back. "Keep it."

He seemed almost amused. "Do you want it to follow you again?"

"It didn't follow me. Someone put it there."

"Perhaps," he said.

Cold fear pooled in my veins. "It's evil," I told him. At the very least it was disturbing. I didn't like how it had shown up in my locker. Or that it had seemed to take on a life of its own.

"It's a tool." He ran his hand over the bundle, like he was testing it. "Our lack of understanding doesn't make it evil."

He would have to say that.

"This isn't something you want to rush," he said plainly. "We'll take our time and do the right thing. If this is nothing, it should be clear if we give it time. If it's more . . . well, we'll have to see what happens."

I groaned. As much as I needed McArio's advice, there were times when I really didn't like what he had to say.

He knew it, too. "You're young."

"Compared with everyone around here."

"And in such a hurry," he continued, as if I hadn't said a word. "Will the world end if you don't have every answer right away?"

I'd like to think so. "Yes."

McArio barked out a laugh. "We're blessed to have you."

"That's one way of putting it."

"If the Lord can have patience, so can I." The twinkle was back in his eye. "Now tell me. Is this the only thing you came to see me about?"

I wanted to say yes. "No."

We watched the puppy settle onto a doggy bed sculpted from a bedpan and topped with one of Father's old shirts. My thoughts traveled back to Galen. "I took the knife out of a special ops soldier. It broke off inside him."

Father's eyes softened. "And he died."

"I saved his life," I said. "Of course that doesn't mean he's willing to tell me where he was when he was stabbed—or even who did it." I flushed, caught up in the emotion of it. "He says he doesn't know that part."

Father nodded, listening. "What else?"

"What makes you think there's anything else?" I asked.

Father simply waited.

Damn, he wasn't going to make this easy.

Somehow, no matter how much I wanted to, I couldn't admit to Father that I'd touched the man's soul.

It was too deeply embedded, too real to explain. It was almost as if saying it out loud would diminish it. And I wanted to preserve that connection. Treasure it where nothing and nobody could touch it. It was the most beautiful thing that had ever happened to me.

Galen had affected me in ways I was still trying to understand.

"Petra?" Father asked.

"I'm attracted to him." There. I'd given him something. "The whole camp thinks we're doing it," I snorted.

Father tilted his head, as if what I'd just told him wasn't completely crazy. "What do you think is wrong with being attracted to a man?"

He had to be kidding. "I'm a doctor!"

Father rubbed at his chin. "He's a demi-god."

"Very much so." I couldn't believe he might actually like me back.

Father gave a small smile. "You haven't allowed yourself to feel. At first, I wondered if it was because of your accident when you first came. Then there is an adjustment to the difficulties of your job and of losing good soldiers. Now I wonder if you've just forgotten how."

He was wrong. I felt plenty. I just couldn't get it out. I swallowed the memories and the pain. "He's still my patient."

"Like that's ever stopped anyone around here." McArio's mouth twisted. "If half the people 'visiting the good father' actually visited the good father, I'd have a lot more company."

"Remember you're talking to a Cajun Catholic. We were born to feel guilt."

"It's more than that," he said gently.

Maybe he was right. Maybe this place had damaged me more than I even knew. I had no idea what normal felt like anymore.

Worse, I realized with a start, this was the first time I'd experienced any real attraction to a man since I'd been with Marc. And he'd been dead ten years.

"Give yourself permission to be human," father said. "You deserve to be happy."

The puppy began to snore, and Father broke out into a big

grin. "Besides," he said, turning his attention back to me. "It's not against army regulations."

I stared at him.

He cocked his head. "Let me guess. You've never read the handbook."

"I've skimmed parts," I said defensively.

"Right. Well, look at it this way. Have you seen how some of these creatures who call themselves gods have acted over the centuries?"

"Good point."

"Some of them have experienced truly tragic attractions. What you seem to be experiencing is quite natural. And healthy."

Too healthy.

Father bowed his head. "Now let's pray."

We bowed our heads as the hellhound lay on his back, dreaming and chasing imaginary hellcats.

I felt a little better as I left McArio's hut. Sure, I still had a dagger in my pocket, and more questions than answers, but he'd given me a lot to think about. And I had to admit Fitz was pretty cute.

Shadows rose up around me as I approached the fork in the road. Maybe I should have taken McArio up on his offer to walk me home. He always seemed to avoid the pranks. I hoped that wasn't because he was pulling a lot of them.

A cold wind blew in from the desert as I glanced back at the light in the distance. No, I wouldn't do it. The man should be retired. He didn't need to be walking me through the minefield in the middle of the night.

I'd made it through once before and I'd make it again. I tightened my jacket around me and checked my watch. At least it was late enough that most of the loving couples should be back from the rocks. Hopefully they'd sprung most of the traps already.

One step at a time. I edged past the Hickey Horns bus, barely avoiding the skeleton of a helicopter, half scrapped for parts. Only this time, it felt different.

Icy cold settled on the back of my neck. It felt like someone was watching.

My torch had burned down while I'd been inside McArio's hut. The low flame cast deep shadows, barely illuminating the ground in front of me. The minefield seemed taller than before, longer. I could see my breath in puffs in front of me.

Breathe in. Breathe out.

I was a doctor. I was logical. Thinking types didn't get scared of the dark.

My galloping heart disagreed with me.

Fuck a duck. I searched for the barbecued VIP shower tent. Where was that charred heap of junk? Lord help me if I got lost in the maze of metal.

It reminded me of being a sweaty-palmed kid in my dad's basement. I could almost feel the beasts lurking in the shadows.

Skreek!

I lurched forward as something landed with a thud behind me. Pranks be damned. I took off running.

Skreek!

It caught my jacket and yanked me backward.

"Oh my god," I darted forward, tearing free. It grabbed for my legs.

I zigzagged like Walter Payton, or more like a panic-slapped doctor running for her life. Holy hell. This had better be a prank.

Skreek!

I could hear it scuttling behind me as I made a mad dash down the path, leaping over rocks and twisted metal. My torch was useless but the moon was high. I focused everything I had on the patch of ground right in front of me. No way was I going to fall down like some horror-movie twit.

It was gaining. I had to find cover. I could feel the ground shaking behind me.

There! I spotted a broken-down jeep to my left. It'd have to do. I scrambled inside as an immense claw struck the ground, sending up a shower of rocks.

No prank.

Blood pounding in my ears, rocks in my hair, I slammed the door.

"What the hell was that?" I'd never seen anything like it.

The inside of the jeep smelled like dirt and decay. I was sitting in the passenger seat, with the driver's-side door across from me closed. Okay, good. The roof looked relatively intact. Hallelujah. And it was a hardtop. I wanted to kiss whoever had ordered a sturdy roof for this hunk of junk.

My eyes watered from the stench of lighter fluid. That's when I realized I was still holding a lighted torch. Oh shit.

I nearly dropped it when a giant claw smashed into the window next to me. The safety glass fractured into a jagged web.

Skreek!

No way the window would hold against another hit. I scrambled for the driver's seat as the creature slammed its claw straight through. It sliced into the seat at head level, sending foam cushion bits flying.

I seared the giant red claw with my torch.

Skreek! The creature shuddered.

Ha! "The monster doesn't like fire." I waved my torch at a claw the size of a guillotine blade.

My palms burned as it clamped around my weapon and yanked the torch straight out of my hands.

The monster held it aloft and as I pressed my back against the driver's-side door, I got a no-holds-barred look at the largest scorpion I'd ever laid eyes on. It was at least six feet long, with a reddened body, grasping claws, and a segmented tail curling over its back into a pointed stinger bigger than my head.

The creature waved my torch in the air before snapping it in half.

Unbelievable.

This thing could tear me apart in seconds.

I checked the backseat for weapons. Nothing. The jeep had been stripped clean.

My heart caught in my throat as the scorpion reached for me, one claw clattering against the dashboard as the other slammed against the front window. The jeep heaved with the impact.

I couldn't outrun it.

But I couldn't stay.

I was going to die in here. If I didn't get out, I was going to die.

Okay. Deep breaths. I twisted the driver's-side door open and nearly fell out onto the hard-packed dirt. Hulks of twisted metal appeared gray under the full moon. I started to run, until I saw an immense creature skitter out from behind the rusted-out bus next to me, its tail curled and ready to strike.

Fuck. Two? Chest heaving, I hustled back inside the jeep and slammed the door. Then I locked it. As if that would stop a giant scorpion. I was so screwed.

chapter seven

The second scorpion was on me in a heartbeat. I yanked my hand away from the car door as a large black eyeball pressed near the glass. Its mouthparts twitched as it stared me down.

Heaven help me. I was dinner under glass.

Skreek!

The first scorpion leapt onto the hood and smashed its tail into the front window. Glass rained down as I dove for the backseat.

The tail was thick as a battering ram, with a curved spike on the end. I gasped as it dripped its poison onto the stick shift, each drop sizzling into the plastic.

I struggled to get back as far as I could. Feet out, I was ready to kick the bastard if I had to. It was a pathetic attempt, but it was all I had. I couldn't run. These things would be faster. And there was absolutely nowhere to hide.

Galen leapt onto the hood behind it, naked except for a pair of pajama bottoms. I'd never been so glad to see anyone in my life.

"Alala!" He bellowed the Athenian war cry, and I about choked as he drove a metal spike through the fat body of the first scorpion.

It lurched forward and let out a piercing yowl, its claws exploding the remainder of the windshield as they tumbled onto the dash.

"Get back as far as you can!" he ordered.

"Right," I croaked.

I wanted to dig a hole in the ground and live there as I watched the creature's spider-like legs scrabble against the hood of the jeep.

If this thing came any closer, I was going to have to make a run for it out the back. If I could even get out that way.

I dragged my knees as close as I could to my chest while the dying predator thrashed in front of me.

Galen leapt off the hood. Holy moley, he was going after the other one. I'd have to finish this one, bash its head in. Numb, I searched for something—anything—that I could use on its head. If it even had a head. It was more like a giant mouth with tentacles coming out.

My heart sank as the blood pounded in my ears. I had nothing.

Outside, the second creature shrieked.

Galen let out a low grunt.

"Get in the front seat!" he ordered, a desperate edge to his voice.

"What?" He had to be crazy.

"Now! Now! Now!"

The air whooshed out of my lungs. I said a quick prayer and tumbled into the driver's seat.

Damn Galen of Delphi if he was wrong.

Skreek!

The seat underneath me jerked as the entire back end of the jeep caved in.

"Galen!" I shouted, on the verge of panic as I was shoved forward into the steering wheel. I pushed away from it, knees slipping into the space below the driver's seat. I dug them against the floorboard as I edged toward the center of the car. Another blow buried the steering wheel into the seat behind it, nearly crushing me.

Trapped, I braced both hands against the plastic under-side of the dash, crouching close, trying to make myself small as possible as I faced the shuddering predator.

I swallowed, trying to breathe. The first scorpion's stinger was an inch from my cheek, dripping poison into the black hole where the stick shift had melted away.

"Petra." Galen's voice drew closer.

I didn't dare move.

"Petra," he repeated, the edge back in his voice.

"I'm here," I said into the plastic.

"Thank gods," he swore. "Hang on. I've got you."

Behind me, I heard the high-pitched rending of metal and steel as he yanked the door off its hinges. The seat that pinned me was wrenched back. "Are you hurt?"

"I don't know," I said, breathing freely again, afraid to turn my head, not willing to take my eyes off the stinger.

"We'll get you out of here." Galen's hand closed over my shoulder. "Follow my lead, okay?"

"Gotcha," I said, trying—and failing—to maintain a shred of calm as I inched toward him.

My back hit the steering wheel.

"Can you bend?"

I felt closed in, trapped in the tiny space. "No." My mind raced. My breath came in gasps. I started seeing tiny black dots in front of my eyes.

Holy hell. I hadn't had a panic attack since med school. I braced my hands on the dirty floor of the jeep and breathed in through the mouth, out through the nose. In through the mouth, out through the nose. I couldn't lose it. Not now or I could fall right into that stinger.

"Hold on." I heard the groan of plastic and metal as the barrier behind me lifted. One arm curled around my waist, drawing me away from the deadly poison. "You're okay. I've got you."

"I'm fine." I tried to swallow. Failed. "Just don't touch me for a minute." I had this handled. I was almost out. Galen had ripped off the steering wheel and a lot of other parts, too. Because, sure, of course—why not slay two giant scorpions and then rip the side off a jeep? I couldn't believe I was even a teeny-tiny part of this. I gave a high-pitched, strung-out laugh. "What are you, Superman?"

"Just your average demi-god."

I tried to croak out another laugh. There was nothing average about this man.

My body was stiff with fear and shock. As soon as I started moving, I came down with the shakes.

"Easy now," he said, catching me when I reached the edge of the seat, making sure I didn't fall face-first into the dirt.

"Oh yeah. Piece of cake," I said, as he pulled me from the wreck and crushed me to him.

He was breathing hard, his neck bent, his chin resting against my forehead. I wrapped my arms around his back and held on. His grip was steady. Mine was not.

The jeep was crushed—with one speared monster on the roof and another on the hood. He pulled me tighter and at the same time angled himself between me and the wreck.

His heart pounded against my cheek. My tears fell hot against his cold chest. We were both so cold.

My breath came in sharp gasps as I clung to him. He'd saved my life. God. He'd saved me.

It felt so good to be safe.

He'd lost his new bandage somewhere along the way. Or maybe the nurses hadn't even thought he needed another one.

He'd be shipping out tomorrow for sure. And while that should have been a relief, all I could feel at that moment was a keen sense of loss.

I wondered what would have happened if I'd met him at a different time, under different circumstances—in a world that didn't involve ancient bronze daggers, the prophecy, or this bloody war.

It was ridiculous. He was an immortal warrior. I was a girl from the Eighth Ward. Yet I felt more connected right there with him than I'd felt with anyone in a long time.

I took advantage of his closeness to run my fingers along the puckered red scar where I'd sewn him together. He inhaled sharply.

"Does it hurt?" I asked, jerking back.

"No." He caught my wrist and held it.

His breath came quick. His eyes glittered like ice. We were completely alone. Hidden in the darkness.

"How did you find me?" I hurried to ask, stumbling over the words, making conversation, refusing to believe what could and would happen with this man if I only let myself have it.

My cheeks flushed. My heart beat wildly in my chest. And it had nothing to do with the two dead scorpions sizzling on the jeep.

Galen knew it. The soldier in him caught every detail, dissected every nuance.

If I didn't want this, I should back away right now.

But I couldn't. I needed it. It was real and good and gut-wrenchingly right. I knew him. I'd seen into his soul and understood without a doubt that Galen was the kind of man I wanted to be with.

He was noble, strong, and loyal. He would stand by me, fight for me.

He was a gift. One I couldn't have. I shouldn't. But one I so desperately wanted to pretend was mine, if only for a little while.

Sparks of pleasure burned through me as he ran his fingers down the side of my neck, and I nearly exploded when he followed with teeth and tongue. "You taste so good," he murmured against my skin.

My breath came in gulps. I tried to think of something, anything other the sweet heat and the throbbing ache between my legs.

Talk. Just talk. Maybe we could talk.

But my throat was hoarse and my voice pitched wildly. "I can't believe you're in one piece."

My nipples tightened as he ran his hands up my sides, over my white tank top. I wished it were my bare skin. "I got lucky," he said, stopping just below my breasts.

God. I wanted him. I wanted this.

I shifted so I could feel him. He was rock-hard and ready. My hands fisted at my sides. I could touch him. I could feel the whole hot length of him in my hand. I could make him gasp again.

I dug my fingers into my palms until it hurt. "So what kind of scorpions were those anyway?"

His gaze turned steely, ripping over me with a ferocity that stung. "Petra," he said, his thumb tracing my lower lip, "shut up."

He gripped my shoulders and edged me against the smooth side of a broken-down Humvee.

For an instant he stilled. Our breaths mingled, fast and ready. Every nerve sizzled, and my senses sharpened. My body thrummed with anticipation. *I shouldn't be doing this.* He'd be gone soon.

I could end this. I could let him leave. But then I'd never know what it was like to slide naked against him, hot and sweaty and eager, his mouth on my breast, his teeth grazing the nipple.

The moonlight framed him like a halo. The hairs on the back of my neck rose as his mouth hovered over mine. He bent his head slowly, and I closed my eyes tight as his mouth touched mine.

His lips were soft, so unlike the rest of him. His kiss was languid and sensual, as if he was savoring every last bit of it, committing it to memory.

I unclenched my fingers and touched them to the hard plane of his chest. The corners of my mouth curved up and I slipped closer, fitting him against me. He groaned and pressed tighter, his mouth gentle, his fingers sliding through my hair.

I'd never expected this. Him. Galen the big, bad special ops soldier was kissing me slow and sensual and raw.

He had to be on an adrenaline high. Hell, I knew he was. But he didn't push. He didn't shove. He took it painfully and achingly slow.

He kissed the edges of my mouth, dipped in, teasing me with his tongue. It was earth-shatteringly intimate. Strong, cool Galen of Delphi had a tender side. But hadn't I known that? I'd seen it in his soul.

Fear crept into the corner of my mind.

I'd never imagined anything like this, like him. My entire body was alive, lit up from the inside.

I couldn't share that with him. It was too much.

But we could have something else. I knew he wanted me. I nibbled his lower lip, ground hard against his arousal.

He groaned low in the back of his throat. I trailed my fingers down his belly, to where his taut skin disappeared under the pajama pants. I yanked the ties open.

"What do you want, Galen?"

"God damn it, Petra," he hissed as I slid my hands around the edge, then underneath. And then he went perfectly still as I ran my hands over his hips and down his lean, hard thighs.

"Tell me what you want to do to me, Galen."

His hot breath scalded my cheek. "I'm going to kiss you until your juice is running down your legs. Then I'm going to strip you naked, lick it up, and suck on your clit until you come."

"Oh gods."

He shoved me back against the side of the Humvee and pinned me there with an eating, devouring kiss. I wound my hands through his hair, yanking him closer. There was no more thinking. No more doubt. I wound myself shamelessly around him, raw and primal and powerful. This was how it was supposed to be.

He shoved my scrub pants down. I kicked them off as he arched my leg around his neck and fell on his knees in front of me.

I jerked my head back as I felt his mouth on my inner thigh, the rough brush of his cheek. God, I was so wet. He lingered, kissing his way up to the core of me. I wanted to scream, thrash, make him go faster.

At last his lips and tongue found me. His shoulders shook as he tasted me. Slowly, he licked the very center of me.

"More," I pleaded, my heel at his back, squirming closer. "Galen."

He broke at the sound of his name, groaning out loud as

he devoured me. My body reeled at the tidal wave of sensation. My legs quivered. My hips thrust. There was no holding back, not anymore.

His hands tightened on my thighs, opening me wider,
pushing me harder as I came with a scream.

He kept with me, never letting up. The force of it ripped
through me.

And then boneless, panting, and shuddering, I watched as
he ran his tongue along the inside of one quivering thigh,
then the other. I was riveted, shocked, and I grew even wetter as he lapped up my juices. He was slow and indulgent.

He reveled in it.

"Galen, I—" I began, gasping for breath, for sanity.

He gazed up at me, his blue eyes piercing, his mouth wet.
"I told you what I was going to do."

He caressed me as he stood.

Both of us stiffened as screams pierced the night. He
whipped his head around, as if he could see into the darkness.

"Imps," he said, "here in the minefield."

I was still half submerged in a mix of searing excitement
and bone-drenching lassitude. "How do you know?" I asked,
clawing my way back to the real world.

The scar across his right eyebrow furrowed as he gave
me a you've-got-to-be-kidding look.

"You're still in danger," he said, retying his pajama pants.
He found mine on the ground and returned them to me.
Hands shaking, I tugged them on.

I could see the outline of his cock, long and thick under
the thin cotton. I still wanted to touch it.

He saw me staring and grinned. "I've created a monster."

I laughed at that, wondering just how true it was.

He sheltered me behind him as a hissing crackle pierced
the air. I looked on top of the jeep and saw the assassin's
body smoke and bubble, folding into itself, boiling down
into the caved-in roof. The metal groaned and collapsed. I
gasped as it took the stinger of the first scorpion with it,
along with the entire front end of the vehicle.

I stared, wide-eyed. "Please tell me they're dead at least," I said, barely finding my voice.

"They're definitely not going anywhere." He glanced over his shoulder at me. "Let's help this last one along."

Galen took two steps backward and located a long piece of steel that might have been a stretcher support or perhaps part of a helicopter blade. No matter. He lifted it like it weighed nothing, his broad shoulders steady, the muscles in his back flexing.

Holy heck. To think I'd ordered this soldier into a wheelchair.

I watched as bounded up onto the front of the jeep.

Legs spread, he plunged the improvised spear into the abdomen of the scorpion on the hood.

The metal hissed as the creature's flesh crackled around it.

He used an arm to wipe the sweat from his face. "I must have missed the heart the first time," he said, dodging a sizzling pile of goo.

Oh sure. That was it. "If I had a nickel for every time that happened to me."

"Do you have a smart answer for everything?" he asked, jumping down.

"Not lately." I swallowed hard. "What are they?"

His chest and shoulders stiffened. "Carnivorous scorpions."

"Carnivorous?" I wanted to bend in half and cry like a baby.

He wore a calculating expression. "Come on," he said, leading me past the giant bugs. "They were sent by the old gods," he added, glancing sideways at the wreck, "or at least that's who usually uses carnivorous scorpions."

Holy hell. What if the old gods knew I could see the dead? What if they were after me?

Horrific screams pierced the night. The imps were getting closer. "Faster," he said, taking my hand.

chapter eight

"Imps never come into the minefield," I said, glancing behind us as we made it back onto the path. Father McArio warded our camp extremely well.

Galen handed me the upper half of my torch. "I doubt you have killer scorpions, either."

Touché.

I was all for hightailing it out of there, but what I'd give for another few minutes up against that Humvee. I felt raw under my clothes, ready. Galen was like gourmet chocolate: One taste just wasn't enough.

Next time, I wanted him as buck naked as I was.

If there was a next time.

God, I was so hopeless.

"Hold up," he said.

I dug my standard-issue lighter out of my jacket pocket and set fire to the torch while Galen searched the area around us.

"Earlier," he said, keeping an eye on me, "when we went out walking, I could tell something was following us. I just didn't know what."

It sank in with sickening clarity. "These things were stalking me?"

"Only two," he clarified, as if that made a difference. I supposed it did if you were fighting them, like Galen did.

He stopped in front of a heap of twisted metal. His shoulder and trunk muscles flexing, he yanked a formidable-looking bar out of the wreck like a sword. "All set," he said to himself, hefting it in one hand.

"Yeah, well, some of us aren't big, bad demi-gods." I let out another involuntary shudder.

He must have mistaken it for a chill because when he returned to me, he slipped an arm around my back and pulled me close as we walked. It felt achingly good.

His heat wound through me. God, he even smelled like sex.

The rocks crunched under our boots. "I don't think they could get into camp, or they would have," he said, completely focused on the task at hand.

"Oh, well, that's comforting."

"I should never have let you out of my sight," he said, his voice a deep rumble against my ear. He kissed me right where the lobe curved, and I felt my knees buckle.

Both of us pretended not to notice when he propped me up.

"I'm not completely helpless," I said, although the jury was still out on that one.

He laughed. "You hold your own."

I returned his smile, leaning into him. I was amazed we were even here.

"There's one piece of this puzzle I don't understand," he said.

"Only one?"

"When gods order a carnivorous scorpion for a kill, they give them a very specific assignment. Find the one who stole the White Hind of Diana, for example." He looked down at me as if he already knew the answer. "What could they have used to distinguish you as a mark?"

Dread slithered through me. My ability to see the dead? Or maybe the bronze dagger that wouldn't leave me alone.

I was suddenly glad I hadn't left it with Father McArio. I couldn't imagine him on the edge of the limbo wastelands with a carnivorous assassin locator beacon.

"Tell me this," I said, turning it around on him. "How did you make it out of recovery?"

He seemed amused at that. "I'm elite special forces. I know how to sneak around." He brushed some dirt away from my cheek with his thumb. "I'm glad you're safe."

God, what would it have been like to make love to this man? "Thanks for saving me."

He cupped my chin with raw tenderness. "I could say the same to you."

He tilted his head to kiss me, and my entire body thrummed in anticipation. At the last second, his gaze flicked to the darkness behind us. "Quickly," he said.

I glanced behind, unable to see anything but black as we picked up the pace.

"Have you actually fought imps?" I asked. It was amazing how safe I felt with him.

"Yes. Keep your eyes peeled. They like to ambush."

We made our way through the cold night. Me, hurrying. Him, stalking like a predator. Forget about pranks. He didn't even miss a loose rock in front of us. Which was good because I'd seen pictures of imps, with their scaly skin, sharp claws, and rows of scalpel-sharp teeth, but I really didn't want to meet any.

Galen had us out of the minefield with startling efficiency. Below the cemetery, I could see the torches of our camp, and the welcoming light from the hospital tents.

"Your wards are stronger here," he said.

"Good," I said, eyeing the junkyard behind us as if something was going to come jumping out. "I can't believe we walked that fast without tripping any pranks."

"You mean like this?" Galen eased a mummified scarab out of the pocket of his pajama bottoms and held it under the flickering torchlight. "I found it on the way in. Thought it was kind of cute."

"Ew." The thing looked like it had been digested and spit out. "How did you even know it was a prank?"

"There was a sign next to it." He nudged me forward. "Come on," he said, as we started back toward camp.

"You'll have to tell Jeffe you were scared."

"The sphinx? That would mean admitting I snuck out of recovery."

"Don't worry. I think you'll be missed," I said, dreading that explanation.

He grinned down at me. "Escapes are one of my specialties."

That and slaying giant scorpions. I stuck close, glad for the company as we navigated the maze of graves. He was my personal warrior, at least until I shipped him out.

"Tell me," he said, his voice casual while he kept a steady guard against the surrounding night. "You've always been able to see the dead, right?"

I nodded.

"You've kept your secret."

"You know what would happen if I didn't."

I was glad to see even he cringed a little. "Then why tonight? Why now?"

I shook my head. I wasn't sure. "Maybe they weren't following me. Maybe I was at the wrong place at the wrong time." I sure as hell wasn't going to visit Father McArio at night anymore, if at all.

"You want to know what I think?" he asked, scoping the darkness behind us.

"No."

The man would be perfect if he didn't have so many theories.

He glanced down at me before returning to his vigil. "I think we're already on this journey. From the moment you pulled that dagger out of me, it was decided."

I shook my head. "Nobody else saw what happened between us." If they had, I'd have been taken and punished already. I tucked my hair behind my ears. "I know this is going to sound crazy, but what happened back there feels like a shot in the dark."

Unless the knife had attracted them to me. If that was the case, there was nothing I could do.

He gritted his jaw as he worked it through. "That's what

I'm wondering, too. They know there's a doctor out there who sees the dead, and who pulled out the bronze dagger. The gods on either side could have sent the scorpions."

"Wait, so you're saying our side could be trying to kill me?"

"They're trying to stop the prophecy. Which means the first part has already come true."

I brought a hand to my temple. "I think we already had this argument."

"Discussion," he ground out. "Just because you refuse to see the truth doesn't mean it isn't happening."

Maybe I'd go back in and face those imps. It was better than having this conversation.

We walked in silence until we reached the dirt path beyond the funeral pyres.

When we stepped past the wards near the edge of the cemetery I wanted to collapse in relief. "Okay, let's get you back to the hospital."

He barked out a laugh. "I can't go to the hospital. I'm guarding you."

"I've never felt more cared for." Every inch of me. His eyes flared as he caught my meaning. "But I can't have a patient in my tent." Even worse, "Everyone thinks we're doing it."

He broke into a cat-who-ate-the-canary grin. "Aren't we?"

Just shoot me now. I fought off a blush. "It doesn't mean I can keep you in my tent."

He had to see how ridiculous it was. I'd never gotten close to a patient, never dated a patient, and now I'd almost slept with one who was now going to follow me home and stay for how long? I didn't know. Worse, a part of me thought it could be a pretty good idea.

Of course that was the part of me that wasn't thinking about prophecies, seeing the dead, or the bronze knife in my pocket.

The dust wasn't packed down here like it was on the paths, and my righteous stomping whipped up a small cloud. I could practically taste the staleness in the air.

"I don't care what it looks like," he said behind me.

"Obviously," I said, dodging a leaning Celtic cross.

He took my arm and stopped me cold. The playfulness was gone. In front of me stood a fierce protector. "Do you realize what almost happened back there? You almost got eaten. I don't know how you were marked. I suspect you do. And until we get to the bottom of this, you need a bodyguard."

"You said the wards were good," I protested, my body warming like a traitor at the thought.

His eyes swept over me, missing absolutely nothing. "Right now. But there's no guarantee. You need strength and power." He planted his weapon in the dirt. The corner of his mouth betrayed a grin. "Now, are you going to see reason or am I going to have to quiet you down again?"

"You'd like that, wouldn't you?" I hated being backed into a corner, living this nightmare. Because there *were* big, bad things out to get me. Everything he said was true.

"Petra," a voice called from the main path. I turned to see three supply officers, clapping.

They knew we'd been to the minefield. And of course they assumed the worst.

"Oh, grow up," I said, both relieved and disappointed as the moment was broken. I navigated the slope of the cemetery and jumped down the small rise onto the path.

Galen took it in stride. "Officers," he nodded as we passed.

I watched the trio ogling us even after they should have been long gone. There. That just proved my point. "You can't expect me to take you back to my tent now."

Galen walked easily next to me. "Even if what they suspect were true—that I were going back to 'do' you, as you put it—where is the shame? You are an incredibly sensual woman."

He said it as if it were a simple fact. The sun rose in the morning, the gods fought, and I was a sensual woman worthy of a demi-god. I hand't even gotten a date to senior prom. Not that I'd wanted to go. I was too busy studying to get early acceptance into the med program at Loyola. But still.

He almost made me want to be that girl that a demi-god could lose himself in.

Incredible.

He was going to save the world, get the girl, and have hot sex in my tent.

"I hesitate to ask," he said, as if he could see the wheels turning, "but what are you thinking?"

I shook my head. "That out of all the men in this camp, I had to go for a hot warrior with a Superman complex."

He laughed.

"Admit it," I said, knowing I'd hit close to the truth. "You want to save the world and everyone in it."

He shrugged, denying nothing. "What's wrong with that?"

It was impossible. He should know that by now.

He needed to get it through his head. "I don't need saving. Not anymore." This wasn't like the minefield where I was caught alone and completely off guard. "I live with a vampire and a werewolf."

"Good," he said, sounding genuinely pleased. "I can't wait to meet them."

This I had to see. "Really?"

He seemed slightly offended. "Yes. Really. I'd be glad to have help, provided your friends can actually protect you from old-god assassins."

I wasn't so sure I believed that. Galen didn't seem like the type to let go easily.

"This is going to be fun," I said as we headed for the tar swamp. Arguing with the man was like fighting a series of small battles—ones I kept losing. I glanced up at him. "And you'd better mean it when you said you'd let them protect me, too. I don't want you giving my roommates some kind of a test they can't pass."

He seemed mildly surprised at that. "Just the opposite. I'm on your side."

Not if he knew what I was hiding.

I could smell the faint trace of garlic wafting from the mess tent as we trudged together in silence. Tonight must have been spaghetti night.

"I want you to have your freedom," Galen said.

He was talking about more than a walk home.

I stared straight ahead, hands shoved into the pockets of my scrubs. The fingers of my right hand curled around the knife. I could feel him watching me.

We walked through the maze of low-slung hutches.

I was used to being alone. I had it figured out. Anything else? Well, I didn't know what to think.

The closest friend I had was Rodger. He cared. But he'd also drop me like a hot rock if he could. I didn't blame him. Rodger had a family he loved—a wife and kids, relatives, a clan. I'd feel the same if I were him.

Sexy club music thumped from my hutch, and the lights were on. At least Marius was around. Galen would soon see the vampire I had at my disposal. I only hoped Marius wasn't wearing his black silk robe with the butterflies.

I barged in the door. "Lucy, I'm home!"

"Yeek!" Marius yanked the bedcovers around him as the vampire underneath him disappeared in a puff of silver smoke.

Too late I noticed the candles and the half-drunk champagne glasses of blood.

The corner of my mouth tipped up. "Marius, you old devil." I was glad to see he had some company.

The vampire hissed, fangs out. "Do you mind?"

"We used to hang a sock on the door," Galen said.

"No kidding," I said. "Wait, you have women on the Limbo Front?" Not that I didn't want him to date. But really, I didn't like the idea of him hanging out with other women.

"This was in basic," Galen said, planting a hand on the doorjamb.

Okay. Well that was a long time ago. "Ancient Greeks," I said, shrugging it off. I'd heard they liked to party.

"Nah." He played with the rough wood. "Siege of Rhodes."

"You don't say." That's right. He was only about five hundred years old.

"Do you even care that I'm here?" Marius was about ready to start spitting bullets. He had the covers yanked up to his neck and was shimmying into a pair of boxer shorts.

"Did you even think before you stumbled into here like a couple of drunken sailors?"

"Hey," I said. "I'm sorry. We had no idea."

"No sock on the door," Galen added.

Exactly. "Besides, I need you to protect me."

The vampire flipped a lock of blond hair out of his face and gave me a look like I had to be kidding.

In all fairness, it probably wasn't the best way to ask for a favor. Marius's eyes grew wide as we explained about the giant scorpions. I wondered just how much fighting versus nightclubbing he'd done in his former life.

Then again, I didn't want to get in to that in front of Galen.

"Now that you can see I'm quite safe here," I said to my studly protector-wannabe, "let's get you dressed."

Galen had done enough parading around camp in nothing but a pair of pajama bottoms—and make no mistake, Galen was going back.

Marius stood in a pair of black silk boxers, arms crossed over his chest. "Don't look at me."

He was too lanky anyway.

Rodger wouldn't mind lending a few things. I cracked open his footlocker. At least a dozen little dinosaurs scattered, their black scales gleaming in the lanternlight. "Dang it, Rodger."

"What?" Marius asked, a little too curious.

"Nothing." Rodger had told me he only had six. Those things had better not be breeding in there. I slammed the footlocker closed and went for Rodger's beat-up brown side table.

I yanked out a drawer and grabbed a white T-shirt from the top of the heap. Rodger needed to learn how to fold. "Here," I said, handing the shirt to Galen.

And yes, I watched his muscular forearms and chest as he dragged it over his head.

I'm not made of steel.

Only when Galen pulled it down did I see that the shirt read WORLD'S GREATEST LOVER.

"A little premature, don't you think?" he asked, grinning.

"Oh please," I said, returning to the drawer. "Take this, too." I shoved an orange-and-brown shawl at him.

"I like it." He winked. "Only because I know you'll enjoy watching me put it on."

The man was insufferable.

Thank heaven the shawl was big as a tent, obviously knitted by Rodger's wife.

The furry monstrosity covered him like a tarp. Now Galen looked half yeti. Perfect.

Meanwhile Marius was walking around the room, blowing out candles and draining the remaining blood from the glasses. He used one hand to lift the cast-iron stove in the middle of our hut and glared at me as he snatched up a handful of condoms from underneath.

I hadn't realized Marius was such an optimist.

Or a poor planner. Those condoms would have been hard to reach from the bed.

Galen, as usual, missed nothing. "He is strong."

"He is something," I agreed.

"Vain as well," Galen said, inspecting the mirrors over Marius's bed.

"Hey, I hadn't noticed those," I said. Marius must have dug them out special tonight. I couldn't help but whistle.

"You are so immature," the vampire glowered.

I cocked my head. "Have you met the rest of the people in this camp?"

Galen grudgingly inspected the boards of the hutch. "He can't protect you as well as I can," he said, "but you're in a highly populated camp. I suppose you'll be safe enough."

I drew my hand to my chest. "Oh my goodness. A man with an open mind."

His eyes caught mine. "Give me a chance. I'm full of surprises." He paused at the door. "I have one last favor to ask."

"I knew it."

He gave me a long look. "Come say good-bye before you try to ship me out again."

I'd say one thing for Galen. He was good at getting his point across. "I'll come see you."

He nodded. There was nothing more to say. I was on the home stretch. Sure, I still had some kind of enchanted knife in my pocket, but once Galen was gone, I could deal with that.

Soon everything would be back to normal.

Lucky me.

As Galen ducked to go, I found myself wanting to call him back. I didn't know why, or even what I'd tell him. It was better this way. No attachments. No complications. I watched him head out the door.

And run straight into Rodger.

"Ow!" My roommate bounced backward a foot. "Hey, that's my sweater."

"I lent it to him," I called, hoping Rodger was sober enough to get his butt inside and let Galen keep walking.

"Okie doke," Rodger said, swaying into the doorjamb. His hair was even messier than usual, and his gold-rimmed eyes were bloodshot. "Ooh. It looks like a vampire love nest in here."

"It was," Marius seethed.

"Who was he with?" Rodger asked me.

I shrugged, looking to Marius. "I didn't see. The girl was too fast."

"Girl?" Rodger asked.

I stepped back to let the werewolf stumble past. "What else would it be?"

Rodger chuckled as he toppled face-first on his cot. Phew. He smelled like cigar smoke and rum.

Galen had stopped to watch the freak show. I didn't blame him.

"What were you two doing?" Rodger asked, rolling over. "Oh wait. I heard about it at the bar."

"Already?" I asked.

"You went and saw Father McArio." He barked out a laugh.

Yeah, real funny. This was going to be a long night.

Rodger reached for his covers and ended up covering himself with the tent flap from the window. "Did he take the knife?"

Oh no.

Galen stopped, and my heart skipped a beat. If he found out about the bronze dagger, he'd never leave this alone.

"You're drunk, Rodger." I wanted to slam the door, but Galen was already back inside.

"What knife?" he demanded.

"Rodger—" I warned.

"The bronze dagger," Rodger answered like a man who wanted to dig my grave. He waved a hand, as if that could dispel the tension thickening the air. "You probably don't want to see it. It's the same one she pulled out of you."

"Rodger!"

"What?" He sat up on his elbows while I looked on in horror. "He knows he was stabbed. Ohh . . . Skittles." He reached for a few petrified candies on his nightstand. "She tried to get rid of the knife but it showed up in her locker."

"Rodger!"

Galen's expression went hard. "That's why you asked where I was when I was stabbed," he said, cutting each word.

Rodger flopped his head back on his pillow. "Gah. Stop talking so loud. I think my hangover is starting already. That's the last time I mix Hell's Rain with Malibu."

Galen stood in the doorway, looking like he'd been smacked. "It's the prophecy," he said, almost to himself. Anger quickly replaced his surprise. "You lied to me."

"Not really," I snapped. Deny it all. "The knife isn't important."

"That's not what you said," Rodger added.

Perhaps I could smother him with a pillow.

"Let me explain," I said quickly. "The dagger that I took out of you, I showed it to the chaplain tonight, just to see if it was special."

"And?" Galen snarled.

"It's not. There's nothing special about it. Father McArio didn't even want it."

Rodger propped up on his elbows. "Even after it kept following you?"

"Rodger!"

"You didn't tell him that part?" my roommate asked.

Galen looked ready to tear down the hutch with his teeth.

"Of course I told Father that part, but I wasn't going to tell *him* that part," I hissed, flinging a hand at Galen. Rodger had never been able to keep his mouth shut, but you'd think for once that he could give me a break on this.

"Okay. Fine," he said, both drunk and offended. "I won't say anything else."

"There's nothing else to say," I fumed.

"Exactly," he said.

Galen towered over me. "Oh, there's plenty to say."

Fuck. "We're going to have to do this, aren't we?"

"Immediately," Galen answered. "No tricks. No back talk. You tell me what the hell is going on."

"Fine," I said, eyeing Rodger, who was still trying to use the tent flap as a blanket, and Marius, who sat cross-legged and bristling on his cot. "Let's go somewhere private."

"There is no such place," Marius grumbled as Galen led me back out into the night.

chapter nine

We banged out of my hutch and stepped straight into an ice-box. I wrapped my coat tight around me. "Come on. I need coffee and I need it now."

"You're going to need more than that," Galen said, heading for the officers' club.

I grabbed him by the fuzzy poncho. "Not there." I wasn't up for the stench of cigar smoke and half-drunk soldiers. Or the prospect of being overheard.

"Where else do you suggest?" he asked, as if I was going to screw him over.

Okay, so I had screwed him over. He didn't have to get so pissy about it. "Come on. We're going to break into the chow hall."

Galen stiffened. "You want me to get caught, don't you?"

"Truthfully? Yes. But that's not why I'm taking you there."

"It's like you enjoy being difficult," he muttered under his breath as he fell into pace next to me.

He was sure one to talk. I wasn't looking forward to explaining myself to the oversized lout, but maybe—just maybe—I could minimize the damage and convince him to take it down a notch.

Ha.

As long as I was wishing for that, I might as well wish for a pony.

Torches cast shadows over the rocky path in front of us as we made our way past the enlisted tents.

I was almost rooting for giant scorpion or three—anything to distract him.

No such luck.

I knew what he suspected.

A healer whose hands can touch the dead was supposed to be the key to ending this war.

Well, it wasn't me.

I'd hoped for it to be me, prayed for it with everything I had. I'd read the whole prophecy and tried to make it come true. I'd been willing to risk exposure, and certain death, if doing so meant I really could put a stop to this war.

But despite what I'd hoped—and what I put on the line—my grand foray into peacekeeping hadn't worked. It only backfired, bringing disaster down on me and the people I loved.

It wasn't going to happen again.

The mess tent slung low on the far south side of camp. It was usually a rollicking place. At this hour, it sat empty and dark.

Lo and behold, it still smelled like garlic.

The door was locked, but the screened window next to it was broken. I should know. I'd sliced the edge last week in order to slip Rodger a caramel-dipped onion.

I'd gotten him, too. The corners of my mouth tugged up at the memory. It wasn't a big enough prank to use on Kosta, but I'd sure enjoyed it.

My fingers trailed down the edge of the screen. Someone else had widened my original cut. Dang, I'd better keep an eye on my own food.

I tore the screen open the rest of the way and ducked through. It was pitch black inside.

"Watch it. There's a table right here," I said as Galen followed me.

The kitchen was in the rear of the tent. The sand floor crunched under my feet as I slipped past the tables in the dark. The less we were noticed in here, the better.

I walked straight back until I bumped up against the serving area. Ah, good. I followed it with my hand until it skirted back toward meal prep.

When I reached the door to the kitchen, I stopped. "Galen?" I peered into the dark.

"Yes."

I jumped a foot as his voice sounded directly behind me. "Can you at least try to make a little noise?"

"I am what I am."

"No kidding." I pushed through the door and felt for one of the lanterns above the kitchen serving area. "Bingo." I lit it, revealing a hodgepodge of equipment that had been scrubbed to within an inch of its life.

Well-used pots and pans hung from racks above the long metal countertop. Behind it was the prep area, refrigerators and freezers. I spotted a coffeemaker by the sink. Wouldn't you know it? It was already filled and ready to go for the morning shift. I hit the START button and sighed.

"It's the simple things," Galen said.

"Yes," I agreed.

The glow of the single lantern cast shadows over his face. "You can trust me," he said.

I straightened my shoulders. "I know." It was the truth. If I didn't trust him, I would never have moved toward a giant poison scorpion stinger. I gave an involuntary shudder. I would have been crushed in the backseat of that jeep.

He kept his distance, as if he were assessing the situation. And me. "I'm glad we got that out of the way. Because I'm tired of you lying to me."

I crossed my arms over my chest. "I don't owe you anything."

He slammed his fist down on the countertop, sending dishes clattering. "This isn't about either one of us." With great effort, he collected himself. "Lives are at stake."

"You don't think I know that?" I shot back. "I'm the one who put you back together."

Two large strides and he closed the space between us.

"You lied to me. You said you didn't see me on the table." He towered over me. "Admit it. You saw."

"Fine." There was no use denying it any longer. "I saw you. I held your soul in my hands."

His anger vanished. "I remember."

He stood, stunned.

Oh no. He really was remembering something.

"We touched," he said. "It was like grabbing on to a live wire. And then I could see inside you. I could feel it, in my hands, your strength and your dedication. The way you care for people you've never even met before. The way you ached for me. You didn't even know me." He stopped for a moment, as if he didn't quite know how to say it. "You're ashamed of that, but you don't need to be. You don't need to hide from me."

I suddenly felt exposed, raw.

"All I ask is that you respect my secret," I said, although frankly I didn't even know if he was listening at that point. "You know what they'd do to me if the truth ever came out. I'm just trying to protect myself."

His expression was soul searing, intense. "Petra," he said, pure wonder in his voice, "you're beautiful."

I cringed. It was as if he'd ripped down every wall I'd put up, leaving me bare and bloody. "No, I'm not. I'm strong and practical and snappy and damn good at what I do."

His face didn't waver. "You try to hide it, but I saw. Even before I remembered, I knew."

It was too hard to explain. Too painful. "I don't want to have this conversation."

"I know. I won't push you. There's no need. I already see what's there." He watched me with such intensity it hurt. "You don't know how good it feels to know there's someone like you in the world."

Yes. Failed, cranky, and hiding my power.

"So can we keep this between us?" I asked. Because I really didn't want to spend the rest of eternity pushing a rock up a hill, or whatever the gods would do to me.

"We can," he said, easing.

I tried not to fall sideways in relief.

"We'll do this together," he stated.

"What?" Oh no. "I'm not doing anything else. Listen, other than"—I gestured, I couldn't even say it—"that thing that happened with us, talking to the dead isn't what you think." It wasn't what anybody thought. That's why I kept it to myself. I rubbed at my temples as if by mere force of will I could make him understand. "I don't talk to executed mortals or immortals. I don't talk to the souls of hell, and I don't have anything to do with the prophecy."

"How do you know?" he pressed. "The oracle couldn't predict who would be chosen."

"Exactly," I said on an exhale. I turned my back on him and grabbed a coffee cup from a rack by the sink. I was in desperate need of some distance here. "Do you realize how nebulous the oracle can be?"

He stood stock-still, watching me. "The signs are never exact. That's why we have to be open to every possibility. Including this one."

I slammed my cup down. "This is my life you're talking about."

"This is war," he countered.

Oh, great. "One sacrifice for the sake of many. How noble of you."

The kicker was, he thought it would make a difference.

He came from a place that believed in woo-woo predictions. They'd been doing it in central Greece for thousands of years. Of course I came from New Orleans, so I guess you could say the same thing about me.

Then again, I didn't always believe in the weather report, much less this.

He was asking me to expose myself—my secret—in the hopes that I might be the one. And if I wasn't? Well then, there was just one more dead doctor in this war.

No, thanks.

I yanked the coffeepot from the brew station. The steeping brew hissed and crackled on the hot plate as I filled my cup with as much of it as I could get. It was a pathetic little cup.

Galen had taken a spot by the counter. Maybe he thought he was giving me some space, but I knew better. The man was a rock.

"Remember the first step," he said. "The oracle predicts that a healer whose hands can touch the dead will receive a bronze dagger."

"I didn't receive a dagger," I reminded him. "It was thrust into your chest."

"You took it out."

"To save your miserable life!"

"And now the first part of the prophecy has come true," he said, as if I'd just confirmed everything he believed. Galen was taking two separate incidents and twisting them all out of order.

"Keep it down," I hissed. The place might've been deserted, but we were still breaking and entering. "You're asking me to risk eternal torture on a hunch, just because some knife keeps following me around."

His gaze traveled over me. "I saw your pain," he said, as if he was deconstructing me, "but I didn't know it ran this deep."

Glaring at him, I cradled my cup defensively. "I don't want to hear about my pain." Or any obligations he thought I had. "You can't force these things."

The corner of his lip curled. "Watch me."

"That wasn't a dare." And he wondered why I wasn't exactly racing to help him. I took a drink and felt the warm liquid ease down my throat. It should have been soothing. It wasn't.

He stood assessing me. Finally, he said, "I was stabbed at a hell vent just north of here."

I paused over the edge of my coffee cup. "What does that mean for us?"

"I don't know. It was in the heat of battle. I didn't even see who shoved it into my chest."

I sighed. "Do you want to see the knife?" I slipped a hand

into my scrubs and felt its heavy weight. I removed it slowly and handed him the wrapped bundle.

He held it for a moment, as if he couldn't quite believe what he had.

"I sent it straight to weapons waste after surgery. It's standard procedure," I said quickly, trying to soothe his horror. "Anyhow, it didn't stay gone for long. Someone put it in my locker."

He opened it like it was a sacred relic.

"I'm not the one," I reminded him.

He retreated to the door and studied the knife under the light of the single lantern. Firelight played off the strong lines of his face, casting shadows. "You can't know that."

"Yes, I can."

The back of my eyes burned with the memory. He wasn't going to get it from me. He knew too much already. And I absolutely refused to let Galen twist it around like he had everything else.

I'd give anything for an end to this war, to have a normal life. But I'd been there, tried that, and it had been horrifying.

"I know I'm not special," I said, moving out of his sight line. His profile was hard and clean. "I'm just cursed."

He turned to me with warmth in his eyes. "That's where you're wrong."

I clutched my coffee cup, embarrassed in a way I couldn't even express.

"The oracles would see your power. They'd know when it's time," he said. "In fact, once they made their discovery, they'd go straight to the gods. Your attack tonight proves it."

Oh geez. It made sense.

"I stayed to protect you."

"How do we know that?" How could we prove any of this? The strain of the night seeped into my bones. "Maybe this is crystal clear to you, but I'm used to dealing with facts, things I can prove."

"I'll make you a deal."

"Why do I get a bad feeling about this?"

"If you ship me out tomorrow, then it is over."

My heart caught in my throat. It was exactly what I wanted, and it wasn't. I had to get a grip.

"You're healthy as an ox," I told him. The man was skewering assassins, for pity's sake. I didn't understand why he'd make this kind of a deal. "I'll examine you tomorrow," I said. "And I'll make it fair," I was quick to add. "But my guess is, you're going back to your unit."

"Then you'll be rid of me," he said, with too much confidence for my taste.

I dumped my coffee out. "You don't have to say it that way." Not after everything we'd been through.

Then unease settled into my gut. "Why aren't you worried?"

The side of his mouth quirked. "It's a test of faith."

"I'm not so good at those."

The warm light from the lantern played over his features. "I know."

Damned if he didn't look delicious.

And smug.

"I don't believe I'm fated to leave," he said. He wrapped the knife once more. "In fact, I wouldn't be surprised if we receive the second prophecy soon."

"Just what I need." Another prophecy.

He finished wrapping the dagger and handed it back to me. "You'll see."

I eased the knife into my coat pocket. "That's what I'm afraid of."

I walked Galen back to recovery in silence. We'd said everything there was to say. After that, it was a matter for the fates. Heaven help me. He gave me one last, long, lingering kiss. Then I watched him disappear around back, not even wanting to know how he snuck into bed. From Jeffe's shouts, I could tell he made quick work of it.

Back at my tent, sleep was impossible. Not with Rodger snoring and Marius glaring at me. So an hour later I found myself back in recovery.

The charge nurse glanced up at me as I slipped inside.

"I want to prepare some release paperwork," I said, trying to sound as casual as possible.

"You're up early," she said, her blond twist bun flopping forward as she bent to pull out my patient files.

I glanced down at the darkened rows of beds. "Galen of Delphi," I said under my breath, hoping he was asleep.

She shuffled through the charts. "I don't see him," she said, as if we were talking about a pencil instead of a person.

"He's here." Believe me.

"Oh he's here all right." She set a chart down by her laptop. "But he's not yours anymore."

"What?" I barked. "I mean"—I brought it down a notch—"of course he's mine." Until I booked him on the first transport out of here.

"No . . . ," she said, her voice droning as she ran a finger down his paperwork. "You transferred him."

"No, I didn't. He's in bed 22A," I said. Probably awake. And listening.

"Let me look." She began clacking keys on her laptop, and I resisted the urge to start drumming my fingers on her desk. This wasn't brain surgery. This was a simple patient release. I'd done it hundreds of times. It wasn't hard.

She furrowed her brows. "This is something."

"No, it's not." Whatever it was, it was not.

She pointed at her screen, edging the computer around for me to see. "You transferred him to Dr. Freierrmuth."

Okay. Sure. Maybe that's what the screen said. "But he didn't go to the 4027th," I assured her. I tugged at my collar, starting to get a little desperate.

Come on. This had to work. I'd told Galen it would work.

The nurse looked at me over her glasses. "Dr. Freierrmuth died in 1812."

Of all the . . . "I talked to Dr. Freiermuth last week!"

"Well, yes. I talked to Diane, too," the nurse said, as if she were actually helping. "But you didn't transfer your patient to Dr. Freiermuth. You added an *r*, which makes it Dr. Freierrmuth."

"So?" I demanded. My handwriting was messy. Add the fact I'd been writing on a chart braced on my hip. And I'd been a little stressed at the time.

"Different doctor."

"You said yourself Dr. Freierrmuth is dead!"

"Yes. But the transfer paperwork went through."

This didn't make any sense. "So what does that mean?"

"It means Galen of Delphi is under the care of Dr. Freierrmuth."

"The dead woman." I took a calming yoga breath. It didn't work.

"He was actually a man," she corrected. "Dr. Helmut Freierrmuth." She glanced up. "Obviously we'll keep your patient here."

"And transfer him back to me," I said. They'd have to give him back.

"No," she tapped at her computer. "Dr. Freierrmuth would have to sign off on that."

I resisted the urge to scream. "You do realize—"

"He's dead," she concluded. "Yes. I'm not saying it makes sense, but it is army regulations."

I blew out a breath. "I hate the army."

"That doesn't change regulations."

I wanted to pound my head against the desk. "Okay." Focus. "How do we fix this?"

She shrugged. "I'll send a note to headquarters."

"A note? No. You're going to send more than a note." Headquarters was notoriously slow. They were still deciding their position on the destruction of Atlantis.

She stared at me like I was the crazy one. "It'll be a good note."

"No." We needed to do more than that.

She continued on as if I hadn't spoken. "In the meantime, the patient stays here."

"Absolutely not." I said, backing away, not even wanting to think, dream, imagine Galen could be right on this one. I was going to get rid of him one way or another. Today.

I charged out of the recovery room and ran straight into

Horace. "Watch it," he demanded, holding up a box as if I were about to mash it to bits. "What's your problem?"

"I need somebody raised from the dead."

Horace frowned. "I told you to avoid the tough cases."

"I didn't kill him," I balked.

"Good," he said, as the box in his hand let out a series of squeaks.

"That better not be what I think it is," I warned him.

The sprite huffed. "It's nothing."

Really? Horace wasn't hovering high enough. I flipped open the lid, and a tiny dinosaur head popped out.

"You can't have that." I said. "Them," I corrected as a second one shoved its snout out of an airhole.

"Rodger gave them to me," Horace said, cramming the lid back on. "He has too many."

Did he ever.

"Keep them separated," I warned. "Boys from girls."

"How can you tell?"

That was the million-dollar question, wasn't it?

"I'll figure it out," I promised.

He could count on that. But first I had to see a guy about a dead doctor.

chapter ten

I pushed into Kosta's outer office and nearly tripped over a case of condoms. Ribbed for her pleasure. "What is this?" I asked, nudging it out of the way.

The colonel's new assistant poked her head out from behind an entire stack of condom boxes. "Keep it there. I'm counting." Shirley emerged with a clipboard, shaking her curly red head. "That's twenty-four cases . . . eighty boxes per case . . . twenty-five per box . . ." Her head snapped up, horror flooding her delicate features. "How am I going to get rid of forty-eight thousand condoms?"

I surveyed the boxes scattered across the otherwise bare office. "First, you're going to need a few nights off."

She groaned into her clipboard. "Why do I even ask you these things?"

Heck if I knew. "I can set you up with Marius."

She peeked out from behind her inventory sheets. "Isn't he gay?"

"What? I don't think so." Sure, he was neat, but he was an uptight vampire. What did people expect? Then again, I was usually the last one to know about those kinds of things.

I strolled past Shirley and checked the heavy wood door to Kosta's office. It was locked. "Is he in there?"

"Yes," she sighed, "and he's going to kill me when he sees these."

"Oh no, he's not." I needed the colonel in a good mood. I was about to ask a giant favor, and I didn't need any distractions. "How did you even get so many?"

She blew at a lock of curly hair that had fallen over her face. "Supply clerk," she said. "I foisted a bunch of work off on him." She groaned with regret. "I told him to order a pallet of rubbers. You know? Latex gloves. He thought I meant condoms. I mean, whose brain immediately goes to condoms?" she asked.

"A man's," I said. Especially around here.

She rubbed a hand over her eyes. "I'm so screwed."

It was an honest mistake, for those of us who weren't keen on details. Shirley was more of a big-picture person, or at least she had been when she was in charge of games and recreation. She was an outdoorsy type. The outer office didn't even have any windows.

"What in Hades made them transfer you here?" I asked.

Sure, they'd needed somebody after Kosta's last assistant went berserk. The poor selkie was asking for signed paperwork before ducking out to the latrine. The colonel could do that to a person.

"I requested it," she said, smoothing her uniform shirt and sending a smoldering look at Kosta's closed door.

Love could make you do crazy things. It was no secret that Shirley had a crush the size of Manhattan, but I hadn't realized she was that gaga over the colonel.

If you asked me, she'd have been better off with someone else. Even Marius. Sure, Kosta was easy on the eyes, in a Vin Diesel I'm-going-to-kill-you sort of way, but he was a Spartan. They lived for discipline and self-denial, not hearts and chocolate.

I could hear him shuffling on the other side of the door. Lordy. If he was moving, he might be out here soon. I needed him in a good mood.

"Just explain to Kosta that supply messed up."

"Except that he specifically ordered me to handle these kinds of things myself."

"Oops."

"Thanks," she said, miserable.

"Hey, why don't you call Rodger? He'll take these off your hands." We could use them. "I'm thinking water balloons."

Kosta might get to see them yet.

Shirley's eyes widened. "You really think so?"

I had no doubt.

"It's not like anybody would miss them."

She leaned over her desk and flipped on the intercom microphone.

Rodger Woflstein, report to Colonel Kosta's office, she said, glancing back at me. *See if you can't find a couple of orderlies along the way.*

"That's bound to start some rumors," I told her.

"Would you mind helping me move them outside?" she asked.

"Now?" I mean, if big, burly men were going to be moving boxes for me, I'd rather leave them to it.

"If the colonel hears a commotion, he's bound to come out," she said, glancing at the door.

Well, all right. I picked up a box. They weren't too bad. Shirley and I spent the next few minutes banging in and out of the outer office until all twenty-four cases were stacked outside.

A trio of supply clerks whistled as they walked past.

"Petra," one of them called, "you should have let us know. We could have gotten you a discount."

"These aren't for me," I snapped. And why did they always travel in threes?

"Nice going, Petra," called the ungrateful jerk I'd given my dessert to last week. In all fairness, pre-packaged, dehydrated ice cream was no real treat, but still . . .

"These are for Rodger!" I corrected.

"Well, you can't expect them to believe that," Shirley said. "Rodger is devoted to his wife back home."

"Remember, I'm helping *you.*"

"I know you are," she said, missing the point entirely. "Oh look. Here comes Rodger."

"Good. Can we go inside now?"

"Impatient," she said, as she followed me back inside.

I felt for the knife in my pocket. Still there. It was now or never. "Can you get me in?"

"Let me fluff my hair and put on a little lipstick," she said, digging in her desk drawer.

"Okay, but I'm not waiting while you stuff your bra."

A gorgeous and calm Shirley announced my presence and I heard a gruff, "Enter."

Kosta sat behind a desk like Shirley's. It may have been slightly larger, but it was still standard metal, military issue.

Ancient battle shields lined the walls of his office, no doubt trophies from a former life. The colonel had been granted immortality after the campaign against the Persians, but he sure hadn't let it go to his head.

He frowned, the muscles in his shoulders bunching. "You here to talk about the kraken in the officers' showers?"

"No." I didn't start it. I just relocated it.

He steepled his fingers and leaned forward. "What about the cannabis you planted in my vegetable garden?"

"Let's skip over that." I'd told Rodger we needed to hide it closer to the tomatoes.

His eyes narrowed. "You want to explain the snails in my combat boots?"

"That wasn't even me," I said a bit too quickly. Whoops. Good one, though.

"Sit," he ordered.

I took the straight-backed wooden chair opposite his desk.

"What do you want, Robichaud?" He watched me like he knew. He grunted, leaning back in his chair. "It had better not be more surgery cases. You don't have the rank or the seniority."

I squirmed on the hard wood seat. "Not today, Colonel." Although I still hadn't given up on that one, despite all the trouble my last big surgical patient had given me. "I'm afraid it's more serious."

He gave me his full attention. "Yes?"

I crossed my legs then uncrossed them, fighting the urge to sugarcoat it. Kosta liked things short and to the point. "I'm dealing with a bureaucratic mistake. My patient isn't my patient anymore. He was transferred to a dead doctor. I want him back."

"It could take months."

"So I've heard. He's special forces," I explained, knowing Kosta preferred facts over emotion. "He needs to get back to his unit in time for a major offensive." One he refused to tell me about. "I have a feeling we may be looking at an unbalanced army."

Which meant earthquakes, tsunamis, disaster on Earth.

Kosta frowned, the scar over his lip crinkling. "One man can't unbalance an army."

"I know," I told him, "but the kicker is, I think this guy can." Regardless. "He needs to go back to his unit. Only the doctor who needs to sign off is dead."

He sat, unmoved. "Call on another doctor in the unit."

"His backup is dead. They've been dead for eighty years."

Kosta studied me. "I'm sure he's in good hands wherever he is."

It took everything I had to keep my voice even and my butt in the chair. "That may be so, but I want him back. He's my patient." I felt guilty for trying to get rid of him in the first place.

Kosta tilted his head. "What's really going on here, Robichaud?"

Galen of Delphi saw too much.

Knew too much.

Made me feel too much.

Worst of all, Galen of Delphi might be right.

I stood quickly. I needed a walk, or maybe a swift kick upside the head. "I suspect this patient fully recovered," I said, pacing between an Athenian shield and an uncomfortable-looking cot. "He's a trapped war hero who probably doesn't appreciate being stuck here."

Kosta pulled out a cigar from the bottom drawer of his desk. "He's a soldier. He'll manage."

"Why should he have to? Can't you call someone?"

"I don't bend the rules." He bit the tip off the cigar and tossed it in the trash.

"I should have just signed it myself," I mused.

"And you'd have faced court-martial."

I stared at the ceiling. "So the only thing left would be to raise this doc from the dead."

Kosta scoffed. "You know it doesn't work that way, Robichaud," he said, lighting up.

I knew. I'd never seen Kosta use his power, but I knew it cost him every time he did it.

"Powers are a tricky thing," he said.

Tell me about it.

He rolled his cigar between his fingers. "Every action has consequences."

It was the last thing I wanted to hear. "So what do you expect me to do?" I needed him to throw me a bone here.

"Deal with it."

"Lovely."

He took a few puffs. "You may want to start with Shirley. Tell her I said to talk to Pandora at HQ."

"Okay." I could do that. "Thanks."

I turned to leave.

"One more thing." He rolled the cigar in the corner of his mouth. "You say this man's a war hero?"

"Yes," I said, hope blossoming.

He pulled the cigar from his mouth and pointed it at me. "Then I'm going to have to agree with you. He doesn't belong in the hospital tent."

I wanted to twirl with relief.

"Put him in VOQ," Kosta said.

"Visiting officers' quarters?" He had to be kidding. That was for diplomats and generals and important people.

"I'll have them start prepping the tent this afternoon. It'll be ready first thing tomorrow. You give this soldier one final exam and then move him in."

"Oy."

"One more thing, Robichaud. Be sure to tell this hero just how honored we are to have him with us."

I nearly choked. "Believe me, sir. He's made himself quite welcome."

chapter eleven

That night Rodger and I patched up a couple of mechanics from the motor pool who had tried—and failed—to unleash a plague of locusts in Kosta's tent.

We were in the small intake room off the main OR. Two tables, no waiting.

Rodger had been avoiding me all day. Now he wouldn't even look at me as he worked.

Yeah, well, denial would only get him so far.

The mean part of me hoped he had a hangover. Maybe he'd learn from it.

"That's a nasty scrape," Rodger said to his patient.

I shot my friend a dirty look. "It's always good to think before you act."

That went for me, too, I realized as I climbed up on a step stool. I wasn't crazy about heights, and yes, this counted. Still, it was the only way to get a better look at the Russian sitting on my exam table. I touched my gloved fingers to my patient's bald head and craned my arm to adjust the large silver snake light above him.

"There's not much I can do for the bites," I said, examining a particularly nasty one between his eyes. A little Neosporin should do the trick. "Your buddy got the worst of it."

His companion lay prone on Rodger's table, suffering

more from humiliation than his twisted ankle. He tilted his head up. "Next time, we use frogs."

Rodger tossed his exam gloves into the waste bucket between our tables. "It's not your taste in plagues. It's the colonel's wards."

True enough. Rodger and I learned that firsthand when we tried to park a jeep in his office. "He's got his tent warded, his car—"

"His private latrine," Rodger added. He cast a glance my way, testing the waters. "Kosta's a slippery one."

Our patients had made a beginners' mistake. Sure, Kosta's plain tent looked like an easy target. So did his car—a vintage 1959 Cooper T51 racer that he liked to polish with a cloth baby diaper. In fact, I'd be willing to bet that the Formula One racer was Kosta's only luxury.

Back when the vacation pot was only up to a week and change, Rodger and I tried to fill Kosta's race car with gumdrops. We got our candy-laden trash bags to within a foot of the royal blue paint job and the gumdrops started exploding. It was like we were each holding a thousand live firecrackers. Rodger screamed like a girl. I'd like to say I handled it a little better. But I don't like to lie.

No doubt the colonel had been in his tent, smoking a cigar and laughing his butt off.

"That's why the vacation pot is up so high," I said, placing a Band-Aid between the Russian's eyes.

Well, that and the fact that we'd gotten a lot of veteran transfers. You had to put in your whole vacation savings bank in order to have a shot at the jackpot. Some of the immortals had chipped in as much as a day. It was insane.

"It can make people do crazy things," Rodger said, tucking an ice pack into his patient's bandages.

"Like drive a person to drink," I said, tearing open another Band-Aid, not even bothering to hide my meaning.

Rodger took a sudden interest in making sure the Ace bandage clips were tight.

My patient frowned. "Kosta's not the magical type."

Not unless you counted raising the dead as magic. Still, the Russian had a point. "We think there's someone helping him," I said.

"We keep hoping Kosta's magical ace is in camp," Rodger said.

"And corruptible," I added. If we could figure out who it was, and if the person was open to part of the jackpot, we'd be in business.

"Did you two see anybody outside after your prank failed?" Rodger asked. "Anybody checking out the hutch or maybe aiming a few spells at the place?"

"We were too busy running," the man on Rodger's table groaned.

I didn't blame them.

Rodger helped him down and we sent our patients back to their tents with parting gifts of crutches, antibacterial ointment, and Band-Aids, courtesy of the new god army.

The room was deafeningly quiet, save for the low buzz from the overhead lights.

I pulled off my latex gloves. "I'm glad we were on call tonight," I said to Rodger, "or else I would have thought you ran away."

"I haven't been avoiding you," he growled, shoving the Ace bandage roll back into the med cabinet.

"Oh good," I said. Fan-fricking-tastic. "Then you must want to talk about what happened last night."

Rodger tossed a disposable ice pack into the med waste bin. "No. Because I already have a mother and she's in Topanga."

"So, I'm a nag if I tell you that you might be turning into an alcoholic."

He glared at me. "I'm in control."

"Is that a fact?" My heart thumped hard against my chest. "Then why the hell did you tell Galen about the knife?"

"Wait." He threw up a hand. "What?"

He'd better not deny it. "You heard me."

He stood, stunned. "I don't remember that."

I squeezed my eyes shut. "And you don't think that's a problem?"

He ran a hand through his coarse mop of hair. "Hey, I'm sorry. I had no idea—"

Yeah, well, that ticked me off even more. "Sorry doesn't cut it." Apologies meant nothing if he didn't promise to knock it off. "Look, this place gets to me, too." It got to all of us. "But it doesn't mean you have to destroy yourself."

Rodger cocked a brow. "Aren't you being a little melodramatic?"

"No." I sighed. It was like reasoning with a doorknob. "I'm worried about you."

He dragged on his army field jacket. "I got it, okay?"

I didn't think he did. But I'd made my point as best I could.

Rodger started flipping off lights.

I bent over the small desk by the door and signed us out on the log sheet. "You got drunk and didn't bother to think. Now, because of you, Galen is convinced I'm some answer to everyone's prayers."

"Who's Galen?" Rodger bent to add his signature.

"The special ops soldier," I snapped.

Rodger gave me a knowing grin. "Ahh, so now he's Galen?"

"Oh, grow up." I wasn't in the mood. Besides, "Don't you think there's something wrong if you don't remember what you said last night?" I planted a hand on my hip. "What would Mary Ann say?" Maybe I should write to his wife about his drinking.

Although chances were, she could do nothing and it would just worry the snot out of her.

Rodger snarled. His shoulders bunched as if he were ready to pounce.

"What?" I asked. "Too close to home?"

Yellow ringed his pupils as he stared me down. He seemed larger, more menacing as he sucked the air out of the small room.

I rolled my eyes. "Too bad for you the angry-werewolf

thing stopped working about three years ago." And frankly, it pissed me off that he'd even try. "I know you weren't on duty and I know you weren't on call, but what if we'd actually needed you last night? What if a dozen ambulances came screaming in and we needed an extra set of hands?"

He growled low in his throat. "Are you done?"

"No." Because that wasn't even why I was mad. I scrubbed a hand over my eyes and sat back against the desk. "Remember last month?"

Rodger had gotten drunk, shifted, and gnawed the tires off half a dozen ambulances.

He crossed his hands over his large, round chest. "You nailed Marius into his footlocker," he said accusingly.

Way to bring that up. "That was different. I wasn't drunk."

He shrugged one meaty shoulder. "Look. I'm fine. Okay?"

No, it wasn't okay. Something was taking hold of Rodger. I looked up at my friend and knew from the stony expression on his face that he'd shut down.

I didn't know what else I could say to get through to him and that bugged me most of all.

"Rodger—" I blew out a breath. What was I going to do? Tie him to his bed? Nail him in a footlocker? He had to decide he had a problem and he had to want to change. I didn't know how to deliver him to that point. Maybe he hadn't screwed up enough yet. "Let's get out of here," I said.

"Sure," he said, letting it drop. Rodger always let it drop.

It was dark and I was cranky as we trudged toward the tar swamp, crunching over locusts, batting them away from our eyes.

Cursed amateurs.

It had been a grueling day, made more annoying by the fact that I'd been running full-throttle and somehow making things worse instead of better.

Father McArio was no longer the only one who knew I could see the dead. The entire camp thought I was going to use forty-eight thousand condoms. And Galen was a VIP.

I glanced at my roommate as we made it back to the

hutch. Cases and cases of condoms were stacked on both sides of the door.

"You couldn't even put them out back?"

"They're heavy."

And he was wrung out from his one-man party last night—not that he'd admit it now. He didn't have to. Rodger didn't even bother to take off his shoes before he fell face-first into bed.

I figured it would take me a while to settle down, but it was the last thought I had until morning.

Sunlight stung my eyes as I woke to a chorus of swamp creatures squeaking. It sounded like way more than a dozen.

Hades. I didn't want to know. I buried my head in my pillow, hoping they'd go away already, when I realized that the morning was awfully bright.

I grabbed for my watch.

"Ten o'clock?" I shot up in bed, squinting against the suns. "Where are my shoes? I was due at rounds by eight."

Rodger's cot protested as he rolled over. "That's why Horace was banging in the door." He threw an arm over his eyes. "I gave him a little dinosaur and he went away."

Another one? I grabbed my boots and plopped down on Marius's footlocker to drag them on. "You've got to stop giving out swamp creatures. They're breeding."

"I've got it under control," Rodger said, rubbing his arms as he sat.

Where had I heard that before?

I stood up. "Rog, seriously. Do you have it under control?"

He yawned. "Don't worry about me."

Merde. One more fiasco I couldn't control. I planted a boot on the footlocker and tied the laces. "Tell them to keep their little monster parts to themselves."

Rodger grinned, his red hair sticking out at impossible angles. "Thanks for the condoms, by the way."

"I figured they'd make good water balloons."

"Or finger puppets."

"Off to work," I said, grabbing my stethoscope.

"Have fun, dear," Rodger called after me. "Good luck."

"Yeah, yeah," I said, tossing a pillow at his head on the way out. I was going to need all the luck I could get.

"Well, look who decided to show up," Holly drawled as I banged into the recovery tent, two hours late.

"I was on call last night," I said, grabbing a few Starburst from her candy bowl.

"Ah, the old plague-of-locusts excuse. Your two friends from the motor pool were talking about it at breakfast," she said, clacking through patient release charts. "I found half a dozen of the little buggers in my left boot this morning."

"Crunchy?"

"Extra-crispy." She handed me a clipboard packed with rare pink forms. "Here's your hold on Commander Galen of Delphi."

I stiffened. "What makes you think I'm coming in here just for him?"

She raised her brows. "He's your only patient in recovery."

Right. I took the chart. "It's been a crazy week," I said, by way of explanation.

"Technically, he's not even yours," she said. "Captain Thaïs did his final exam. He's clear for release . . . or wherever he's going."

"Kosta wants him in the visiting officers' quarters."

"You don't say." Holly leaned her chin on her knuckles, interest sparking her eyes. "Nice digs. And he's certainly easy on the eyes."

"Don't even think about it."

"Why?" she drawled.

"I'm not being possessive, if that's what you think."

Holly winked at me and straightened in her chair.

Why was she looking so flirty? "Is there something you want to tell me?"

"Hello, Doctor," Galen said behind me. I turned around, figuring I'd be prepared for the sight. I wasn't.

Holly whistled. "Hello yourself."

Galen stood in his combat fatigues, feet set wide, shoulders squared. He wore the black of the special forces, with a Ken rune etched in red on his left shoulder. It was the symbol of flame, sex, action, and heroism. It was the mark of a warrior. A gold commander's star glinted on his collar.

Oh my god. I couldn't believe I'd actually been with this man.

Galen looked like he could charge about a dozen giant scorpions, uphill, and not even break a sweat.

He glanced at Holly. "At least somebody doesn't mind having me around."

My body warmed and I felt a flush creep up to my cheeks. "She doesn't know what you're capable of."

He leaned in close enough to touch. "Neither do you."

Was he trying to give me a heart attack?

Technically, I was supposed to plant him in a wheelchair until he left the hospital, but I wasn't going through that again.

"Follow me," I said, not bothering to see if he did. I had to calm down. I wasn't some simpering female. I was a trained medical professional.

A brisk walk would be just the thing.

All I had to do was show Galen to his tent and then hope he never came out again.

The sky was blue as we stalked across the courtyard. The high-level tents were next to the hospital and administrative offices. You had Kosta, the head nurse, and now Galen—our newest VIP.

Black dragons swooped over a rocky outpost in the distance. Scouts, no doubt, gathering intelligence before battle. We'd be seeing wounded soon.

"I know why you're so worked up," Galen said, falling into pace next to me.

Hades, I hoped not, because I couldn't handle that right now.

"You're mad because I'm right," he said.

Of all the . . . The man was dead sexy and too cocky for his own good.

I stared him right in the baby blues. The uncertainty fled, replaced by hot indignation. Angry I could do. I had a PhD in pissed off. "You think Kosta giving you a cushy tent makes you right?"

He didn't bat an eyelash. "I'm still here, aren't I?"

"For the moment." Until I could figure out what to do about the dearly departed Dr. Freierrmuth.

We reached the plain red tent next to the VIP showers. Galen's new quarters were at least three times as big as my hutch. I always wondered why the bigwigs stayed in tents instead of hutches with doors.

No matter. My job was almost done.

"Here you are," I said. I flung open the flaps to the tent and gasped.

I didn't know what I'd expected. Probably something like Father McArio's private hutch—all business and no frills. This was like a scene out of Arabian Nights.

Plush pillows and low couches scattered across the main room. Ornate copper and glass lamps hung from the bright blue ceiling. And what was that gurgling I heard?

I strained my neck to the left and felt my mouth drop open. "You have a fountain."

He leaned in past me. "Look at that. Let's check it out."

"No." I didn't belong in there. Nobody did.

Besides, I was angry. Wasn't I? I swear this man could ruin a good rant before I even got started.

Galen stood close behind me. I could feel the heat of his body on my back, but I was rooted to the spot. This place was temptation on a platter. Good thing I wasn't used to getting what I wanted.

"Go," he said, nudging me onto the plush carpet floor. Oh sweet heaven. Carpet. I hadn't seen carpet since I left home.

And the fountain . . . the entire thing was done in mosaics. It was a riot of color. Mermaids spilled water from orange and yellow shells into the glistening pool. It was difficult to imagine such a thing could exist in the flat, red wastelands of limbo. I ran my fingers over the tiles. I dipped them into the pool, letting the water lap against my skin.

"Look at this kitchen," Galen said from the back of the room. He slid back a clouded glass door to reveal a mosaic countertop and modern, stainless-steel appliances.

My heart gave a flutter. "What's in the fridge?"

He opened it with a flourish to reveal food. Real food. Like milk and cheese and eggs and, "Blueberries," I whispered. I hadn't had a blueberry in seven years.

I'd never seen Galen so amused. "Come and get 'em."

He didn't have to ask me twice. "Maybe I should rethink this friendship of ours." There was a lot I could tolerate in the name of fresh fruit.

"You cook?" he asked, holding out a little wicker basket of blueberries.

"Used to." I popped one into my mouth and groaned at the burst of sweet flavor.

I grabbed a handful and sank down on the rich carpeted floor, enjoying them one at a time.

"We have an entire quart," he said, inspecting one.

I didn't bother answering. The blueberries deserved to be savored.

The carpet underneath me was plush, woven in an intricate pattern of golds and greens. Yellow paper lanterns hung above the counter.

That's when it hit me. There wasn't a trace of red in the place.

Galen groaned. My first thought was that he was injured, but then I saw him with one hand propped up against the counter. The other fisting a bunch of purple grapes.

"Long time, sailor?"

"You have no idea," he said, sinking down next to me.

"I should warn you that if you eat too much fruit after having no fruit, that could be bad."

"Spoken like a true medical professional."

We both ignored my advice and relished every minute of it.

"There's a note on the fridge," he said, when we'd worked our way through almost all of it. "Food deliveries come every day."

"Will you marry me?"

He snorted. "Demi-gods don't get married. We kill and destroy."

"You also hoard grapes," I said.

He had his eyes closed. I leaned my head back against the kitchen island. He'd been serious. I couldn't let it pass. Not this time. "I know you're not like that, Galen."

"Not always, no." He sat perfectly still. "My mom had a vineyard out back. She used to let me cut grapes with her. Well, she'd cut, I'd run and explore. I used to like to sneak up on her from between the trellises."

"Covert even back then."

"I hadn't thought of it that way." He grinned.

"Come on," I said, "let's go see if you have a bowling alley hidden somewhere in here."

I opened the flaps to the next room and found a step-down bath, big enough for several people. It was filled with warm, bubbling clay.

"Ohh . . . mud bath!" I'd seen these in spa magazines.

Galen didn't look so eager. "I think I'd prefer the bowling alley."

"Are you kidding?" I said, walking around the massive tub. "This is probably world-class mud."

He stopped a few feet short. "I've been fighting in the mud for hundreds of years."

"You'd enjoy this," I said, dipping a hand into the bath. The warm mud comforted me like a hug. "I'd like to sink down naked into this."

His lips quirked. "Now, there's an idea."

I looked at him from under lowered lashes. What would it be like to slather this man in mud?

More than I could handle, that's for sure. I cleaned off on one of the softest towels I'd ever felt. Dear lord, was there anything in this place that wasn't drop-dead amazing?

My eye caught a pair of deep gold curtains. "I wonder what's back there?"

I ripped open the curtain and found myself staring at the largest bed I'd ever seen.

His bed.

I wasn't so sure I wanted to be here anymore.

Sweet heaven, it was draped with sumptuous coverings. It was nothing like my single sleeper with the scratchy wool blanket.

This thing was massive, both luxurious and elegant. I licked my lips. This wasn't the bed of a soldier. It was the bed of a god.

I could feel him behind me. His fingers whispered along my scalp as he tucked a strand of hair behind my ear. "Want to try it out?"

"Not in a million years." This wasn't just any bed. This was Galen's.

There's nothing like being in a man's bedroom for the first time. It's always nerve racking. One part giddy anticipation, another part antsy at just how far it could go.

I knew better than to push Galen.

In the minefield, I could tell myself that sex stemmed from the moment or the danger or the insane attraction . . . or that things just *happened*. But alone in his bedroom? It became a choice.

"It's okay," he said against my ear. "Touch it."

He knew how bad I wanted to.

"Are we still talking about the bed?"

He chuckled behind me. "Yes."

"Okay, then," I said, leaving the doorway. Maybe just this once. Only to see what it felt like. I ran my hand over the sumptuous silk, fleece, and mohair wool coverings. I groaned despite myself.

Galen laughed, bracing his hands on either side of the doorway. "It's only a bed."

"You are so wrong." I said, enjoying his amusement, sinking down onto the bed, taking what I wanted before I could think about it too much.

My heart skipped a few beats as I lay on the softest mattress known to man. I'd never felt anything like it. Not even before I'd been dumped into limbo.

The bed shifted as Galen lay next to me. He exhaled slowly

as he felt the bliss that was this mattress. "I thought the hospital beds were good."

"You're kidding." I'd lowered my voice without even thinking about it.

He stretched out next to me in those drool-worthy black combat fatigues. I wondered what he'd look like naked, sprawled out over this bed.

He found a lock of my hair on the pillow and wound it around his finger. "I usually sleep outside on the ground."

My heart thudded in my chest. We were so close. We both knew where this was going.

But was I okay with that? With him? With us?

I could get up and go.

His breath whispered over me.

I didn't. He lowered his mouth and kissed me once, twice. I didn't want to go. I kissed him back hard. Our tongues tangled as we ate each other. The fury took over and he climbed on top of me. Mouths and hands frantic, his big body on top of mine, I rubbed against him like a cat, wanting more, needing . . .

I gasped as he went to work on my neck, his hand sliding under my scrub top. He bared inch upon quivering inch as he worked his way up, layering kisses along the edge of my rib cage.

His hand cupped the underside of my breast and I about shot off the bed as his thumb grazed my nipple.

I tugged my shirt off, tossing it onto the bed next to us. Flushed and more than a little afraid, I sat back on my elbows, open to his gaze.

The look he gave me, one of pure adulation, nearly brought tears to my eyes. If this was what it meant to be worshiped, I was all for it.

He braced himself on one arm, his hand caressing my chest, my rib cage, the curve of my waist.

He bent his head and took my breast into his mouth. I watched him. I couldn't take my eyes off him as he adored first one nipple, then the other with his tongue. He worked them until I was weak-limbed and wet with pleasure.

I closed my eyes and let the sensations take me.

He was so dangerous. If I got used to this, or to him, I'd never leave.

"Gods, I want this," he murmured against my throat. "I want you."

"I can't believe you're real," I said, my breath coming quickly. Couldn't believe I was in a sumptuous bed in the middle of the desert, with Galen the demi-god. "It's like a fantasy."

His fingers found my waistband and I lifted my hips. A thought flittered through my mind: I could have stopped him. I could have chosen to go slow. But I didn't want that. I wanted him.

He loosened the tie of my scrubs, his eyes catching the blue swirling Fleur-de-Z tattoo on my hip. He ran a thumb over it, then his tongue as he stripped the pants from me. He kissed my bent knee, my thigh, my clit right through my soaked underwear.

"You are so incredibly wet," he said, rising over me, his elbows on either side of my cheeks. "I want to know just how wet you are. I want to feel your juice sliding through my fingers."

I let my legs fall open as he slipped his hand under my panties.

He touched me where I was aching, slippery, and ready for him. He slid his fingers through my wet folds as I strained against him, growing even slicker for him.

Only for him.

"I can't believe how drenched you are," he murmured, his breath scorching my ear. "You are so god damn hot."

I swallowed. "I want your fingers inside me." I wanted to feel him penetrate me, stretch me. I wanted him to make room for his cock.

There was nothing stopping us and I didn't care anymore. This was so good, so right.

He lined himself up against me at the perfect angle to slip inside, if only he'd strip off his pants.

"You're teasing me." I imagined my juice soaking into his combat fatigues, wetting the tip of his cock.

His jaw was tight. "I'm about to go out of my fucking mind."

Hades, I was so ready for this. My orders required me to be on birth control. I even had forty-eight thousand condoms at my disposal.

Naturally, they were on full display outside my hutch.

Damn, this was really going to happen.

I let out a nervous laugh.

"It's fate," he said, kissing the curve of my ear. "Us finding a place like this. Us sliding wet and naked against each other," he said, kissing the tip of my nose. "This is the universe telling us we're on the right track."

What? "No," I said, barely finding my voice as his thumb caressed my cheek, his other hand closing over my hip bone, holding me as if he were already inside me. Sleeping with him meant I was lusting after a god. It did not make him right. "This is lust."

Our bodies were perfectly aligned, ready. Eyes slit with desire, he rocked his cock against the core of me. Did he know what that did to me?

"We're here because Colonel Kosta needed to put you somewhere. Nothing more."

The disappointment showed on his face. "You still don't believe we're part of something bigger here. That there's a plan behind this."

"Other than the one to turn me into a raging nymphomaniac? No."

"What is it with you?" he asked, braced over me. "Why don't you want peace?"

"Oh, all of a sudden I don't want peace?" Unbelievable. He was the hardened killing machine. I sat up and so did he. I crossed my arms over my chest, chilly without him. "I want this war to end." I always would. "But not by forcing it. Not your way."

"Why?" he demanded.

"I could ask you the same thing. Why does it have to be your way? Your show? You may be a god, but you're certainly not perfect. I know this may come as a shock, but you don't have all the answers."

He was as surprised as if I'd smacked him. "And you do?"

"No one does," I said, my voice kicking up a notch.

This was such a mess.

He'd suffered. He'd lost. I wished I had a way out for him, or at least a way to make him understand. I tried to get a grip, calm down. "Look, I can't take the risk. Okay?"

"I don't even know what that means," he thundered.

Oh yeah. Way to get pissy. I reached for my shirt, my mouth twisted into a bitter smile. "Nothing."

"What aren't you telling me?" he demanded as I forced myself to get up off the bed. I found my pants on the floor. "I think I deserve to know why you're so adamant about this." I'd never gotten dressed so fast in my life. "Why the hell are you leaving?" he demanded as I walked away.

I turned. "Oh, I'm sorry. I didn't realize I owed you my life story."

He got up to follow me. "Do you want to calm down and talk to me about this?"

His placating tone pissed me off. "So now you're the reasonable one?" I asked, fighting through the yellow curtains.

He made sound that was half snarl, half utter exasperation as he followed me through the living room. "I'm going to be on you until you tell me what's going on."

Yeah, right. "I'd like to see you try."

"Remember you said that," he called as I stalked out of the tent.

chapter twelve

Okay, so first I couldn't shut up and now he couldn't keep his opinions to himself. Only one thing was clear to me and that was that Galen and I had no idea what to do with this insane attraction.

We were in bed. In his *bed* and we couldn't even pull it off.

Argh. He was the most frustrating man I'd ever met. I wanted to kiss him one minute and bash him over the head the next. At this rate, I'd be a born-again virgin forever.

Not that there was anything wrong with that. I'd been doing fine for the last seven years. I didn't need a hot special ops officer, or his big, soft bed.

Fuck.

What I needed was chocolate. The Post Exchange was always out.

I had to get my head on straight, focus on something else. I cruised through post-op to see if they needed any help, but of course they had it handled. So I headed back to my hutch.

My bunk squeaked as I flopped down and reached for the shoe box on my nightstand. It was my snack box, and today it held Fruit Stripe gum and three packets of saltine crackers from the mess tent. Yum.

The soft bubbling from the tar swamp next door wasn't as comforting as it usually was. Today it just smelled. I unwrapped a stick of grape and popped it in my mouth. It was stale and left my mouth feeling dry and dusty.

I hoped he had blue balls.

Not that I was thinking of Galen. Because I wasn't.

I unzipped the screened window over my roommates' cluttered shelf and tossed the nasty gum into the swamp.

Good riddance. I didn't need Galen or his massive bed. And once Rodger took down his laundry, I'd even be able to walk across our tiny hovel without getting hit in the head by surgical scrubs and *Star Trek* T-shirts. I mean, who really needs more than one?

My hutch might not be as plush as Galen's, but it was mine. I bunched a pillow behind me. It used to be lumpy. Now it was flat from overuse. Official new army regulations said I had three more years to go before the next pillow reissue. Ten years, one pillow. That seemed reasonable.

I dug around on my nightstand and pulled on a pair of sunglasses. The suns were especially bright this afternoon. That's probably why there weren't too many people out walking, or stopping by.

Galen was probably lonely as hell in that big tent by himself. Well, it was his fault that we weren't sweaty and naked on his bed.

I had to think of something else.

Books! Yes, I could focus on the books I'd brought down here with me. Who cared if I'd read them a few times before?

I settled in to read *Undead and Unwed,* one of my all-time favorites. It amused me to no end that most people topside thought it was fiction.

But today Betsy the vampire had her work cut out for her. My mind was skittering all over the place.

My sunglasses slid down my nose as a lingering unease tugged at me. Where was everyone? It was never this quiet. Normally I couldn't get through a chapter without someone bothering me about something I couldn't fix.

I pushed my sunglasses back into place and glanced at Marius's footlocker. No doubt the vampire was snoozing inside. "It's just you and me, buddy."

The way it ought to be, really.

At last, I lost myself in the book, like I always did. I'd just made it to chapter fourteen when Rodger banged in the door. If possible, his hair was scruffier, his cheeks pinker, and his expression even more wingding than usual.

"Best day ever." He paraded straight past me to get a good look at the suns setting over the tar swamp. He turned around, almost surprised to see me. "Chocolate-covered cherry?" Rodger asked, popping two into his mouth at once. He held out a half-eaten box.

Dread seeped over me. I knew VIP contraband when I saw it. "Where did you get those?"

He plopped down on Marius's footlocker to eat a few more. "Where do you think?"

Great. While I was alone all afternoon, Galen was yucking it up with my friend. I brought my book up between us and settled back onto my pillow "You can keep your ill-gotten chocolate."

"You can't be serious," Rodger said, through a mouthful of cherries.

"What? You think Galen is so wonderful?" It was just like a god to have to be the center of attention.

"He's really cool," my roommate said, picking through the candy. "I showed him that picture of Mary Ann and he said the same thing you did."

"She looks like Rachael Ray?" Rodger's wife was the spitting image.

"Yep," he said, his ruddy face breaking out into a grin. "And I told him about Gabriel getting that part in *Joseph and the Amazing Technicolor Dreamcoat*." He leaned back, his mind back at home. "Of course now Mary Ann's got to make Gabe a coat. Knowing her she'll glue it instead of sew it. Can't even sew buttons on straight. I used to sew the buttons. Did I ever tell you that?"

"Yes, you did." About once a week.

"Oh and I didn't even tell you this," he said, leaning forward, the chocolate forgotten. "Mary Ann was downstairs the other night and baby Kate got hold of one of her brand-new blue pumps—the ones she bought for church. Chewed the heel right off. Mary Ann was fit to be tied, but I wrote her back and reminded her that the poor pup's teething." He sounded half amused, half proud. "I chewed through my dad's entire vintage baseball card collection once upon a time."

Okay. So Galen had let Rodger talk (and talk, and talk). No harm in that. "Did he tell you what he said to me this morning?"

"I gotta show you this new picture of Stephen," he said, digging under his bed and drawing out a shoe box. "The little guy lost another tooth." He popped the lid and began lifting pictures out.

It was like talking to a big, hairy wall. "Rodger," I began.

"What? He pissed you off, you pissed him off. It's not my fault you two can't get it together. Now look at this," he said, handing me a photo of a fresh-faced seven-year-old pup.

Righteous anger tugged at me. Rodger made everything sound so simple, and it wasn't. Still, I couldn't help but grin at Stephen's lopsided smile. "This is really cute."

"I know," he said, taking the photo back and smiling at it. "Thank god they look like their mother." He gave a small sigh.

"Okay, so tell me about Galen," he continued, as if I were about to show him my world cruise vacation photos. "Do you want me to pass him a note in math class?"

Har-de-har-har. "It's not like that." Not really. Yes, I wanted him, but it was ridiculous to even feel that way—as evidenced by this morning when he tried to use my attraction to him to justify his crazy theories.

Why couldn't he just leave it alone? I wasn't against enjoying what time we had together.

No one had ever spoken to me or touched me the way Galen did. He knew my most secret fear. He'd seen *into* me, for cripes sake.

But he was obsessed with that damn prophecy. He didn't seem to care if I got drawn and quartered as long as he had a shot at stopping the war—which he didn't.

The gods always thought they could tamper with fate,

change the rules to suit them. And who paid the price? People like me.

"He's just . . ." I tried to explain it to Rodger without sounding like an over-eager schoolgirl. "Galen is such a god."

"So?" Rodger shrugged.

"You and I were supposed to go creature fishing," I said, grasping a little. True, I hadn't wanted to see anyone this afternoon. And we hadn't actually made concrete plans so much as we'd talked about maybe going. Still, it wasn't the point. Rodger had forgotten me. In a way, he'd chosen Galen over me.

"You don't even like sea serpents," he said, missing the point entirely.

"They're better than you fawning all over Galen," I said, trying to get back into my book.

"Fawning?" Rodger snarfed. "I'll tell you who's in danger of fawning."

"You know what? Let's just drop it." I didn't need Rodger and his stale popcorn. I was happy reading. *Undead and Unwed* was a great book. A keeper.

"I'm not the one sleeping with him," he said.

"I'm not sleeping with him," I shot back, the injustice of it twisting in my gut.

"You're crazy," Rodger said. "Any girl in this camp would kill to be in your place. In fact, there were a couple of them lined up outside his tent this afternoon."

"Fuck off." I grabbed the box and lobbed a cherry at him.

"Cut it out!" he said, reaching for the cherry and catching it like Hank Aaron. "You're wasting them. Besides, Galen wasn't flirting back. I'm only telling you because I know you won't ask. He wouldn't even let them in."

I hugged the pillow to my chest. At least that was something.

"You must be having some fun, at least," he said, popping the cherry into his mouth. "I could smell you all over him. I, for one, think it's great."

"You'd be the only one," I said, wishing Galen could have kept his opinions to himself this morning.

"Do I need to help you two along? Maybe draw you some diagrams?" I prepared to toss another cherry. "Hey, cut it out. I told Jeffe he could have some."

The box tipped off my lap.

"Real smooth. Thanks, Petra."

He peeked under the overturned box. The cherries had smashed into the canvas floor of the tent, leaving a sticky mess.

"Oh well. Kind of reminds me of home." He scooped up the crushed candies, using the mangled box as a trash can. "At least this gives me an excuse to go back to Galen's. I'm going to have to give Jeffe the entire box of turtles now," he muttered under his breath.

"What's Jeffe doing over there?" I could see Galen making friends with Rodger, because who wouldn't. But the sphinx? The last time Jeffe noticed Galen was when he was pulling a special op sneak-back-into-bed mission. That couldn't have gone over well.

Rodger fished an Orange Crush out of his medical coat pocket.

I gasped. "I love orange soda."

"I know," Rodger said, holding it out of my reach. "That's why I snagged you the last one."

"Great. One day with a hutch of his own and Galen is more popular than me."

"No offense, but when has it ever been your goal in life to be popular?"

"Good point." I'd just wanted Galen to miss me a little this afternoon.

Rodger went to the counter between his bunk and Marius's. "You got a bottle opener?" he asked, rifling through the picture frames, action figures, and other assorted junk on his half.

"I haven't even seen a bottle in seven years," I said, getting up to help find something, anything, to pry off that lid.

I hadn't had an Orange Crush since my dad and I went to Cooter Brown's Oyster Bar about a week before the new god army showed up at my door. I rummaged through Marius's dresser drawer, and mine.

In fact, it was getting dark in here. I fished out a book of matches and lit the lanterns above each of our beds.

While the light was nice, I didn't see anything that would help us pry open the bottle. "Maybe we can bang it against the edge of the dresser," I suggested. I may have seen that in a movie once.

"No way." Rodger frowned. "I'm not going to break it. Galen probably has an opener."

"Like we need him." Maybe we could use surgical pliers.

"I don't know what's making you both so miserable," Rodger began.

"He's miserable?" I asked hopefully.

"Well, not exactly miserable, but. I don't know. Why don't you go over and talk to him? Galen's a good guy."

Of that I had no doubt. But he could come over here, too.

Rodger turned, his jacket sleeve knocking Marius's obnoxious Roman fertility statue off its display base. "Whoops."

I tried to reach around him and missed. "You'd better not crack the penis off again." We were out of superglue.

Rodger returned the well-endowed figurine to its base. "He's fine." The statue wobbled but held as he took another go at the soda. "Hey, look. Twist top."

Rodger twisted and the bottle fizzed open.

"Lovely," I grumbled, but I didn't turn him down when he offered me the first swig.

It was sweet and bubbly and amazing, just like I remembered from when I was a kid. I closed my eyes and leaned against the counter to take another long, sweet drink.

Heaven.

"Galen's got Jeffe playing a Trivial Pursuit world championship," Rodger said.

I opened my eyes to find my werewolf buddy lounging on the sleeping vampire's footlocker.

"I don't believe it," I said, handing him the bottle.

"Well, it's not really the world championship," he said,

eyeing the Orange Crush. I'd drunk about half of it. "They just call it that for fun."

I'd treated plenty of demi-gods and I knew they were the type of guys to party large and surround themselves with big groups of friends, but Galen was a warrior, a decorated commander, and a general expert at killing things. Jeffe was scared of spiders, couldn't start a conversation without it turning into an interrogation, and spent most of his time doing crossword puzzles and collecting stamps.

Rodger shrugged. "Galen asks him questions. You should see Jeffe go. He's really good at geography. Fills his entire plastic pie up with blue pieces."

"So Galen is letting him cheat." It figured. Galen wanted me to break the rules, too.

"They're having fun." Rodger laughed. "You should try it sometime."

"Hey," I said, reaching for the bottle. "I'm fun."

He handed it to me. "So how much fun did you have with Galen this morning? I could smell you in his bedroom. And the bed was rumpled."

He left the bed rumpled? I wondered, with hope. Maybe he couldn't bear to straighten the blankets. Maybe he missed me.

Maybe he was being a man and didn't even notice that beds have sheets.

"What is with you two?" Rodger mused with a smile.

Marius rattled in his footlocker. Rodger jumped.

Saved by the bell.

The suns were almost completely down now. "You'd better get up before Sleeping Beauty gets pissed," I said.

"I'm out of here." Rodger stood, leaving me the bottle. "Oh hey." He grabbed a stack of note cards off my nightstand. "Four by six. These are perfect." He banged them against his hand. "You have any more?"

"Sure." Tons. I used them as reminder notes. "Why do you want my note cards all of a sudden?"

"We ran out of the ones Shirley gave us from supply," Rodger said, cramming them into the pocket of his scrub pants. He shrugged off his white medical coat and tossed it on top of the table he shared with Marius. "Jeffe is off tonight. I'm going. So that's three of us. We don't want to run out of cards."

"At Galen's," I said, a dull thud forming in my chest. I was afraid to ask. "Doing what?"

It was like they were having a big party and I couldn't go without losing face. I was taking a stand against Galen, and he needed to know that.

Rodger dug through the chest of drawers next to his bed. "Galen has this theory. Says you're nothing without hope. Which makes sense, you know?" He pulled out one of the ponchos his wife had knitted. "Anyhow, Hume has been feeling down in the dumps."

"Nurse Hume?" He was more than depressed. He was a walking ghost.

"Yep." Rodger began pulling the poncho over his head. "So Galen gets to talking to him in the mess hall today—"

Wait. I couldn't hang out with Galen, but Nurse Hume could? "What? Is he having dinner parties now?"

"No," Rodger said slowly. "Just dinner in the mess hall." He shrugged. "Galen likes to be social. You should come to breakfast with us tomorrow."

My head was starting to hurt. If I went, I couldn't ignore him. And Galen would probably twist it and think he'd won.

If I holed up here, I'd just be wondering what they were doing. "I don't suppose I could ask you to stay away from Galen?"

"What—are you telling me who I can spend time with?"

"Wouldn't think of it." It would never work anyway.

"You should come with us," he said, as if that were the issue. "It's fun." Rodger found his fishing cap. "Like in the mess tent, Galen is talking to Hume and learns the guy had one bright moment in his whole miserable life down here."

"I shudder to think." Hume had been a ghost of a person for as long as I'd known him.

He slapped his hands together. "About fifteen years ago, he won a year's subscription to *Reader's Digest*."

I stared at Rodger.

"He entered their monthly joke contest and he won."

My fingers played along my soda bottle as I tried to process what Rodger was getting at. "Hume isn't funny."

"That's what you think," Rodger said.

Of all the . . . "You think so, too."

Rodger shook his head. "Doesn't matter what I think. You should have been there. Hume lit up like I've never seen him. So Galen decides to get Hume some hope."

"It doesn't work that way." You couldn't go out and get hope, like you'd pick it up at the store or something.

"Yes, it can," he insisted. "Ha!" He spotted another stack of note cards and reached under my bed to get them.

Amazing. I hadn't seen Rodger this gleeful since his last letter from home.

He waggled the cards. "We're helping Hume win the Dr Pepper sweepstakes," he said. "Enter as often as you like. No purchase necessary. Every postcard could be your ticket to fabulous prizes."

"Okay, fine." I stood. "This I have to see. And I'm going to make it very clear to Galen that I am not there to see him."

"Whatever you say." Rodger was already ahead of me and out the door.

There was no reason to stay behind. Galen couldn't get to me if I didn't let him.

Besides, Marius's footlocker was rattling again and he wasn't going to be happy to see Rodger had used his cuff links to fix a rip in the screen door.

We picked up a couple of torches from the path outside our tent and headed for Galen's place.

I was not giving in, I was not crawling back, and I didn't want anything from him.

Maybe this wasn't such a great idea.

My feet felt like lead. Rodger was practically skipping.

Galen was trying to change things around here. And I was happy to see some of it. I was. But he needed to know when to quit.

The night was growing colder by the minute. I didn't think I'd ever get used to the chill of limbo after dark. We didn't pass many people as we made our trek back. No doubt most were in their hutches staying warm. I walked with nervous anticipation swirling in my belly. Rodger whistled the theme song from *The Price Is Right*.

Light glowed from inside the immense red tent. The flaps hung closed. "Yo, Galen," Rodger called.

I wasn't that polite. Heart hammering, I flung the flap back.

Galen stood just inside, looking breathtakingly gorgeous in those damn midnight-black combat fatigues. He trained his eyes on me the same way he had right before he went down on me in the minefield. It made me feel exposed, naked, and sexy as hell.

I broke contact. *Think of something else.* Like Jeffe on the floor next to Galen. The sphinx bent over stacks of note cards, his tail curling around a cardboard box filled with even more cards in neat, rubber-band-bound stacks.

Galen moved toward me with all the grace of a predator. He knew I'd be back. His manner said it all. I silently cursed myself for making it so easy for him.

He scooped a bowl off the edge of the couch as he approached.

"Blueberry?" he asked, lifting the bowl to me like he was offering the apple from the forbidden tree.

Oh yeah. He was good. And judging from that sexy grin, he didn't doubt my answer.

"I didn't come here for treats," I said, realizing too late that I hadn't quite turned him down in the way I'd hoped.

He fixed those damn blue eyes on me and the raw hunger I saw in them sent needles of anticipation down my spine. "I'm glad you came," he whispered, closing the distance between us.

I remembered exactly how it felt to be in his bed together and so did he.

"I missed you," he said. He looked like he could eat me alive.

His breathing grew heavy as he slid a ripe blueberry between my lips.

It was luscious and sweet. Perfect. I hadn't even known I wanted it. Now I could hardly think of anything else.

But even as I savored it, I knew it was trap. I raised my eyes to his. "You always get your way, don't you?"

"Not always," he said slowly. His lips curved in the barest hint of a smile. "But I sure as hell try."

I'll bet. I trailed a finger down his battle fatigues. "You think you're so smart."

"He's very smart," said Jeffe, almost giddy.

My stomach quivered. I'd forgotten about the sphinx. And about Rodger.

"Get a room," my buddy whispered not so quietly in my ear as he slid past me. "How's it going, slick?" Rodger asked the sphinx, strolling over.

So much for showing Galen he wasn't all that and a box of crackers.

I tilted my head to the side. "I'm not here for what you think I'm here for," I said, wincing inside as I said it. Color me smooth.

No question Galen had me rattled, but did he honestly think I was going to hand my life over to him just because we'd connected on a soul level? Or because of the chemistry between us?

A muscle in his jaw twitched. "Then why are you back?"

"Okay, how can I say this?" I wondered aloud, my face warming. God, what would it be like to touch him again? To be alone in that bedroom again? To have one more chance?

It didn't matter. That wasn't the point. I was here to tell him to stay out of my business. I paused to gather my wits. "I know we've shared some things. And I like you. I do. But I don't like it when you push me. I'm not going to put up with it—anytime, anywhere, and especially not in bed."

That hadn't come off as steely as I'd wanted, but damn it, he was way too close and way too large and way too *male* for me to keep my focus.

"Fine." He gritted his jaw. "I think I can handle that."

"Really?" I asked, wary. Maybe we had a shot at this yet. I wanted to believe he meant it.

"I won't push," he said. "You'll see soon enough that the first prophecy has come true."

And just that quick, hope crashed and burned. "I should leave," I said, turning to go.

"Wait." He touched my arm. "Stay. I want you here. We all do."

"What? So I can watch Jeffe address postcards?" I asked.

Jeffe's head cocked up at the sound of his name. "See how I write. Are they not beautiful?" Bold geometric designs edged the cards. He'd drawn scarabs, lotus flowers, and, of course, the occasional guard sphinx. "You don't just want to write a name. You want to draw symbols for good luck and prosperity."

Rodger stood over the sphinx. "I think you've got something there."

Jeffe tilted his chin a little higher. "Tomorrow I start writing questions for trivia night! I am in charge as long as no one gets eaten."

Nurse Hume burst through the front flap, holding an empty milk crate. His hair was pale, his skin was pasty, but his face was alive. "I just mailed batch six!"

A cheer went up from the group.

Come on. They must get thousands of entries every day. "He might not even win," I told Galen.

"But I might," answered Hume. His cheeks took on a flush I'd never seen before. "Imagine how I'd look in a brand-new silver Camaro."

"They might even let you pick the color," Rodger suggested.

I was all for roses and sunshine, but, "Don't you people realize we're in the middle of a war zone? We have jobs to do."

Hume clucked his tongue. "Well, aren't you a buzzkill?"

"You've got to be kidding me." I looked to my friends for support. Naturally, they ignored me.

Hume gave a small smile as he bent down to take the almost full box from the table.

"I've gotta get out of here," I said to myself more than anyone. It was too much too fast and if I wasn't careful, I was actually going to join in.

I was aware of every muscle as Galen stood and closed the space between us.

"I'll walk you home."

I took two steps back. "Let me rephrase that. I want to get some distance from you."

He stood over me, determined. "Let me be blunt. There are assassins after you."

I cleared my dry, aching throat. He would have to remind me. I glanced past him, hoping Jeffe and Hume hadn't heard. We didn't need any more rumors floating around. "I thought you said I'd be okay in camp."

"With protection after dark," he said. "I don't want you going home alone tonight."

I didn't want to be alone tonight, either. My belly tanked and my breath caught. What would have happened with this man if we hadn't met this way?

Forget it. There was no use wishing for things I couldn't have.

I stood in the open doorway. "Rodger, I need a bodyguard."

Rodger was stretched out on a colorful rug, admiring Jeffe's artwork. "Come on. We just got here."

Galen braced an arm on a tent post. "Are you afraid of what might happen?" he asked, a bit too amused for my taste.

I looked past him to the colorful Moroccan lights swaying in the cold breeze from the night. "Of course not."

Not in the way he thought. Maybe I'd been without a man too long, or maybe I was just in denial. But Galen was exactly the kind of strong, sensitive, braver-than-death guy who made me want to forget just how responsible I was.

Yet he was too dangerous. He was getting too close.

And he was stubborn as hell.

"Let's go," I said, before I changed my mind.

We walked across camp in silence, his boots crunching in the dirt along with mine. The moon was purple tonight. It hung, large and luminous, over camp.

The air blew colder than before. I could almost feel the heat burning off him. He was close enough to touch. I missed that about him. Touching him. Kissing him. Making him gasp.

It was completely insane because I couldn't get attached. He didn't belong here. He'd eventually realize his theory was bunk and despite the current paperwork mix-up, he would be leaving this place, returning to the front lines or to whatever secret missions he ran.

For as much as we were both a couple of control freaks, neither one of us could control that.

When we reached my tent, we found Marius on the bed, his eyes closed, blocking out the world.

Galen stood at the threshold. "Let me in."

I wanted to. I deserved to have someone. Hell, he did, too.

"I can't," I said as I slipped through the door.

chapter thirteen

The next day I didn't hear anything from Galen. I tried to tell myself it was a positive step. Maybe he had finally given up.

But I missed him. I didn't know what he was thinking.

I refused to ask Rodger where he was going, and where he'd been when he came back, humming. And Rodger didn't even tell me.

He'd lain off the alcohol, which surprised me. He wrote pages and pages to Mary Ann. At this rate, she'd know more about what was going on than I did. I was feeling hopelessly out of the loop.

The next day I was halfway through folding a stack of laundry when Horace popped up outside my screened window. "I've been asked to bring you these."

"What?" I asked, unzipping the window flap.

The sprite tossed a stack of paperbacks on top of my whites.

I grabbed for them. "Lora Leigh, Charlaine Harris, Sherrilyn Kenyon." And they were new. *New books.*

Rodger sat on the bed behind me, polishing his boots. "He misses you, you know."

I held the books to my chest. "How did he know I have a serious romance addiction?"

"I might have told him."

"Rodger!"

"It's not a big secret. Besides, he could have seen those authors on your shelf."

Maybe. "How did he even find these?" I asked, giving in to some serious book fondling. There were no bookstores in limbo.

"VIP interdimensional lending library," Horace said. "Want me to take them back?"

"No." I held them tight. "Maybe I'll skim a few." The books felt new, smelled new. Their spines were perfect.

The sprite nodded. "Okay well I have to get back to the construction site."

"I don't even want to know," I said, lining my new books up on my bed.

That didn't stop Horace from telling me. "We're refurbishing the burned-down VIP showers over in the minefield."

"Why?" I asked slowly.

Rodger gave Marius's footlocker a guilty glance. "Our vampire buddy needs some privacy."

I planted my hands on my hips. "Are you saying this because he superglued your sheets to your bed?"

"No," Rodger said, "that was just to get back at me for the cuff links. I get that. This is different. Galen's in charge. In fact, wait up, Horace. I'll go with you." Rodger dragged on an old pair of tennis shoes. "We've got some blackout curtains, some mirrors for the ceiling. Hume says he may be able to win a clock radio."

It was like I'd been dropped in an alternate universe. "Why are you doing this? Galen's not even part of this camp."

Horace notched his chin up. "Yes, he is. Do you know he leaves me pennies every day?"

Well, if that was all it took . . . "I have pennies."

He flashed a hand. "Save them. I don't want reluctant charity."

I wasn't reluctant. I just didn't realize how things could change.

"You know hope isn't always a good thing," I reminded them. I wanted things to get better. I did. The small improvements were nice, although it burned me up I didn't think of them first. But giving Marius a spot to call his own, or Jeffe a trivia outlet, or Hume a reason to be optimistic didn't mean Galen was right about everything.

In fact, he was proving himself to be the type of guy to force change. Sure, that was good when it came to cheering up Hume or giving Jeffe his own trivia night (lord help us on that one). But it could spell disaster if he tried to force any prophecies.

I'd made that mistake already.

I stifled a groan. It was just so unexpected. Galen was supposed to be a killer, a brutal special ops soldier, not *this*.

"Just don't expect me to join the party," I said, grabbing up a copy of *No Mercy* as they barged out to the minefield.

By evening, I'd come to realize resistance was futile. Marius's new "lair" had been cobbled together on the flat strip of space between our hut and the tar pits. And so I went out to investigate.

I was fine with the limited view of the bubbling swamp. What I didn't get was how excited Marius was. I stood a short distance from him, Galen, and Rodger as they admired their handiwork.

Marius tossed back a shock of blond hair. "It's divine," he said. "A triumph."

Galen held his torch aloft, inspecting some of the seams. "I think we did pretty well with what we had."

Marius couldn't get enough. "I can sit in the dark and brood. I can stand. I don't have to lie in a footlocker all day with my knees smashed against my chest while you two use it as a footstool."

"And we did some soundproofing so you can play your music as loud as you want," Rodger added.

That had never been a problem for Marius.

Rodger jogged over to me. "You should check it out."

"I will." In a minute.

I was insanely curious. Galen had brought more excitement to this camp than the last three USO shows combined. And that's not just because I wasn't into Homeric plays, feats of strength, and other entertainments the new gods seemed to think we'd enjoy.

Still, I refused to fall all over him just because everyone else did. I hadn't done it for the cool kids in high school and I certainly wouldn't do it now.

Rodger stood grinning next to me. "I tell you. Galen is the coolest guy."

"Why? What did he ever do for you?"

Rodger shrugged. "I'm having fun."

Galen caught my eye and I felt my toes curl. Frick, I was in trouble.

"Well done," Father McArio said as joined our little party, a mess tent cup of coffee in one hand. He patted Galen on the shoulder. "I can't tell you what a pleasure it is to have you here, son."

Oh, brother.

I made my way over to the priest. "How's Fitz?"

"Happiest hellhound in limbo," he replied. "That reminds me." McArio fished in his pocket and handed Galen a key. "I don't know what you'll get out of him. He's been chasing lizards all day. I left him sleeping in the woolly daisies behind the hutch."

Wait. He couldn't possibly have gotten to Father McArio, too. "Why are you giving Galen a key to your place?"

"His leash and treats are inside," Father continued.

Galen pocketed the key. "I used to train guard dogs."

"Of course you did."

It was bad enough he'd barnstormed his way into my roommates' affections. And Jeffe's. And Horace's. Now he had to go after my mentor, too.

"Where'd he get that?" I grumbled, watching Marius drag an ornate rug into the lair. Galen ran over to help him.

"VIP tent." Father sipped his coffee, watching. "He's great, isn't he?"

"He's the bane of my existence."

Father watched me frown. "Funny." He tilted his head. "I heard the commander saved your life."

"How did you know?" Shock made me stand taller as I tried to figure out what that meant.

"Galen shared with me what happened. He's worried about you," Father said, as if he knew my fear. "Be careful, Petra. Stay in camp."

"Just don't tell him about what I did when I first got here," I cautioned.

"Of course not." McArio seemed surprised I'd even had to ask.

I didn't like the father talking to Galen. Even though I knew he wouldn't betray my past, it made me uncomfortable. I couldn't count on anything anymore.

Galen walked among the gathering crowd, his torch held high as he directed my companions. He wore his command like a second skin, his voice rich and warm.

Rodger was making sure everyone heard exactly how Galen had salvaged the lumber from the decimated VIP showers out in the minefield. Horace directed the onlookers with god-like glee. Several maintenance workers were busy smoothing out a path to connect to the main route, complete with torch holders.

In a quiet spot set apart, Father McArio had taken it upon himself to offer a small, silent blessing, which I wasn't sure was entirely appropriate for a vampire lair. Once the priest had lowered his hand and opened his eyes, Galen joined him, speaking in hushed tones.

Galen wasn't even Catholic. Was he?

My roommate couldn't get enough of the attention this spectacle had afforded him. He flipped his hair and preened like he was on the red carpet.

Well, if the vampire wasn't going to be using his dark retreat anytime soon, I wasn't one to turn down a quiet spot.

I eased past the canvas hanging over the door and ducked into the vampire's lair. Two steps and I practically had my nose pressed up against the back wall. So much for luxury. The thing was the size of a bathtub.

An old red lantern banged me in the head, its flame reflected in dozens upon dozens of mirrors in all shapes and sizes. Most were broken. Some were obviously from discarded makeup compacts.

Most of the salvaged lumber was warped and stained—and was that a showerhead poking out of the ceiling?

The canvas flap rustled behind me. "He's hoping to eventually have one big mirror ceiling," Galen said, his shoulders level with my face. "We couldn't fit the mirrors from his hutch in here."

He was suddenly very close. His presence wound around me in a way that made me flush.

"Ah," I said. No, not much would fit in here. "It's very broody."

Galen seemed to follow my train of thought. "It's his."

I hated to admit it to him of all people, but, "I like it." I'd never seen Marius that happy.

He lingered so close that I could have easily reached out and touched him. Tiny waves of pleasure vibrated down my spine when I realized I'd like to do just that.

I cleared my throat. "You did good."

Galen leveled a slow sexy smile at me. The warmth of it soaked me to my toes.

Get a grip. It was all too much—the changes, the bizarre notion of hope, him. I had to get out of here.

Run.

But before I did, I was going to take advantage of this private space to make myself clear.

I cocked my head and did my best to ignore the way the lamplight played off his features. "You think you can do anything you want and people will just follow you."

He stilled. "I don't think anything," he answered, genuinely perplexed. "We're at war. I'm doing my best to make sure we survive it."

Maybe so. We'd all tried to carve out a way to stay sane. "Why do you care about Marius and Rodger and Hume and Jeffe?" And whoever else he was helping.

"They're good people." He ran a hand over the bottom of his face. "They didn't ask for this any more than you or I did. I don't have all the answers. I'm not completely divine, but I do what I can to fix things."

I planted my hands on my hips, shaking my head. "You just can't leave well enough alone."

"No, I can't," he said, without any trace of regret. "But I tell you, for once, it feels good to do it with a hammer and nails and not at sword point."

So take-charge Galen was going to fix the world, one person at a time.

I stood stock-still as he touched my shoulder, his fingers trailing down my arm. "I know we don't see eye-to-eye on some things, but let me in. Let's see where this takes us."

For a moment, I wanted that. I'd give anything to feel safe and protected, to be in control of something bigger than myself, to make a dent in my own destiny.

I wanted to know how he did it. What he did to twist words and circumstances until suddenly the solution to everything was to trust Galen of Delphi.

But I couldn't. "Your price is too high." I could smell his clean masculine scent as well as a hint of blueberries. He wanted total compliance and I couldn't do that.

An inch more and we'd be chest-to-chest. Sure, we had no room in this place, but I couldn't get over the idea that he was doing it on purpose, to tease me.

Yeah, well, two could play at that game.

I touched his cheek. I could see the stubble on his wide-set jaw, feel the coarseness of it under my fingers as I drew them down to the smooth tan skin at his collar.

Perhaps I didn't need to give in—in order to enjoy him.

His breathing quickened, and a small part of me rejoiced that I'd gotten to him just as he'd gotten to me. His gaze raked over me with a ferocity that made my heart race.

Shadows smoothed the rough edges of the hut. It truly was a place apart.

We were alone, hidden from the world.

Galen dipped his chin until it was inches from mine. "You want to finish what we started in my bed?" His voice was raw, earthy. "I love the sounds you make when you come."

The lanternlight caught the mirrors like dozens upon dozens of flickering candles. Knees clenched, I remained where I was, bracing against the unnamed emotions he stirred in me.

"I'm tired of being alone," I murmured.

"Me, too," he said against my mouth before he consumed me in a burning, eating kiss. There was no gentle teasing as there had been before. Galen dragged me against him, ground his body against mine as we kissed desperately.

I knocked an elbow against the wall. He hit his shoulder as we pressed and tangled in the tiny space. I had to get closer. I wanted to crawl all over him, get inside him.

He was so lean and so hard and so delicious and all mine. For here. For now. It was all I could ask.

His mouth caught my breast, teasing me through the thin fabric of my tank top. A riot of sensations washed up from where his teeth grazed my nipple and his tongue scorched it, wet and hot.

"God, I love your breasts," he said, yanking down the shirt and feasting on my bare skin. I wrapped around him, clung to him until I ground my core against his rock-hard cock.

I wanted to touch it, to taste it.

He nipped at my breasts, sending molten pleasure straight to my groin.

"Harder," I moaned, thrusting against him as his teeth closed over one aching nipple.

An industrial flashlight zapped us, stinging my eyes. Ohmigod.

"Fuck." Galen turned me away from the light.

It took a moment for our change in circumstances to penetrate my passion-soaked brain. My breasts ached. Galen's uniform felt coarse as they pressed against it.

Shirley poked her head into the lair. "A little crowded in here, isn't it?"

"Can you give us a minute?" Galen asked, his voice rough. He eased me down onto the ground.

"I didn't mean to intrude," she said, her face a shadow as she continued to blast us with her beam. As Kosta's assistant, Shirley was issued the new army version of high-tech. Didn't mean she knew how to use it.

My knees felt wobbly as I pulled my shirt back up over my breasts. Galen watched, as if he were itching to start up again.

"I wouldn't interrupt," Shirley said, clearly not understanding just what she'd barged into, "but it's here, Galen. The guys are setting it up right now."

He nodded curtly, his breath harsh as his eyes wandered over me. "Good to know. We'll be there in a minute."

Yes, well we would have been doing something a lot more fun if he didn't have eighteen projects going on.

He gave me a smoldering look that said he'd been thinking the same thing.

"Come on," he said, lacing his fingers in mine.

Wait a second. "Why do you need me?" I asked, as we followed Shirley. I wasn't going to get drawn into this.

The only problem he could solve for Shirley would involve Kosta in bed with a bow on his head, and although Galen had proven himself quite talented, I didn't think he was that good.

And if he was, I sure as hell didn't want to be a witness.

We ducked outside, and he pulled a torch from the ground near the front of the lair. "You didn't hear the real news, did you?" Some of the tension left his face, as if he were relieved. "No wonder you didn't come to me."

"Confident, much?" I asked, gazing past him, realizing that Shirley had bugged out.

Shadows lengthened around us as the few remaining members of the crowd retrieved their torches and faded down the path.

We were alone. "What's going on?"

Torches bobbed in the distance as people rushed toward the mess tent, or huddled in groups talking.

He squeezed my hand.

"Horace?" Galen called to the sprite as he zipped past. "Want to tell Petra what happened?"

Horace flew down to us and hovered, impatient. The cave light he wore on his head flickered. "The first prophecy came true!"

chapter fourteen

I about fell over sideways. Horace didn't notice.

"It happened last week, evidently," the sprite said. "Although I have to say I'm surprised it didn't take us even longer to hear in this backwater dump."

My heart raced. I couldn't believe it. My actions, my pulling the dagger out of Galen's chest had to have been the start—unless some other doctor who could see the dead came across a bronze dagger. It could happen.

Holy hell.

I yanked at Galen's hand. "What if you're actually right about this?"

"What if?" He raised a brow, apparently too classy to rub it in.

I broke contact and wandered down toward the main path by myself. My temples pounded. I rubbed at them—as if that would help. "What are we going to do?" I said to myself more than anyone.

Horace dropped down right in front of me. "Why, PNN of course."

"What?" I didn't get it. My head was racing. Was I breaking out in a rash?

"Paranormal News Network," the sprite answered, as if I'd hit my head on a rock. "Really. I have to go." He took off toward the mess tent.

People rushed past us as we hit the main drag. "I know about the Paranormal News Network." I barked out a laugh, a breath away from really losing it. PNN was our world's answer to CNN. "But I'd like to see how you'd get a TV in limbo." Even if any of us could afford to ship one down here, it would short out on the way through the portal.

A pair of cafeteria workers rushed past us.

"I put Shirley in touch with Dumuzi's people," Galen said, as if this was supposed to make sense.

"Dumuzi?" I asked. "The Babylonian god of fertility?" And what was Galen doing talking to Shirley?

"I helped her contact his harem, specifically." Galen handed me a torch. "Evidently she had something they wanted pretty bad. Forty-eight thousand condoms, to be exact. We have a real television set up in the mess hall," he said. "Pre-oracle coverage has already started."

"Pre?" I tried not to drop my torch.

How did everyone seem to know the procedure for this? We hadn't had a new oracle in most of our lifetimes. We hadn't had one this important in thousands of years.

I couldn't get over the idea that I could have started this entire thing. Me. I was a do-gooder, not a leader. I couldn't start making historic prophecies come true. I'd screw it up, like I did the last time.

My stomach had morphed into lead by the time we reached the mess tent.

Leave it to my colleagues to throw a party. The long room buzzed with talk and laughter as chairs and tables were dragged across the floor and slapped together.

And there, along the right side of the long hall, bolted to the menu board, was the ugliest television I'd ever seen. It was one of those old 1970s cabinet models with the carved wood and the curved gray screen.

You'd think it was a sixty-five-inch HD plasma flatscreen from the excitement pulsing through the room. The area in front of the television was packed with chairs. Some people were even sitting on the floor. Shoved-aside tables cluttered the middle. Dozens more sat on top of those. A beach ball bounced through the crowd.

The cafeteria workers had set out a make-your-own peanut-butter-and-jelly sandwich bar on the back serving line, along with a bunch of jugs of orange drink.

Galen and I found a spot on top of a table, near the front. The picture on the screen flickered. An orderly sitting on a stool next to the television stood up and banged on the side of the set a few times. Everyone cheered as the picture steadied.

A perky blond reporter stood at the bottom of a sheer cliff face with a cave cut into the rock. She wore a chunky gold necklace, a pink suit, and a perennially amused expression.

"I'm BeeBee Connor reporting live from the Oracle of the Gods where just yesterday we saw the oracles come out of an intense soothsaying session in order to wail and tear at their hair."

Tiny rocks pelted BeeBee as the mountain behind her shook.

"Look at that. Did you catch that, Rob?" she asked, delighted.

"The mountain has been shaking all day," she went on, ignoring the rocks raining down on her perfectly coiffed hair. "A sure sign that our oracles are hard at work. And if you look below me, you can see the boiling lava surrounding Mount Lemuria."

The camera panned to where her spiky pink heels hovered several yards above a bubbling, churning lake of orange.

"The crowds haven't been too bad, due to the fact that Lemuria is a lost continent," she said, in that perfect news monotone. "Still, we are getting some boats out in the water as the wait goes on. Officials are warning people to keep their distance. According to my sources, the lava hasn't flowed like this since the oracle predicted the destruction of Atlantis." She tilted her perfectly pointed chin down. "And aren't we glad we listened then?"

Hellfire and brimstone.

Palms clammy, I clutched the table below me.

She was just too perky, and this was just too much.

They panned back to the studio where an overly tanned werewolf sat behind the PNN news desk. "Any word on when we might hear something, BeeBee?"

She tilted her head. "My sources aren't saying. But one thing's for sure. This new prophecy is going to be hot, hot, hot."

The newsman delivered a toothy smile. "Thanks, Bee-Bee. This is Stone McKay and you're watching PNN twenty-four-hour live coverage of Oracle Watch MMXII. More of day five after this break."

My elbows weakened. "Day five?"

I did the math again in my head, but I knew already. It had been five days since I'd pulled the bronze dagger out of Galen. Five days since I said there was no way what I was doing had any bearing on any kind of prophecy. Five days since I'd started telling Galen he was wrong when oh my god he might be right.

Galen drew a steadying arm around my shoulders, which was good because I was about ready to fall right off the table. "You're okay?" he asked.

"Sure," I replied, voice weak. I wanted to do something, say something, but all I could manage was to sit where I was and wait through the endless barrage of commercials for portable caskets and shapeshifter sheaths (shift without wrinkles, every time).

How could these people even be thinking of clothes and vacations when we were waiting for the second oracle?

"And we're back," said a smiling Stone McKay. "It's Oracle Watch day five and in case you missed it, the oracles left their cave yesterday to wail and tear at their hair."

PNN cut to footage of three middle-aged women in long white dresses appearing at entrance to the cave. They cried and yanked at their long hair and clothes.

"Can we get a freeze frame on that?" Stone asked as the camera shot stilled. "If you look, you'll see that's Ama on the left, Radhiki next to her, and Li-Hua on the far side, holding up a large femur bone, presumably from a small dragon or a large cow."

What was I going to do?

What if the second oracle asked me to expose myself? Could I do that? Was I sure enough?

"Here's another angle on the wailing and the tearing of the hair," Stone continued.

I'd told Galen I needed real proof, and here it was. The oracle had come true on the day I'd pulled the bronze dagger out of his chest. What were the odds?

The idea of peace was too momentous, too wonderful. But not if I had anything to do with it. I'd screwed up badly before. I'd misinterpreted the signs and brought horror to the people I loved. What if I stood up and I sacrificed and I gave everything and it happened again? I couldn't take it.

The world, and PNN, didn't seem to care.

"For those of you who are just tuning in, we are on day five of the Oracle Watch."

A banner scrolled along the bottom: BREAKING NEWS: ORACLES WAIL AND TEAR AT THEIR HAIR.

"What am I going to do?" I asked myself, voice shaky.

Galen drew me closer and said nothing.

The PA system crackled.

Attention. Attention all personnel. Incoming wounded.

I leaned my chin against my chest. "Holy bad timing, Batman."

It's going to be a doozie.

Chairs skidded and boots slammed down on the floor as everyone made their way to pre-op. I wasn't on call tonight, which meant I was backup in surgery.

I could see the lights from the helicopters approaching in the distance.

In the locker room, I dressed quickly, listening to the shouts from the yard and the mechanical screech of brakes as ambulances pulled in.

I was getting ready to scrub in when Kosta grabbed me by the arm.

"See me after this," he said, dragging a surgical cap over his bald head. "We have a problem."

Oh no. Had he found out about me?

"What kind of problem?" I asked. If it was bad news, I wanted to know now.

Kosta frowned. "One that I'll tell you about when we don't have two dozen casualties coming into camp. Now move it."

The operating room was packed. I was at a table on the far left. They brought me a young private with an artillery shot to the shoulder. His eyes darted wildly.

I placed my hand on his arm. "I've got you. You're going to be fine." I always hated to promise that, but in this case it seemed like a safe assumption. And it was something he needed to hear.

He drew a deep breath and nodded as Nurse Hume cleaned the wound and I prepared my sutures.

"Somebody needs to bring the TV in here," Rodger said from the table a row in front of mine.

"Nothing's happening," Marius grunted from his table behind me.

"Yeah, but day five. That's a big day," Rodger said, tossing a piece of shrapnel onto a metal tray. "It never takes them longer than five days."

I winced. "Can we talk about something else?" There was nothing we could do about the oracle anyway, at least not right now.

"Sure," Rodger said.

"I can't believe Galen got us a TV," Marius said.

What was it with these people? "Let's not talk about Galen, either." Nurse Hume had finished cleaning the wound. I threaded my needle.

"Why not?" Rodger asked. "I saw how long you were in Marius's lair. Believe me, there's not that much to see."

Oh yes. Announce it to the group.

"If the lair is a-rockin', don't come a-knockin'," droned Hume.

I lost the thread out of my needle. Damn.

"I'd date him," Rodger added.

"Why are we talking about this?" I asked out loud, trying to rethread my needle.

"I prefer blonds," Marius said.

"Hold him steady," I said to Hume, ignoring them all as I set to work on the soldier in front of me. His breath hitched as I began sewing him together. Poor kid.

"Is this your first time?" I asked him.

He gave a small nod. "Just joined up in August."

These soldiers were brave, every last one of them, but there's nothing like being on an operating table for the first time.

"You volunteered?" I asked, wishing I could go easy on him.

He nodded, squeezing his eyes shut in pain.

Once again, I found myself lamenting the fact that anesthetics—or even painkillers—didn't work on immortals. They were with us every step of the way.

"It's not like they said it would be," he gasped. "It's way worse."

I had no doubt of that. "War is hell."

He was about halfway done. The wound was deeper than it looked, and I had to use more stitches than I'd planned.

It was already starting to heal on its own, which meant I had to get this lined up or it could heal wrong.

A fine sweat gathered on his forehead. "They had more guys out there than us today."

I gripped the needle tighter. "Is that so?"

"They're talking about an unbalanced army."

I didn't even want to imagine.

Galen had said something about it—how things were hitting a crisis point. Heaven help us if he was right about that, too.

We operated for twelve hours straight. Marius left us right before dawn, which added to the load. Afterward, I pulled off my cap and sat on a bench in the locker room, head down, elbows on my knees as I listened to doctors tell the same story over and over.

The injuries are worse.

The casualties higher.
The armies are becoming unbalanced.

We were in deep trouble. Tired, I stood and let down my hair. Even that didn't feel as good as it usually did. I tossed the ponytail holder into my locker and slammed the door shut. I leaned up against it, drawing a hand down over my face, waiting for it to all go away.

But I couldn't avoid this. Not anymore. And besides, I had to go see Kosta. I could only imagine what he had in store for me.

chapter fifteen

I changed out of my scrubs and into a pair of rust-colored new army uniform pants. Might as well try to look official. Events were in motion. I couldn't deny it.

Naturally, I had no idea where I'd left the belt portion of the pants, so I just smoothed my white tank top over the copper button.

The matching field jacket hung in the back of my locker. It was stiff from lack of use, practically new. I shrugged that on as well.

The first prophecy has come true. The armies are on the move and unbalanced.

It still felt like a dream. I wished it was. I could use a few z's. We'd been in surgery all night and into today. My eyes felt like somebody had rubbed them with sandpaper.

The heat of the day had already gone from stifling to unbearable. I squinted against the suns and kept my heavy head up as I hiked next door to Kosta's office.

Shirley was on the phone when I walked in. She sat at her desk, banging a pencil about 180 miles an hour. Her fiery hair was curling out of its loose twist. A fan blew the hot air around, solving absolutely nothing. "Try looking under Fiction-Human-Irrelevant."

"Is Kosta in there?" I asked, aiming for his office.

"No." She swung her chair toward me and lowered the

phone. "He had to deal with an issue in post-op." She tucked the pencil behind her ear and held a finger up. "But don't leave."

Phone propped between her chin and her shoulder, she turned back to her desk and began shuffling through the closest of about six different stacks of files. The top papers fluttered in the artificial breeze. "I have something on Galen you're going to want to see."

"Something good?" I asked. See? I could be hopeful.

Shirley's forehead wrinkled. "Depends on your point of view." The phone squawked and Shirley yanked it up to her ear. "Yes. I'm still waiting." She frowned as she listened. "You didn't find it?" She rolled her eyes. "Try Fiction-Human-Anthropological."

She sighed, her eyes flicking to me. "I'm trying to get a few things for the new TV," she explained. "Tell me. How do you think the army film depot would file season one of *Dynasty*?"

Geez. I didn't know. "Couldn't you get *True Blood* instead?"

Shirley pointed a warning finger at me. "That is why I'm not telling anybody about this."

"Okay. Fine." I rubbed at my eyes. No need to get testy.

"Just keep looking. I'll call you back," she said, hanging up and resting her head on her desk. "This deal's costing me an entire case of Thin Mint Girl Scout cookies. With my luck, we're probably going to end up getting season three of *Green Acres*."

"Ooh." I liked *Green Acres*. "Remember when Oliver rented a rooster?"

"You're not helping, Doc."

"I'm just glad to hear Galen has Girl Scout cookies."

"He doesn't," she said, shoving through the paperwork littering her desk. "Besides, I can't trade anything from the visiting officers' tent. I get one case of cookies a year from my great-great-great-niece. One. And I refuse to accept substandard entertainment."

"Hey, you could get a romantic comedy. Something about a surly Spartan who finds love."

She gave me a long look. "I don't think that exists. Besides, Kosta doesn't watch movies. He's going to flip when he finds out we have a TV." She shook her head. "Something's going down. He hasn't even noticed the television, and Kosta notices *everything*."

Like we needed any more issues. "Do you have any idea what's going on with him?"

"Not yet."

She stopped at a brown file on top of the largest teetering stack. "Here it is. Galen's medical history file."

"At last," I said as she handed it to me.

"It came with the final transfer paperwork."

"What?" He was leaving? I felt a keen sense of loss. He couldn't walk away—we couldn't end it. Not now. Besides, a new oracle was coming down. I needed him.

"No worries, babe," Shirley said, reading my face. "He's still getting transferred in. This is the army we're talking about."

Okay. Well. For once it was working in our favor. I leaned against the edge of her desk and cracked open the file. It was thick, as it should be for a man who had been at war for nearly five centuries.

Clipped to the top was his original intake picture, from when he was a new recruit. Only this happened to be a photo of a very large, very detailed full-body oil painting, and he was completely naked.

He was larger, sexier, and more cut that I'd ever imagined, and believe me, I could imagine quite a bit.

I slammed the file shut as a shivery warmth shot through me. No doubt, Galen would be happy to strip for me in person, but I felt kind of funny lusting after his picture with Shirley sitting right there.

"What?" Shirley asked.

I went a little breathless. "There's a naked picture. Right on top."

"Like you haven't already seen Galen's goods," she snorted.

"Why does everybody think that?" I asked, resisting the urge to crack open the file again. "You didn't look, did you?"

"I'm not a doctor."

"Right." I said, leaning away from her and opening it once again. The medical files I was used to seeing had drawings or photos of old injuries, when they were relevant. I'd never seen a healthy, full-on nude shot.

Naturally, they'd posed him like the Greek demi-god he was—his wide shoulders squared, a well-defined arm holding aloft a sword.

It was completely unnecessary. Not to mention mouth-wateringly delicious.

He had deeply tanned skin over hard lean muscle. His smooth chest tapered down to a narrow stretch of hair that began just below his belly button and—*my, my, my.*

He could make a girl forget her good sense.

I was never going to be able to get Galen's naked body out of my mind—not that I wanted to.

"You are cracking me up." Shirley sat tapping the phone receiver against her shoulder. "It's just an identification photo."

"That's right." In person, he would be even better. The gods certainly had no qualms when it came to nakedness. "I can't imagine posing for such a bare intake picture."

She grinned. "You never would have survived the old regulations. We used to have to wrestle a boar to prove our worth."

"Pass."

"No kidding. Those things stink."

"I'm glad they made a few changes before I was recruited," I said in the understatement of the year.

Shirley jumped as the phone rang. "MASH 3063rd. Sergeant Macdha here."

I opened the file again, more tingly under the collar than I should have been. While Shirley talked, I folded the photo in half and slipped it into my pocket.

The man was built to command and conquer, on the battlefield and in the bedroom.

Seven hells. I had to stop thinking about sex.

It might be easier if I'd actually had any in the last ten years. Or if Galen and I could manage to finish what we'd started.

I moved on to the main folder. Inside, handwritten reports on thick parchment paper detailed the rise of a decorated—and damaged—war hero. He'd been wounded 112 times before the day he'd died on my table. Galen had received the Soldier's Medal twice for conspicuous gallantry by risking his immortal life in situations that went beyond the call of duty. It was the new army equivalent of the Medal of Honor. I was both amazed and humbled at Galen's courage.

And as I made my way to the more modern, typed accounts, I couldn't help but wonder how he'd survived this long.

He'd been terribly wounded. I'd seen the scars streaking across his chest. There had to be others as well. But he still believed in peace. He had hope. I didn't understand it.

"Did you see his lineage?" Shirley asked.

"No," I said, shuffling through the pages. All I saw were military reports.

"It's the page right under the naked picture," she said, still on the phone.

No wonder I'd missed it.

And Shirley said she hadn't looked.

"Hello?" She asked the person on the other line. "Yes, I'm still here."

I shuffled faster. A demi-god's lineage was the key to his divinity. Well, if you considered them divine. I didn't. They were a different form of supernatural creature, really.

They had powers, like Marius or Rodger or even me. Only they were stronger, and the pure gods had a definite complex.

I flipped to the front and found a yellowed parchment page. It was a hand-drawn family tree. Nothing fancy. It was obviously done by a medieval intake officer.

Galen of Delphi had been born in 1473 to Aletheia, the Greek goddess of truth.

No kidding. I lowered the file. It made sense. He could see

people. I'd bet anything that was his special power. He had a heightened sense of what people were feeling and what they needed.

He'd certainly gotten to me.

But what about Galen himself? If he could read people so well, why had I seen such overwhelming loneliness inside him?

I wondered if he still felt that way now, surrounded by my friends. Or if he was alone in a crowd, like me.

His father was listed only as Santo, a mortal lieutenant in the Ottoman–Venetian War. I wondered how much attention young Galen of Delphi had received from Aletheia. Goddesses weren't known for their mothering skills, and his father had been fighting against the Greeks.

I flipped to the report on his latest injury. He'd been with a special operations unit doing reconnaissance right on top of a huge hell vent, about ten miles from our camp. No notations about bronze weapons, or who had stabbed him. I couldn't imagine what our army would be doing near any entrances to Hades.

Galen was no match for a demon—none of us was. That's why the old and new gods were so powerful—they were willing to step in and use their supernatural gifts to hold back the forces of the underworld. And if that meant they interfered in the lives of the rest of us, it was a price we were willing to pay.

"I wish I knew what this meant, Shirl," I said, closing the file and hugging it to my chest. And how the knife fit in.

She didn't hear me, of course. She was still busy on the phone, this time with the supply depot. I was glad to see she had her ledger sheets out and was filing her own orders.

The door banged open as Horace rushed in. "Hurry," he said, bobbing up and down, sprinkling the floor with glitter. "They're going to announce the second oracle!"

"Are you sure?" I asked, pushing off the desk, excited and nervous as well. Six days seemed fast. Maybe they wanted to take more time with this.

Shirley hung up on supply. "Let's go," she said, grabbing her purse from under her desk.

"Wow." This was really it. My nerves tangled and my knees went weak. They'd better not start talking about a doctor who drinks orange soda who is supposed to slay a dragon or something.

Or that I was destined to lust after a smoking-hot demigod for the rest of my life.

Come to think of it, that last one might not be half bad.

Shirley and I jogged for the mess tent while Horace zigzagged across camp, banging on doors and alerting clerks and mechanics, maintenance staffers and technicians. He skipped the post-op tent, which was good because I could hear Kosta out back, cussing.

As if he had problems.

The mess tent was packed with bodies. Everyone was talking at once. Shirley broke away from me and headed for the serving area. The food was gone. Now rows of people sat on long steel counters. The room was at least ten degrees warmer than Shirley's office and I felt the sweat against the back of my neck as I jostled toward the tables where Galen and I had sat before.

After a few false starts, I spotted his wide shoulders and strong profile. He held a hand up. My insides fluttered. He looked the same as he did in that file photo, and for the first time I could clearly imagine his hard body under those special forces blacks.

Shake it off. Yeah, right. I could practically feel the heat radiating from that man.

He caught my eye, and a wave of desire sluiced through me.

He sat back down, his body spread wide. As soon as I reached him, he closed his legs and eased over so that I'd have a seat.

"It should be anytime now," he said, assessing me as an unspoken question hung between us. He knew something had changed. Damn it. I was an open book. Or maybe he was just a little too good at sensing the truth.

"Are you nervous?" he asked.

"Yes," I said, quickly.

It's not that I want to strip you down right here, right now, for an up-close and personal look at what is under that uniform.

I scooted back as far as I could on the table, trying to sandwich myself into the crowd, so close to touching him it was killing me.

We hovered close, yet apart, the briefest touch separating us. I wrapped my fingers around the edge of the table.

The Paranormal News Network was just coming back from commercial. The same perky blond reporter from before smiled down from the television. She'd changed into a furry blue sleeveless sweater, which was entirely inappropriate for the occasion.

"I'm BeeBee Connor, reporting live from the Oracle of the Gods, where just one day ago we saw the oracles come out of their intense soothsaying session in order to wail and tear at their hair.

"Now we hear that the oracles may have the second prophecy." She paused for effect, her green eyes twinkling. It was just as well, because the peanut gallery around me began to cheer and throw popcorn at the TV.

BeeBee smiled as the kernels bounced off her forehead. "Right now, as we speak, the oracles may indeed be using their blood to transcribe the oracle onto the living rock of the cave behind me. Let's go back to the studio."

"Right, BeeBee," said Stone McKay from the newsroom. "We're going to show you an illustration of what may be happening as we speak."

"Or what may not be happening," I murmured. Was this news or conjecture?

The video cut to a green screen of a rock wall. Stone McKay strolled over in front of it like a PNN weatherman. "Now what should happen is that each oracle will take a sacrificial ivory dagger and slash her wrist about half an inch below her palm."

The camera got a close-up of Stone's over-tanned wrist, as if any of us had a doubt as to what the underside of a wrist looked like. "They will use a slashing motion," he said, as if this were news, "then they will take turns writing the second prophecy on the wall, like this." He drew his imaginary wound over the green screen.

I swear these newscasters thought we had the brains of gnats.

Yes. I needed to focus on that and not the fact that the next phase of my life was about to be written in blood, and it was looking more and more like I was powerless to stop it.

"Wait," Stone held his hand up to his ear. "We have breaking news from the field."

Galen and I traded a glance as the camera cut to BeeBee Connor. "I'm standing here live as the oracles have come out of the cave. Li-Hua has tossed the bone she was holding into the molten lava below me, which we can only take to mean that she doesn't need it any longer. I'd venture to say a decision has been reached."

I let out a shuddering breath.

The camera caught a close-up of Li-Hua as she crouched outside the cave, way nearer to the cliff edge than I ever would have ventured. Her straight black hair whipped in the wind.

She spoke—at least her lips moved—and I felt my throat go dry.

BeeBee Conner zipped up to her in an instant, microphone out. "Could you repeat that, please?" she asked, voice quaking.

Galen's warm hand closed over mine.

Li-Hua stared into the camera with haunted almond eyes. "With the dagger, she will save lives," she said, her voice low and grainy.

He gave my hand a small squeeze.

Okay, that didn't seem so bad. I saved lives as often as I could. In fact, I'd like to save more lives. Hope flared in my chest.

Dang, my heart was beating like crazy.

The oracle looked dazed. Her eyes were bloodshot. "And . . ."

Her labored breathing was amplified by the PNN

microphone shoved under her nose. "And"—the oracle's lip curled into a hiss—"she will arrest the forces of the damned."

The mess tent erupted in cheers.

"Oh hell no." I choked. No way was I going anywhere near any forces of the damned.

"Petra." Galen slid off his seat and stood in front of me. At least he looked worried as snot.

"Did you see that?" I demanded. "I'm not doing that." I wasn't going to start running around, arresting hell spawn. "I don't even know what the damned look like." And I didn't want to find out.

People were rushing past like we weren't even there, trying to get closer to the television to see the replays. The rest had started a party.

Galen stayed by me, like my own personal port in the storm. "It's okay. I've got you," he said, as if I had any idea what that meant. "We can do this."

"Lovely. So we're going to leave camp and you're going to fight off giant killer scorpions while I go around poking the damned on the shoulder and making citizens' arrests?"

"Don't be ridiculous," he growled.

I leaned back against the table and tried to think. This was so much worse than I'd imagined.

He wore his determination like a second skin. "We're going to approach it systematically, with military precision."

My head swam.

But he didn't let up. "Let me help you," he said.

"Help me do what?" I barked out a laugh. Expose myself? "Get killed?"

"We'll go out together. I'll bait the damned. I'll weaken them and then you finish them off."

"No," I snapped, voice eight octaves higher than usual.

That was the worst plan I'd ever heard, second only to the oracle's plan from about two minutes ago.

We were not forcing fate or running around chasing damned creatures.

I met his focused glare with wild eyes. "Me and my knife are staying right here."

I was doing fine in our MASH unit. Sure, it was a dump and infested with Rodger's swamp creatures and the water in the women's shower was always cold, but this was my home. Besides, there were assassins after me the minute I stepped outside of camp.

He stood, resolute. "There are forces at work here that go beyond you or me." He stopped, as if he were afraid to tell me more. He seemed to make a decision. "I believe I was sent here to guide you and to guard you through this."

Unbelievable. "You don't care what happens on Earth, do you?"

He sighed, exasperated. "I care, but I'm looking at the big picture. There are forces at work, things you don't understand."

Oh please. I planted my hands on my hips. "Is this a god thing?"

He seemed surprised at that. "Yes, this is a god thing. Sometimes the gods have to make tough choices that lead to bad things. And sometimes we—they—get cursed for it. People blame the gods all the time, and nobody knows what we have to deal with. Bad things happen for a reason."

"Now I've heard everything," I grumbled.

But he wouldn't let up. "In a way, mortals are lucky. You don't have to make these kinds of decisions."

"Oh sure. I'm feeling really lucky right now." Merely dealing with a suicide mission. "Look. I appreciate what you did out in the minefield with the scorpions," I began. A young sergeant glanced at me on the way past and I lowered my voice. "This is totally different."

"You're going to do this. This is war," he said, jaw clenched, as if he didn't want to say it. "We have to be willing to sacrifice one for the good of all."

"Fuck you." I slid off the table and stepped sideways, away from him.

"Where is the dagger?" he asked.

"In my pocket." It was always in my pocket. No matter what I did.

Horace zipped above the crowd and hovered over us, his

wings hitting us with a nice breeze. "Kosta wants to see you, Petra."

I lifted my head. "Now?"

Horace shrugged. "He's pissed you didn't find him first."

Could this day get any worse?

I'd tried. "Did you tell him I was outside his office before?"

"No," he said, his nose wrinkling. "I'm not your messenger boy."

That's right. He was Galen's pet.

"I'll go with you," Galen said, leading the way. The crowd parted for him. "If the fates work fast, we may not even have to go hunting."

"You think this is our sign?" I didn't want to imagine. "Kosta doesn't control anything outside our unit." And he sure as heck wasn't going to allow any damned inside camp. That's what the guard sphinxes were for.

Camp was deserted outside the mess tent. It seemed like everyone really was inside watching.

Galen waited outside Kosta's office as I made my way in.

What if Kosta asked about my power? Should I lie? Would he turn me in?

The colonel sat with his back rod-straight behind his large desk, but I didn't miss the dark circles under his eyes or the hint of fatigue in his voice.

"Sit down, Robichaud." He rubbed at his forehead.

"Oh no. Do you want to talk about the prophecy?"

He reared back in surprise. "Prophecy? What prophecy? I've been trying to make sure people don't die. In the last month, we've seen the biggest increase in wounded that we've had in four hundred years." He shook his head, resigned. "Now we've got something else." He eyed me. "A special assignment."

chapter sixteen

I stared at Kosta, from his bald head to his wide hands, palms down on the large metal desk. Bronze battle shields lined the wall behind him, like soldiers at the ready. He was a man used to getting his way, and unfortunately I had a pretty good clue what he wanted.

"I'm not special," I said, just in case he was getting any ideas.

His eyes narrowed. "Not you, slick. The assignment. This one is coming straight from the wilds of limbo." He seemed amused at that, or more likely, energized by the challenge.

The drawer at the front of his desk rumbled as he opened it to pulled out a cigar. "We got a call in from an enemy MASH unit. They've got some of our soldiers—four critical casualties." He flicked his eyes up. "They can't treat them."

Wait. "They have to help our people. It's in the Waset Convention."

The gods didn't always obey it, just like armies didn't always stick to the Geneva Convention back home, but I'd never expected this.

Kosta didn't offer an opinion. Either he didn't have one or he wasn't sharing it with me. "They've been put under orders to neglect our wounded despite the conventions." He dug a battered lighter out of his pant pocket. "That doesn't sit right with their commander. He wants to get the injured out, but the situation is tense. We're going against regs." He stopped, his lighter forgotten. "He made us a highly unusual offer," he said. "We can go get our soldiers."

It was never that easy. "There's got to be a catch."

He pointed the Zippo at me. "Two doctors. No weapons."

I about choked. "Oh well, that seems fair."

He lit his cigar and took a puff. The caustic smoke carried a hint of cherries. He glanced at me. "You're going."

Holy hell. I was going to get thrust out of camp, just like I'd been forced to take the knife from Galen. It was like I had no free will.

She will save lives and arrest the forces of the damned.

My pulse pounded and my palms began to sweat. There had to be a better way—one that didn't involve me venturing out of camp, trying to dodge the giant scorpion assassins on my tail while trying to decide the best way to get a headlock on the forces of the damned.

"You don't understand," I said, as I stood, my chair skittering out behind me. I racked my brain to figure out something, *any*thing to say that might change his mind. "I can't go. I've never been outside of camp."

Not that I was opposed to leaving. I'd been dying for some kind of a field position that would take me to strange and exotic places, but meet-and-greets with enemy units didn't count.

Besides, I didn't know if I could live up to the weapons ban. I had this knife I couldn't seem to shake.

Kosta stood with great deliberation, his features set in a snarl. "What I understand, soldier, is that we've got men who are dying out there. I don't give a rat's ass whether you want to go. This is your assignment."

I stood frozen, numb. The prophecy said I was going to leave and bang—I was on my way out.

It didn't matter if it was smart or right or if I was walking straight into an ambush.

I'd been pissed off more times than I could count since I'd set foot in limbo, but I'd never been this afraid.

I tilted my chin up. "Yes, sir," I said weakly. "Fuck, how did this happen?" I muttered, almost to myself.

He was asking me to drive an ambulance into hostile territory. Kosta hadn't said as much, but I knew I'd be on my own if something happened out there.

Kosta took the cigar out of his mouth, sympathetic. "Their commander is an old buddy of mine," he said, tapping it out onto a flat stone tray on his desk. "We go back to the Battle of Tanagra. Hell of a war," he added, almost to himself. He cleared his throat. "He's a good man. Sheer dumb luck he ended up on the other side. This deal is strictly off the books."

My voice felt dry. "So if I get captured?"

He tilted his head. "I'll have to tell them you wandered out of camp."

"Lovely." I wasn't even supposed to wander alone in camp.

For the first time, I wondered if I should tell Kosta about the attempt on my life, the bronze knife, everything. Sure, the commander was a hard-ass, but he was also a practical leader. He'd faced off against the worst of this world, and the one above, for centuries.

The knife weighed heavy in my pocket.

Pistaches. What could Kosta do? Take back the prophecy? It didn't even sound like he believed in it.

I realized with a jolt that I was looking for some way, some*one* to take the burden. I wasn't a soldier like Kosta or Galen. I was a doctor. I didn't want to lead the charge. I didn't want to go on clandestine assignments, or carry a weapon, or arrest forces of the damned.

But as much as I wanted to take some of the load off, I knew this was my cross to bear.

Kosta walked along the wall of orphaned battle shields. "The patients are stable for now. Meet-up is in two hours, and it'll take you about that long to get there." He stopped. "If this doesn't go well, the mortal soldiers will die. The immortals will be imprisoned for eternity." He shook his head. "Damn awful way to go."

I gave an involuntary shudder. Prisoners of war were held by the Shrouds, cursed creatures who fed on life like parasites. They moved like silvery shadows, sucking the life and souls from humans and endlessly torturing immortals to the brink of death.

His nostrils flared as he took a deep breath. "Sorry, kid. I couldn't send Marius on this. He needs to sleep during the day. Rodger is a loose cannon."

Rodger also had a wife and kids who needed him.

He leveled his eyes at me. "Frankly, you're the best we've got."

His confidence filled me with unexpected warmth. Maybe because I hadn't gotten many "atta girls" in this godforsaken place.

"I'll take good care of them," I said. This was the reason I got in to medicine in the first place.

If this was what I had to do, I'd do it. Maybe there'd be four fewer empty shields in the world.

Besides, walking away from these forces of the damned could also impact the prophecy. If I didn't go, if I was the one who tried to influence the second prediction by refusing to go, well, I didn't want to think of the consequences.

"The camp is due south. Shirley can give you the map."

"Okay," I said, thinking of what I needed to pack. "What am I going to find when I get there?"

Kosta moved to the charts on his desk. "Two mortals with thoracic hemorrhaging, an immortal missing most of his lungs—"

I found myself nodding. I was the only thoracic surgeon in camp. A fact the army seemed to remember from time to time. "Do we have a donor?"

"We've got a pair coming in if you can get the patient back here alive." He handed me four hastily written charts. "We also have an immortal in need of a complete arterial repair job."

Right up my alley. Until Galen, busted hearts were the only real cases I'd gotten.

"It'll be you and Dr. Thaïs."

Lovely. I'd been avoiding Thaïs since our locker room tête-à-tête when I'd found the knife. He had the personality of Yosemite Sam, only I couldn't toss him down a cliff.

Still, it made sense. Thaïs was an immortal. It would take a lot more than packs of wild imps or enemy soldiers or whatever came out of those hell vents to kill him. Too bad I wasn't that lucky.

I paused at the door that led to Kosta's outer office, clutching the charts.

"The ambulance is packed and waiting outside. Shirley has the keys."

"Gotcha."

"Good luck, Doctor." He placed a hand on my shoulder. "Those soldiers are depending on you." He gave me a squeeze. "I am, too."

"Thanks," I said, unsure of what I was supposed to say. In fact, there wasn't much else to do. I was ready—well, except for the knife in my pocket. And I knew exactly what I had to do with that.

Thaïs was already waiting outside the door. Luckily Rodger wasn't here or he would have started whistling the Mister Clean theme song. It always put Thaïs in an even worse mood than usual.

"Doctor," he sneered as he passed. Only he could make it sound like a put-down.

"Grime fighter," I answered, just to tick him off.

This was going to be a fun trip.

Galen stood next to Shirley's desk. She was back from the PNN party. "Hey." I spotted a white doctors' coat on her desk. "Can I borrow this?"

"It's Marius's," she warned.

"He's asleep," I said, tossing it over the charts Kosta gave me.

"What did the commander have to say?" Galen asked.

"Come here." We headed for the corner by the outside door.

Hades. How to explain it.

I glanced past his massive chest to Shirley. Of course she'd followed us. "Can we get some privacy?" Galen growled.

In this camp? Ha.

Then a thought occurred to me. "Hey, Shirley, before you go too far, can you get Jeffe in here?"

She planted her hands on her hips. "Sure. I live to please."

"I owe you about eighteen chocolate bars," I offered. Which I'd never have.

"You're lucky I like you," she said, picking up the microphone for the PA system.

Galen gave me a questioning look.

Will Jeffe the sphinx please report to Colonel Kosta's office? Jeffe the sphinx.

As if there were any other Jeffe.

"Now we need our privacy," Galen said, with a pointed look over my shoulder at Shirley.

"And here I thought this was my office," she said, cigarette in hand as she strolled past us, banging the door closed behind her.

Who knew how much time we had? I dug in my pocket for the wrapped-up knife. "I need you to take this," I said to Galen before he could quiz me any more about what had just happened with Kosta.

He drew back as I pressed the bundle into his hand, but I knew he wouldn't let it fall. "Petra," he said, his voice full of warning, "it doesn't work that way."

"I'm hoping it does." At least this once. I needed to catch a break.

His eyes narrowed.

Well, tough. I didn't like this, either. But I didn't have a choice. I wasn't going to be responsible for the deaths of two soldiers and the eternal imprisonment of two others.

"I've agreed to go on a little field trip for Kosta. Two doctors. No weapons. Thaïs is in there right now getting our orders."

"You can't leave camp without me," he said, as if it was the craziest idea in the world. "It's not safe."

"Believe me, I know." I liked my skin as much as Galen

did—probably more. But this was the right thing to do. "We've got a situation." I explained to him about the wounded. And the Shrouds. "I can't risk these soldiers' lives just so I can carry a weapon I don't know how to use."

Galen didn't even get that. "What's there to know?" he thundered. "You hold it and stab."

I hated to break it to him, but, "I'm no hero. I don't even know if I can kill." Frankly, I thought the whole concept was ludicrous.

Besides, my knife and I would be no match for the long swords the enemy guards tended to carry. Not to mention the soul-sucking Shrouds. They didn't even need weapons. They'd wrap their filmy white bodies around me and I'd be finished.

Galen wasn't happy. Yeah, well, neither was I. "I have to go," I told him. I was a doctor. "You of all people should understand duty."

A muscle in his jaw tightened.

There was no way I was going to take a weapon. He had to see that. "I don't want to piss these people off." Kosta may be an iron-fisted asshole, but I trusted him. If he said we'd be okay with no weapons, two doctors, I had to accept that. I wasn't about to screw up the plan.

Galen's expression went raw. For the first time since I'd met him, he didn't know what to do. I don't know which one of us that scared more.

He closed his eyes tight. "How are you going to arrest the forces of the damned when you're unarmed?"

I touched him. "How would I do it anyway?" His muscles were tight, ready to unleash their power, only we had no enemy to fight.

His eyes opened to slits. "All right. If this is how the fates have arranged it, then I'm coming along."

Jeffe eased through the doorway behind Galen.

He glanced back at the sphinx before bringing his full attention back to me.

I touched his arm. "I don't want you following."

He barked out a laugh. "Too bad."

I shook my head, already feeling regret. "My orders are clear. Two doctors. No weapons."

The side of his mouth turned up. "They didn't say anything about demi-gods."

I had a feeling it was implied.

Then again, this was Galen. "I've got to protect you," he insisted.

"You're going to get me exposed and you're going to get me killed." I had to trust Colonel Kosta on this one. "Any trying you do is going to influence the prophecy, and I can't let that happen."

His expression hardened. "I won't leave you out there alone." To him, it was absurd. Just like he wouldn't leave me in the middle of a freeway during rush hour, he wasn't about to let me do this on my own.

He left me with no choice. "Jeffe," I said. "Arrest him."

The sphinx leapt forward. "Gotcha, boss!"

Galen snorted, not even taking his eyes off me. "You're going to have to do better than that."

Jeffe whipped out his claws like a cat and jammed them into Galen's leg.

Galen stood his ground. "Jeffe," he said through gritted teeth, "you're making a big mistake."

Galen's eyes widened slightly. His expression was still set in a snarl as he tipped straight forward. I caught him, barely, bracing myself as his full weight came tumbling down.

He almost took me with him as I eased him to the floor. "Thanks for the help," I gasped.

"No problem," Jeffe said, standing next to me, watching as I struggled out from under Galen. I rolled him over onto his back.

"What did you give him?" I asked, slightly out of breath, staring at the zonked demi-god next to me.

Galen was out.

Jeffe shook out his mane. "I gave him the Egyptian treatment. Did you know that it takes the average sphinx only one point two seconds to knock down prey? Your Galen is strong."

"He's not my Galen."

Jeffe leaned over Galen's splayed body. "He still looks mad."

He sure did. But I couldn't have him following me. "How long until he wakes up?"

"At least three days. Sometimes five or six. It takes that long. Usually, I'd have to start devouring him now, and that can take a while. I am not big. Did you know it takes the average sphinx twenty minutes to devour a small squirrel? I prefer rabbits, myself. But do not worry. I like Galen. I won't eat him."

"Thanks, Jeffe." I hated to have Galen out of the picture that long, but at least this was going my way.

Galen took up a good portion of the area in front of Shirley's desk. "Will you call a few orderlies to get him back into his tent?"

"Right-o, boss," Jeffe said cheerfully.

I scratched my neck, uncomfortable. "I'm not really your boss."

"Yes, you are," Jeffe said, his long hair swooshing around his shoulders. "It is in the handbook."

I had to find my copy one of these days.

The door to Kosta's office burst open and Thaïs stormed out. "Are you ready to go?"

I grabbed the medical charts and my white jacket off Shirley's desk. "I was waiting for you," I answered, wincing as he stepped over Galen.

Shirley was outside, cigarette in hand. I would have told her that was bad for her, if her kind could get cancer.

Smoke trailed out of her nose. "Can I go back in my office now?"

"Yes," I said, juggling my charts. "Sorry about that."

She wasn't impressed. "You owe me one."

"Also about Galen. He's laid out on your floor."

She took one last drag. "Never mind. We're even."

chapter seventeen

True to his word, Kosta had an ambulance parked outside. It was rusty red, same as the limbo landscape, with the Ankh—an ancient symbol for life—blazoned on the sides. The Ankh was painted in gold, and resembled a cross with a loop at the top.

I wore the same symbol on the sleeve of my field jacket. It was painted on the roofs of our medical tents. It was our version of the Red Cross, really.

Thaïs walked ahead of me, with his trademark limp.

Not even bothering to look back, he swung open the heavy metal door and climbed into the driver's seat. What a male move.

I trudged around the front, toward the passenger side. It was just as well. I hadn't driven a car since I'd parked my bright blue Mustang at my dad's house before leaving.

My heart squeezed a fraction.

It didn't do any good to think about it.

"You're out of uniform," Thaïs barked as I stepped up into the modified truck.

I slid onto the vinyl seat and stashed my white coat and the charts on the dash. "I'm a doctor, not a soldier."

"Obviously," he grumbled.

Thaïs fired up the engine as I slammed the door. The sound of it vibrated through the metal interior like a tuning fork.

The driver's cab smelled like the dust and heat of the limbo desert. Out of habit, I reached for a seat belt. There weren't any. *Merde.* Not everyone was immortal.

The entire ambulance rattled as Thaïs hit the accelerator with enough gusto to launch the charts into my lap. Jeffe sat outside, waving as we pulled out in a cloud of dust.

Teeth rattling, we whipped past the hospital and a puzzled Rodger, who was just about to go inside.

Not many people left camp. I fought the butterflies in my stomach as I dragged off my field jacket and laid it next to me. The sun felt good on my bare arms. The ambulance bumped over the uneven road between the recovery tent and the supply depot, toward a side road that led due south.

A hand-painted sign informed us that we were indeed on the HIGHWAY TO HELL.

Too bad it couldn't be Galen sitting next to me. He'd probably been down this road before.

I dragged my hands through my hair. I couldn't believe I'd actually knocked him out. That would put a crimp in our relationship.

Before this afternoon, I hadn't exactly known how sphinxes took down their prey. I'd figured it wasn't pleasant. But really, I didn't have a choice. I had to complete this assignment without Galen following me.

And without killing Thaïs.

"Where's the map?" I asked, locating it on the scratched up floor between us.

"Don't bother," Thaïs hollered over the droning engine. He pointed to his head. "I have it right here," he said, tapping.

"Oh please," I ground out. "And here I thought your head was full of hot air." With a few cobwebs in the corners.

I unfolded the map, fighting it as the edge flapped in the breeze.

When Kosta said we had to head south, I figured we'd be heading toward Hades, but I wanted to know just how far he expected us to go. I certainly wasn't going to depend on Thaïs's ego to tell us when to stop.

I rolled my window up and braced a knee against the two-way radio receiver on the dash in front of me. Better than the siren button.

Okay. I ran my finger down the colorful map that detailed hell vents, raised terrain, and very few roads. The Highway to Hell speared down from our camp.

It looked like we needed to head thirty-two miles due south until we hit a bottomless canyon. Well, that should be easy to spot. At the canyon, we'd turn left onto a dirt road for another mile.

"Told you we were going the right way," Thaïs said as I refolded the map and stashed it under my charts. "I don't need you telling me where to go," he said to himself, gripping the wheel with both hands, "or slowing me down."

"Oh, well," I said, "forgive me for tagging along."

Wouldn't Thaïs be even happier to know we could have some assassins on our tail?

At least we'd be able to see them coming. The rusty red desert stretched for miles. Here and there, I'd spot an outcropping of rocks in the distance.

Hopefully I'd be back in time to be with Galen when he woke. I could tell him how I'd done this on my own—how we'd fulfilled the second prophecy. Lord help us.

Wind thundered through Thaïs's window and echoed throughout the cab. As we rode farther and farther south, the whole thing started to smell like someone was cleaning an oven.

"I could do this myself," Thaïs harrumphed.

I knew the silence was too good to last. "You can treat four casualties at once?" Impressive.

To think, I could be back in camp hanging out with my bronze knife, or hearing more about the prophecy.

Thaïs tightened his grip on the wheel. "You don't have any respect for this war."

"No," I said, gazing out onto the unending desert, "I'm partial to the kids I treat."

"They're not kids," he balked. "They're trained killers."

Not the one laid out on my table last night. He couldn't

have been more than eighteen years old. He was lucky I didn't have to do anything but sew his shoulder shut. Next time, it might be worse. And there would be a next time.

There always was.

I glanced at Thaïs in all his determined glory. "It's a dumb war." For every battle-crazy soldier like Thaïs, there were half a dozen others who just wanted to go home.

He glowered at me. "That's treason!" I could tell I'd shocked him, which meant he really didn't get out enough.

I rested my head on the back of the seat. "Let the gods fight it out themselves."

He acted like I'd suggested they take up belly dancing. "Hand-to-hand combat is beneath them."

I lolled my head toward him. "I was thinking more like Parcheesi. Jeffe can moderate. As long as he promises not to eat anyone."

"This is not a joke," Thaïs cursed under his breath.

"I know." People were dying. If we weren't careful, there'd be four more dead today.

I just had to trust myself that this would work out. I'd do what I had to do in order to bring those soldiers back. Anything else was out of my control.

I glanced out the window to my right and nearly fell out of my seat. "What the hell is that?" A leathery black creature dashed across the desert, straight for our ambulance. It had the rolling gait of a chimpanzee, only it was about twice as big and ten times faster. I spotted two more in the distance.

Holy shit. Assassins. And I'd chucked my knife and knocked out Galen.

"Ha!" Thaïs barked. "They're just imps."

Spoken like a man with a death wish. Imps were minions of the devil. They could tear your heart out in one swipe. They had razor-sharp teeth, crushing jaws, hell, even their spit was lethal.

Heart racing, I braced my hands on either side of me and searched for something I could use to clock them. This weapons ban was going to kill me. "You don't get it. Those monsters are after me." The cab was bare. "Why don't we have any weapons?" This was the fucking army!

Thaïs—the jerk—seemed to be enjoying himself. "You haven't been out of camp much."

"No," I snapped, wide-eyed, "I haven't." And now I knew why.

The imps had drawn into attack position. All three of them ran beside the ambulance on my side, their mouths set into snarls. I could see their glowing yellow eyes and the ridges of bone on their foreheads.

"For god's sake, close your window," I yelled. Or maybe not. Let them eat him first.

"Watch," Thaïs said, two seconds before he hit the brakes.

"Shit!" I grabbed hold of the dash as the impact shoved me forward.

"See?" Thaïs hollered. He still had the damn window open.

"What?" I pleaded.

He pointed out the window. The imps had slowed to match our pace.

"What are they doing?" I demanded. Stalking us?

"They like to run alongside cars."

"Huh?" I stared at my annoyingly smug colleague, then back at the creatures. They loped next to us, tongues out. I stayed there for a minute, catching my breath, not quite believing any of it. "They're not going to attack?"

"Oh, they probably would if we stopped and had a picnic," Thaïs said, "but right now they're just having fun."

"They're minions of the underworld," I protested, watching them jostle for position alongside my window.

"Exactly." Thaïs shrugged. "They deserve a break."

I sat back in my seat, arms shaking. "I am never doing this again."

The corners of his mouth tugged up, but Thaïs didn't comment. We drove in silence, the limbo suns bearing down hard on the metal shell of the ambulance. Still, I didn't open my window for anything.

The imps stayed with us for at least ten miles. Then they

dropped off and dashed toward a leafy green hell vent on the horizon. I shivered despite the heat, watching them go.

I'd seen a lot of screwy stuff in my life, but this was right up there.

"My sister used to have a flesu," Thaïs commented, out of the blue.

"A flesu?" It took me a second to register what he'd said. It sounded more like a sneeze than a name. "I don't even know what that is." I hadn't given much thought to Thaïs or his family, either.

"Half imp, half gargoyle," he said, pleased. "They're very rare."

"I'd say." I wouldn't want to be in charge of that breeding program. Gargoyles hunted imps.

"She called him Romeo," he said, as the ambulance bounced over a rough patch. "Rode him in countless battles."

I couldn't help but notice the past tense. "What happened to him?"

"I don't know," he said, voice tight. "She was killed in the Battle of the Three Points."

Five years ago. "I'm sorry."

"I'm not." He drew his shoulders back. "It was an honorable way to die." His mouth twisted. "Instead of spending eternity on the sidelines."

I shook my head, willing to bet there'd be a line of demigods willing to trade Thaïs a bum leg for a ticket out of the combat corps.

"Look," I pointed. "Up ahead." The desert surface dropped off into a canyon.

"That's us." Thaïs barreled up to the edge before making a hard left onto a dirt road. We hugged the rim of the bottomless pit, like we were on some twisted carnival ride.

What the fuck were these people thinking? I mean, who built a road on the side of a cliff when it could have been ten feet back?

Make that twenty.

"You mind driving us over there?" I snapped, pointing to the endless desert.

"And break an axle?" Thaïs balked. "No way."

"You want to plunge down a cliff?" I barked.

"I'd be more worried about that hell vent." He pointed dead ahead to a leafy expanse of jungle. Colorful birds swooped over a cluster of trees. It looked like a page out of a resort brochure. "I'll bet the enemy camp is on the other side," he said, as if we were driving through a friend's neighborhood, looking at house numbers.

Thaïs skirted way too close to the hell vent, but I refused to give him the satisfaction of another reaction on my part.

The air was sweeter here, lush and vibrant. I could hear the chatter of exotic birds, the screeching of monkeys. Illusions, no doubt. I wasn't going to get close enough to find out.

I held my breath. It was cooler now, as we caught the breezes off the trees.

Shadows moved among the trunks. I'd read reports that people had seen children in the forest, or at least heard the sound of young laughter. I didn't trust anything except the rattling of the ambulance.

Thaïs began humming the theme song to *Rocky,* whatever that meant. He was half crazy on a good day.

I breathed a sigh of relief once we made it around the vent and picked up the trail again.

We hadn't gone more than a mile before we spotted two troop trucks parked on either side of the road ahead. Two jeeps with stretchers attached sat behind them. Thaïs slowed the ambulance.

"Checkpoint," I said under my breath as I grabbed for my white jacket. This had to be it.

The soldiers climbed out, carrying broadswords. There were at least a dozen of them. Huge demi-gods wearing the muted tan of the old army. Etched in green on their sleeves was the double-headed eagle of the infantry corps.

They were followed by at least as many archers. Their arrow tips glistened with the blood of Medusa. It glowed with an unearthly fire. One touch would rot a mortal from the inside out. Several of them knelt in firing position while others stood.

Oh boy. My palms were clammy as I shoved the door open on the ambulance. They certainly didn't go over this in medical school.

Hands up, I approached them slowly. Out of the corner of my eye, I was relieved to see Thaïs on the other side.

They held their arrows steady, pointed right at us.

Every step forward, I had to remind myself why I was doing this.

"We're doctors," I called, when I'd drawn within a baseball's throw. "From the MASH 3063rd."

I sure hoped they'd gotten the memo.

Thaïs stood with his hands on his hips. "Drop your weapons and turn over your prisoners," he demanded.

Real smooth.

"Stop right there," a soldier in the front ordered.

We did. Thaïs and I stood side by side in the middle of the road, waiting. My throat went dry while the rest of me slicked with sweat.

"You want to put your hands up?" I said under my breath.

He scoffed. "I'm a demi-god."

"Well, in that case . . ." I raised my hands higher for the both of us.

This wasn't the time to play games. I was willing to do anything it took to get those soldiers and hightail it out of here.

A sharp breeze from the hell vent blasted us in the back and I wondered again just how I'd gotten into this.

I'd gone to a few personal extremes already. I'd knocked out Galen. I'd found a way to get rid of the knife.

Thaïs stood next to me. The fervor on his face spelled trouble.

"Do not screw this up," I hissed under my breath. This was too important.

He merely smiled.

Oh, fuck.

The sun beat down. I held steady, afraid to move. My arms ached, but there was no way I was taking them down. I didn't want to get shot over a misunderstanding.

Thaïs inhaled sharply, and I followed his gaze. A dark shadow had begun to form behind the troop transports. It billowed like a cloud, rolling forward, the mist stretching out into the line of soldiers.

Stale air enveloped us, smelling of sulfur and death. The demi-gods tensed, but held their own as the smoke began to take form behind them. Tall figures emerged from the mist. Heads bowed, faces hidden, they floated above the limbo plane. They were flat and gray, and rippled with a life of their own.

Shrouds.

This couldn't be necessary. No way anyone needed to use Shrouds. Some said they were spirits. Others claimed they were flesh and something else. There was no way to know for sure.

Shrouds came straight from hell. They were the oldest of the soul eaters. They'd damn mortals in an instant. Immortals they'd torture for eternity.

Both sides used them, but I'd never seen one until now.

I stared at the one straight across from me and sucked in a breath when it lifted its head. There was no face, no eyes. Just blackness.

My heart pounded in my ears. I didn't sign up for this.

Why the hell didn't I let Galen follow us? He'd know what to do. I had no idea.

And now I was trapped. I had to see this through, come hell or . . . I didn't want to think about it.

Figures emerged behind the Shrouds, skirting the damned, careful not to draw too close. A hard, leathery doctor and several orderlies led out four patients on stretchers. They made a wide berth and emerged on the left flank of the soldiers.

"That must be Kosta's buddy," I said under my breath to Thaïs.

He frowned. "I should have known Kosta had friends on the other side."

Didn't everybody? It wasn't like this was exactly a sane situation.

Every nerve on high alert, we stood, waiting.

After a moment's hesitation, the doctor began to move again, toward the middle of the road. The soldiers eased their weapons. I clenched my shoulders. *God, let this be over soon.*

A soldier in the middle stepped out front. "Stop the transfer."

Every sword tip and poisoned arrow pointed at us.

"They're armed," he announced.

My belly flip-flopped. "Oh shit." Was my knife back?

It couldn't be. I was supposed to arrest the forces of the damned, not get eaten by them.

I reached down for my pockets, willing them to be empty. The archers drew back. I had to keep going. I had to know.

I kept my hands flat. *I am not going for a weapon.*

My hands slammed into my sides. There were no lumps in my jacket. I felt again, my heart soaring. No weapons.

"I'm clean!" I shouted, ready to faint with fear, or take off running.

There was a solid second where nobody moved.

"He's got a blade!" the soldier hollered.

What? I froze for a moment, stunned.

"For death and glory!" Thaïs drew a curved dagger from under his shirt and charged.

I dropped to the ground as the archers launched a volley of arrows. This was it. I was dead.

The air erupted with shouts. I squeezed into a ball, covering my head as I felt the poisoned tips slam into the ground around me.

One nick and I was done.

Now would be a great time for Galen to make a heroic save. But no—I'd tricked him and knocked him out.

So that I could die alone in the desert.

And they said I was the smartest one in my class.

"Get her." Soldiers dragged me up roughly by my arms, which meant I was alive. Thank God. I was alive.

Damn Thaïs and his death wish. He could die a hero on somebody else's mission.

The soldiers dragged me forward, toward enemy lines,

their fingers bruising and their pace quick. My head swam as I tried to take it all in. Thaïs lay on the ground, riddled with arrows. They'd punctured his neck. He'd taken two more to the sternum. One in the belly.

They forced me past him. The poison would be working by now.

The head guard, the one who had spoken before, wrapped an arm around my shoulders and dragged me back against his hard armor. I strained to get away, to stand on my own two feet.

"We've got her, Colonel Spiros." He pressed the tip of his knife into my side. It penetrated my fatigues, stinging my skin. "Don't you dare move."

I swallowed hard, glancing down. It was one of those knives that broke apart inside the body, shredding you from the inside out. A chill snaked through me. No doubt it was poisoned as well.

"Look at me, soldier," the leathery commander ordered. He had small, piercing eyes. "Kosta put you up to this?" He smelled like metal oil and sweat.

"No," I said quickly. They had to see Thaïs acted alone. "My partner here is crazy."

The colonel frowned. "You broke the deal."

chapter eighteen

"He broke the deal," I protested, voice cracking. "He paid the price." I couldn't help Thaïs as he lay bleeding on the ground. Maybe I could still convince Spiros to let me save those soldiers.

The old colonel stared me down with that same imperceptible expression Kosta got, as if he didn't know whether to take me seriously or throw me out.

I straightened, calmed, still very aware of the knife point against my ribs. "Don't make these soldiers suffer because of a crazy man."

The injured lay in pain on the ground behind him, like spoils to the victor. Blood soaked through their bandages.

The Shrouds clustered barely an arm's reach away, shifting in agitation, impatient. The soldier nearest to the creatures eased back a step, as if that would help.

It was the creepiest thing I'd ever watched—these hellish creatures, preparing to dine.

"Light the torches," the colonel ordered.

His soldiers laid out a semicircle of fire around our little party. It felt like a sacrificial altar.

Spiros stood with his back to the impending carnage, clearly in control. I wondered how he'd harnessed the damned. Never mind. I didn't care. I just wanted to get out of there.

The torches crackled in the dry desert air.

There'd been too much suffering, too much death already. I couldn't stop most of it. Damn. I couldn't even stop Thaïs, but I had to convince this commander that I was on his side.

I shook my head, willing him to understand, to find some of the mercy he'd shown by the sheer fact that he'd allowed this meeting in the first place. "I'm not a demi-god," I said. "I'm not a warrior. I'm a doctor. Let me save these people."

The shadows of the setting sun played over his sharp features. Whether it was the darkness or the centuries of command, Spiros was unreadable.

My head swam with the injustice of it. He wanted it. I knew he did or he wouldn't be standing there. "Haven't you seen enough useless suffering and death?"

He tilted his head up. "I have." He eyed me. "You've put me in a difficult position. We can't fly under the radar on this."

Because Thaïs had spilled blood.

I glanced back at my colleague, relieved to see he was at least moving. He kicked his legs and let out a groan as he dug his hand inside his uniform shirt.

He couldn't treat himself. This was a disaster.

And then I felt a heaviness in my pocket.

No.

The familiar outline of the knife pressed into my skin.

Fuck no.

My body thrummed, every nerve on high alert. I didn't want this. I didn't need this.

But there was no question about it. The knife was back. I refused to touch it, fought the urge to look down at the lump in my pocket.

Pretend it's not happening.

I had to get through this.

Blowing out a breath, I focused my full attention on Spiros. "I know it's bad." I was used to that. Bad never meant impossible. We could work it out. Tell a story. Get these soldiers—and my knife—the hell out of here. "As far as I'm concerned, my colleague tripped."

I could feel the soldier behind me chuckle, the blade of

his knife rubbing against my skin. I winced. At least I'd succeeded in surprising Spiros.

"Get that knife away from her," Spiros ordered, waving his hand. He frowned. "I admire your wish to set things right, Doctor. Damn shame it can't be solved that easy."

"She's armed!" a soldier shouted.

Fuck, fuck, fuck.

Spiros snarled as they dragged the knife out of my pocket and handed it to him. "What the hell is this?"

No. He had to understand. "I didn't plan this, I swear." My mind raced for some way, any way, to get him to believe me.

He inspected the dagger. "This is the Knife of Atropos," he said, awe coloring his words.

"Who?" You could have knocked me over with a feather. "Wait. Atropos is one of the Fates."

"This is a powerful artifact," he said, suspicious again, his fingers tracing over the blade. "Where did you get it?"

Before I could say anything else a shout went up from the guard. "He's got a bomb!"

I twisted to see Thaïs as another cry went up from the soldiers. "He's rigged!"

The guard surged forward. The warrior behind me released his grip and I dropped forward onto the ground. Boots caught my shoulder with a searing crush. I covered my head with my arms, wrapped myself in a tight ball as the battle ignited above me. There was nowhere to go, nowhere to hide.

I tasted stale dirt and my own fear.

"Man down!"

Spiros fell next to me, blood soaking his gut.

"No!" There came a shocked cry from above. I stared up at the soldier who had held me. He clutched a bloody knife and stared in horror at his colonel.

Blood spread over the colonel's tan uniform shirt as I scrambled to his side.

"Is it poisoned?" I screamed above the chaos. The guard didn't seem to hear. I grabbed him around the leg and shook. "Your knife," I demanded.

The burly soldier surfaced from his daze. "No. Not mine. Shit!" He leveled the weapon at me.

A sliver was missing from the tip. We both saw it at the same time and from the sheer revulsion on his face, I knew what had happened.

Spiros choked up blood. "Stay with me," I ordered, turning back to my patient.

I ripped open his shirt. I'd done this for Galen. I could do it for him. "Get me a knife that's not going to break apart," I ordered the soldier behind me. "And for god's sake get me some light."

The colonel's stomach was bathed in shadow. It was almost full dark. The knife had pierced below the sternum, just under the costal cartilage. Okay. Good. I used my sleeve to wipe away some of the blood. I needed more light. I needed to see where the shard went. Please let there be just one.

It would break apart soon enough.

Sweat slicked my palms. No. I'd get it out.

"There." I saw it. Right below the skin, traveling toward the heart. "Damn it. I need that knife!"

The guard handed me a small military dagger with a three-angled blade. Perfect. Torches blazed down. Good. "Now get out of my light."

I traced the bulge of metal with the tip of my knife, following its deadly path under his skin until I got ahead of it. I sliced, pulse pounding as blood pooled in the wound, blocking my view. I didn't have a nurse. I didn't have suction. But I could do this.

I spread my fingers, adding pressure on either side, coaxing the tip out.

My breath hitched and I fought a flood of panic. "Where is it?" I didn't see it.

Spiros bucked. "Hold him down."

Shit.

"Wait." I saw it. Two inches above my incision, still heading for the heart. I adjusted my angle, my shadow falling long over the colonel's heaving chest. I could do it. I just needed to get a better look. One more second.

And then it split.

My throat closed.

It split again.

One shard disappeared into his body. Then another. Cold fear swamped me as I realized I'd never be able to get them. At that moment, I realized Spiros had been watching me. A soldier braced his head. Another held his arms. His small eyes glittered with pain.

I held his gaze. "I'm sorry," I said. For what, I wasn't even sure. For coming here, for being blind enough not to suspect Thaïs, for failing to save his life.

The old colonel knew he was dying. And unlike the movies, where it's a peaceful, even reverent moment, this one sucked. Spiros lurched forward, coughing blood.

My jaw grit as I showed his soldier how to hold his commander's head at a more comfortable angle and used my coat to wipe the blood from the Spiros's mouth. There was nothing else I could do.

The light intensified above us and I looked up to see a ring of soldiers, weapons drawn and expressions tight.

The sun had set all the way. Darkness pressed in behind them.

"I'm sorry," I said. I had no doubt Spiros was an honorable commander. Death was never fair.

Even an immortal like Spiros could lose everything in this war.

He'd stopped choking, his face red. I used my clean sleeve to wipe some of the sweat from his cheeks and forehead. I moved aside a bronzed basilisk tooth he wore on a leather chain. It was glacial to the touch, even though his body was burning up.

I wiped his neck and shoulders. I had no doubt he was just trying to protect his people, like I was.

The soldiers stiffened as they realized their colonel was indeed dying. I saw grief, and fear.

"He controls the Shrouds," one of them said.

Hold up. "What?" My mind raced to process the ramifications of that as I stared down at my patient. His eyes flew open as another coughing fit seized him. "What are you talking about?"

I knew they had to control the Shrouds somehow, but they couldn't leave it up to one man. Even if he was supposed to be immortal.

The soldiers began pulling away. I took full hold of my patient as they eased his arms and head down onto the dirt. I turned him onto his side as he spewed blood onto the ground.

"He won't lose his soul," said the guard who'd held the knife on me. "He'll die. His soul will be saved."

"But when he dies—" another began.

Understanding crept over me. Oh hell.

"Pull out!" The soldiers made a coordinated dash for their vehicles.

"You got that bomb?" one called to another. "Get rid of it."

"Wait," I hollered, my hand still circling the colonel's back, trying to give him some dignity, some comfort as he drowned in his own blood. There had to be another way. Kosta would have had a backup plan. Spiros had to have one, too.

The soldiers thundered past me, in full withdrawal, some firing up the trucks as others continued to climb in the back.

The ground shook as a bomb detonated somewhere off in the open desert.

"Go, go, go!" a sergeant hollered as he ran past.

"At least take the patients!" The humans might die. The immortals would suffer. But these people deserved to keep their souls.

The torches danced. The Shrouds stirred, restless and hungry. Waiting.

"Oh boy." I rubbed at Spiros's back, mind racing, trying to think of something—anything—I could do.

I could run. Leave. Let Spiros die with his face in the dirt. It wasn't right and it wasn't honorable but in the all-out battle against terror, it was hard not to think that way.

Damn Thaïs and the old army.

If Thaïs was even alive anymore.

Spiros doubled over, grabbing my coat as he pitched forward. He clutched at the bronze tooth at his neck, ripping the cord. He fisted it, shoving it against my coat, holding it there as he died.

Holy hell.

I watched the colonel's spirit rise up out of his body. He looked to his troops, in full retreat as they sped down the road. Then he turned slowly back to me. He nodded before he faded away.

The tooth in his fist flashed like lightning, blinding me. Electricity sizzled in the air and I realized the spell had broken.

The soldiers were gone. It was me and the injured. And the Shrouds.

Blinking against orange spots, I desperately peeled the dead man's fingers from the necklace.

The Shrouds closed in.

"Back!" I yelled, holding up the tooth, praying it would be enough.

They recoiled as a unit. I wanted to collapse in relief.

But they could still go for the soldiers. The flames crackled from the few remaining torches as I eased away from the commander.

I said a quick, silent prayer of thanks that I'd made it this far. The necklace had to be some kind of talisman. It burned cold against my skin. No doubt this thing was meant for a god, or a demi-god at least.

I saw my bronze dagger on the ground and took that, too.

The Shrouds let out a low, rustling hiss as I dashed toward the soldiers. I tripped as I reached them, knees in the dirt, hand closed tight around our only protection.

It was making me dizzy, weak. I could feel it draining me.

The Shrouds knew, too. They hovered, waiting. The big one on the end rocked back and forth, as if it were itching to pounce. I could feel its hunger.

I climbed back to my feet, doing my best to stand strong in front of the soldiers, afraid to look back. The talisman grew more and more frigid, searing me with ice. I held it tight, fighting it even as it drew the very life out of me.

My knees gave way once more and I knelt in the dirt. The night had gone black, the winds chilling.

It was hard to breathe, impossible to think.

I felt the heat and the energy seep from my body. This must be how my patients felt as they died.

Squeezing my fingers, I concentrated, focused, tried to hold on to the talisman. I knew I was dead the moment I let go. That's not what stopped me. It's what would happen to everyone else.

The Shroud on the end inched forward.

I couldn't hold on much longer. I was too weak. Too cold.

My fingers loosened and I felt the talisman slip.

The Shrouds rushed forward and I held them back with the knife.

"Petra!" Galen's voice echoed across the desert.

How did he get here? I wanted to tell him to run, get away. The Shrouds whipped their bodies in a frenzy of need, waiting to be unleashed.

My body felt dry, used up, like it could blow away in the wind.

My fingers were numb. I couldn't feel the talisman. *It was gone.*

A flash erupted below me. The spell broke. I wanted to cry for it, but no sound came out.

The Shrouds shrieked and charged.

I stabbed at the rotting, filthy soul eaters with my dagger, crying in dry heaves. Their moans scratched like sandpaper as putrid dust rained down.

The ground shook as Marius landed to the left of me.

"I got her," he said, scooping me up under my arms. My body went light and I realized we were flying.

My face pressed against his shoulder. My head swam.

"The Shrouds," I tried to explain, voice tight.

"Are a problem. I know." We hit the ground with a thud and I heard Marius ripping open the back door of an ambulance. "You drove them back with that knife, but nothing kills them.

"Sit," he said, planting me on the back rise. "I'm going to get the wounded."

Sweet Jesus. I'd driven back the Shrouds.

My hands shook, my body felt like rubber. I'd lost the knife. Hopefully back where Galen could find it. Marius hadn't taken me far, I realized, my fingers clenching against metal. This was our ambulance.

I coughed, trying to get my bearings. I was facing the black of the desert; I could see the halo of light from the battleground behind me.

The second oracle had come true—I'd arrested the forces of the damned.

I blinked and Marius was back, sliding a stretcher into the ambulance next to me. Then another, moving at super-speed. "Tell Galen to wear the talisman around his neck," I managed to remind him, through the haze.

"He's holding his own," he said, buckling a man into place. "For now at least." A lock of blond hair fell over his eye as he double-checked the other patient. Then he was gone.

I wanted to scream. I wanted to rant and rave and find the talisman and do something that would actually make a difference. I slid off the back of the ambulance, struggling to focus.

Gripping the metal side, I fought to stand as I watched Galen holding back the Shrouds. They writhed and twisted like snakes as they stalked him. Sword at the ready, talisman up, he backed across the desert, leading them away.

Sweet Jesus, he'd better not die out there trying to save us.

I fell straight forward.

My cheek and shoulder slammed into the dirt, along with the rest of me. But those were the parts that hurt the most.

No telling how long I lay there until Marius's boots crunched in the dirt next to me. "Damn it, Petra."

He shoved me into the back like a sack of potatoes.

"Go, go, go!" Marius hollered as he slammed the door closed.

The ambulance lurched forward, throwing me across the floor.

"Wait," I creaked, my voice refusing to work. Had Galen made it back?

Marius was already working on patients as I tried to pick myself up.

The rocks in my head made it hard, as did the thrashing of the ambulance as it bounced over the desert. The metallic tang in the air made me sick to my stomach.

"Is she okay?" Galen barked from the driver's seat.

I closed my eyes. Thank heaven.

"Yes. Drive," Marius answered.

My eyes refused to open and I gave in, letting Marius take charge. He was a good doctor, one of the best. It's what had doomed him to eternity with Commander Kosta, but at the moment, I was sure grateful for it.

"Sorry I don't have a spot for you, roomie," Marius said, laying me out on the floor and bundling something soft under my head.

I wanted to tell him that was okay, but I blacked out instead, dreaming of phantoms chasing us across the desert.

Even in my dreams, though, I knew it was only a fantasy. It had to be. Otherwise we'd be dead already.

There was no telling how much time had passed before I was awoken by a bright light and the overwhelming stench of Drakkar.

"Physically, you check out." I opened my eyes to see Marius hovering above me. The motion of the ambulance jostled him from side to side.

"Thanks," I said weakly, grateful to be able to say anything. "What about our patients?"

His mouth formed a thin line. Marius wasn't the type to sugarcoat it. "We lost both of the humans. They bled out." His eyes held regret. "Kosta and Rodger are prepping for surgery back at the post. I'm taking the third. We should be there in a few minutes."

I started to sit up as the ambulance took a hard left. "Wait." My head swam and I lay back down, wincing. "Three?"

"Thaïs is hanging in there."

I swallowed, trying to process it. "I could have sworn he was dead."

Marius's mouth twisted into a wry smile. "So you didn't

hear him screaming. I neutralized the poison. Now he's just full of holes."

Damn Thaïs. He survived while good men died.

"I can assist," I said, trying once again to sit. My body ached like I'd fought an entire battalion by myself.

"Like hell you will." Marius held a hand to my back, helping me up. "I'd put you under observation if I thought I could get away with it. You don't have any physical damage that I can tell, but the Shrouds drained your strength."

"It wasn't the Shrouds"—at least I didn't think so. But we were getting off the subject. "I'm actually feeling better," I said, sitting on my own. That would show him. I fought a wave of nausea. Oh geez. Who was I kidding? I was a mess. "How did you even find us?"

"You were at the checkpoint. As soon as we had full dark, I flew."

Right. Thank goodness for super-vampire speed or I would have been toast. I braced my head in my hands. "Thanks, buddy."

"Don't suck up," he said, easing me back down as Galen made another sharp left. "And you owe me a white coat."

I looked down at the one I'd borrowed. It was spattered with blood.

Marius glanced out the back window. "We're here."

The ambulance ground to a halt and the whole thing rocked as the back doors flew open. Rodger and Kosta pounded in.

"What have we got?" barked Kosta, already examining the immortal on the top bunk.

"Lung function compromised. We're down to about twenty percent, thoracic hemorrhaging, I neutralized the poison on Thaïs. Arrow wounds near his heart need repair," Marius said as orderlies scrambled to unhook the stretcher. "Petra was drained, lost consciousness."

I winced. Fine MD I'd become.

"Get them out of here," Kosta barked. "Let's move."

I grabbed hold of the side of the ambulance and heaved up to my feet. "What can I do?"

Kosta didn't even spare a glance. "Stay out of the way, Robichaud."

He jumped out and Galen replaced him, his face a mask of calm concentration mixed with worry. His black special ops uniform was torn and dirty. "Come on. Let's get you out of here."

I examined the arm wrapped around me as he led me outside. The chill of the night helped clear my head. "How are you okay?" I'd seen those Shrouds. I knew what they could do.

He huffed. "This is from Jeffe," he said, poking a finger through a hole in his field jacket. "He stashed me in the mine-field."

Rodger barked commands as orderlies rushed one of the immortals into surgery.

"I'm sorry," I said.

"So am I," Galen growled. I had a feeling we'd be talking about that later. "Lucky for you, I'm a fast healer." He steered me past rushing medical workers as we walked through the chaos of the yard. "I used the amulet on the Shrouds," he said, "drove them into the hell vent."

I missed a step and almost tripped. "Why didn't I think of that?"

"Because you were half out of your mind." Galen said. "You're not a god."

But he didn't say I shouldn't have touched it. We both knew I'd had to do it.

"What happened to the Shrouds in the hell vent?" I asked.

He shrugged. "Rustle, rustle, burp. I don't care. They're gone."

I stopped in front of the OR. "I need to help out in surgery." I might not be on a table, but I could assist. I could hear them working inside—Rodger, Kosta, Horace.

Galen glanced at the closed door. "Let them handle it. They're good."

I knew that. I wanted to be a part of it. I squeezed my eyes shut. "This is my one chance to make a difference and I can't." I could barely stand up straight.

Surprise skittered across Galen's face. "You already did."

Weak bulbs cast pale yellow light over the yard. He tipped my chin up, his thumb caressing my tearstained cheek. "You think the only way to save lives is to be a doctor? It's not, you know."

The strength in his voice, the surety of his words made me want to believe him. I could see why people followed this man. He came at the world from a different angle. He acted with complete clarity. It almost seemed effortless in the way he drew the right people behind him at the precise moment to make a difference.

If I was science, he was art.

He'd even motivated a persnickety vampire.

I gave one last, long look at the closed door of the OR. "What else can I do?"

"Come on," he said, leading me away. "I'll show you."

chapter nineteen

I shivered as the cold desert breeze blew in from the north. The sleeves of my coat were clammy, wet with the colonel's blood. My entire body ached.

Galen wrapped an arm around me, avoiding my bad shoulder, as he led me across the yard toward the visiting officers' quarters. EMTs were already clearing out the back of our battered ambulance, prepping it for next time.

We passed the cluttered bulletin board that gave the latest count on the vacation pot—three weeks, one day, seven hours, and forty minutes.

A loudspeaker crackled above, hanging crookedly on the old dead trunk of a palm tree. I had a new appreciation for whomever had dragged that out of the closest hell vent. And I could have sworn I saw one of Rodger's sea creatures slink behind the supply tent.

Nothing changed at the MASH 3063rd. That usually drove me nuts. Now it settled into my bones with a familiar comfort, like returning home from a long journey.

My legs were still wobbly, but it wasn't why I leaned against Galen. The truth was I needed him. I craved the kind of comfort he offered. I rarely allowed myself that type of weakness, but either I had to accept some support or I was going to give in to a crying fit. Nobody wanted that—least of all me.

"You're doing great," he said, tugging me closer.

I let out a slightly crazed laugh. Tonight was the closest I'd ever come to death. Both my own and losing the people I cared about. I'd barely held on. In fact, I hadn't. I'd collapsed. I'd have been Shroud bait if Galen hadn't shown up when he did.

And Thaïs. He wasn't just an asshole, or a traitor to the cause. Tonight, he'd shown himself to be a homegrown terrorist.

"Thaïs attacked those soldiers," I said. We'd come in peace. "He had a bomb."

He'd been struck down. He'd gotten what he deserved.

Still, for as much heartache as he'd caused, I didn't want to see him die, either.

I almost felt guilty about that after what happened to Colonel Spiros.

We reached Galen's tent. The torches outside burned high, illuminating his handsome features in the firelight as he untied the front flaps. "It's over now," he said. "You did the best you could. And if Thaïs survives, I'll kick his ass myself."

I tried to smile, but I couldn't. I'd failed tonight. It tugged at me. I should have prevented Thaïs's insane suicide charge. I should have known. If there was one thing I'd learned in this hole, it was to be aware of the people around me. "There had to be something I missed."

"Some situations, some creatures you can't predict," Galen said. "You just deal with them as they come." There was rock-hard assurance in his voice, a grim determination that no matter what we'd face—be it scorpions or Shrouds—he'd have my back. He touched my arm. "We'll get through this."

"Which part?" I asked, overwhelmed.

He held my gaze. "All of it."

God, I wished he wouldn't look at me like that. It was just one more thing that could go wrong.

"I'm a mess," I said, ducking inside the tent.

After the events of tonight, the sheer luxury of this place was lost on me. Galen sat me down on a plush purple couch and slipped my white coat off from behind. He wadded it up and tossed it into the kitchen garbage.

"Hey," I said, in halfhearted protest. Oh, who was I kidding? Marius's coat was toast.

He squatted in front of me, running his hands up my arms, checking for injuries.

"It wasn't my blood on the coat," I said, half impressed by his methodical search, half turned on. I swallowed hard. "I just got kicked around," I insisted as he ran his hands up my sides, his touch warm against my white tank top.

We were finally alone together and I felt like death warmed over. My breasts grew heavy as he lingered on the blossoming purple bruise on my shoulder.

"I'm fine," I insisted. I was pretty clean. "That's not even my blood on my pants." Although there was quite a bit of it, now that I really looked. Still, you couldn't really tell against the rusty red of my uniform.

"They're bloody," he said, tugging open the buttons.

His touch was certain, and unfair, considering this was just a mercy undressing.

Unless . . . God, was I even considering it? We'd just been through hell.

Galen stripped the pants off my legs. It felt good.

I found I wanted them gone. I wanted to be rid of the blood and the grime and the feel of the desert.

At least I'd worn my barely there lace bikini bottoms.

He tried not to stare.

My mouth twitched in a smile I didn't quite feel.

He liked them. I could see it in his hitchy movements as he stood, the way his eyes traveled everywhere but on me.

I felt the tightening between my legs as I shifted my hips on the couch. "Is it okay to be turned on?" I wanted to forget about blood and death and simply feel.

"It happens," he said, his voice a bit hoarse. "But you don't need me to jump you right now."

Ah, but that's where he was wrong. I needed to forget. I needed to find a place far gone from the suffering. I needed to feel valued, cherished, loved.

"At least take your shirt off for me," I coaxed. "It'll make me feel better."

"Stop it." He stood, backing out of my reach. "I'm pissed off and I'm taking care of you," he grumbled, but I could hear the desire underneath his words.

He strode through an open tent flap and toward the bubbling mud bath. He pulled a towel from a freestanding rack.

"Fine," I said. If that's how he wanted to play, "I'll take my shirt off."

Galen dropped the towel.

He stared at me as I seductively inched my white T-shirt up, freeing my breasts. My muscles ached and my arm stung, but I didn't let it show in the sexy smile I gave him. I tossed the shirt at his feet.

Yes. This felt good. No pain, no fear. Only desire.

He stood with his arms at his sides, absolutely motionless. "Shit, Petra. I'm trying to be noble here."

I toyed with the soft skin between my breasts. "What if I want you to be hard instead?"

He couldn't tear his eyes away. I don't even think he blinked.

I let my knees fall open. "Do you want to know what you do to me?"

His breath was ragged. "I don't think I'd survive it."

He swallowed hard as he retrieved the towel and held it under the gurgling fountain. He wrung the fresh, clean water onto the floor as he returned to me.

Oh yes, he was hard. As he stood over me with the towel, I could see his swollen cock fighting against his black combat fatigues. He bent at the knees, and I caught him in my hand.

He hissed and grew even more as he crouched in front of me. I inched my hand up his chest, over flesh and muscle, as he sank down all the way.

He closed his eyes, fighting for control as he came level with my breasts.

His muscles shook as I drew my hand up farther, baring his chest. "I thought you wanted to make me come," I said, brushing my thumb over a flat, hard nipple.

His eyes blazed. "Gods." He lowered his gaze and took a shuddering breath. "I'm not going to grab you and shove my cock into you," he muttered, as if he were about to rip off my panties and fuck me right there. "I have to make sure you're okay."

I lingered on the idea of his cock. Hot and ready. Moisture beading at the tip before he drove it inside me. I felt myself grow wet.

The muscles in his chest and jaw tightened as he brought the cool cloth up to my cheeks and neck. He cleaned me gently, lingering on my jaw. The pain and the chaos of the night faded away.

He worked slowly, taking extra care with my bruised shoulder. He eased the cloth down my arms. He took my hands in his and wiped the blood away from my palms. Then he ran the cloth over each finger, gently pulling, his head bent as he worked. Every stroke of his fingers spiraled straight through me. His eyes caught mine, hungry.

We both shivered as he drew the cloth over my aching breasts, again and again, like he was fighting some kind of battle in his head and this was the line of demarcation.

As long as he was cleaning me, he was taking care of me. Never mind the fact that I didn't have any blood or dirt on my breasts. He held the cloth in a death grip, rubbing, stroking.

My nipples tightened to painful points. My skin flushed. I pushed into him. God, it felt good.

"Fuck." He exploded, dropping the towel, dragging me into his mouth. He closed over one breast and then the other as he took turns kissing and sucking and worshipping them both. I shoved my chest forward and my head back. Yes. This was exactly what I needed.

Pleasure threaded through me, making me even wetter. I wound my fingers through his hair and squirmed my hips closer. I wanted him to feel my soaked panties, to know how ready I was for him.

"Hades," he cursed against my trembling skin, "I should be taking care of you tonight."

"You are," I said, as he rose up over me.

He kissed me deeply, over and over, like he was afraid to stop. I clung to him, kissed him, loved him.

He jerked away, his mouth glistening. "I almost lost you tonight. It scared the hell out of me."

I was tired of fighting, this and everything else. "Then make love to me, Galen. Make me forget."

"In here," he said, lifting me like I weighed nothing and carrying me to his bed.

My pulse raced, my heart pounded. Finally. I wanted this. I wanted him.

I'd never allowed that for myself. Never expected to find it after Marc was taken and killed. God, that seemed so long ago.

It was.

Galen lowered me onto the sumptuous bed. He lit the candles, one by one.

Warm light bathed the room as he moved back to me, his large hand cupping my jaw, cradling it in his palm. "You are so beautiful," he said, lowering his mouth.

His lips brushed against mine, strong and warm. He caressed me, avoiding my hurt shoulder and arm. He was so good. So noble.

He was mine.

He wrapped an arm around my waist and drew me flush against him.

I could feel him—all of him—hard against me.

"Strip," I whispered against his ear. "I want you to strip for me."

He raised up over me, his hips straddling mine. His muscled arms and chest flexed as he pulled his T-shirt over his head. With a wicked grin, he tossed it behind him.

"Mmm . . . very nice, soldier."

He tilted his chin down, eyes on me. "I aim to please, ma'am."

He slid off the bed. Soon his combat boots were in a heap with his shirt. He stood in front of me, wearing his fatigues and nothing else.

I raised up on my one good elbow. "Very nice. But I'm not letting you back in bed until I've tasted your cock."

His hand froze on his top button. "Holy hell. You're like a walking wet dream."

"Strip."

He shoved down his pants and unveiled a tapered waist, strong thighs, and the most beautiful cock I'd ever seen. It was long and thick, with a glistening drop of pre-cum at the tip.

"Oh my god."

"That's right," he said, grinning.

Yeah, well I knew how to wipe that smile off his face. I reached out and caught him with my tongue. He groaned as I circled his tip and then took the whole of him in my mouth. He tasted rich and salty—alive. I slid a hand between his legs to caress his heavy balls.

"Holy fuck."

I took his whole length again, working him with my tongue.

"Enough," he grunted, lifting me up and slamming us both back down onto the bed. I ground against him, raining kisses against his chest as he ripped off my panties and buried himself inside me.

I hissed as I felt the full length of him, kissed the sweat-dampened line of his neck.

He gasped and withdrew, his tip hovering outside my entrance. We both wanted it again—the sweetness of that first invasion. I wrapped my legs around him, and we both groaned as he slipped inside of me once more.

He plunged his tongue into my mouth.

Yes.

I kissed him back with everything I had, reveling in the feeling of him on me, *in* me.

His wide shoulders were corded with tension. He watched heatedly as he took me. He was so hard and powerful. He held nothing back.

He was perfect.

I reached a hand down between us and touched the place where he pumped in and out of me. I felt my juices on his cock, whispered my fingers through it as he penetrated me.

"Like this," he said easing my hand over my clit. He pressed it there. I gasped, reveling in the weight of him sliding in and out of me, stroking me, my fingers pressed down, the pleasure spiraling.

He tensed, never taking his eyes off me as the speed and depth of his strokes increased. It was delicious. Searingly beautiful to be held by him, loved by him, owned by him in the most primitive way known to man.

The friction built, spiraling into warmth and then, and then, I reached for it, thrust down harder, bucked against him.

I screamed as the full force of it slammed into me.

Galen wrapped his other hand around my backside and held me there, forcing me to take it, to feel it. He drove into me until I flew apart.

I came so hard my shoulders leapt off the bed, trying to get closer, to feel more, to take more as the sheer pleasure of it streaked through me. It was too much. Too hard. Too long. I gave a hoarse cry as wave after wave of it crashed over me.

He threw his head back and shouted as it captured him. He gripped my hips with both hands as he poured into me over and over again.

chapter twenty

When we were both shaking and utterly spent, he collapsed over me. Eyes closed, I drew circles on his back, enjoying the weight of him on top of me. I couldn't stop touching him.

After a long moment, he spoke. "I think I broke something."

"You'd better not have," I murmured, licking the salt from his shoulder, "because I plan to be doing this a hell of a lot more."

He chuckled and flexed his hips, still half hard inside me. "Lucky for you, I heal quickly." He gave me a long, lingering kiss. "Come on. Let's get you under the covers."

"Still trying to take care of me?" I asked as he snuggled us both under the blankets. Me with my head on his chest. Him holding me close.

"You have no idea what you do to me," he whispered, his voice tight.

"Oh, I have some clue," I said, drawing my fingernails over his side, pleased when his breath hitched in response.

He snaked his body over mine, heavy and warm. "You'd better be careful. More of that and I'm not responsible for my actions."

I ran my tongue along his collarbone. I loved the way he moved, the way he felt. It humbled me the way his eyes glittered with want for what I could give to him. For me.

But damn, didn't I deserve a little happiness? Didn't we all?

I touched the short, stiff hair above his ear, caressed the back of his neck. "Thank you."

He drew my hand down and kissed it. "For what?"

There were so many things. "For coming after me tonight. For protecting me. For leading me through this mess." Before, I'd been hesitant to admit I needed him. Never again. "I don't know what I would have done without you."

"You would have done it without me," he said, with more surety that I'd ever felt. "You would have found a way." He held himself over me. "You're one of the strongest women I know."

I looked away, to the darkened doorway. "It's not because I want to be. It's because I have to." I'd been taking care of myself my entire life. "I can't quit," I told him, "even if I want to every day."

"I know," he said simply. "I want out of this war, too." His expression grew tight. "When I was stabbed this last time, I knew it was different. I thought it was fatal. It was almost a relief."

"That's awful." I could only imagine the pain he must feel. I wished I could take some of it away.

"Hell, I know," he said quickly, misunderstanding me. He shook his head, his eyes clouding over with what? Shame? "I shouldn't even think it."

"Why?" As far as I was concerned, it was good to get it out.

"It's treason, you know," he said, his tone grim, as if he could hide his sorrow and his hurt.

"What? To have feelings? To be overwhelmed by death and violence?" It was absurd to expect anything less.

"I should be above that," he said, steeling himself.

"Nobody is," I said, coaxing him down next to me. I propped myself up on my pillow, resting my head on my arm. "You're only half god. You don't have to keep up the shtick all the time."

"Shtick?" he said, slightly entertained at the word.

"You know what I mean." For once, I was glad my mother was a selfish, derelict fairy. At least she wasn't a god.

"It's not about my mother," he mused.

I gave him the you've-got-to-be-kidding-me look.

"Okay, it is sort of about my mother." He rolled onto his back. "She got me into this." He glanced at me. "Do you know how it works?"

I shook my head no.

"She dropped me off at the Abaddon Hell Vent when I was eleven."

Yikes. "I wasn't allowed to go to the mall alone when I was eleven."

"It's where we used to train back then," he said, looking up at the ceiling, thinking back. "That's where I learned to be *strong and noble, heroic and true*." He recited the virtues like items on a checklist.

"Those are all good things, you know."

"I know," he said, the words hollow.

"I'll bet she's proud of you."

He shifted to face me. "I don't know. I never saw her again."

I was shocked, not only at his mother's callousness, but also at his grim acceptance. It was sad. This was a man who deserved to be loved, not abandoned.

"Maybe you should seek her out." I had to imagine she'd be proud. "You can show her what you've become."

The thought of it did little to cheer him. "I'm not sure that's how it works. But sometimes, I think she knows."

He drew me into his arms and we held each other tight. He kissed me on the head. "Let's talk about something else."

"Okay," I said, warm and safe against him.

We lay still for a moment. Then I felt him smile against my hair. "At the risk of being kneed in the balls, I have to congratulate you on the second prophecy coming true."

I poked him with my pinkie finger instead. "I did arrest those suckers," I said, letting it sink in. Or at least I'd stopped them. Last time I read a dictionary, *arrest* was a synonym for *stop*.

There was no way Kosta or anyone else could have forced that. Spiros dying, the Shrouds breaking free—none of it should have happened. Somehow, the oracle knew.

I studied the arm he'd laid over me, the pure strength of it. Candles flickered. Shadows danced over the walls of the tent. "I'm afraid," I admitted.

"You should be," he said against my hair. "Fear forces you to be vigilant, to prepare." He kissed my shoulder. "Fear keeps you alive."

"I can't believe you do this day in and day out." He fought on the front lines and watched his men suffer and die.

All this time, I thought I was the one who stood alone. But Galen did, too. He commanded. He inspired. But he had no one to prop him up.

I found myself wanting nothing more than to reach out to him and ease his pain.

"Not quite like tonight," he said, the muscles in his chest tightening. "That was something new, even for me."

"Really?" A moment of understanding passed between us.

I couldn't quite believe that this immortal warrior was here with me. That he'd chosen it.

It was more than I'd ever imagined.

"Petra." I tilted my chin up as he tucked a wisp of hair behind my ear. "I was missing something before. I have been for years. I didn't know what it was until I met you."

His admission filled me with joy and at the same time, a stark awareness of him erupted through me. I didn't know if I could take it, that kind of closeness—that kind of responsibility. "I don't know what to say."

He gave a small smile. "You don't have to say anything."

He held me close. I closed my eyes and sank into him. I felt so warm and safe. Content. Like I'd made it back home.

I woke to his tongue snaking across my hip. I lifted the covers to watch as he dipped it into my belly button. It tickled.

"Stop laughing. I'm trying to seduce you." He grinned against my skin.

My stomach growled. "What time is it?"

"Just after noon. Want to get something to eat?"

He tugged me to a sitting position, and I followed him out to the kitchen. "That's right. I forgot the number one reason why I'm here."

We both knew I was lying through my teeth. We were barely out of bed and I already wanted him again.

He opened the fridge to reveal shelves full of meat, cheese, and fruit.

"Ooh . . . sliced pineapple," I said, nudging past him.

"We could have fun with that fruit fixation of yours," he said drily. He stood with his hip braced against the counter. God, he was beautiful. I felt him down to my toes.

I popped a slice of fresh, tart pineapple into my mouth, enjoying this playful side of him. "At ease, soldier."

He closed the space between us. "Just so you know, you're the first person ever—mortal or immortal—to take me prisoner."

"Sorry about that."

"No, you're not," he said, stealing a slice of pineapple.

I fed him another slice, the sticky juice running down my arm as he sucked at my fingers. "Jeffe said you'd be out for three days at least."

He laughed. "Jeffe underestimated me."

No kidding.

"Did it hurt?" I asked. I'd never intended to cause him pain.

"It was strange," he said, examining the skin at the back of one very perfectly sculpted calf. "I was dizzy, I tried to take a step, then—nothing."

Wait. That was unheard of for an immortal. "You didn't feel them moving you?" It was actually good, because Jeffe might have dropped his head a few times. "You didn't dream?"

He searched his memory. "No," he said, surprised.

"Amazing," I said, leaning against the counter, my mind going a mile a minute.

"Don't act so happy," he said, brows furrowed as he commandeered my fruit bowl.

"Do you know what this means?" I asked, ideas tumbling over and over in my mind. "We might be able to develop an anesthetic that works on you people."

I opened the lid on the trash container in the corner, looking for my discarded medical jacket to see if it had a pocket light. "What is this? An incinerator?"

"Yes."

Lovely. We had a junkyard and the VIPs had incinerators.

I pointed a finger at his bare chest. "I want you in the clinic tomorrow."

"No problem." He looked at me with enough admiration to make me blush. "It would be amazing if you discovered an anesthetic."

"I'd like to discover an end to the war."

He nodded, his mouth twisting. "You didn't need to knock me out."

"You were going to follow me," I pointed out. I appreciated his need to be involved with the people around him, but, "you could have influenced the prophecy." It was a fine line, one I didn't intend to cross.

He frowned. "What's with you and this fear?"

I sighed, the burden of it weighing me down.

"Tell me," he said. It was more of a plea than a demand. He wanted to understand.

So did I.

"I didn't . . . It . . ." I couldn't form the words. My voice cracked as I tried in vain to say some thing coherent. Letting out a heavy breath, I gave it another shot. "Look, I tried to stop this war," I said, my voice thick as lead. God, I could barely look at him. How could I explain how horribly I'd failed? "A few months after I arrived here, after I saw the death and destruction, I tried to be the one." It had sounded so damn simple. *A healer whose hands can touch the dead will receive a bronze dagger.* "I could see the dead. I figured that was close enough. All I needed was a dagger."

"So you tried to get one?" Galen asked.

I crossed my arms over my chest, embarrassed. "I ordered a bronze dagger off eBay."

He barked out a laugh.

"What?" I shot back. "You can find anything on eBay."

He couldn't seem to argue that.

"You don't know how hard it was," I said, staring at a pile of purple and gold pillows on the other side of the counter. "I spent a year's salary to bribe an operator at computer command central."

"You're lucky you didn't get caught," he said. Computer access was restricted to approved personnel only. I could have gone to prison.

It had been a gamble on so many levels. "The day it arrived in camp, disaster struck." I closed my eyes, trying to block the pain of it. "My home in New Orleans was wiped away, my father was killed, and the rest of the city was chewed up and spit out by a hurricane."

He touched my uninjured shoulder. "I'm sorry."

Me, too.

"I'd heard that messing with a prophecy might have consequences. I never imagined how terrible they could be." I shook my head and pulled back. "I don't want to make the same mistake again."

He leaned closer. "Listen to me—"

But I was beyond hearing at that point. "I caused a failure. I killed thousands of people, including my own father. And I'm not about to let you or anyone else tell me I should push this."

I was Catholic. I'd confessed to Father McArio. He'd taken the knife and forgiven me. But I didn't think I'd ever be able to forgive myself.

Galen was quiet for a long moment. "It wasn't the right time."

"I know that. And I know this could be the right time. But I'm not going to force anything." I took his arm and held on. "This has to happen naturally."

He nodded. "I understand. We'll wait. We'll be strategic." I knew what it cost him to hold back, which made me appreciate it even more.

"We'll listen to the next prophecy no matter what," I vowed. If we played it right, we could have everything.

"We will," he said, drawing close. "No matter what."

He nibbled at my ear. I couldn't think with him doing that. Then again, maybe that was the idea.

"Trust me," he said, trailing kisses down to my collarbone.

His touch undid me. "I do," I murmured, catching him in a searing kiss. The thrill of it slapped through me, the intensity of what I'd finally admitted and what this man meant to me.

Hands everywhere, we tried to make it back to the bedroom and made it as far as the couch. He was so powerful, so amazing. I cupped his perfect ass and rubbed against him. God, he felt so good. Having him here like this made everything worth it.

He drew back and we both watched his hands as they smoothed up my sides, his thumbs caressing my breasts. He stared at me with raw intensity, as if he couldn't quite believe we were here, at last—together.

This was the man who believed in the impossible. He'd made me believe, too.

I pulled him toward me as he shoved us both back down on the couch. Hands searching, bodies sliding, I poured all my desire and love and fear into that moment, sharing it with him. Being with him.

It felt so good, so right. I drew my hand down between us until I found the full length of him. I remembered the feel of him inside me, of touching him as he made love to me. I rolled my hips against him. He shuddered and groaned against my mouth.

His attention wandered south and it was my turn to tremble. Molten pleasure wound through me as I worked his cock, reveling in the feel of him kissing my breasts.

A banging on the tent post made me open my eyes. "Knock knock!" Horace called. "Is Petra in there?"

I buried my head against Galen's crisp, clipped hair. "No."

"Go away," he groaned.

"Kosta needs her," Horace said. "It's urgent."

So was this. "I'll be out in a minute," I called to Horace.

Galen kissed my shoulder, his warm breath sending a new wave of lust though me. "Tell Kosta to make it quick."

We sat up, still entwined, my breasts rubbing against his bare chest. Whoa boy.

I threw my head back. "Oh frick. I don't have any clothes."

"You're trying to kill me, aren't you?" Galen unwound himself from me. "Hold on a minute," he said, heading for the bedroom.

He came back with clean clothes—a pair of his fatigue pants and a black undershirt.

"Thanks," I said, standing.

His eyes caught on the blue swirling Fleur-de-Z tattoo on my hip.

I slipped into the pants. His fatigues were huge. Didn't matter. Once I had them on, I pulled on the shirt.

Meanwhile the pants fell down. They had adjustable waist tabs, so I ratcheted those in as far as they'd go. With that done, I was the proud owner of a pair of special ops hip huggers.

"All dressed," I said, trying to tuck in his massive T-shirt.

"Now, that is damn sexy." Humor glinted in his eyes.

Yeah, yeah, the shirt was more like a nightgown. I gave up and tied the excess material into a low knot at my waist.

He watched me as I tightened the knot on the shirt. "God, you're beautiful."

"I love a man who's biased." It felt good to smile again. "Don't go anywhere, soldier."

He walked toward the door, flattening me against it with a searing kiss. "Don't be too long."

chapter twenty-one

Horace hovered next to me, bobbing up and down as if to hurry me along. "Kosta is very upset."

"He can join the party," I said, tugging up Galen's pants while walking. I'd been about to have a lot of fun.

A burst of laughter echoed from the officers' club down the way.

At least they were holed up in there and not watching our little parade.

Horace's golden eyebrows speared downward, as if he were chewing on a thought. "I'm glad you're alive," he said, as if he wasn't quite at home with the sentiment.

"Thanks, bud." I still owed him those pennies.

He zipped in front of me, sprinkling a fine gold dust. His pointy ears were drawn back. "Wait," he said, blocking the way, "while we're alone, I must tell you to watch your step." He glanced behind him. "Thaïs thinks you died. He told Kosta you were attacked."

I stared at Horace. He nodded vigorously as the truth sank in.

"Unbelievable." I fought the urge to punch something. After all Thaïs just put me through. I wanted to scream. "He nearly killed everyone. Now he's trying to play the victim?"

Because he thought there were no witnesses.

The world had gone to hell and left me holding the bag.

Horace gave a half shrug, half wince. "He *is* the son of Caerus," he said, as if that answered everything.

"Oh well, there you go." I threw my hands up in the air. I wanted out. If I could walk back home I would. And I'd take Galen with me. To Hades with the immortal army.

Horace just flittered there and watched.

I crossed my arms over my chest. "Who in the hell is Caerus?" I could never keep track of the thousands of gods.

"God of opportunity." Horace glanced across the road toward Kosta's office. "Come on."

Oh yeah, sure. No sense keeping the immortals waiting. I shoved my fists in my pockets and started walking. "That lying, stinking . . ."

"Asshole," Horace added.

Yeah, he could say it, but he didn't mean it. My gut clenched. In the end, it was the immortals versus the mortals. Always had been, always would be. The gods thought they could do whatever the hell they wanted, screw the consequences.

It was what was wrong with this world and this war and well, hell, my entire life.

I gritted my teeth. "God damn gods."

"Don't go bringing the rest of us into it." Horace fluttered beside me on golden wings. He planted his hands on his hips. "You have to admit Thaïs made a valid assumption. No mortal should have survived a direct assault by an armed enemy unit."

I sent him a withering snarl as the truth of it settled over me. Thaïs never planned on me making it out of there alive.

"This day's just getting better and better." I was a mortal, which meant expendable to a lot of these gods. It was yet another reason why I wanted away from this place and out of this war.

"Now you're Kosta's surprise for Thaïs." Horace halted outside the door to Kosta's outer offices and pumped a fist, as if that was some kind of a victory.

Jesus Christ on a biscuit. "Is that what this war is for you people? Entertainment?"

He didn't even have the decency to look ashamed.

I banged inside.

"Petra!" Shirley whipped her chair away from a desk littered with at least half a dozen coffee cups.

She rushed over to us, giving me a giant hug and a mouth full of hair. I gave her a pat on the back as I got a huge whiff of cigarettes and coffee.

She pulled away, holding me at an arm's length. "What happened out there? You were attacked?"

Leave it to Shirley to screw with my mood. "Something like that," I said, smoothing Galen's oversized shirt. Buttoned-down military, that was me. "I have to give my report to the colonel."

Kosta was in his office—yelling. His words might have been muffled by the thick wooden door, but the message was clear: *Somebody is going down.*

"Been like this all day?" I asked.

"Since he got out of surgery this morning," she answered, sharing a glance with Horace. "Kosta's in rare form."

"They shot at me for no reason," Thaïs's voice screeched from Kosta's office.

Oh goody. I'd get to be the one who enlightened the colonel. I rubbed a hand over my eyes. Most of these demi-gods liked to stick together, which meant I'd have Thaïs and his buddies trying to smite me for the rest of my life.

I glanced at Shirley, who looked like she could use some sleep, too.

"God damn it, Doctor. Get in here," Kosta bellowed.

"How'd he even know I was here?" I asked her.

"Gird your loins," she answered.

I yanked up my droopy pants, squared my shoulders, and headed in to meet the firing squad.

Kosta paced behind his desk, cigar in hand, ashes scatting as he waved it around. He zeroed in on me, flushed red all the way up to his bald head. "Close the door."

Thaïs turned and I had the distinct pleasure of seeing his expression go from shocked to horrified.

Take that, asshole.

Thaïs was visibly pale. He had a gauze bandage wrapped around his neck and he was standing kind of hunched, but he was among the living.

It was more than we could say for Colonel Spiros.

I glared daggers as I stood at attention next to him.

He was visibly quivering now. "You're—"

"Alive. I know. Sorry to fuck up your night."

Thaïs straightened, trying to recover. "You're also out of uniform."

"Yeah, well my other clothes were a little bloody, thanks to you."

Kosta wasn't amused. "At ease. Robichaud, what happened?"

I eyed my colleague. "We arrived at the checkpoint as we were ordered." My jaw clenched as I spoke. "The patients were there, waiting for transfer." Everything should have gone off without a hitch. "Spiros was in charge. The assignment was going exactly as planned until Thaïs pulled out a knife."

"That's ridiculous," he shouted. "We were ordered not to bring weapons."

"Which is why I was shocked when you tried to detonate a bomb," I snapped. "No wonder you assumed I was dead." It was like he'd been trying to get us killed. "If you want to go on a suicide mission, that's fine and dandy with me. But next time, leave me out of it."

Thaïs towered over me, injuries forgotten, every overgrown immortal inch of him quivering. "You don't want to die in glory. Sniveling cowards like you can die on the ground. I saw you with your face in the dirt pleading with the enemy for your miserable, insignificant little life!"

"*You* want to be on the ground?" I demanded, shoving him backward. I could at least kick him in the balls before he tore me in half.

"Stop." Kosta ordered. His voice hit me like cold water.

My heart raced and my brain boiled over. How dare Thaïs accuse me of being the coward? "How brave is it to fuck up a chance to save four soldiers?" Two of them might be alive right now if it hadn't been for him.

"Enough!" Kosta slammed his fist into the wall. The office shook with the impact.

Damn Thaïs.

"What is this about a bomb?" the colonel demanded.

I trained my eyes on Thaïs as I answered. "The guards shot Thaïs." With good reason. "I tried to smooth things over with Spiros, but one of the soldiers shouted about a bomb." My pulse hammered as I relived the moment. "I turned and Thaïs was reaching for something. All hell broke loose. I didn't see what happened after that. But I know they somehow got it away from him and detonated it."

Thaïs stared me down as he answered. "There was no bomb." He bit off every word. "She's lying about all of it." He sneered. "Ask Marius if he saw a bomb."

Oh yeah, right. "It was a crater in the desert by the time Marius got there."

But then it hit me. What would I do without proof? I had nothing that said Thaïs was anything but the immortal Boy Scout he was making himself out to be.

"I've heard plenty," Kosta said in a low, even voice that shut us up. He chewed at his cigar, staring past us both.

I needed Kosta to take me at my word, but when push came to shove the colonel was one of Thaïs's people, not mine.

Mortals couldn't even testify in demi-god courts, much less bear witness in a crime against an immortal. And here I was, asking him to condemn Thaïs with no evidence, no witnesses. Nobody on our side, at least.

A hollow feeling took root inside me. Kosta was more open than most. But Thaïs had served under him for three centuries. The colonel had boots older than me.

Kosta eyed us, his lip curled in disgust. "Thaïs, you're under arrest."

His eyes widened. "But I'm a demi-god."

"So am I," the colonel ground out. "MPs!"

A burly cyclops banged into the office.

The eye in the center of his forehead trained on me before moving to Thaïs. The officer was followed by two more military police. The lumbering, one-eyed giants set up behind Thaïs.

He believed me. Thank god he believed me.

The colonel appeared sad, but resolute. "I'll need you to testify before the tribunal," he said to me.

"I can do that?" I had no idea.

"You believe her?" Thaïs protested at the same time. The MPs secured him on either side. "You're going to take the word of a mortal?"

I hated to agree with him on that one.

"It's unusual," Kosta conceded. "But a tribunal is not a court. And I do believe her."

"Unheard of," my colleague sputtered.

Yes, it was. Just when I was starting to hate everything about this war, Kosta had to go and do something like that.

"You blew it, Thaïs." Kosta walked around the desk to stand in front of him. "You turned a peaceful mission into an act of war for your own asinine pride. You put soldiers at risk. One of the kids we almost lost is the son of Dellingr."

"Who?" I asked, before I could hit the EDIT button.

Kosta scowled at me. "He's an old Norse god. You probably know him as Svipdagr."

Oh, sure.

"Fertility god and a real asshole," Thaïs said, by way of defense.

Kosta wasn't amused. "His son Dagr, god of hope and light and fertility and all that bullshit, almost died tonight because you had to play solider."

Holy hell. "He was one of our patients?" The pure gods almost never put themselves in harm's way. If the god of hope and light had gone down under our watch, they would have held me and Thaïs personally responsible. Mostly me.

"Nobody told me that," Thaïs protested, looking to the MPs for support. They merely blinked at him. "You can't blame me."

"It's not my job to explain why I send you on a special

mission. It's your job to take orders and make sure nobody gets killed!" Kosta thundered. "Get him out of here."

The MPs led Thaïs out while I stood there, hands on my hips, contemplating the bullet I'd just dodged.

Mortals didn't get the justice or the respect that the gods seemed to have for one another. I might have spent the rest of my life in prison. And eternal lockup didn't have luxuries like Fruit Stripe gum, beds, and three meals a day. In fact, sometimes the gods forgot that mortals needed to eat and entire prison populations would starve.

Shake it off. It didn't happen.

"We'll assemble a solid tribunal, but he may not even make it through the first interrogation," Kosta said, matter-of-fact. "Watch yourself."

I nodded, reading between the lines. Thaïs had friends. And I'd just stepped way above my station. At least that's how a lot of immortals would see it.

Kosta consulted the paperwork on his desk. "I need you to file a report and pick up his shift."

"Of course."

"I'll have Shirley put out a new schedule."

One that would be worse than before. That wasn't what worried me, though.

I cleared my throat. "Did the old army know what they had?" I asked Kosta.

Kosta took a seat behind his desk. "Not in the higher ranks. They would have tortured him, tried to dig out information. The kid didn't know anything." He opened a drawer and pulled out a fresh cigar. "Spiros sent me word. We worked out a plan to get that boy the hell out of there."

"I'm sorry," I said, pulling up a chair.

Kosta nodded, turning his cigar over in his fingers. "What happened to him?" he asked quietly.

I tried to think of a nice way to say it, and finally just settled on the truth. "It was an accident. One of his own men stabbed him. I did everything I could to save him, but the knife came apart on us."

The colonel sighed, accepting it like the enduring soldier he was.

"Did he . . . ?" He ticked his chin toward the heavens, and I could see the fear behind the question.

"He died quickly and well," I said, glad I could offer my commander some comfort.

The colonel dug a fist against his desk and stared at it for a long moment.

He cleared his throat. "Thanks, Petra." He expelled a long breath. "You know he had a wife and kids topside."

"On Earth?" I hadn't realized. It wasn't overly common. Most of these warriors had been down here too long.

He shook his head, a wry smile tickling his lips. "Met her on leave. Could hardly do without her."

I wasn't sure what to say, so I waited. He deserved to be able to talk about his friend.

Kosta's gaze wandered. "Damn shame" was all he said.

He lit his cigar and blew out a few puffs. "Before you go, I've got to give you the heads-up." He planted his elbows on the desk. "The armies are unmatched. Nobody can deny it. Not anymore." He let out a low whistle. "Something big is going down. We've come close to losing the last several battles. Now the armies are massing to the north."

"I'll be sure to rest up." We'd have a tougher time of it now that we were down a doctor.

"I don't think that will be enough," he said, regret coloring his words. "I just got word they're going to be pulling our soldiers out of recovery."

That didn't make any sense. "They can't take wounded men." It was completely absurd, not to mention counterproductive. "Without proper medical care, some of those soldiers could die."

The lines on Kosta's face had deepened, and he looked older than his immortal forever-mid-forties physique. "The new army needs every warrior it can get. Even if they take all the wounded from every MASH unit, I hear we're still outnumbered."

Which meant disaster on Earth.

"Galen said there was something in motion." He'd said it was a military secret.

"Commander Delphi," Kosta corrected, almost as a reflex.

Yes, yes. Whatever. "His information might be outdated now," I feared. He'd been away from his troops for too long.

"He couldn't tell us anyway," Kosta said. "Intelligence issues. But don't be surprised if they take him, too."

"They can't." I couldn't afford to lose him. Not now.

"You're not his doctor."

Kosta was right. And even if I had been Galen's physician, that didn't seem to matter anymore—not if they were pulling the injured out of recovery.

The prophecy was supposed to bring peace. It was supposed to stop this.

I'd done everything they wanted. I'd gone to the edge of hell and back.

And for what?

"What are you thinking, Doc?"

"That this is wrong. It's not supposed to turn out this way. The prophecy—"

"Prophecies are pigeon crap," Kosta thundered. "We need a savior in the next two days, three tops, or the world is going to hell."

chapter twenty-two

Dismissed, I left Kosta's office more miserable than when I'd gone in. Shirley sat in the outer office with her phone to her ear.

"Wait," she said, placing a hand over the mouthpiece. "Did you hear? There's a new prophecy coming up."

Hope surged. "You mean now?" I could use a break.

"Not yet, I don't think." She spoke into the phone. "What are they doing now?"

After listening, Shirley glanced up at me. "They're wailing and tearing at their hair."

Naturally. "Who are you talking to?"

"Elise from the 8071st. She's stuck at her desk, too."

"Right." Despite the sleep I'd had at Galen's, I was exhausted. Shirley had to be feeling ten times worse. "When are you getting out of here?"

She gave me a look that said, *Come on,* and I wondered why I even brought it up. We all knew the drill.

"Everyone's watching PNN down at the mess hall," she told me. "I'll meet you there after I get off."

"If you get off," I corrected, "and no thanks." I stretched my arms and realized I'd forgotten to put on a bra. "I'm going to bed."

"Those pants say you already did," she called after me as I banged out into the courtyard.

Everybody was a comedian.

Oh well. Let her laugh. At least now it was true.

She'd be at her desk or in front of a television while I'd be getting mine—barring prophecies, medical emergencies, or the end of the world.

Camp was quiet, save for the party going on down at the other end. Smoke billowed from the kitchen behind the mess tent. The chatter of the crowd echoed across the terrain.

I'd take a hot demi-god warrior over twenty-four-hour PNN coverage any day. *My* hot demi-god warrior. Oh my. My body warmed just thinking of it. Smiling, I headed to Galen's haven across the road. I knew exactly where I was going.

Of course I hadn't taken five steps when I heard Rodger. "Well, look who's not going home." The cheer in his voice was forced. He sounded tired.

"I'm a walking billboard," I said, turning around, displaying my oversized special ops duds. "No out-of-uniform jokes, okay?"

But there was no danger of that. Rodger just stood there outside recovery, looking pale and worn to pieces. His hair stood out at odd angles from under the sagging surgical cap he'd forgotten to take off.

"Hey, thanks for jumping in back there," I said, strolling over to him. I didn't like the expression on his face, like he'd seen a ghost. I was the only one who was supposed to see ghosts. I glanced at the ward behind him. "How are my patients doing?"

"Recovering well," he said, his voice curt. "What, were you just going to go back to Galen's and not even talk to me?"

Come on. "So now you're jealous about Galen?"

I really didn't need werewolf drama. I just wanted to reunite with my studly warrior and find a safe place to sleep for about a week.

Rodger rubbed a hand over his face. He looked like hell and needed a shave. "That's not it. I don't care what you do with your boyfriend. I've got a family to worry about."

That got my attention. "What? Is there something wrong with Mary Ann or the kids?" In the last month, Gabriel had gotten stuck in the dryer, Stephen decided to play Superman and jumped off the roof with a cape tied around his neck, and Kate shoved an entire rainbow of Skittles up her nose—again.

Frankly, it seemed more distressing to Mary Ann than the kids. And there was nothing we could do from down here.

"No," he said miserably. "Mary Ann and the kids are just fine and dandy. Perfect."

"Right." Something was definitely going on with Rodger. "You want to talk about it?"

Rodger stood stone-faced and glum.

"Okay." When my buddy wasn't ready to talk, no amount of prodding could get him to have it out. I'd have to wait to figure out what was up with him.

I hitched up the waist of Galen's pants. "I'll see you tomorrow, okay?" Maybe he'd be ready to talk after a good night's sleep. "In the meantime . . ." I glanced over to Galen's tent, positively swamped with anticipation.

"Gods"—Rodger rolled his eyes—"bring back my jaded friend."

"She's on vacation."

"I can tell."

Yes, well, Rodger needed to snap out of it. "You should be glad to see me alive."

"I'm glad you're alive," he said, like a kid asked to recite math problems.

"Good," I said, tugging off his surgical cap and shoving it against his chest. "I'll see you tomorrow."

Galen rose as soon as I entered the tent. He wore fatigues and nothing else. "What happened?"

I sighed, burying my head against his chest, snuggling in as his arms wrapped around me. "Thaïs is in lockup."

"Good." His chest rumbled under my cheek.

"Mmm . . ." I wanted to forget Thaïs and Kosta and Rodger and everybody.

I let him hold me, indulging in the comfort, and—I'll admit it—taking a little rest.

It was like coming home after a long day. Only this time, I was sharing a tent with a devastatingly attractive demi-god who liked to feed me blueberries.

"Now where were we?" I asked, trailing my fingers down his side.

Galen chuckled, shaking me out of the catnap I'd begun to take. "You can't keep your eyes open," he said, as if that was the most amusing thing in the world.

"Can too," I said, trying to find his pant buttons with my eyes closed.

"Come on," he said, leading me to the bedroom.

"Well, if you insist." I wasn't going to argue locations with the man. And from what I recalled, his bed had been heavenly.

He pushed back the curtain to the back room.

Twinkling lights were strung across the ceiling, mimicking the night sky.

Those were new. "What'd you do?" I asked sinking down onto the softest mattress in the world.

"I took the time to turn them on."

"Ahh . . ." We had been in a bit of a rush.

As I picked out the Big Dipper in the starscape above, an uncomfortable thought tugged at me. "Kosta said the army is calling up soldiers out of recovery."

I wanted to hear him say it wouldn't be him.

The bed dipped as Galen eased down next to me. "That's always been their plan in case of emergency."

Wrong answer. "It's that bad," I said, unease settling over me.

"It's been getting worse for about a year now." He ran his fingers through my hair, sending little shivers down my spine. "We've mostly been able to even the score by going in and taking out vital positions before the big battles."

I rolled to my side and propped up on one elbow. "That's what you've been up to." I'd wondered what he did with the special forces.

"Yes. Me and my men," Galen lay opposite me, parallel yet

not touching. Not yet. "The situation is dicey. You've heard of the earthquakes and eruptions on Earth."

I had. It was getting worse. "What do you know?" I understood all about the army and the fact that I didn't have clearance. He didn't have to tell me and probably shouldn't. Still. "If we're going to try and stop this, I need to know."

He hesitated. "I am allowed discretion," he said slowly.

Ah, now this was getting interesting. "So you can tell me if you want."

He tensed. "For security purposes only," he said, as if testing out the thought.

I shifted my hips on the mattress. "And not because I can give you mind-numbing orgasms?"

He snorted. "Definitely not."

Galen touched the soft spot at the crook of my hip where his borrowed pants stopped and a slice of bare skin began. "The enemy has been steadily working its units north, toward the Mountain of Flames."

"I've heard of that," I said, inching closer to him. I'd never been north, but those who had said it was this massive hell vent with a mountain smack dab in the middle.

"Our side captured it shortly after the last peace."

"In 1593?"

His brow knit. "I'm not sure of the mortal year, but yes, I'd say that is accurate for our conversation." He brought his hand to rest on my hip. "As you know, hell vents can let loose demons and imps. They're also immense sources of energy for an army that has the knowledge and the resources to exploit the power. The Mountain of Flames is the only remaining entrance to the underworld. At least the only one that lets you leave after you've finished your business."

"So why haven't we done it?" I wasn't for unbalancing the armies, but if we needed a leg up, then maybe our gods needed to get on the horn to the gods of the underworld. There were at least a dozen: Osiris, Hades, Pluto, Erlik, Mantus, Yama—and that wasn't even counting the Mayan death gods. Wait. We had to be talking at least thirty.

The whole lot had refused to take sides in the war, but

that didn't mean the denizens of the underworld weren't above simple bribery.

"We tried to do it," Galen admitted, reluctantly. "My former commander was one of the ones who was present at the negotiations."

"Okay." We could work with this. "So what does he say?"

"He was killed more than three centuries ago. But what he said at the time was that the terms of the underworld gods were completely unacceptable."

"So the new gods couldn't make a deal."

Galen shook his head. "Many of them were tempted. Several pushed for it. But in the end, they declined." His hand tightened on my hip. "We've gone to great lengths to keep control of the Mountain of Flames ever since. If the old gods ever made it to that negotiating table, they would have no problem making the bargain."

Hell's bells. I didn't like the sound of that. "What did the rulers of the underworld want?" I felt my hands ball into fists. It was no accident that he hadn't mentioned it. He hadn't wanted to tell me. Which meant it was bad.

He swallowed. "They wanted the soul of every mortal in our army."

Oh my god. I shot up, hands over my mouth. "And our side had to debate?"

In a single motion Galen was next to me. I backed away.

"You know what some of the gods are like," he said. "They only think of themselves. This was an easy solution for them."

Oh. Sure. Real easy. "Who's going to run their army?" At least half the people in our camp were mortals—probably more. I couldn't imagine me, Rodger, Father McArio—tossed into hell for eternity without a second thought.

These gods were insane, vicious in their complete and utter apathy.

"Hey." Galen knelt in front of me. "Focus," he said, gripping me by the shoulders. "We didn't do it. But they will."

My heart hammered in my chest. "So every mortal on the other side is going to get swallowed up."

I had friends on the other side, colleagues. These were

people like me who had been drafted, taken, forced to give their lives for this war. The gods might not shoot us outright, but we were still casualties.

They hadn't chosen this any more than I had.

"Petra," he said, his gaze eerily steady. "I'm going to be honest with you."

Oh no. "What?" How much worse could it be?

Galen's blue eyes held sadness and fear. "I have my suspicions that if it came to the point where we were going to lose the Mountain of Flames—" He paused, clearly trying to find a way to say it.

I did it for him. "Our side will take out the mortals first."

The air whooshed out of me. I couldn't even comprehend it.

Galen held me steady. "If there's any way I can join the fight, I will," he said, shaking me with every word. "I'll fight to the death. I'll do everything I can to make sure you make it out of this."

I simply stared at him. Here I'd been fighting to keep my secret, to save my life, when I was really at risk of losing my soul.

I ran my hands over my arms, feeling goose bumps, trying to think.

Galen seemed almost relieved. "That's why I was pushing you so hard. That's why this prophecy is so important. It's all we have."

Heaven above, he was right. Now not only did I have to deal with suicide doctors and Shrouds, but our next move could mean the difference between life and eternal damnation for me and everyone I cared about.

But Galen wouldn't let up. "Prophecies come in threes. We've completed two. We only need one more."

I felt sick. "How can you know that?"

"I don't," he said with his trademark conviction. "Come here." He gathered me in his arms. "I just feel it. I do. You have to believe it, too."

"You know who you're talking to, right?" I asked, sinking into his embrace.

He held me close, his cheek against the top of my head. "There's skill in battle. The right amount of training, preparation, strategy. But after that, you have to listen to your gut. We'll approach this next prophecy with intelligence and ability. We also need to be open to what we can't see. In those spaces between, you find your edge. You find the truth."

I was shaking and I couldn't stop, even though his arms felt warm and safe. I nudged closer. "You and your damn demi-godness of truth."

He held me tighter, his chuckle ruffling my hair. "I'm so glad my divinity impresses you like that."

"Oh, stop it. You already got the girl."

He laid a kiss on the top of my head. "We will get through this."

I nodded against him, hoping he was right.

"The stakes haven't changed," he said. "You just know about them now."

I shuddered.

Galen eased around so I could see him. "Are you sorry I told you?" He was so sincere, so earnest.

"No." I needed to know.

He gave a small, reassuring smile. "We're still in this fight. Events are starting to come together—for the worst and for the good. We'll make it through."

I barked out a laugh. "I almost believe you."

"You should." He kissed me on the cheek. "Here," he said, helping me nestle my head down against his chest.

"Wait." I tried to sit up again.

He rested his hands on my shoulders. "Lean into me," he said, rubbing at my tight muscles, finding the places where I was most tense. "At this moment, we're safe. We're together. Let's take it for what it's worth."

I rested my head against his chest, still keyed up. I understood the soldier's mentality—how it was important to rest when you could. Still, I would have loved nothing more than to storm out of the tent and do something—anything.

The problem was, there was nothing to do yet.

His fingers dug into the tightness at the back of my neck and I felt myself begin to relax.

Galen was right. This moment was precious. I didn't want to waste it.

"Calm down," he said as his fingers traveled to the soft spot where my hair began.

Galen was both a warrior and a protector. He'd lived with this secret. He'd fought me as I'd tried to dismiss the danger. And now he was comforting me. His fingers worked through my hair as he gave me the most amazing scalp massage known to man.

He worked my aching head, easing the tension, finding that tight spot at the back of my neck and rubbing the stress and the ache and the pain away. He drew his fingers through my hair with light, gentle tugging motions until there was nothing to do but groan at the pleasure of it.

I felt completely and thoroughly safe as he eased me into sleep.

It was morning by the time I woke. I rolled onto my back and gazed up at the blue skyscape over his bed. The mattress was blissfully soft under me.

I almost felt guilty for having slept so well after what I'd learned. But Galen was right. The rest had made me stronger, more ready. I took stock of my body.

My headache was gone, my mind clear. I rolled over. I needed to talk to him, work out a plan.

The other side of the bed was empty.

Wait. I ran a hand over the sheets. It didn't look like he'd even slept next to me. Which meant . . .

I stared, stunned and horrified. Did he leave to go fight?

Was that what he meant when he said he'd protect me?

I scrambled out of bed. "Galen?"

Nothing.

"Galen, are you here?" I demanded, searching the kitchen, then the front room with its gurgling fountain. "Galen?" I even went back to the mud-bath room. He wasn't anywhere to be found.

Damn the man. He couldn't leave now. I needed him here. There was no way I could do this by myself—no way I wanted to.

The purple couch was empty. The tent flaps were tied closed. He wasn't here.

I swept the counters and tabletops. No note. No indication where he'd gone.

Galen wouldn't just leave . . . unless they'd taken him.

Right now, he could be on his way to defend the Mountain of Flames. And this time, he'd fight to the death. He said it himself.

But no. *Get ahold of yourself.*

He could still be here.

He had to be here.

"Galen!" I ripped open the flaps and stormed out of the tent.

chapter twenty-three

There was no sign of him outside. "Galen!" I called, drawing stares. Half the camp seemed to be walking past at that exact moment. What was this? Rush hour at the MASH 3063rd? I'd never seen so many people out at seven o'clock in the morning. Or maybe I'd just never noticed.

"Galen!" I shaded my eyes against the glare of the rising suns.

"Nice pants, Petra," a skinny mechanic called.

"Can it, Mitchell," I barked, scanning the growing crowd.

"At least she's getting some," a supply clerk called out to a chorus of snickers.

He wasn't among the now staring faces. Damn. My heart sank. Of all the stupid times for him to be leaving me, this had to be the worst.

I leaned back against a wooden tent support. "Demi-god or not, I'm going to kill you."

"What'd I do now?" Galen asked, walking up to me buck naked save for the towel draped around his waist. Water droplets clung to his upper body and his hair was slicked back.

The tension whooshed out of me. "You were taking a shower?"

He glanced at the crowd, puzzled yet amused. "What? You didn't think I needed it?"

"Everybody's watching," I said under my breath.

He gave me a very public kiss on the head. "That's what happens when you start yelling."

Just shoot me now. He was right. Our audience was growing.

My body tingled with embarrassment. Here I was, standing outside his tent in full morning-after mode, wearing his pants while he was in a towel.

All right. Fine. "Yes! I'm fucking him," I announced. "Are you happy?"

Half the camp burst into cheers.

"I have to go." No way was I heading back into the tent with Galen while the peanut gallery whooped and did hip gyrations like drunken hookers. Besides, I could stand a shower, too. And I had to take Thaïs's shift. Morning rounds started at eight o'clock. "Just promise me you won't go anywhere."

"I can't promise that," he said, his expression guarded, and my heart sank a little.

"At least promise you'll come tell me if you have to go."

He softened. "I'd never leave you without saying goodbye."

Somehow, that wasn't as comforting as I'd hoped.

One day at a time.

And so I left him.

I crossed the compound, nodding at a cascade of "About time" and "Keep up the good work."

"I'll do my best," I said as I made my way through the gawkers. "Now shoo." Amazing how nosy people could get when there was nothing else to do.

The suns beat down on my shoulders and made me squint. I also realized that I'd forgotten my shoes, not that I was going back for them now.

The rocks in the path dug into my feet. "Why aren't you people watching PNN?" Somebody had to keep track of what was going on.

A burly maintenance worker shrugged. "They have a panel of experts talking about what the oracles might be thinking as they wait for the signs."

"That sounds productive." I walked proudly and hoped my pants would stay up.

"Not the seventh time around."

Okay, I could appreciate that.

The entire walk of shame only took about five minutes. Our camp wasn't that big. But it felt like an hour.

My hutch had never looked so good.

I dropped in on Rodger as he sat reading a letter on his bed. Laundry hung from the ropes on the ceiling and I could swear I felt a drip on my head, but from the look on my roommate's face, I decided not to push it.

"News from home?" I asked, sitting down on my cot to brush the sharp little rocks and dirt from my feet. He'd been upset last night. I hoped he was ready to talk about it.

Rodger bent over the single-spaced, scrawled pages. "Everything's perfect."

I watched him for a moment, not wanting to let him get away with it, knowing he'd fight me if I pushed.

"Okay," I said, standing. If he needed more time, I could give him that. I found my flip-flops and a set of my own clothes, took my shower kit, and headed out.

I wished I'd also grabbed my sunglasses as I weaved through the tents toward the three-stall wooden shower hutch. As far as showers went, it ranked just above the ones I'd grown up with at Girl Scout camp. That's only because our showers didn't have any spiders. Limbo was too harsh for the little buggers. Chalk one up to living in a wasteland.

My clothes went on one hook, my kit came in with me. I turned on the lukewarm water and praised the heavens I was the only one in here. I liked quiet showers. They let me think.

Cracking open the generic new army shampoo, I gave my head a squirt and tried to make some sense out of a world gone insane.

I felt like I should do something, know something. We were less than a hundred miles south of the hell vent that could destroy every single mortal in this camp, and here I was washing my hair.

Galen was a rock. No wonder he'd wanted to influence the

prophecies, to stop this. He wasn't drunk on power, he was determined to save me and every other mortal in this camp. I didn't know how he could stand the secret for so long. I wanted to rush out and tell everyone I knew to run, hide, go topside. But of course that was impossible. There was no escape.

The only thing I had was the next prophecy. And I couldn't even watch the coverage until I finished Thaïs's shift.

Damn Thaïs.

The water went cold in under five minutes, like it always did. So I finished up my shower and put on fresh clothes.

There's nothing quite like being clean. With a heavy sigh, I combed my fingers through my hair. We'd get through this.

Somehow.

Rodger was still crabby when I made it back to our hutch. "Can you not bang the door so loud?"

He held the pink bottle of his mate's scent against his chest while he re-read the letter.

Enough was enough. "What is with you?" I asked, dumping my shower kit under my cot. "If Mary Ann is fine and the kids are fine, why do you look like you're going to break out a bottle of scotch?"

"I would, but I'm on shift in half an hour."

That wasn't what I'd meant.

He kicked out his feet, knocking over pictures on the table like dominoes. A plastic Leonard McCoy bobblehead fell and banged against Marius's footlocker.

"Ouch." Poor vampire. "Is he in there?"

"No," Rodger said grudgingly as he snatched up his things. "Marius has retreated to his lair."

Good for him. "Look, I don't need your attitude right now," I told Rodger. And certainly not while sharing a twelve-hour shift. "Either tell me what's chewing on your tail or go find someplace to brood yourself, because I can't help you when you're like this."

He glared at me. "It's Mary Ann, okay?" he said, shoving the scent bottle into his pocket. "Look at this," he lurched out of bed and thrust the letter at me.

Before I could read it, he took it back. "The pilot light went out on the hot-water heater on Monday," he said, mockingly.

Okay.

Rodger read from the letter. " 'I was afraid to light it myself, so I called Bob over.' "

Dread settled over me. This could be bad. "Who's Bob?"

"Our neighbor from next door," he said, as if Bob had the nerve to live there. His finger traced along the page as he read. " 'Bob knew exactly what to do and he relit the pilot light with no problem at all.' "

"Well, that was nice." I hoped.

Rodger threw his arms up in the air. "That's my pilot light."

"Technically, yes," I said, getting a little sick to my stomach. I didn't know how I was going to patch him together if Mary Ann moved on. I didn't think she'd do it, but if a soldier was down here long enough, with no hope of ever coming back, it happened more often than not.

His face reddened. "That's my wife and my responsibility. I always lit the pilot light when it went out. Now Bob has been over to fix the banister and clean out the dryer vent."

Ouch. "Maybe Bob was being nice?"

Rodger was having none of it. "She even invited Bob over for dinner the other night because he's in his seventies and doesn't get out much."

There you go. "See?" What a relief. "Bob's not a threat."

Rodger sat down on the bed. "She doesn't need me, Petra."

"Oh hey." He looked so sad. "Of course Mary Ann needs you."

"She's gotten used to life without me," he said, his voice empty. "She said so in this letter."

I didn't believe it for a second. "She couldn't have meant it that way."

He carefully folded the letter. "She probably didn't, but it's true. Mary Ann is happy without me."

I took a seat on Marius's footlocker. "Look, just because

she's not dwelling on how hard it is doesn't mean she doesn't miss you. If anything, I'd say she's trying to cheer you up."

Head down, he creased the letter over and over.

As much as we went through down here, it was easy to forget how hard it was for the people we left behind. "We're drowning in blood and guts and war. She doesn't want to burden you with what she's going through."

"She seems happy."

"I know. I did the same thing when the person I loved was called into this war."

He glanced up at me.

I didn't like to talk about it, but at that moment he needed to hear it. "I think I told you about Marc."

Rodger shrugged. "Maybe a little."

"I met him when I did my residency at Tulane. He helped me find my way around."

That got a snarf out of Rodger.

"It's true. I had a rough time starting out. I don't know if I would have made it through without him." Even now I could picture him and the names we made up for these two doctors who liked to give me trouble. "Marc was our head resident. We started dating. He did his fellowship at Tulane so we could be together. He used to bring me beignets on my breaks." I knew I'd told Rodger plenty about beignets.

"From Café Du Monde?" he asked.

"No. Frank's Fish Market. It sounds weird, but they're amazing. Anyhow, Marc and I would sit in the cafeteria, just being together, until I had to go back in." In my off time, he'd taken me to concerts and parties and restaurants, but those quiet times sitting in plastic cafeteria chairs were the times I treasured the most.

I sighed. "Then the old god army did a recruiting sweep of New Orleans. They took him," I said, once again feeling the pain of it. "We didn't even get to say good-bye."

"At least I had a day or two with Mary Ann and the kids," Rodger said grudgingly.

They gave that to spouses, not to people you intended to marry.

But we weren't here to talk about my issues. Marc was in the past. I folded my hands in front of me as I leaned forward. "My point is, I wrote him letters all the time. It was how I got through that year he was gone. But I never told him the bad stuff. I didn't get into how much I missed him or how hard the program was or how miserable I felt." Rodger glanced up at me. "I stayed happy because I knew he was going through hell." He was in a war zone, an expendable mortal MASH surgeon. I wouldn't have the last words he heard from me be sad or depressing or down. I'd be his strength.

For the first time, I saw hope. "So you did it for him."

I nodded, glad that Rodger at last understood. "Marc was killed about a year later during an evacuation. The unit had to bug out, but they had a patient who couldn't be moved. Marc had done an arterial reconstruction and it was too soon."

Rodger gave a small smile. "He was brave."

"I know." I didn't like to talk about it. I didn't want to now. "So do you understand why Mary Ann doesn't tell you the bad stuff?"

"Aside from the Skittles up the nose?"

I couldn't help but grin. "That's not bad and you know it."

"One is bound to hit baby Kate in the brain one of these days," he said, shrugging.

I let out a sigh. "You know what I mean."

"I do." He smiled. "Thanks."

All righty then. I went to go look for a hairbrush.

"Marc would be proud of you."

It cut me deep to hear someone else say his name. "I know," I said, digging through my dresser drawer. I'd put him to rest. Marc was my past. Galen could very well be my future.

"I like Galen," Rodger said. "He's good for you."

He was. "You know, Galen is the first guy I've been able to really see myself with since."

"So what's going on?" Rodger asked.

He was sitting back in his cot, the folded letter on his chest.

"I don't know," I said, brushing my hair.

Still, talking about Marc had freed something inside me.

It had let loose the kind of hope I hadn't felt in a long time. "I feel like I have a shot at this, whatever it is between Galen and me." If we could just make it past this next hurdle. I lowered the brush. "Let me ask you this, Rodger. Do you believe people are sent into your life?"

He nodded. "I do. Everything happens for a reason."

Strange. I'd never really believed that. Now I wanted it to be that way. I craved it on a fundamental level.

"You about ready?" Rodger asked.

"Sure," I said, slicking my damp hair back into a ponytail.

I couldn't shake the thought as Rodger and I made our way to start our shifts in recovery. Galen was here, with me, for reasons I was just beginning to understand. Together, we could have a real shot at peace—and something more.

It stayed with me as I made my rounds, this sense of peace, the idea that for the first time in a long time, I had a true partner.

Our shift was busy. Most beds were full, and thank heaven the new army hadn't yet seen fit to start taking injured back to the front. I prayed it would never happen.

I spent most of my time on a yeti claw infection to the spine and a bowel resection. Immortals healed wrong from time to time. I hated to go back in. It was surgery without anesthesia. Once was bad enough.

The first patient we'd saved while on special assignment was doing well. Sleeping. I replaced his chart and headed off to see the other in intensive care.

The ICU was located between the OR and the recovery unit. I pushed my way through the double doors to the semicircle of curtained patient rooms.

I could tell which one held my guy from the pair of cyclopes guarding the entrance.

"Dr. Petra Robichaud," I said, fishing for the ID on my white coat. I was glad I hadn't forgotten it this morning. ID seemed kind of redundant when I had my name sewed on my coat. And when everybody knew me. But orders were orders and I knew they were playing this one by the book.

They moved aside and I entered the room of Dagr, god of

hope and fertility and probably a few other things Kosta hadn't seen fit to mention.

He lay on his back, strapped to beeping heart monitors and an IV bag administering the anti-inflammatory drugs we gave for long-term exposure to parasitic entities. Injured, he would have experienced an acute reaction to the Shrouds. If the bodies of the gods overcompensated for the energy drain, it could put them into shock.

Dagr was pale, but his breathing looked good. Dang. He reminded me of a young Ricky Schroder. I took the chart from the end of his bed. His oxygen counts were still low, but that was to be expected.

"Hi, Doc," he murmured.

"How are you feeling?" I asked, moving to the side of the bed so he could see me better.

"Fine."

"You look good," I told him. And he did. Based on his chart, most soldiers with his kind of injury would be in recovery.

I had a feeling we'd be hiding him here until it was time to let him leave. Although I had to think that the double guard outside the kid's room was giving away the secret.

"I just want to fight," he said, clearly miserable. "They're afraid to let me do anything."

"Sounds like you showed them," I said. His wound could have easily been deadly if we hadn't reached him in time.

He watched me. "I told her I'd be a hero."

"Who's that?"

"My girlfriend."

"Ahh . . . now, that's something worth fighting for."

"Anybody can be a god," he sighed. "It's harder to be a hero."

"To be counted among the stars." And I wasn't kidding. The gods made their stars into stars. Look at Hercules. "That's a lofty goal."

He shifted in bed, facing me as best as he could. "Give me your honest opinion. As a girl. Would that impress you?"

"As a girl, yes. As a doctor"—I stood—"why don't you try and be a little more careful next time?"

He folded his hands over his chest. "You doctors are all alike."

"I wish," I said as I replaced his chart and headed out.

My shift was over and I had a hero of my own to see, for as long as I had him.

I glanced back at the cyclops guard as I left, feeling a tug of sympathy for the young god and his dreams of war and glory. It was immature in a way—and damn dangerous. But I could imagine how hard it would be to want to be a soldier, to be trained and given the uniform, only to be told that you couldn't actually go to war with your friends.

Shaking my head, I ducked outside. At least we had one more kid off the battlefield. He'd survive this war, even if the rest of us didn't.

The twin suns were setting with a rosy glow.

Attention all personnel. Attention. Shirley's voice crackled over the loudspeaker. *As you know, Colonel Kosta has forbidden us to make any official announcements about the prophecy. Therefore, I will not tell you that PNN says the oracles are coming out of the mountain right now.*

People began emerging from the tents and buildings around me.

I repeat. There is nothing to see—unless you want to go down to the mess tent.

I shared a glance with a nurse across the way. Holy heck. I began jogging with the crowd.

This was it. Our final assignment. I only hoped I could handle it.

chapter twenty-four

Galen stood outside the mess tent. "I saw you heading this way."

My heart gave a squeeze. How long had it been since someone had waited for me to get off work?

He treated me to a long hug and a lingering kiss that had me gripping the lapels of his fatigues and yanking him closer.

"Are you ready?" he asked.

"Heck yes." After that, I was ready for just about anything.

The mess tent was even more crowded than before. There was a line six people deep just to get inside, the buzz of voices reminding me of an overstuffed beehive.

Once we'd made it through the door, we jostled through the crowds lingering between the long tables.

There were all kinds of people parked on the tables as well. Others had pulled most of the metal folding chairs up to the front. Still more created a mass of bodies on the floor in front of the television. The serving area that had held snacks the last time was filled with people. Horace and some of the winged orderlies hovered along the sides.

Everybody who wasn't on shift was here. Well, except for Kosta. Excitement flowed through the mass of onlookers like an electric current.

"Turn it up!" hollered someone in the back.

A nurse jumped up and twisted the big round volume knob. Stone McKay's voice blared over the crowd. ". . . along with updates from the front . . ."

"Turn it down!" everyone yelled as he adjusted it lower.

The overly tanned newscaster was as cheerful as a game-show host. "Remember, you can follow the oracle excitement on our blog at www.pnn-network.com. We'll have the latest news and developments, live streaming video, and the *Ask an Oracle* quiz show where you can submit your questions to our own PNN soothsayers. It's all at PNN-Network.com."

I stopped in my tracks. "Quiz show?" Didn't they understand what was happening here?

Galen took my hand "Come on."

The crowd made way for him. I liked to think it was because he held an air of command, but I also saw how most of the women gave him a second look. And sometimes a third. I couldn't help but smile. Yes, this man was with me—and every single one of them knew it.

We found seats by Shirley near the front. People were passing king-sized bowls of popcorn.

A banner scrolled along the bottom of the television screen. BREAKING NEWS: TWELVE VAMPIRES DEAD AFTER FALLING ASLEEP AT OUTDOOR ORACLE WATCH PARTY.

"How'd you get off?" I asked, sliding in next to Shirley on the table.

"Kosta is pissed," she grinned, tying back her hair in a colorful bandanna. "He wanted me out of his sight."

"You don't seem too bothered by it," Galen commented, making himself comfortable on the other side of me.

Shirley shrugged. "You've got to push a man's buttons every once in a while." She grinned. "It used to be Kosta didn't notice me. Now he watches me. And he really reacted today."

"No kidding?" I'd never been good at intrigue or the games that went on between men and women. But, hey, I was all for having a plan. I hoped this one worked out for her. At least she'd gotten the night off.

"So you really think it's going to happen tonight?" I asked.

"When it comes to you, I'm easy," Galen murmured in my ear.

I rested a hand on Galen's thigh, pleased when he leaned even closer. "That's not what I meant." Although I'd be more than willing to go another few rounds with him. I was going to enjoy this man for as long as I could. "Are we sure anything is even happening?"

The PNN screen was now shared by three guest soothsayers. "Tell me," Stone's voice sounded as each guest was shown in his or her own little on-screen box. "What are the oracles doing inside the mountain right now?"

"They're drinking the energy," said a man in an orange turban. "It's spiritual."

"No," snapped a blond woman. "Inside the mountain is a riot of color and light."

"You're both wrong," a man in a plaid bow tie interrupted. "They will sleep until it is time to—"

The woman frowned. "How can you say they're sleeping when we hear them wailing?"

Plaid-bow-tie man snarled. "Back in 1232—"

But the woman was already talking over him. "We know from reports that they see colors and—"

"Can I talk? Can I talk?" demanded the man.

She raised her voice. "Colors and light and—"

"It's a peaceful, spiritual awakening," the turbaned man yelled.

"We know from history—" Plaid bow tie joined the fray.

Oy. This is why I'd avoided the Sunday-morning news shows back home. Glad to see some things never changed.

People at the front started throwing popcorn at the screen.

I braced a hand behind me as the din grew louder. "You know I started off as a journalism major."

"You never would have made it," Shirley said, eating popcorn.

"Thanks for that," I said, as she went back to talking to the woman next to her.

At least I'd still be topside.

Doing what, though? Blissfully going about my life, most likely. There was a certain freedom in ignorance.

Damn it all. I hated to think it, but given the choice I'd rather be down here. At least I was living with my eyes open. And maybe I could change things.

The screen broke over to Stone McKay, who wore a grave expression for the camera. "We're going to have to interrupt our discussion for some breaking news from the front."

Oh no.

Galen took my hand and I held on tight.

We were in this together.

A square-jawed reporter with perfect hair and three-hundred-dollar sunglasses grimaced as explosions sounded behind him. He stood in a state-of-the-art flak jacket, fresh out of the box, as soldiers wearing old army tan marched behind him. "Chip Dobson here in the ninth quadrant where the old army is advancing on the new army stronghold of Hades Gate, also known as the Mountain of Flames."

This was it. I felt my heart speed up.

Galen gave my hand a squeeze.

"The new army has held this territory for the last fifteen hundred and twenty-three years. They are firmly entrenched, but from what I'm seeing here, Stone, the new army is out-numbered by about two to one. This is the first time we've seen this large an imbalance in the armies."

He paused as screeching winged dragons flew overhead. "I tried to speak with representatives from the old army, but they've all refused the opportunity to speak on camera. I have been told by multiple sources on condition of anonymity that the old army plans to take the stronghold within the next twenty-four hours."

I about choked. "Twenty-four hours?"

Grim, Galen didn't take his eyes off the reporter. "Wait."

"Did they say how they plan to take the stronghold, Chip?" Stone asked, as if the old army had pulled out their strategy documents and offered to share.

Fuck. This was ridiculous. We had a day to fix this, Galen

was cut off from any classified information he could have gotten from his unit, and we were counting on PNN for the intelligence we needed to save countless souls.

The reporter held on to his earpiece. "We don't know details, but I can tell you that I've never seen a troop amassment like this. It's obvious that they have been planning this for some time and that the Mountain of Flames must be a key objective for them."

I barked out a laugh. Key in that it would get us all damned. Gods. I wanted to jump up, run, do something.

Galen planted a hand on my shoulder, steadying me. "Patience." I puzzled at the utter confidence in his voice. "We have to see how this unfolds."

"But—"

"We can't go running off until we have a firm objective."

We didn't have time for that. We didn't have time for anything. "You heard what they said. Twenty-four hours."

His jaw ticked. "I've pulled off the impossible in less time than that. I'm betting you have, too."

Nothing of this magnitude.

Stone McKay stared into the camera, as serious as the grave. "More on the front as soon as we have it."

A PNN news graphic spun up onto the screen. "Stay tuned to learn Five Things in Your Lair That Can Kill You. Why the prophecy could mean impending death. And a funny little story about a kitty caught in a tin can. That's up next—on PNN."

Wait. "What?" Now the prophecy could mean death? We were counting on this thing to save us.

It was probably just the newscasters overdramatizing everything.

I took a deep breath, then another, watching my mortal colleagues as they murmured to themselves. The fear in the room was palpable. No doubt they worried about their families back home, how the imbalance of the armies would impact the people they'd left behind. Little did they know, worse was coming.

"Popcorn?" Shirley asked, as a bowl made it over our way.

"I can't eat," I said, waving it off.

"See? Stress makes me eat," she said, taking an extra-big handful.

Me, too. Usually. Although nothing was ordinary about today.

I glanced at Galen, who seemed deep in thought. Damn, he was handsome. His stark cheekbones complemented by a strong jaw that worked as he thought. I sure hoped he was hatching a way to get us out of this.

Stone McKay was back. "And now: Five Things in Your Lair That Can Kill You. But first, let's check in with Bee-Bee Connor, who is standing by live at the Oracle of the Gods."

Perky BeeBee wore a fire-engine-red jacket over a leopard-print top and seemed thrilled to be hovering at the bottom of a sheer cliff face. Above her was a gaping hole in the rock that held the cave of the oracles.

She leaned forward, like she was telling the audience a big secret. "I'm BeeBee Connor reporting live from the Oracle of the Gods, where my sources tell me the soothsaying session has indeed concluded. The oracles are now drinking from the pond of wisdom before they emerge to tell us their findings."

"Thanks, BeeBee," Stone said. "Now, how long between the drinking from the pond and the announcement of the oracle?"

"It could be days," BeeBee responded, delighted.

My throat grew dry. We didn't have days. We had twenty-four hours.

BeeBee continued to lean forward, displaying copious amounts of cleavage. "The lava has really been boiling here at Mount Lemuria, which is another good sign that this prophecy will be a biggie."

My head pounded. "Then let's get on with it," I ground out. I wanted to scream.

"Now, aren't the armies afraid that a third prophecy so soon could force a cease-fire?" Stone asked.

Dirt and debris rained around BeeBee as the mountain

behind her shook. "It is true that we're well on our way to a forced peace. Some here think that's why the old army has moved so quickly to initiate major combat. If there's any peace to be had, they want to end up on top before it happens. It's up to the oracle now, though, Stone. We'll just have to wait and see."

My nerves tangled. Wait and see. While mortals suffered and died.

"I hate to interrupt you, BeeBee," Stone said, clearly relishing it, "but we have breaking news from the new army."

They panned to a live shot of a two-star general dressed in rusty red combat fatigues. He had a regal bearing and a steady gaze. The general moved to stand behind a podium, holding a sheaf of papers.

Galen leaned closer. "That's General Howzer."

"Do we like him?"

"He's a good soldier."

For the immortals. I could read between the lines. "So he might not have good news."

Cameras flashed as the general began his announcement. "The new army is announcing today that we have a secret weapon."

Confused murmurs erupted from the news corps.

The truth of it hit me. They were calling up the gods of the underworld, which meant the new army was about to sell our souls straight to hell.

Howzer glanced up. "The old army is fully aware of the capabilities of this weapon. And we will not hesitate to use this weapon if they do not draw down their assault on the Mountain of Flames."

Oh no. "We could have less than twenty-four hours."

Galen's grip tightened on my waist. "Have faith."

"Why?" I asked, sick and tired and, well—done with it. "Why should I trust anything these people do?"

He shook his head. "Not in them," he pressed, "in me. In us."

How could he even say that? I wasn't ready for this kind of a leap. "I'm a doctor, Galen. I need to see things." Or at least be able to prove them, to know them. This went against everything I thought I knew.

He tipped my chin to face him. "You will do this." He swore under his breath. "I believe it. Why can't you?"

Because I was a nobody. I wasn't the first in my class. I wasn't the smartest or the bravest. Sure, I believed in peace. But when was that ever enough?

I fisted my hands in my lap. "I want to make a difference, Galen. I do. But I just can't believe in it like you."

"Nobody has to have faith all the time. That's impossible." The sincerity in his words blew me away. "When the time is right, you'll understand what needs to happen."

I swallowed hard, overcome with the enormity of it. At the same time I knew I'd do everything I could to stop the tragedy that was about to happen. "Okay." I'd stand up for what was right. I knew that much about myself.

I would protect these people. I would make a difference.

I'd even die if I had to.

The armies of the gods would not sell me, my friends, my colleagues into hell.

The mess tent crowd grew louder and I focused back on the television to see the oracles emerging from the cave. Cheers erupted all around us as I stared at Galen.

This was it. I slapped a hand down on Galen's thigh. "They're coming out with a verdict."

He grinned like he was the one who'd done it. "We can do this."

We can do it. His words stayed with me.

"I'm BeeBee Connor, reporting live from the Oracle of the Gods. The oracles are about to announce the third prophecy." She pursed her lips, her green eyes sparkling.

Oh come on.

"My sources say they have indeed transcribed the oracle in blood onto the living rock of the cave behind me." She pointed, as if we didn't know where the blasted cave was. "And here comes Li-Hua."

I leaned closer, despite myself.

"She's the leader of the group." The camera panned in on

Li-Hua as she squatted at the edge of the cliff face wearing what appeared to be a bloodstained sack. Her straight black hair tangled around her face.

My fingers tightened on Galen's leg.

The oracle let out a guttural moan, her lips moving. I could feel my palms go clammy.

BeeBee Conner whizzed up to the oracle, microphone out. "Could you say that again?" she asked.

Galen pulled me closer.

Li-Hua gazed into the camera, her eyes sunken and ringed with dark shadows. "As armies rage," she rasped, "the life-saver will join bodies in love."

I about choked. *In love?*

He didn't love me. He didn't know all my faults yet. There was a lot to learn.

If my goal was to shag Galen, I could definitely do that. But *love*?

The oracle hissed out a breath. "And after, she will find new peace as he finds death."

My heart slammed in my chest. Oh hell no.

Galen gave no reaction. He simply sat rigid, like the soldier he was.

He couldn't even be considering . . .

"I'm not going to kill you!"

"Shhh . . ." Shirley elbowed me.

Galen shook his head, "Petra, I—"

"I'm not going to kill you," I hissed. I wouldn't. I couldn't. It was against everything I stood for. I didn't kill people, I saved people. And Galen wasn't just any person to me. I cared more for him than I had for anyone in a long time, and it was wrong and sick and disgusting to ask me to kill him.

He turned to me slowly. "I'm a soldier."

"I don't care." Fear trammeled through me. I was prepared to make the final sacrifice. I could die to save the people in this camp and countless other mortals. But I couldn't fathom killing Galen. He'd burst into my life and he changed it around and he actually made me *feel*. And now that I'd had that and had him, I wasn't about to let him go.

He gave me a gentle, tight-lipped smile. "I do what's right. I fight. I die so others don't have to."

"I'm not going to kill you." There had to be another way. But even as my mind scrambled to find one, I knew there was no hope.

It felt like a joke. A sick, sick joke.

He looked me straight in the eye. "It didn't say you were the one who had to kill me," he said, as if that made a difference.

I couldn't believe we were discussing this. "That's not the point."

Galen—damn the man—was as stubborn as a rock. "It's not up to us."

It had to be. My mind swam as I fought back rising panic. "Fuck." It didn't make sense. It was so unfair.

So wrong.

"Petra." With a groan, he hauled me close. His hands caressed my arms, my shoulders, my neck until he cupped my face. Then he lowered his mouth to mine.

He kissed me like a man on a mission, his fingers shoving upward into my hair, tangling in it as he commanded me even closer. He shook against me, his arms taut with tightly held emotion. It moved me that this man who had so much to give was so willing to give it all away.

I wrapped my arms around his neck, stroking it, doing my best to comfort him as I moved my fingers to the spiky hair at the back of his neck. He was vulnerable, even if he didn't want to admit it to me or the rest of the world, even if he was trying to protect us.

He kissed me long and deep. Tongues entwined, I gave back with everything I had. Because this time it was different. This wasn't the same as the passionate kisses and urgent touches we'd shared before. This time, he was beginning to say good-bye.

chapter twenty-five

It was too much. I had to get out of there. I broke the kiss and took one step back from Galen, then another.

Fear welled up inside me and I dashed for the exit, pushing through the mass of bodies. They were oblivious, talking a mile a minute, blocking the aisles with their animated chatter. I had to get out. I had to get away. I had to go somewhere, do something. Nothing made sense anymore.

"Hey, Petra." Rodger grabbed my arm not five feet from the door. I hadn't even seen him. I'd been too focused on the darkness outside. "What do you think?" Rodger beamed, and it took me a second to remember he was talking to me. "Isn't this fantastic? Do you know what this means?"

I stared at him. "No." I didn't know what any of it meant anymore.

Only that this prophecy was no cause for celebration. It was wrong and degrading and tragic. I didn't want to lose Galen that way.

How could I make love to him, knowing I was going to kill him?

But Rodger couldn't stop smiling. "Aw, come on." He clapped me on the arm. "I know PNN is a little crazy. But if this prophecy comes true, I get to see my kids again. I can go home."

"That's right," I managed to choke out. If I went through

this, soldiers like Rodger would get to be with their families again. It was the one thing he lived for down here, his only hope in the middle of this barren wasteland.

I didn't want to have to be responsible for the souls of thousands of innocent people. If I didn't stop this, I was banishing soldiers like Rodger to hell for all eternity.

He'd never see Mary Ann and the kids again—not even when they were all dead.

My eyes grew hot with tears. I couldn't do that to him. I couldn't do that to anyone.

There had to be a different way.

"Galen!" Rodger waved over the crowd.

"I gotta go," I said, ducking away.

"What'd I say?" Rodger called after me as I ran out into the night. I didn't want to see him, or Galen, or anyone else. I just wanted to run, leave, and never see this place again.

They'd check my hutch first, so I went the opposite way, past the motor pool and through the cemetery.

I was used to deciding between two bad options—which wounded soldier needed to be on the table first and which would wait for care. Whether to leave my family for good or try to explain I was part fairy.

Whether to save Galen or sacrifice him.

And so I ran. I kept running until I saw the red lantern burning outside Father McArio's hutch.

I stopped, out of breath. Hands on my hips, I turned to look at the path behind me. Shadowy hulks of machines littered the minefield.

Amazing. I'd made it through without tripping any of the booby traps.

I sniffed and wiped my nose and eyes on my sleeve.

God, why was I here? For all I knew, Father McArio was back in the mess tent. And if he wasn't, what would I even say to him?

A collar jingled, and pretty soon I had a hellhound jumping on my leg. He yipped, his red eyes glowing in the night. I hesitated for a split second, but after what I'd been through, hell, who was I to judge?

"Hey, Fitz," I said, reaching down to pet his velvety head. I melted a little when he tried to press his entire body against my hand. "Oh come here," I said, picking him up and just holding him for a moment. He wriggled like a piglet, but I didn't care. He was soft and warm, his fur stubbly against my cheek.

"I see you found Fitz," Father called, his lantern bobbing as he ambled down the path.

"More like he found me." I swallowed and shoved some of the hair out of my face. I was a mess.

Father saw, and his expression softened. "Come on inside."

Once we made it into the father's hutch, Fitz was eager to attack a table leg. I sat on a camp chair. Father hung his lantern and, calm as ever, took the chair across from me. He didn't press. He just waited.

I sniffled and wiped at the tearstains on my cheeks. Thousands of thoughts and emotions collided, but I couldn't get a handle on them. I couldn't force the words out. It left me feeling turned around, helpless.

It was too much to take. Impossible to explain.

Father placed a hand on my knee. "Start from the beginning."

The tears threatened again. It was almost as if speaking out loud would make it real.

I wanted out. I needed a do-over. Whatever I did to bring us to this point, I wanted to take back. Destroy it. Burn it. Scatter the ashes and hide.

But there was nowhere to run anymore. I was trapped, with this knowledge, this fear eating a hole inside of me.

I took a deep breath, gathering my courage. Before it slipped away, I said, "Galen told me about the Mountain of Flames," I swallowed, "how the new gods made a deal with the lords of the underworld."

I glanced up to find Father leaning forward, elbows on his knees, his hands clasped in front of him. "I'm not sure I understand what you mean."

My head pounded and my body ached. I closed my eyes

tight. I didn't want to tell him. I didn't want to be the one who changed this good man's view of the world forever. Father believed in something more for every single person in this camp, something better. And now I got to shatter his illusions, tear at that belief, hurt him while he tried to help me.

But there was no other way. He deserved to know the truth. He'd earned my candor. And maybe, just maybe, he'd help me figure a way out of this.

I explained to him about the underworld gods and their offer to back the army that delivered the souls of its mortal soldiers and staff. As I told it, I still couldn't imagine any creature—god or not—willingly brutalizing another for all eternity. Hate rose up in my belly.

They'd gladly send someone like Father McArio to hell.

His eyes widened as he grasped the enormity of it, the complete and utter wrongness. I laid it in his lap, watched him shrink into himself as the worry lines on his face deepened and his fingers instinctively found the silver cross he wore around his neck.

The old gods would damn us in a second. The new gods vowed to destroy us before the old gods could use us. They were playing chicken with our very souls. I wiped at my eyes. "The armies are attacking right now."

Father gasped and began to cough. I rose to help him, but he waved me away. "But the prophecy," he choked.

Acid crawled up the back of my throat. The prophecy. If I never heard that word again, it would be too soon.

How could he possibly understand?

Father watched me expectantly. Oh god. He actually had hope.

"Petra?"

The back of my throat tightened as I let out a sob. This was so impossible.

Say it. Just say it.

"'As armies rage, the lifesaver will join bodies in love. Afterward'"—I forced myself to finish—"'she will find new peace as he finds death.'"

Father leaned back. "I see."

No, he didn't. I didn't even understand. "How could I do that?" Be intimate with Galen, share everything with him, give him my body—and then kill him? Every fiber of my being said *no*.

"Galen is a good man," I protested. Surely Father understood that. "He's the reason I've gotten so far." He'd pushed me as I'd fought him. He'd let me rile against him. "He saved me from the Shrouds in the desert. I wouldn't be here, doing this, if it weren't for him and now I have to end him?"

And I couldn't say it out loud, but I knew. I knew in my heart that sleeping with him might not be enough.

Fuck it all. I had to open my own heart up. I had to love him and I couldn't do that. Not now.

Father folded his hands in his lap, his expression grave. "How does Galen feel about this, Petra?"

"That's what makes it worse. He's willing to die." Ready to sacrifice. And I could kill him and it wouldn't be enough.

I stared at the red lantern above Father's head until tears blurred it. He was so willing to give, but me? No. Maybe it was because I'd had so little for so long. I thought I'd learned to live without comfort, affection. Love.

But now I felt like a part of me was being ripped out whole. I'd never be the same again.

He'd die in glory and I'd be alone. Always alone.

I knew it was selfish and I knew it was wrong, but what about me? Bit by bit, he'd cracked open my defenses. He'd slipped past the barriers that had kept so many others out.

He came to me. He saw the real me. He'd wound his way into my heart, and now he was going to march off into the sunset. His death would kill me, too. There would be nothing left whole and good anymore.

I broke down, letting the tears come. I was tired of fighting. "I don't know what to do."

Father placed a comforting hand on my shoulder. "I'm sorry."

Me, too. I was sick as hell of people I loved being noble and dying. I knew I was supposed to applaud them, but the selfish, lonely, scared part of my being wanted to ask: What about me?

What about the person who gets left behind?

"I'm not strong enough for this." I'd survived through blood and guts and war, but I was at my limit. "I can't take it."

Father touched my shoulder. "It's the nature of sacrifice. To be willing to suffer for what you know is right. It applies to the one who leaves, and maybe even more to those left behind."

It wasn't fair.

I should know by now that nothing about war is fair.

Another horrible thought slammed into me, confusing and angry. "If I do this. If I go to Galen now, it would only be to make the prophecy come true. I'd be trying to influence it." We both knew the disaster that could come from a move like that.

"I don't know," he said, looking as lost as I felt. "I just don't know."

"At least you're honest."

He gave a small smile. "Have faith, Petra," he said with utter conviction.

"You realize who you're talking to." I didn't know how he did it, how he believed so much.

Father's eyes flicked to the ground, then back at me. "I'm sorry this had to happen," he said. "I had the highest hopes for you two."

I nodded, lips pressed together. "So did I."

I still didn't know what to think as I said my good-byes to Father McArio. Nothing was clear. My world would never be the same. It hurt more than I could have ever imagined.

Father lingered by the door. "I'd really rather you stayed here."

"No." I needed to go. I didn't want to talk anymore.

I didn't know what I wanted.

Father nodded. "Take this," he said, handing me one of the lanterns he'd made.

"Thanks." It was a whimsical piece, welded from scrap parts into the shape of a star.

Somehow it only made me feel more bleak and alone.

I held it out in front of me as I trudged down the path toward the minefield. A flame burned from the center, and tiny holes all around gave off their own flickering light.

Of course I knew not to get too attached to the beauty of the flame. By morning, it would be as dead and lifeless as the dirt under my feet.

Imps screeched and chattered out in the desert. Maybe one would eat me and put me out of my misery.

As I reached the turnoff for the minefield, a shadowy figure stepped out from among the twisted debris.

My heart skipped a beat when I realized who it was.

"Galen." I didn't know what else to say.

We each stood alone for a moment, cloaked by the night.

I was so scared to lose what we had. I knew without words that he felt the same. There was nothing as terrible as being torn from the one who made you whole, the one who made you feel.

He'd been alone for so long.

So had I.

"Petra." He closed the distance between us. "I didn't want to surprise you."

I leaned against him, enjoying the simple act of letting him hold me. "What were you doing in the dark?"

"Looking for you." He kissed me on the head.

I drew back, my fingers tracing the outline of his face. "I'm sorry."

For running, for struggling, for not being able to accept what he had to do.

For not being able to live up to my part.

He caught my wrist and held it. "You don't need to be sorry." He scanned the darkness behind me as hellhound barks echoed up the path. "I have something I need to tell you. Kill your lamp."

I didn't understand, but I did it. And when I'd blown out the light, he led me farther into the darkness.

"Wait," I said, "the camp is over here."

Galen glanced back toward the minefield. "Not that way."

"Why?" I didn't know what he was getting at.

"Come with me," he said, a note of urgency in his voice.

What could he possibly have to tell me that wasn't already clear?

He was going to stop this insane act of the gods. He was going to bring hope back to countless mortals who didn't even know they were about to lose everything.

He was going to die.

I walked with him. He deserved that at least.

He'd known about the Mountain of Flames before I'd ever met him. He'd carried the burden alone. Now I would at least try to share it with him.

We traveled the path until we came an outcropping of rocks. It took me a moment to realize where we were.

Stones rose from the base of the desert, washed black by the night. Some were large, with nooks and crannies big enough to be considered small caves. Others squatted like giant, bald eggs.

"So this is the rocks," I said.

Galen surveyed the area. "You told me about this place."

My heart skipped a beat. I wasn't ready. "I know what you're going to say," I told him—and what he wanted. I would have wanted it, too, under different circumstances, but not here. Not now.

"Listen." My stomach churned as my words failed. "I know you think this will make a difference, but it won't." Deep down, I was sure he understood that, too.

And while I wished I could make love to him one last time, doing it, taking that, without being able to give him the one thing he needed would tear me apart.

He stood, strong and accepting in the light of the low, luminous moon. A part of me broke when I saw he'd embraced his fate. He was willing to go it alone, willing to be abandoned again, to accept this final battle as he had all the countless ones before. "Then maybe this is good-bye. I've been called to the front," he said simply. "I leave tonight."

chapter twenty-six

He touched his forehead to mine. I closed my eyes. Hadn't I known this moment would come eventually? I wasn't ready. I'd never be. We stood for a moment, as the cool breeze from the desert whistled between the rocks.

His fingers glided up my neck to cup my jaw. "I promised I wouldn't leave without saying good-bye."

"Wait." I drew back. It was too soon. The starkness of it blindsided me. "Good-bye? That's it?"

He was truly willing to leave without anything else?

"That's all it can be," he said, looking as torn and wretched as I felt. "I can accept that." He caressed my cheek. "I'll always be grateful that I met you."

He glanced back at the path that led toward camp. "I've already risked too much by coming to find you." The muscles in his jaw tightened, and I saw the pain in his eyes. "They have an instantaneous transport official waiting. I leave immediately."

"No." Goose bumps skittered down my arms. "It's too soon." I knew I was going to lose him. I wasn't ready yet. I never would be.

He was going to leave and he was going to die.

And this was it.

I swallowed my fear and longing, afraid it would overwhelm me. "What about . . ." Now that he was here and we were alone, I found I had trouble saying it. "You know . . ."

It was a poor substitute for what I really felt. I'd gotten so good at blocking out emotion. Before I met Galen, I'd existed on humor and light companionship, enough to get by. I'd been starving, living on scraps.

There were no uncomfortable questions. No commitment. Rodger never pushed me. I'd never let anyone else close. Truth be told, no one had even tried. The world was content to pass me by.

But Galen had seen me. He'd roused me.

Galen had broken through. He'd drawn me out slowly, like a neglected animal he needed to tame. He played the waiting game, letting me come to him.

He'd challenged me, protected me. He'd stirred up the kind of hope and joy and soul-deep connection that I'd never let myself think was possible. It was too raw, too exposing.

It was too late.

I wanted this man in the most elemental way. I wanted to show him how much he meant to me. I wanted to have a moment with him, a true coming together, before I lost him completely.

He ran his fingers through my hair, and the raw desire in his eyes almost undid me.

"The prophecy claimed we would join together," I said, voice cracking.

"You're talking about sex," he said, his voice rough.

"Yes." The kind of raw wicked sex that had me screaming his name. In my mind, I could almost feel our naked bodies, sliding together, aching for each other.

"Maybe if we had more time," he said, regret coloring his words. He wasn't talking about sex anymore. We both knew it.

It seared me to the core to realize that I'd squandered my opportunity with this man, that I was about to let him go because I didn't know how to keep him. I was broken on a fundamental level. Damaged in a way that I couldn't repair. Now nothing I could do would ever fix it.

I stood there knowing that I'd regret this moment for the rest of my life.

"I can't lose you." I ran a hand to his chest, searching for something I couldn't even name. "Not yet." I wasn't ready. I'd never be.

"You can never lose me, Petra." He looked at me with such tenderness, it stole my breath away. "I love you." He cupped the back of my head and his mouth came down on me and I was lost. His kiss was raw, almost pleading. I answered, desperate for his touch, for him.

He loved me. Oh my God this man loved me.

I relished the way he held me, the way his thumbs stroked the edges of my cheeks.

No one had affected me the way Galen had. He was light. He was hope. I loved that I was the one who made him groan and press tighter. This demi-god, this immortal soldier wanted me. Loved me.

Kissing him was pure pleasure, and pain. I wanted to cling to it. To live in it. To treasure it and hold it for just an instant longer.

His hands traced my spine, sending ripples of torment down to my toes. He cupped my butt and my knees nearly buckled as he brought me flush with him. I could feel him, all of him, pressing into me. It was as if we couldn't be close enough.

I needed more. Now. I unbuttoned his flak jacket, finding body armor underneath. "Take it off."

He did. The Velcro ties hissed as he tore them open, then lifted the armor up and off. A black T-shirt clung to his arms and chest.

"The shirt, too, soldier."

"Petra—" He winced.

But I pressed on. "Give me this. At least give me this."

He did. As he lifted the shirt away, I could see his scars in the moonlight. They streaked his chest and shoulder with a brute kind of beauty. Galen was a man of action, a defender of his soldiers and of me.

I touched my fingers to his scars, lingering on the jagged

slice above his heart where the dagger had torn through skin and muscle. I remembered how overwhelmed I'd been when I'd held his soul in my hands, when I'd seen his true strength and beauty for the first time.

I'd saved his life that day, only to lose him now.

"Petra," he murmured, drawing me up for an aching kiss. I clutched his shoulders, needing to hold on to something, to anchor myself in the middle of the storm that was Galen.

He moved to my collarbone, raking his teeth along my skin, worshipping every inch of me.

His bittersweet tenderness decimated me. It was too pure, too perfect.

In my life, I'd never experienced anyone like him. This man who believed in the impossible and was willing to die for it.

A man who knew I could save him, but didn't demand it. He didn't even ask.

He ran his hands up my sides, cupping my breasts, his thumbs against my nipples. My breasts felt heavy and I heard myself whimper. It was too much. I couldn't think when he kissed me like that. I just felt. I savored this moment and this man. I burned it into my memory.

I didn't want this to end. It was too soon to say good-bye. It was as if he teased me with everything I wanted and could never have.

"I need to go," he said, his voice low and rough.

He looked at me with such utter desolation that I wanted to hide away. My chest tightened. I wanted to run, to protect myself and him.

But I didn't this time. I allowed myself to see him, to feel him, even as it tore me apart.

"Why?" I asked. Why now? Why not five minutes more? One minute more.

He was hurting. He was in pain. This sacrifice wasn't any easier for him than it was for me. It was impossible and horrible and it was coming sooner than either of us ever imagined.

"They're looking for me."

The blunt truth of it slammed into me. This soldier, this

commander had broken the rules for me. He'd lingered when he should have left. He'd come to me. He'd found me.

He'd kept his promise.

That's why we'd hidden my light, why he'd led me in the opposite direction of camp.

I knew I needed to let him go, but I couldn't. Not yet.

Tears welled in my eyes as I braced my hands against his bare chest. "Stay for just a few more minutes." I knew I was asking too much. I didn't care. I wanted to burn him into my memory. Relish the feel of him one last time.

Give back to him the only way I knew how.

Galen always did the right thing. He served. He sacrificed. Now it was my turn to appreciate him. To caress him, to feel him, to be with him in the most potent way a woman could be with a man.

Before he could pull away and deny himself this pleasure, I kissed him. I devoured him.

I poured everything I had into that fiercely exquisite kiss, afraid to stop, because stopping meant he was leaving.

He flinched and then moaned as I ran a hand down to touch him.

Everything about him made me long to hold him, possess him, be with him for this brief moment. His readiness, his command of himself, the stark knowledge that he was like no one I'd ever known.

He worshipped my mouth as I drew my fingers up to skim along the edge of his fatigues.

He kissed me with such sweet hunger as, one by one, I slipped the buttons free. Fingers trembling, I reached inside. He bucked as I found him and slowly drew him out. I touched him everywhere, ran my thumb around the slick tip of him.

He groaned as something broke free in him. Galen shoved me against the rock. He lifted away my tank top and gazed at me in wonder for a moment.

"God, you're beautiful," he said, as he bent to kiss the tip of one breast, then the other.

Before I knew it I was lost. He devoured me, his mouth

hot and eager. I threaded my fingers through his hair and writhed against him, the ecstasy of it pouring through me.

He stripped me bare and feasted on my body like a man starved. I wound my legs around him, kissing his shoulders, his neck, any part of him I could reach.

I needed him. I was empty without him.

I loved him.

He shuddered as I slid down the rock and brought my body flush against his. I stripped his fatigues away and lifted my mouth to his. Our tongues and bodies twined, skin on skin, desperate and needy, just as I'd always imagined it could be.

His breathing grew ragged. "Wait," he said between frantic kisses.

He was ready, poised at my core. I groaned with sweet torture as the very tip of him found me.

It didn't matter anymore. I was going to lose him. This man was too noble, too brave to go off to die without knowing how much he was loved.

Beads of sweat slicked between us. "I need you," I murmured. Just this once.

"I—" He swallowed.

I found his eyes, dark with desire. "I love you."

His mouth crashed down on mine and I lost all reason.

There were no words anymore, nothing else to say. I would hold him and I would love him—even if it meant his death, I would love him.

He would leave and he would die and he would break my heart. But he would leave knowing that he was my world.

I held him as he slipped inside me with wrenching ecstasy. "Petra." His breath feathered against my cheek.

He moved slowly, deliberately, each touch deepening my desire, my painful yearning for one more kiss, one more stroke, one more moment to show him how much I loved him.

The pleasure built and I moved with him, meeting him thrust for aching thrust. I reveled in the torment, the sheer joy of having him with me, loving me.

He slid his hands down my sides, cupping my behind and

driving himself harder. Claiming me. Completing me. Finding me.

Tears spilled down my cheeks. I wanted this. I wanted him. I clung to him, kissing his shoulders, his collarbone, his neck.

I felt every inch of him as he moved inside me, filling me up, declaring me his own.

He took me with an edge of desperation. His breathing rough, his kisses crushing and achingly sweet.

This was meant to be. This had to happen. It was inevitable that Galen would be mine. We fit each other perfectly.

His body wound tight. His breath came in sharp pants.

I felt him, whole and complete. I matched him, thrust for thrust, and the world narrowed down to our corner of the universe, our rock in the middle of a vast desert, to the sensation of our bodies joined together under the moonlight.

Gasping, we clung together as the pleasure built, swelling over until I broke apart, my orgasm rocking through me.

Galen was right behind. He gave a hoarse shout as he poured into me.

Eyes closed, we clung together as if we never had to let go. And once more, I felt the swell of the breeze, I heard the rhythm of our breathing, heavy and spent.

He touched his cheek to mine, and I felt the rough scrape of skin. "I love you, Petra."

My heart swelled. "I know."

The world might be crashing down around us but for this moment, we held each other safe.

We were cherished.

We were loved.

Deep inside, an aching part of me eased.

He closed his eyes. My heart wrenched as he slipped away. The cold breeze iced our sweat-slicked skin. Once again, I was empty and alone.

We dressed in silence. I relit the lantern. I already felt hollow without him, but I wouldn't push him anymore. We'd already given each other everything we had.

And so he took my hand, and together we walked back to camp.

chapter twenty-seven

Galen held Father McArio's lantern out in front of us as we wound our way through the minefield. The star cast a red flickering glow over the rocky path.

Hulking metal skeletons blocked the moonlight in many places, and I could hear scurrying from some of the banged-up heaps.

The wind picked up, whistling through the debris. It bit at my skin and I slowed, drawing nearer to Galen. "This is where we saw the giant scorpions," I said as we passed the mangled ruin that had been a jeep. It seemed like a long time ago. Everything had changed since then.

"I don't think you need to worry about them anymore." He drew an arm around me, taking away the chill as he scanned the darkness. "The gods are disturbingly practical," he added pointedly. "Now that the prophecies have come to be, there's no reason to kill you anymore."

I almost didn't care.

"It seems we've solved everything," I said, other than the fact that the man I love was going to die.

I hated the gods and their prophecies and the way they ruined lives without as much as a thought. Every single stinking one of them deserved a firsthand look at Hades.

We eased past the Hickey Horns bus. The old VW rattled with faint clicks and gloppy footsteps.

I didn't want to go back. I'd rather wander through a junkyard, as long as I was with him.

Put that on a Hallmark card.

I looked up at his profile in the moonlight. This would be my last time with Galen. I would always remember the feel of him next to me, his hand in mine.

As if he could read my thoughts, he stopped and stood over me. The lantern cast harsh shadows over his face. "It's out of our hands now."

He kissed me once, twice. I luxuriated in the feel of him, so warm against me. Losing him would be like cutting away a part of myself.

I only wanted one more day, one more hour. One more minute back at the rocks.

"It's time," he said, pulling away.

I nodded.

We pressed on, we kept moving. We sacrificed because it was who we were. And a part of me died when we reached the edge of the minefield and saw the lights from camp.

Galen stiffened, his body instantly at the ready.

"What?" I asked. Then I heard it, too, the faint ring of alarms.

My breath caught. "They've sounded the alert."

I began to run. The shrill clanging had gone off only once before and that was right before the bombing that killed Charlie. Kosta would only order a high alert in cases of immediate emergency or attack.

My heart beat wildly as we zigzagged through the cemetery, toward the skeletons of long-dead funeral pyres. It was the shortest route. The bells grew louder the closer we got. My colleagues scrambled over the camp like one of the gods had kicked over their anthill.

"Jeffe!" I called, tasting dirt as I half slid, half fell down the rise that separated the burning yard from camp. "What's going on?"

He bounded toward me. "Prisoner escape," he said, his mane flying out behind him, his tail sticking straight up. "Level one emergency!"

"What prisoner? I was having trouble hearing over the racket. "Thaïs?" *Please let it be Thaïs.* He was a fundamentalist nutball, but he wouldn't endanger the camp.

"No, no, no." Jeffe shook his head. "The patient. Dagr. God of hope and fertility."

Great. Our high-profile babysitting case. He must have been more dangerous than I realized. "How did it happen?"

Jeffe's eyes were wide. "Kosta sent his guards looking for you. They were only gone a minute, but the son of a god was fast."

Shock slapped against adrenaline, muddling my brain. "Kosta sent guards after me?" I wasn't even on call. Even if I was, it didn't make any sense. I was a mortal. Disposable. I could fall headlong into the tar swamp and nobody but my friends would notice.

Jeffe wrinkled his nose. "Not you." He pointed behind me. "You."

Galen. I turned and was shocked to see only darkness.

Jeffe snarled, baring his teeth. "I see you lurking in the shadows. You may be good at sneaking, but you cannot fool a guard sphinx. Well, maybe once. But not twice!"

Galen stepped out from the shadows of a spent funeral bier, his face hard. He wore a stillness about him, a distinct aura of danger.

Galen the man had already morphed into Galen the soldier.

He navigated the rise with a warrior's grace and approached the sphinx, his steps measured. "At least allow me turn myself in," he said.

Jeffe shook out his mane and pawed at the ground. "That I can do. But no more funny business."

Galen stood at my side, his body pressed against mine. "I told you I wouldn't leave you."

"Without saying good-bye," I finished, every word tearing at me.

He lowered his mouth for a bittersweet kiss. I savored it, and him.

"Ack. Please," Jeffe said. "I don't need a show." He nudged

our legs with his shoulder. "Now come with me. Kosta is having fits."

We walked hand in hand through camp, ready to face the firing squad.

MPs rushed past in squads of three, going hutch to hutch, searching for Dagr, the god who had most likely fled to the front.

Dagr had wanted war. He'd wanted glory. Frankly, I hoped he made it. Let him battle like ten gods, be a hero. Let him try to even the score for the rest of us.

But even I knew that was futile. There were just too many to fight.

A troop truck carrying a detail of red-robed imperial guards sped into camp just as we reached Colonel Kosta's office. They began piling out even as the brakes creaked to a stop.

I craned my neck to watch them fan out in groups of two. "They're going to tear this camp apart." I could see it in their eyes.

"I've heard stories about Dellingr," Galen said. "He has no sanity, no reason where his son is concerned."

"That's what I was afraid of." I gritted my teeth and followed Galen into Kosta's outer office.

Shirley sat at her desk with her head in her hands as two sprites clanged a series of thick bells in front of the PA system.

I touched her shoulder and she jumped a foot.

"Petra." She let out a whoosh of air. The poor woman was frazzled from her twin ponytails down to her combat boots. She pressed her mouth closed when she saw Galen with me. "Go on in."

I wasn't sure if she was only talking to Galen or if it included me, but I pushed into the office behind him anyway. I wanted to know where he was headed, and when.

The door closed behind us with a *whomp*, and the level of the incessant clanging grew fainter.

Kosta glared at us from behind his desk, his ears red. "It's about gods damn motherfucking time!" He slammed his hands against the metal and stood. "Do you know what you helped cause here? An incident, that's what." He strode around the desk until he stood eye-to-eye with Galen. "Dagr's daddy's gonna chew my hide and when he gets done with me, you're next."

Galen stood at attention. "I'm aware I didn't report as requested."

"Didn't report?" Kosta reared back. "Didn't report?" He leaned into Galen until their noses almost touched. "You're AWOL, soldier."

"He was with me," I said quickly. "Helping me."

Kosta leveled a glare in my direction. "Shut your fucking mouth."

He stepped back from Galen as if he couldn't bear to breathe the same air for one second longer. "You screwed up, Commander. And I just got your punishment straight from the top."

Kosta shot me a glance as he made his way over to his desk. It was as if he was daring me to try to stop this.

I knew better. Jumping in would only hurt Galen.

So I waited, stomach twisting, hands at my sides, helpless once more against the wrath of the gods.

Kosta snatched up a sheet of parchment from his desk. I knew that golden glow and the way the red script stood off from the page. It was directly from headquarters. He held the missive out in front of him. He glanced up and I almost caught a glint of sympathy. Or maybe I imagined it.

Kosta tightened his fingers on the page until it crackled and read in a clipped, rusty tone that brooked no argument.

Galen of Delphi
Rank: Lokhagos
Decorated unit commander and head of the Green Hawk Special Forces
Is to join his unit immediately at Grid N1738.5.

I couldn't help it. I had to ask. "Is that by the Mountain of Flames?"

Kosta gave me an almost pitying look. "Kid, that's inside it."

He looked almost weary as he returned to the dispatch.

As punishment for his vile act of disobedience, Galen of Delphi will be stripped of his immortal status.

He will lose all rights as a demi-god and be forced to live out the remainder of his life as a mortal.

I turned to Galen. He was visibly shaken. It was the first time I'd ever seen him knocked off his game.

Kosta did his best to ignore us as he cleared his throat.

Signed, Huitzilopochtli, god of war and the sun

Co-signed, Pele, goddess of fire, lightning, dance, volcanoes, and violence

"This is a death sentence," I protested.

"Yes," Galen said, his expression unreadable.

"Don't tell me you're accepting this." He'd served those gods for more than five hundred years, fighting for them, killing for them. He'd been viciously wounded time and time again, gone back without question—and this was how they treated him?

Kosta dropped the golden parchment on his desk. "None of us would choose this," he said, "but orders are orders."

"I broke the rules," Galen said, his jaw tightening with the emotion of it. "I was the perfect soldier for five hundred twenty-three years. And now I'm not." He tucked a lock of hair behind my ear. "And I don't regret one second of it."

My heart swelled with his admission, even as it threatened to break. "What they're doing to you is wrong."

He gave a small smile. "I can still fight."

As a mortal. At the mouth of Hades. Against an overwhelming immortal army.

Kosta opened the top drawer of his desk and pulled out a squat jar with a round gold lid. It was filled with some kind of blue liquid.

A shiver ran down my spine. "What is that?"

"My punishment," Galen responded, his voice tight.

"Heaven have mercy," I murmured as the bravest soldier I'd ever known stepped forward to accept the judgment of the gods.

Kosta placed the jar in Galen's hands and stepped back two paces.

Galen held it, his lips pursed together as if in prayer. Then he slowly raised it to the level of his heart and removed the stopper from the jar.

I forgot to breathe as a thin blue cloud of smoke wisped from the opening. The temperature of the room plunged. Goose bumps raced up my arms as the cloud unfurled around Galen, sending his collar ruffling, whispering through his hair, calling out to him with a thousand ghostly voices.

My heart ached for him as he held on, brave and still.

Bit by bit I saw silver flecks in the cloud, like dew caught in a spider's web. I realized with a start that it was his immortal essence. They drew it out of him until it hovered, suspended and naked in front of us.

We watched as it was sucked up by the bottle until Galen stood before us, mortal.

For a moment, no one moved.

"On the desk," Kosta said.

Galen placed the jar on the edge.

With a crackle, the jar caught fire. Heart pounding, I was ready to jump in, to put it out. But Kosta stood stoic, wiping the sweat from his brow. Galen waited in silence, letting it burn. And so I did, too.

I watched it grow into a bright blue flame.

The letter caught fire as well, burning gold.

Within minutes, they were both consumed, leaving nothing on Kosta's desk—not even ashes.

Kosta cleared his throat. "They know you've accepted your fate. You have to go now. The instant transport official waiting outside."

Galen nodded, and drew me in for a long embrace. I held on tight. I could still smell the musk from our lovemaking.

"Are you sure they really changed you?" I asked.

He held me close. "Yes," he said against my hair.

"Let's go. Now," Kosta said.

Together we walked outside to the waiting jeep.

Dawn was breaking as Kosta gave Galen a final salute. "It's been an honor to know you, Commander. Fight well."

He returned the salute. "I will, sir."

Galen turned to me. With regret and determination in his eyes, he kissed me on the forehead, the cheek, the chin. I reached up and gave him one last, long, aching kiss before he pulled away. "Good-bye." He gave me a small, faltering smile.

"Good-bye," I choked.

"I love you," I whispered.

As I watched him depart for the mouth of Hades.

chapter twenty-eight

I walked back to my hutch, empty and aching with the hopelessness of it. I'd done everything. I'd accepted fate. I'd braved the Shrouds. I'd given Galen my heart. I'd let him go.

Would it be enough?

I didn't know anymore.

How many times had I faced this in my career? The wrung-out knowledge that I'd done my best and it still wasn't enough? I'd given everything and still the armies marched.

Rodger leaned over his footlocker as I banged into our hutch. "What are you doing here?" I grumbled. He should be watching PNN with the rest of the masses.

Rodger gave me the kind of look people usually reserve for funerals. "I was just hanging out with Shirley, trying to get a message to my wife."

"I didn't see you."

"You walked right past." He closed the lid. "I figured you and Galen needed some privacy," he said, sitting down on my cot. "And that you might want some company now."

I joined him. "I don't know what to do."

He swallowed hard and nodded. "There's nothing more we can do."

That part hurt worst of all.

We sat for a moment, no words coming. I watched the tar bubbling up in the swamp beyond Rodger's window.

"What did you want to tell Mary Ann?" I asked. It was almost impossible to get any messages out, except by letter, and that could take weeks.

Rodger wiped at his eyes. "Topanga is on a fault line, or near one anyway. I told her to pack up the kids. Now. And take them to her sister's in Utah."

I rested my elbows on my knees. "Did she get the message?"

He stared blankly ahead. "I think so." He dropped his head. "I don't know."

The world had gone to hell and all we could do was stare at tar. "Do you want to go see what's happening on PNN?"

He caught my eye. "Do you?"

Now that he mentioned it, I wasn't sure.

"Rodger!" Holly, the charge nurse, pounded on the door. She opened it before we could bother to tell her to come in. "You've got to take these." She backed in through the door, holding a box of squeaking, wriggling swamp creatures.

"Rodger!" Had he been giving them out to the whole camp?

Rodger leapt up to take the box. "I told you to separate the boys from the girls."

"They're babies," Holly protested. "What are babies doing having babies?"

"I don't know," Rodger said, nudging an escapee back into the box.

"Which is why they need to go back into the swamp," I told him.

He shook his head. "I tried it. They climb back out. See for yourself."

The three of us went outside to the edge of the swamp. "Now watch," Rodger said, as if he were some kind of high school science teacher. He turned the box on its side and nudged at least twenty little scaly monsters back into the tar.

They'd barely gotten their feet wet before they glopped right back out, squeaking and trying to climb Rodger's legs. "They think I'm their mother."

I took in the situation, trying to comprehend. "How many

are there?" He'd had six, which had probably turned into sixty, and then Holly brought hers. Add that to the two I saw Horace carrying around . . .

"Don't we have bigger problems?" Rodger asked, in the shameless diversion of the year.

Unfortunately, he was right.

Rodger's footlocker was already packed with a throng of sea creatures, so I lent him mine. He set a water bowl down into it as I cleared out my clothes and snagged three pennies from the bottom. We didn't want the babies to choke.

"I suppose we can leave the lids open," Rodger mused as a handful of the relocated sea serpents immediately went to sit in their water bowl.

"As long as they stay in the hutch," I ordered, already knowing we were doomed.

Marius was going to have a fit when he came back from his lair.

Afterward, Rodger walked with me as we made our way to the mess tent. We hadn't talked about it or decided to go, we just knew we should. I didn't say as much, but I was glad to have my friend with me.

There were fewer people inside now that the oracle had been read. We ignored a pitiful-looking donut display and found spots on the floor near the front.

Stone McKay glared down from the screen. "The old god armies are advancing on the Mountain of Flames. The new gods have dug in, as they attempt to thwart the attack. Still, by all estimates, they are outgunned and outnumbered. The best they can hope to do is to delay the inevitable."

PNN cut to footage of a vast army, clad in tan. "When will the new army break out their doomsday weapon?"

They showed the most massive hell vent I'd ever seen. A volcano thrust from the top of it, spitting chunks of heated rock and debris. The steam cut through the desert air, and as the helicopter flew over and panned down, I saw nothing but blackness and lava.

"So that's Galen's objective." Rodger whistled under his breath.

All I could do was nod.

He'd never survive. Not as a mortal.

A giant *boom* sounded from the mountain, like one of those jaw-rattling Fourth of July fireworks I used to hate as a kid.

"Is it beginning?" Stone demanded. "Where did that explosion come from?"

The camera jerked and panned over the volcano, down the mountain. The old army had almost made it to the hell vent. The new army was dug in right in front. This was it.

I forgot to breathe as the old army attacked. The new army opened up in a volley of artillery fire. It tore into the lines of tan soldiers, but they kept coming. They surged, wave upon wave, like a living mass of death and destruction.

Old army cannons shot volley after volley onto the Mountain of Flame. The impacts sent showers of rock down into the hell vent and left superheated purple fires burning on the volcano.

The two fronts collided, cannons exploded, and the camera zoomed as warriors fought in hand-to-hand combat, to the death. The wounded were crushed under the advance of the old army.

"I can't believe they're showing this on TV," I said, horrified.

The ranks of the new army began to falter and break.

I wanted to look away, but couldn't. I owed it to Galen to witness this, to watch.

Purple fires raged on the mountain as the new army fell back. "Holy hell," Rodger whistled.

Shouts went up among the troops. "Wait." I clutched the edges of the table. The old army had stopped. "What are they going to do?"

Dragons zoomed overhead, and I half expected an aerial attack to wipe out our side in one deadly, fiery moment.

Rodger pounded me on the arm. "They're falling back."

"No, they're not," I barked. The old army had no reason to retreat. Except that they were backing away. "What the hell?"

A shout went up among the troops. A battle cry? But they didn't charge.

"What in Hades is going on?" I demanded, throat tight.

Rodger simply stared at the television.

They cut to a very confused Stone McKay. He held a parchment with raised red lettering. "We interrupt this, ahem, war to bring you a bulletin." He pulled out his reading glasses and consulted the parchment. "The old gods are calling an immediate cease-fire"—his voice rose in wonder—"in order to meet with the new gods over a more important matter."

"More important?" I choked. I wanted to fall over with disbelief and elation and fear and sheer exhaustion and about a hundred other emotions I couldn't begin to name.

A murmuring went up from the crowd around us. I'd almost forgotten they were there.

"What? I don't get it," Rodger said.

Neither did I. "Wait," I said.

We watched as Stone accepted a rolled parchment. He slipped a nervous finger under the seal and it broke apart with a hiss. "Another highly unusual development," he uttered, trying to fill dead air.

"The gods always could get a letter out," Rodger said, almost to himself.

After seeing the one they'd sent to Galen, I had to agree.

Stone's eyes flicked over the missive. "Cavillace, virgin goddess of fear, patron of the old god army has"—the newscaster's eyes grew wide—"joined with Dagr, god of hope and fertility. The resulting pregnancy scandal makes it imperative for the gods to call an immediate cease-fire to discuss this matter."

I grabbed Rodger. "We have peace?" Is that what they meant? It couldn't be what they meant. It couldn't be that easy.

"Wasn't Dagr your patient?" Rodger asked as photos of the two lovers went up on the screen.

Yes! There was the Ricky Schroder look-alike, along with a photo of a raven-haired goddess.

"He escaped," I said, trying to put it together myself as I spoke. "I thought he was going back to the front."

"Instead, he was off banging his girlfriend." Rodger grinned. "The virgin."

"Not anymore." I couldn't believe it. Sheer amazement and euphoria collided until my head swam with it. Who would have thought fear would get together with hope and bring peace?

"The gods are going to be pissed," Rodger said. Nobody screwed with the order of things.

"Let 'em," I said, grinning for the first time in I didn't know how long. We did it. We actually did it.

We had a cease-fire.

Stone's voice spoke over the video. "All forces are being pulled back, including members of the Green Hawk, Gold Scepter, and Red Dragon Special Forces teams called to the scene."

"That's Galen," I said, grabbing Rodger's arm way too tight.

"It looks that way," he said, letting me shake him up and down a little. I couldn't help it. It was just too much.

"You can see them coming down the mountain," the anchorman said, as an aerial shot showed a line of troops weaving down the volcano, staying clear of the impact zones.

Galen was alive. He had to be. Oh my god. I couldn't believe we'd done it. He'd made it. I wanted to cry with the sheer relief of it.

PNN showed the armies as they began to back down. The helicopter flew over the volcano once more and I found myself leaning forward, trying to peer inside. As if that would work.

I couldn't wait to see Galen again. To hug him and tell him how much I loved him. We did it. He'd survived. And even if I couldn't see him right away, even if he had to rejoin his unit, just to know he'd lived through this—it was more than I could have ever imagined.

The corners of my eyes crowded with tears. I was just wiping them away when the mountain exploded, sending a massive shock wave of purple fire searing down into the hell vent.

A reporter screamed. The armies braced against the impact. I sat in shock.

The Mountain of Flames broke apart. Fiery rock tumbled down into the hell vent, splashing down into the lava. Onlookers cried out in horror as the entire mountain crumbled and was consumed into the depths of Hades.

At that moment, I knew Galen was dead.

"I don't believe it," Stone announced. "One of the most feared hell vents is . . . gone."

Gone.

I sat as the crowd cheered around me.

I didn't have the emotion to move or to cry or to beat my fists and scream at the injustice of it all. Demand that they mourn for the soldier who gave his immortal life and soul so that they could carry on, alive and whole.

It was done. I'd chosen this.

It was the sacrifice I'd made, the deal Galen had accepted.

I just couldn't believe it was over.

chapter twenty-nine

Rodger stood next to me. "You don't know he's dead."

"Don't fuck with me," I said, sliding off the table. I'd seen his unit trailing down the mountain. I'd watched it crumble into hell. "I've got to get out of here," I said, fighting my way through the jubilant crowd.

"You don't know anything for sure," Rodger called, following me.

"How can you say that?" I demanded. It was cruel. "We just watched it happen."

I banged out of the mess tent. The suns were high, and the desert heat beat down. Nothing changed in the MASH 3063rd.

Fucking army.

"Look at what just happened," Rodger said as we left the crowds behind. "There's peace. There's hope again. It must have taken a miracle to make that happen." He jogged next to me.

"A miracle?" I choked out a laugh.

"Have some faith. He could have made it out."

"This had nothing to do with a miracle. And it wasn't about faith, either. It was about minute decisions. It was about the small things."

Rodger squinched his face in confusion. "Okay. Sure. Whatever you say."

We walked for a moment. I toyed with the idea of stopping in Galen's tent, but it was empty. Galen was gone.

"I can explain," I told him. I had to tell somebody. I desperately needed to understand it myself. "But you're sworn to secrecy on this."

Rodger shrugged. "Who would believe me?"

Good point.

"It was about the prophecies," I said. "The first one came true when I saved Galen's life and got that bronze dagger."

A healer whose hands can touch the dead will receive a bronze dagger.

Rodger's brows knit. "You can't see the dead."

My heart skipped. "Not literally," I lied. "But we've all seen war dead."

He nodded.

"You saw the dagger," I said, trudging a foot in front of him, purposely moving on from the topic.

He let it go. "Okay, what about the second one? *With the dagger, she will save lives and arrest the forces of the damned*?"

I dug my hands into my pockets, almost missing the feel of the god damn knife. "I saved Galen's life, so he was there to help stop the Shrouds and save Dagr's life."

Rodger caught up to me, eyes wide. "It's what made the second prophecy come true."

"And set up the third." It all fit. I could see it now.

Rodger glanced at the recovery tent as we passed. "So, the third one said, *the lifesaver will join bodies in love*." He rolled his eyes. "You've certainly done that enough."

His face fell as he recalled the second half: *After, she will find new peace as he finds death.* "Oh shit. I'm sorry, Petra."

Me, too.

"Galen found me before he left. Kosta raised the alert and Dagr escaped in the confusion."

"You're the reason the god got out?"

"If I hadn't delayed Galen long enough to—never mind." Rodger knew already. But if I hadn't made love to Galen, Dagr might not have escaped.

"And him shagging the virgin put a stop to all this."

"It did." Holy hell, if I hadn't fulfilled the second prophecy, Dagr would be dead. It wasn't about magic or mysticism. Well, maybe with the knife. But not with the rest.

It was about decisions, the details I took for granted that could change fate—that could change the world.

Rodger seemed to be thinking the same thing. He stopped in front of the OR. "Little pebbles start avalanches."

I didn't even know I was doing it. I couldn't have chosen how events unfolded. I really had gone on faith. It was both humbling and terrifying. What would have happened if I'd lost Galen, like I'd lost Spiros? What if the Shrouds had taken us that night? They'd come so close. What if I'd refused to follow Galen through the dark and insisted we return to camp right away?

"Hey," Rodger said, mistaking my quiet for grief. "I still say he could have made it."

"They took away his divinity. He went up the mountain as a mortal. No one can survive that."

"Heroes do it all the time. Maybe he's coming back."

"The prophecy said he'd die."

"But it never said when. He's mortal now. He could die at the ripe old age of eight hundred. Who knows? There's still hope, Petra. Have faith."

I felt the pain of it deep inside. I wanted to believe, but it was so hard. I had no proof.

Still, a glimmer of hope took hold. "If anyone could have made it off that mountain, it would be Galen," I said, feeling some of the weight of it ease.

Perhaps hope was more of a conscious choice than a feeling.

"He's a hell of a soldier. He can make it." Rodger clapped me on the shoulder. "Come on. Let's go home."

I dragged my feet. "It's full of swamp creatures."

"I thought you were trying to look at the bright side from now on," Rodger said, nudging me along.

"Okay. Fine. Maybe they taste like chicken."

Helicopter blades pounded overhead. I hoped it was VIPs instead of wounded.

As we walked, I tried to imagine what the recent battle had meant. It had destroyed one of the last major hell vents, and prevented the damnation of countless mortal souls. We had peace for the first time in centuries. I had hope.

And for a brief time, I'd had Galen.

If he'd made it, if he did survive, he'd be sent back to his unit. I'd never see him again.

Yet even if I was alone for the rest of my life, I knew I'd stood up for him. I'd let him know I loved him.

"Um, Petra, about going home . . . ," Rodger began.

I about fell over when I saw where he was pointing.

"Rodger!" I gasped as I stared at our hutch, not quite believing my eyes.

A chorus of sea creatures chirped inside. They covered the floor, the cots, the stove. They pushed at the sides of the tent, straining the canvas walls and window netting.

"Look at this," I demanded as a fat one by the window popped out one, two, three, squirming, slimy little dinosaurs.

Rodger cooed. "It's the miracle of birth!"

"On my cot." Another one slithered out as we spoke.

"It's not on your cot," Rodger said, a bit too academically for my taste. "They're on top of the other swamp creatures."

"What are we going to do?" I wasn't about to go in there.

"Roll down the light-blocking shades," Rodger said, reaching for the drawstrings on the outside of the hutch.

"Oh yes. Hide them. That's a great strategy."

"Just until we know where to put them."

"How about back in the swamp?" Where they should have stayed.

"You know that won't work," Rodger admonished.

I was going to kill him. This time, I was really going to kill him.

"Okay, what now, Sherlock?" I asked, once we'd pulled all the shades. And locked them down. Marius needed the locks, and, well, we did, too.

It sure didn't cover the squawking.

Which was getting louder with every birth. They were multiplying like maniacal rabbits.

"What are we going to do?" Rodger ran his hands through his hair, making it stand up on the ends. "I was just trying to give them a good home," he added, walking in a circle, "better than the swamp."

"Okay, Rodger." The pit closest to our hutch was huge—the size of an Olympic swimming pool. "Maybe we could put your creatures in there and build a fence." It sounded ridiculous even to me. Besides, I knew it was too late for that. The buggers could climb. I'd seen them scaling our walls as I brought down the shades. Rodger had taken them out of their habitat and messed with their mating drive.

Rodger dug his hands in his pockets and cast a guilty look at our place. "I wonder how long until they break out of the tent."

"Petra?" Galen called.

My heart leapt. Was that really his voice? My breath hitched as time itself seemed to slow down. I held on to the moment as hope swelled inside. I wanted to believe. I needed it with every cell in my body.

I turned and caught sight of him.

"Galen!" I couldn't believe it. Could scarcely comprehend it. We met halfway around my tent. He was whole and uninjured and, "You're alive." I wanted to laugh and cry and scream and ended up doing all three as I hit him with the bear hug of the century.

"Hello to you, too," he said, hugging me fiercely.

"You're back!" He'd survived. I wanted to shout it to the heavens.

"The front was brutal, but as soon as the cease-fire orders came down, it forced Pluto to shut down the immortal gate."

"I can't believe you're here," I said, inspecting him. His face was painted with camouflage and he wore a dagger, a rope, and a fully loaded weapons belt.

He shook his head, the corner of his mouth tipped up.

"No one was allowed to die in the battle for fear that casualty numbers would influence the discussion of what to do with the star-crossed lovebirds up there." He captured me and pulled me close. "The lords of the underworld were forced to heal everyone. Pele was a little pissed, but my men are safe. We're all safe."

Tears clouded my eyes. "Thank god."

"Thank Dagr," he said, bending to kiss me on my cheek, my jaw. He brushed a heart-stopping kiss over my lips. "With the cease-fire, they've released us all back to our previous assignments."

"You mean?" I could hardly believe it.

"See what happens when you have a little faith?"

"You just love being right," I said, laughter bubbling from me. But I knew. I understood, even if I couldn't quite put it into words.

We were rewarded. We were whole. I couldn't believe I actually had him back.

Except . . . I wiped at my eyes. "I'm so sorry about what happened to you," I said, running my hands down his arms, his chest, so amazed to have him back, unharmed, that I had to keep checking.

He was mortal now, in a god's army.

"I'm not sorry," Galen said. "It was worth it. We did it."

Damn the man. The way he looked at me made me want to celebrate. Large.

I gave into it and nudged him with my hip. "Want to go mark the occasion?"

His eyes darkened with desire. "Hoo-rah."

"Don't mind me," Rodger said, strolling up to us. He clapped Galen on the arm. "Welcome back, Commander."

Galen's hands slid down to my butt. "Thanks for watching out for this one, Rodger."

Rodger snorted. "You and I both know it's the other way around."

I was still thinking up a witty reply—and in my defense it was hard to think with Galen's hands on my ass—when a jeep rolled up in front of our hutch. I leaned sideways to get a better look. Nobody ever drove around camp, at least not down to the living quarters.

In fact, a small crowd had gathered for that reason. Even more people were poking their heads out of hutches.

Kosta jumped out, with a rolled parchment in hand. He didn't see us by the swamp. Instead he headed straight for the hutch and banged on our door. "Galen of Delphi in there?"

Pistaches. He was going to—"Wait!" I hollered as Kosta opened our hutch.

A flood of sea serpents swept out, lifting Kosta right off his feet. He went down under hundreds of little squeaking dinosaurs. They rolled end over end, quickly righting themselves.

Dinosaurs toddled all over the area in front of our hutch and Kosta sat among them, momentarily speechless.

A great cheer went up from the crowd.

Horace swooped in next to me. "You did it," he said, banging me in the arm with his fist. "You got Kosta!"

I looked at Rodger, who was just as surprised as me.

Rodger let out a whoop. "We did it! We got Kosta!"

I couldn't believe it. For all the planning and work and pranks we'd tried, it came down to a bunch of horny swamp monsters.

We could split three weeks off. We'd be free! I could go back to New Orleans. Rodger could see his wife again, his pups. He'd be the one to fix his own pilot light, to mow his own lawn, to be a part of his family.

He'd be home.

I looked up at Galen and it hit me. I was already home.

"You know what?" I nudged Rodger on the arm. "It's you. You got Kosta. You take the entire pot."

He'd earned it. He deserved it.

Galen and I had everything we needed right here.

Tears filled Rodger's eyes. "Thanks, buddy."

I grinned at him. "Just don't go making any more pups."

"Are you kidding? I'm going to do my best and then some."

The colonel stood, shaking off creatures and trying his

damdest to appear annoyed. "I trust that you'll get these creatures back to the swamp."

"Yes," I lied. I wasn't going to push it when Kosta had dinosaur afterbirth on his forehead.

We'd figure out something.

The colonel strolled up to us, parchment in hand. "This is for you," he said, handing it to Galen.

Galen stood at attention as he accepted it. Then, with a glance at me, he cracked open the seal and the letter unfolded.

"What is it?" I strained to see. Maybe the gods changed their minds about his demi-god status.

"It's a commendation," he said, reading, "for saving Dagr."

"But you're still mortal," I said, taking in the flowery praise of the gods, trying not to let the disappointment seep into my voice.

"Thank you, Colonel Kosta," he said, re-rolling the letter.

The colonel stood his ground in front of us. "You never know what can happen, Commander. Bravery is rewarded in this army."

I'd had enough heroics to last me for the rest of the war. "Let's hope we don't have to find out." We'd succeeded in stopping the war for at least a while. We'd saved lives. We'd made a difference.

Maybe now I could get to work on that anesthetic for immortals. I could probably talk Jeffe out of taking a break from his Trivial Pursuit contest to give me some samples from his claws.

"Okay then." Kosta gave one last withering look to our hutch, which had taken on a definite lean to the left. "I want you to clean this up before you submit your leave paperwork," he said to Rodger.

"Yes, sir," my roommate said with glee.

I couldn't help but smile.

"And you." He pointed to Galen. "HQ paperwork is a mess. You're still here indefinitely."

I loved the army.

"Too bad Rodger won't be around to see the car," Galen said, watching Kosta strut away.

"What car?" Kosta would never let us touch his car. We'd tried.

"Didn't you hear?" Galen asked. "Nurse Hume won a silver Camaro."

My mouth dropped open. "Not the Dr Pepper sweepstakes."

"What?" Galen asked, too amused for his own good. "You doubted?"

I shook my head. "Never again."

"Come on," Galen said, reaching down for a dinosaur. "I'll help you get this sorted out."

"And after that," I said, walking my fingers up his arm.

He flashed a wolfish smile. "Well, I do expect to be rewarded."

I nudged my hip against his leg. "Pushy, aren't you?"

"Always." He wrapped his free arm around me and nipped my ear.

Oh, this was going to be fun. "Lucky for you I find that endearing."

"I promise it will be worth your while," he whispered against my ear.

"All right, soldier. You're on."

Read on for an excerpt from the next book by
Angie Fox

IMMORTALLY TAKEN

Coming soon from St. Martin's Paperbacks

Medusa, serpent-goddess, executioner of men, scourge of Kisthene's plain, stabbed a clawed finger in my direction. "Tell me the truth, human," she hissed. "No more lies."

I straightened my spine and fought the urge to rub my temples in a most unprofessional way.

Why did the gods have to be so dramatic?

Medusa coiled on the examination table in front of me, wearing a light blue, open-backed gown. She stared at me, her eyes glowing red as her clawed hands shredded the white sanitary paper.

"I am outcast," she said in a gravelly voice. Her rattlesnake's tail swished, nearly taking out my freestanding EKG unit. "I am the damned," she declared, face twisted with fury. I held on to my clipboard as the examination tent vibrated with her power. "I am the destroyer!"

I nodded. Some patients took longer than others to adjust, but it didn't change the fact. "You're also pregnant."

"Impossible," she spat, even though we both knew that wasn't true.

I made a few notes in my chart while she threw her head back and let out a screech that shook the tent.

Ouch. I tried not to wince.

In my professional opinion, screaming often did help.

"Doctor," she hissed, smoke curling from her nose. For a moment, she was unable to form the question. Her perfectly sculpted brows knit as she brushed a hand through the wild mane of snakes on her head. "How?"

I gave her my most reassuring smile. "The old-fashioned way, I assume."

She should know. The gorgon was nearly three thousand years old. And from what I'd seen of the ancient Greeks, they certainly knew how to party.

She drew her hands slowly, almost reverently, down her green-scaled torso to the perfectly flat stomach under her examination gown. "I'm cursed," she hissed, "I'm barren. My body is poison!"

"Don't be so hard on yourself." Sure, my fingers went a bit numb when I was checking her blood pressure, but all in all, she was far less dangerous than the ancient Norse dragon in need of an enema this morning.

That had taken two doctors, three orderlies, a set of ambulance drivers, and Jeffe the guard sphinx. Although to be frank, all Jeffe did was warn us not to set the motor pool on fire.

I whipped out form 3871-K, which was actually a little slide wheel designed to help me calculate the gorgon pregnancy cycle. "I'd estimate you're fifty-three days along, which is seven weeks and three days pregnant. Your gestation time is slightly shorter than the average human, longer than the average goddess." I slipped the chart back into the pocket of my white coat. "Still, I don't think we need to see you again until the end of your first trimester."

I opened a drawer in the medical cart next to the examination table where we kept basics, including samples of prenatal vitamins. "Because you're over thirty-five years old," I said, handing her a pack, "we'll want to do an ultrasound at your next appointment, along with a few other routine tests."

The pale skin on her neck and arms flushed as she took it all in. She growled low, "My parents are going to kill me."

Well, I couldn't offer her any advice on ancient marine

deities. Besides, the grin tickling at the sides of her mouth
told me more than I needed to know. Once she recovered
from the surprise, she'd be tickled pink. Or at least a light
green.

"It's just that," her gaze wandered as she nibbled on a
talon, "I haven't talked to my mother since I turned her lover
to stone."

"About that," I said, setting her chart on top of the medical
cart. "You're going to want to try to control your temper.
Stress isn't good for the baby."

Medusa snarled at me, then caught herself. "I'll try," she
muttered.

"Do," I told her.

Ever since the cease-fire in the war of the gods, we'd converted our MASH unit into one of the premier (and only)
supernatural clinics in the area. That was saying something,
considering we were located in limbo, just north of a major
hell vent.

We were known for taking in all patients, regardless of
their origins or ability to pay. Which was the way it should
be. It was also the reason why we got the interesting cases.

"Go ahead and get dressed. I'll see you in five weeks," I
told the gorgon. "The nurse out front will set your appointment."

I ducked out of the examination room and handed the
chart to our charge nurse, Holly, who was one of the only full
humans in our unit.

She tilted her head, flipping her blond ponytail to one side.
She'd gone from red streaks in her hair to pink. I liked it. It
softened her up.

"Rough one, Dr. Robichaud?" she asked.

"Nah, everything's going to be fine," I replied. "Even so,
you'll want to keep your eyes averted when our patient comes
out," I warned her. Just in case.

Flesh-to-stone injuries were painful and time-consuming
to treat. We needed Holly on her feet.

I followed her to the front, where she had her desk.

We'd converted the surgery recovery tent into a makeshift clinic, with curtained rooms running the length of it—eight on each side. At the front sat the nurses' station, which was basically a red metal desk with a portable file cabinet behind it.

"It's quiet around here," Holly said, slipping behind the desk and starting a new file for Medusa.

"I like quiet. Quiet is good."

Peace had broken out exactly three weeks, one day, and six hours ago. It was an uneasy truce. We all knew it wouldn't last. Still, at the MASH 3063rd, we were going to take what we could get.

The younger gods had revolted against the older gods right around the time Troy had fallen. Before this month, neither side had even called for so much as a cease-fire in the last seven hundred years.

A lot of them didn't want peace now, but my hot Greek boyfriend and I had fulfilled a prophecy and screwed them over on it.

Hah.

Holly had refilled her M&M jar, the foul temptress. I stole a handful.

The prophecies came in sets of three and shockingly enough, they were about a healer who could see the dead. Me. They gave nebulous warnings about disasters and opportunities, sending me scrambling as fate came crashing down. If I passed the test, we were spared. For a while. If I failed, well, let's just say it hadn't happened. Yet.

To make things worse, my involvement had to be kept secret from everyone, including my closest friends and colleagues. The gods had outlawed my particular gift. Exposing myself would mean a slow, painful death. If I was lucky. More likely, I would be tortured eternally by something creative and mythical, like being tied to a rock while a python devoured my small intestine or set on fire upside down while spiders nested under my toenails.

Still, I was glad I'd taken the latest risk and bought us a little peace. At the moment, patients were living instead of dying.

If they survived their injuries, immortals healed fast. The last of our soldiers in recovery had gone home a week after the cease-fire began.

So we'd adapted. We'd changed. Now we were treating real problems, instead of endless battle injuries. We were making these creatures' lives better. As far as I was concerned, that was the way things were supposed to work.

Of course there was no telling when the gods would start up again, or who would fire first. I leaned against the edge of the desk, finishing off my M&M's.

Holly eyed me, as if she knew what I was thinking. "The colonel has us stocking up on everything."

"Good." We'd kept our heads on our shoulders this long by being prepared, fast, and more than a little lucky.

Unfortunately, luck can only get you so far.

Once Medusa had made her way out, with her vitamins and all of her questions answered, I signed out of the clinic. Technically, I'd been coming off duty when I'd grabbed her chart. Still, it seemed like the gorgon had needed a friendly female ear. Or at the very least, someone who wasn't squeamish around snakes.

I banged out the door and into the heart of the MASH 3063rd. I'd gotten into medicine to make a difference, to treat the creatures that others couldn't—or wouldn't.

Then representatives from the new god army had showed up at my door. I'd been drafted, forced to leave my practice in New Orleans, for this.

It was hard to believe sometimes that it had been only seven years ago. Most days, it seemed like a lifetime.

The suns were setting low over the limbo landscape, throwing off brilliant oranges and purples. A wide desert stretched beyond the tents of our MASH unit.

Underfoot, and as far as the eye could see, the bare, red landscape was littered with rock.

It was how I'd pictured Mars as a kid.

The entire place was flat, save for the cemetery. We had a hard time digging into the limbo rock, so it was more efficient to make a dirt hill for the bodies.

"Hold up!" I heard from two buildings down. Shirley was stubbing out a cigarette in front of Colonel Kosta's office. She worked as the company clerk, and the commander's private secretary. "Have you heard?" she asked, red hair sticking every which way out of her bun as she jogged toward me.

"What? That the USO is sending us a Sycion lyre quartet?" I'd heard. "I wish the gods would appoint somebody new to the entertainment committee." I'd settle for anybody whose idea of a good time went beyond lutes, fire-eating, and ancient plays. My life was already a Greek tragedy.

"No." She stopped in front of me, her eyes swimming with sympathy. "Galen just got called back."

Cold apprehension seized me. Hell and damnation. I knew this was coming someday, but that didn't stop my stomach from turning to lead. Galen of Delphi was the commander of the Green Hawk Special Forces team and, well, let's just say we'd been enjoying the break in the fighting a little more than most. He was on leave from his unit, due to a paperwork mistake that I'd hoped it would take the Army a long, long time to rectify.

My throat felt tight. "Where is he?"

She glanced toward the shadows past the cemetery. "I think he went out to Father McArio's."

Our unit chaplain. "Okay, thanks." I headed straight across the common area. Father lived past the graveyard and through the junk depot, in a little hutch on the very outskirts of camp. He claimed to enjoy the solitude. I suspected he was secretly ministering to the lost souls of limbo.

I scrambled up the rise toward the cemetery, almost thankful for the energy burn. My mind was racing. It was too soon to lose Galen. We'd barely dated. I didn't know where this was going.

Wooden grave markers of all shapes and sizes stood at

attention. These were the doctors and the nurses, the mechanics and the clerks. People like me, who would never make it out of limbo. Not unless the war ended for good.

"Petra," Galen called, emerging from behind a tangle of burned-out Jeeps. He strode toward me and I took off in a run.

He wore black combat fatigues with a Ken rune etched in red on his left shoulder. It was the symbol of flame, sex, action and heroism, and the man had all four in spades.

"I just heard," I said, dodging graves, rushing into his arms. He held me tight and squeezed. God, I was going to miss him. I closed my eyes. "When do you leave?"

"In an hour."

My eyes flew open. "What?"

That was ridiculous. He had to pack, prepare. We had to say good-bye.

He stood in front of me, all brute force and power. He was built for combat, but he couldn't fight this. "You know the army."

Did I ever. I understood it the moment I'd sat in my little paranormal clinic in New Orleans and opened the New Order Army draft notice.

My dad couldn't even see me off as they led me out into the depths of the bayou to a portal that hung like a misty cloud amid a tangle of cypress trees. Before I could say, "Bad idea," I was in the red, flat wastelands of limbo.

Still, Galen should have been different. He was with an elite unit that took on the most important, and deadliest, missions. In the past, he'd been given special consideration. He was one of them—the immortals—until a risk he took for me drew the ire of the gods.

They'd stripped him of his demigod status. Now he was human, and he was leaving to fight immortals.

I might never see him again.

"It's too soon," I said, running my hands down his uniform. I wished there was something I could do to stop this, to buy more time.

He lowered his mouth to mine in a searing kiss. It was like coming home. I gripped the collar of his combat fatigues, drawing tight against him. I couldn't imagine giving this man up.